The
MUSEUM
of
ORDINARY
PEOPLE

Also by Mike Gayle

Nonfiction

The
MUSEUM
of
ORDINARY
PEOPLE

MIKE GAYLE

GRAND
CENTRAL

New York   Boston

Copyright © 2023 by Pizza FTD LTD
Reading Group Guide Copyright © 2023 by Hachette Book Group, Inc., and Pizza FTD LTD

Cover design by Shreya Gupta. Cover illustration by Cannaday Chapman. Cover copyright © 2023 by Hachette Book Group, Inc.

Grand Central Publishing
Hachette Book Group
1290 Avenue of the Americas, New York, NY 10104
grandcentralpublishing.com
twitter.com/grandcentralpub

Originally published by Hodder & Stoughton in the UK.

First Grand Central Publishing Edition: May 2023

Grand Central Publishing is a division of Hachette Book Group, Inc. The Grand Central Publishing name and logo is a trademark of Hachette Book Group, Inc.

The publisher is not responsible for websites (or their content) that are not owned by the publisher.

The Hachette Speakers Bureau provides a wide range of authors for speaking events. To find out more, go to hachettespeakersbureau.com or email HachetteSpeakers@hbgusa.com.

Library of Congress Control Number: 2022947547

ISBNs: 9781538740842 (paperback), 9781538740859 (ebook)

Printed in the United States of America

LSC-C

Printing 1, 2023

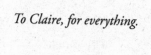

To Claire, for everything.

Prologue

On the morning of my final day at Mum's, I awoke suddenly to the sound of footsteps coming along the hallway. For a split second I imagined that it was Mum, and the past few weeks had been just a terrible dream. But then I heard the sound of boyish laughter and remembered how thin the walls in these terraces were and realized that it was the young kids of the family next door.

After packing my things, I lugged my mattress out to the dumpster, then went back inside the house for one final check to make sure there was nothing I had missed. Satisfied that everything was as it should be, I was about to pick up my bags to take them out to the car when there was a knock at the front door.

"Oh, hello, love," said Maggie, trying her best to sound casual as Dougie looked on. "We know it's your last day here so we thought we'd just pop over and see how you're getting on."

"I'm all done," I said, trying to sound upbeat, "so I'm afraid I won't be able to offer you a cup of tea or anything because I gave away the kettle yesterday. But come in anyway."

As they stepped inside, they looked around the empty front room in disbelief.

"I know it's a daft thing to say given what you've been up to all week," said Dougie, "but it's just so bare."

"Sorry, I should've warned you," I said, suddenly aware that I wasn't the only one to have suffered Mum's loss. They had been her friends for years and of course were grieving too.

"It's okay, love," said Maggie. "It's just seeing the place like this takes some getting used to."

"I can't believe you've done all this on your own," said Dougie. "We kept calling Luce, asking if you'd changed your mind about needing help, but she insisted you were fine."

"We thought it might be too much for you," continued Maggie sadly, "but you've proved us wrong."

"It wasn't easy," I admitted, "but I don't regret it. It was something I wanted to do for Mum, something I needed to do."

"Of course, love," said Maggie, wrapping me in a hug. "She would've been so proud of you."

In an effort to ward off tears, I headed to the kitchen and returned carrying the Pyrex dish that Maggie had brought round at the start of the week.

"Thanks so much for the food. It was lovely. Just what I needed to keep me going."

"I only wish we could've done more," said Maggie, taking the dish. "Your mum meant the world to us."

"I know she did, and she loved you both too."

I noticed Maggie staring at the cardboard box by my feet and the five grocery bags stuffed with my set of encyclopedias next to it.

"Is that all you're keeping of your mum's?" asked Maggie.

I nodded guiltily, ashamed by my poor attempt to effectively curate the life of my wonderful mum. "I know it's not much. To be honest, if I had the room, I would've kept everything. As it is, I don't even know where I'll put this lot."

Maggie and Dougie fell silent, momentarily lost for words; then finally Dougie sighed heavily and asked if I was driving straight back down to London.

"That's the plan."

"I suppose it's best to set off early before the traffic really gets going," he said, and then stepped forward to hug me. "You will look after yourself, won't you, love?"

"Of course," I said, and then he let go and Maggie took her turn embracing me again.

"Let us know if you need anything," she said. "Anything at all, even if it's just a chat, pick up the phone, any time."

I waved them goodbye from the doorstep, and once they'd gone I closed the door and sat at the bottom of the stairs having a last moment alone with the house and all its memories. It was eerily quiet without the ticking of Mum's clock, the gurgling of the old fridge; even the perpetually creaking joints of the place were unusually still. It was as though without Mum the house had lost its life, and now without her things it had lost its soul too.

At the start of the week I'd been convinced that the task I'd taken on was beyond me—to get Mum's whole house emptied, and every last one of her belongings dealt with in one way or another. But now here I was just a week later and the deed had been done. In the process I'd learned the hard way that Mum was everywhere and nowhere at the same time. She'd been in the largest of objects and the smallest too, and as I'd never known exactly when or where she might appear I could only conclude that my decision to do this job alone had been the right one.

It meant that I could look, listen out for, and sense Mum's every last farewell without ever having to temper the scale of my reaction. When I'd come across an old family photo that made me want to rage at the injustice of my loss, I'd done so as loudly as I'd liked; when the sight of Mum's handwriting on an old shopping list stuffed at the back of a kitchen drawer had reduced me to tears, I'd sobbed until my eyes were red and raw; and when, as I'd done many times that week, I'd felt the need to just sit quietly in a room, eyes closed, reliving my favorite memories, then I'd done that too, until the peace and comfort I'd longed for descended on me.

It was just after eleven by the time I made it back home to London. Parking the car in the street, I collected my bags from the trunk, made my way up to the tenth floor in the lift, and let myself into the apartment. Although my life in London with Guy in his Canary Wharf apartment was only a short two-hour drive away from Mum's little Northampton terrace, it might as well have been on another planet for all that the two places had in common.

He'd bought it just before we got together, with the help of a healthy deposit gifted to him by his wealthy parents, and I'd moved in with him about a year later. Although I quite liked the views across central London the apartment offered, I'd never really warmed to its ultra-modern, slick minimalist styling, preferring old Victorian buildings with rooms that have features and character. Guy's place used to be the show apartment and he'd bought it fully furnished, which is why it was full of the modern so-called design classics that were clearly used by the developer as shorthand for quality and excellence. When I'd first moved in, I'd tried arranging some of my colorful Indian throws, and other bits and pieces like candles and cushions, around the place to make it feel more homely. But they just looked wrong and so eventually they ended up stuffed in the cupboards above the wardrobe.

As I closed the door behind me, I was greeted by silence, Guy having thankfully taken my advice and gone ahead with his bike ride. Once again I felt guilty for misleading him about my arrival time but I was grateful for having done so. There was still so much to process, so much to understand, to come to terms with, that the silence of the apartment felt like a welcome friend.

It took me three more trips to empty the car and as I dumped everything in the hallway I felt a pang of guilt at having so quickly turned this pristine space into something resembling a jumble sale. Unsure what to do with all the treasures I'd brought back from Mum's, I decided to concentrate instead on unpacking my clothes and putting on a load of washing. Afterward I stuffed my empty bags into the storage cupboard in the hallway and then turned my attention to the rest of it.

In an ideal world, or at least a world where I only had myself to think about, I would've simply decanted the contents of the box around the apartment. I would've temporarily put Mum's vinyl on display on a shelf, with the intention of perhaps ordering some of those frames specifically designed for albums so that I could hang them artfully on the wall.

In an ideal world I would've hammered half a dozen nails into one of the walls in the bedroom, then draped Mum's scarves from them, so that I could not only see them every day but also once in a while be reminded to put one on and wear it to work or on a night out.

In an ideal world I would've shifted Guy's expensive Eames House Bird ornament, his fancy silver Tom Dixon bowl, and his towering Georg Jensen vase out of the way and replaced them with Mum's broken duck ornament, her knock-off Mason Cash mixing bowl, and her blue vase from Anglesey. But this was far from an ideal world; if it were, Mum would still be in it. Instead I took the box into the bedroom and slid back the wardrobe door. Unlike Guy's side, which was perfectly organized—his work shirts, suits, and ties all color coordinated, his off-duty wear of jeans, T-shirts, and jumpers all neatly folded on the shelves—mine was chaotic in the extreme. Every hanger strained under the weight of multiple items of clothing, T-shirts and tops were stuffed randomly into every nook and crevice, and lower down there was a muddled pile of footwear, everything from flip-flops to work shoes.

As I tried my best to make a space amongst my clutter, I couldn't help wishing I was more like Guy, more thoughtful and ordered in my approach to life rather than dealing with everything it threw at me in a haphazard fashion. Picking up the box of Mum's things, I wedged it into the wardrobe and then quickly pulled the door back into place. For a moment I felt good, like it was one more thing ticked off my to-do list, but then I remembered the bags of encyclopedias sitting in the hallway. For half an hour I stalked around the apartment looking for somewhere to hide them, but every single centimeter of storage space was already full, mostly of my things from before I moved in with Guy. Out of options, I shoved them up against the wall in the hallway underneath the coat hooks as neatly as I could and told myself I'd deal with them later.

Overcome with exhaustion, I returned to the bedroom, closed the blinds, shed my clothes straight on to the floor, and crawled into bed, then allowed the wave of grief I'd been holding back all day to crash over me.

One Year Later

1

❧

I'm in the middle of pouring myself a glass of wine when I hear Guy come home from work. The upside of my job as a receptionist is that at five thirty on the dot I'm out of the door whereas Guy, who works in finance, rarely, if ever, makes it home before eight.

"Guess what?" he says excitedly as I open the cupboard door and take out another glass.

"What?"

"The estate agent called to say that all the slots for viewing the apartment at the weekend are already fully booked."

"Wow, that didn't take long," I say, filling up the glass and handing it to him.

"Just think," he says, pausing to take a quick sip of his drink, "with a bit of luck we could have an offer on the table by Monday. How mad is that? This time next week we could be in a position to make an offer on our very first home together."

"It's all happening very quickly," I say, trying my best not to sound panicked.

"But that's good, isn't it? There's no point in hanging around now that we've made the decision, is there? Talking of which…" he says, giving me a look that I can't quite discern. "I know you really struggled with the decision to put your mum's house on the market but you should be really proud of yourself for going ahead with it."

"Thanks," I say, wondering where this is going, "it was difficult, but like you said at the time, I was just putting off the inevitable."

"Well," he continues, "I'm glad you've said that because I've been wondering if you might be up for making another difficult decision."

My stomach flips. "What about?"

He pulls a face, a mixture of awkwardness and embarrassment, and then looks pointedly toward the front door and in that instant I realize what this whole pantomime has been about. It's about books, specifically the thirty-odd volumes of the 1974 edition of the Encyclopedia Britannica that have been sitting, stuffed into carrier bags, by the front door since I'd brought them back to London after clearing out Mum's a year ago.

"Look," he says. "I feel awful bringing this up. I know what they mean to you, of course I do. It's just that when the photographer came to take marketing photos of the apartment, I had to keep shifting them to make the place look tidy."

"And with people coming on Saturday for viewings you need them out of here," I say, finishing off his thought. "I'm sorry, Guy, I should've done something with them months ago. Leave it with me and I'll get it sorted."

When I finally got around to putting Mum's house on the market a fortnight ago, I never thought for a moment it would lead to this. Really, all I'd been hoping to do was draw a line under my grief, to shake the feeling of exhaustion that had been with me all year. Because that's the thing about grief no one ever tells you: it's greedy. You don't notice at first because you're still in shock, and there's so much to do, from obtaining death certificates to canceling utility contracts, but hour by hour, day by day, it eats up every last scrap of energy you have, leaving you spent and empty. Perhaps that in part was why, as time passed and the world kept turning, as friends got engaged and others had babies, selling Mum's house simply got pushed to the bottom of my ever-growing to-do list.

Instead, I'd concentrated what little strength I possessed on getting myself through twelve months of firsts without Mum: the first Mother's Day, the first birthday, and then of course Christmas, all the while being only too aware that the hardest "first" of all, the first anniversary of losing her, was still ahead of me. As the day grew nearer, I'd made myself all sorts of promises. If I got through it—and I hadn't been at all sure that I would—I told myself I'd start looking forward to the future. The truth is, I was tired of being sad all the time, of feeling like I was just going through the motions, of constantly being trapped in the past. I don't know how long grief is supposed to last—some say three months and others six—but I really was pinning all my hopes on twelve being the magic number, the point in time that would mark a kind of new beginning. I needed to try to get some of my old life back, to be a better friend, a better partner, to really start living again.

While the first anniversary of losing Mum was every bit as awful as I'd imagined it would be, I'd made it through. It didn't finish me off. It didn't send me spiraling off the deep end or leave me permanently curled up in a ball. And so, the very next day I'd put Mum's house up for sale, and to my surprise a week later someone had made an offer. At first I was thrown; I'd thought I'd have longer to get used to the idea, to convince myself I was doing the right thing, and for a while I'd even considered turning it down. But then I'd thought about the past year, and how much I wanted this coming one to be different, and so I'd accepted, never thinking for a moment that it would result in Guy asking me to buy a house with him.

After dinner I help Guy clear the table; then he opens his laptop to do an hour or two of work, leaving me free to take a closer look at the encyclopedias. I pick one up at random. The faded gold lettering on the barely hanging-together spine reads, "Livingstone—Metalwork," and when I open it up a page falls out and flutters to the floor.

Sitting down in the hallway, hugging the volume to my chest, I think about the day this set of encyclopedias first came into my life. I remember it like it was yesterday. Aged eleven, I'd come home from school one afternoon to discover them piled high on the dining room table along with a card that read, "For you, my sweet Jess, never stop learning! All my love, Mum."

Mum had never been what you might call a big reader. She'd left school at sixteen with barely any qualifications, and had always complained that books were too slow for her liking. While she was more than happy to take me to the library every week, the only books in the house that actually belonged to us were a dog-eared edition of *Gone with the Wind* she'd been cajoled into buying at a school fête, a copy of the New Testament she'd been given by the local vicar on leaving primary school, and a coverless copy of the Be-Ro baking book that had been my gran's. So, the sight of all of these books sitting on a table in my house took my breath away.

At that age I'd only ever seen encyclopedias at school or in the library and it had never occurred to me that normal people like Mum and me were allowed to own such things. And though they were clearly second-hand and had seen better days, I absolutely adored them.

When she'd arrived home from work at the supermarket later that afternoon, she found me sprawled on the carpet in the living room poring over them. She'd told me she'd bought them to help me with my homework.

"You'll be at secondary school soon," she said, "and studying things I won't be able to help you with, so I'm hoping these will come in handy."

At the time her explanation made complete sense and I took it at face value. It wasn't until I was much older, and far less self-absorbed, that it dawned on me that this gift had been Mum sending a message: that coming from a black working-class single-parent family didn't have to define me. That I didn't have to get pregnant at sixteen like so many girls at my school did. That I didn't have to take any job, anywhere just to make ends meet as she herself had done over the years. In short, she was saying that I didn't have to compromise. That I could be a doctor, an astronaut, or anything else I dreamed of becoming for that matter, if I studied hard and wanted it badly enough. I think that's probably why I brought them back to London with me. Because they were more than just a set of tatty out-of-date books. They were a symbol of Mum's hopes and dreams for me. But did I really need to hang on to them to remember how much

Mum had loved me? Did they need to physically occupy space in my home when what they represented took up so much space in my heart?

Over the past year they'd crossed my mind several times. I'd thought about piling them artfully in the corner of the bedroom, or perhaps clearing a space on the sideboard in the living room and arranging them in pride of place. But every time I thought about doing it I'd imagined how at odds they'd look set against the backdrop of Guy's apartment, with all of its clean lines and designer furniture, and I ended up just leaving them where they were.

Perhaps Guy is right, I think, returning the copy in my hand to the bag I'd taken it from. This is just like Mum's house; I'm hanging on to them just for the sake of it. Maybe now is the time to finally let them go.

The following evening after work I head over to Soho to meet Luce for drinks.

"Sorry I'm late, mate," she says, plonking herself down on the sofa next to me and hugging me tightly. "Work was like being trapped in some sort of never-ending nightmare. Every time I thought we were wrapping things up, someone else would bring an issue to me and that would be another twenty minutes gone. Three times it happened! At one point I felt like screaming: 'Will you people just stop banging on about your problems so I can go and get smashed with my bestie!'"

"You sound like you need a drink," I say, rummaging in my bag for my purse. "What are you having?"

"I'm just telling you now, I'll be needing more than just 'a' drink tonight, more like half a dozen!" She takes off the red wooly hat she's wearing and runs her fingers through her short blond curls. "Work has been manic all day. And if anyone is going to be getting the first round in, it's me." She hugs me again. "It's so good to see you looking brighter, mate. You've been through the wars but you've come through it."

I reach into my bag, take out a small tissue-wrapped parcel, and hand it to her. "For you," I say brightly. "I've been meaning to give it to you since forever."

Luce eagerly tears into the paper, eventually removing a small ceramic duck.

"Captain Quackers!" she says, holding up the ornament that had sat on Mum's mantelpiece throughout virtually all of our childhoods. "How much did we love playing with him when we were kids? I can't take him. He belongs with you."

"Don't be daft, he's yours. I've got more than enough to remember Mum by and anyway, it's the least I can do given it was your dad's superglue that saved me from being grounded for life."

Luce smiles warmly at the memory. "Ah, the great indoor gymnastics incident of '96. Even thinking about it now makes me shudder. Can't believe your mum never found out!"

I point to Captain Quackers' wonky beak. "Look at the state of that! Of course she knew; she just didn't say anything, that's all."

"That was your mum all over," says Luce fondly. "Always willing to give people a second chance."

I feel a sudden flood of warmth toward my old friend who knew Mum almost as well as me. There weren't many people in my life here in London who did; even Guy had only met her a handful of times.

"This is going to take pride of place in the flat," she says, carefully rewrapping the duck and slipping it into her bag. "Leon can find somewhere else to stick pictures of his stupid nephews; this duck is going to go where everyone can see it." She stands up and picks up her bag. "Right, I'm going to get us a drink and then we'll raise a glass to the one and only Maria Anne Baxter!"

Luce is my oldest and closest friend in the world. Our parents were best friends and we grew up living across the road from each other. As kids, if ever my mum wanted to know where I was, her first port of call would be Luce's, and if ever Maggie and Dougie wanted to find Luce, it was always my house they came to first. Across the years we'd always remained close, even sharing a flat together when I'd first moved to London. Now she works for a homeless charity as a fundraiser and lives in Brixton with her long-suffering boyfriend, Leon.

When Luce returns from the bar, she's carrying two large luminous yellow cocktails she picked at random from the menu, and after raising a toast to Mum we catch up on each other's news. She tells me all about the promotion at work she's thinking of going for, Leon's agonizing over what to do after his PhD, and her parents, who have recently made the decision to get fit.

"They've even got themselves a personal trainer," she says incredulously. "That said, they did get him through Groupon and Mum said when he turned up for their first session he had a bigger beer belly than Dad's."

We laugh so hard over this we end up doubled over, coughing and spluttering, our faces wet with tears. It feels good to laugh. Life-affirming even. For a while there I genuinely thought I might have forgotten how to.

"Anyway," says Luce once we've recovered. "That's enough about me; tell me what's going on with you? How's all the house stuff going?"

"Pretty well actually," I say. "Guy's place only went on the market yesterday and he's already been inundated with people wanting to see it… which reminds me, I need to ask you a question. You remember my old encyclopedias?"

"How could I forget?" says Luce. "Those things are part of our history. Do you remember that one summer when instead of playing outside like normal kids we used them to set each other projects like we were at school?"

I smile fondly at the memory. "We were such little geeks back then."

"True, but at least it kept us out of trouble. Anyway, what about them? They live in your hallway now, don't they?"

"Well, they have been," I reply. "But with people coming round to view the apartment at the weekend, I sort of need them gone and I was wondering if you'd like them."

Luce sets down her glass. "You're getting rid of them?"

"To be honest, I'm not even sure why I brought them back from Mum's in the first place. They've just been sitting in the same spot for over a year now doing nothing. I haven't even taken them out of the bags I lugged them back in. The fact is I'm never going to do anything with them, so I thought I'd try and find them a good home."

Luce looks completely unconvinced. "Firstly, you know yourself how small my place is. Leon and I barely have room for our own stuff. Add in a full set of encyclopedias and we'd have to sleep standing up. Besides, I don't buy what you're saying for a second."

"What do you mean?"

"This whole 'I'm not quite sure why I brought them back with me' act. You know exactly why you didn't want to get rid of them; it's because they mean something to you. This has Little Lord Fauntleroy's fingerprints all over it."

Luce and Guy have never really hit it off, although for the most part they tolerate each other for my sake. Luce thinks that Guy is "a bit up himself," while Guy thinks Luce is "a bit full-on." The funny thing is each of them probably has a point but I love them both regardless.

"Don't call him that," I snap. "It's not Guy's doing, okay, it's *mine*. I'm the one who's decided that I don't want to keep them anymore."

"Well, if that's true, then it's a mistake," says Luce. "Just like … well, just like … you buying a place with Guy is a mistake."

"Don't start this again," I say. "I thought we agreed you'd let it go."

"Let it go?" repeats Luce. "How can I let it go when you're about to make the biggest financial commitment of your life with a man who this time last year you were on the verge of leaving?"

2

It's raining as I emerge from Holborn Station on my way to work the following morning. Popping up my umbrella, I cross the road and walk the short distance to Capital Tower, the twenty-story office block on Kingsway where I work. It had never been my intention for this to be anything other than a temp job, a way to tide me over until I finally got my career off the ground, but somehow five years later I'm still here.

I swipe my card to open the door, then, shaking off my umbrella, duck inside and make my way to the staff room where I find the other two receptionists, Maria and Zofia, having a coffee before our workday starts.

"Morning," I say, nodding toward the ancient coffee machine as I hang up my coat. "I see you managed to get that thing working again."

"I almost lost a nail doing it," says Maria. "But yeah, I got it done. Want one?"

"Oh, yes please," I say, gratefully taking a steaming mug of work's distinctly average coffee from her. "It's really coming down out there, and this should at least warm me up."

Before I can even take a sip of the scalding-hot liquid, however, the door opens and Christine, the office manager, pokes her head round.

"And here was me thinking you'd all been abducted by aliens," she says. "There's an empty reception desk that needs staffing, ladies, so drink up and let's get to work."

One by one we troop down to reception, slip on our headsets, and turn on our computers. For the next few hours I'm busy greeting clients, answering and directing calls, and signing for parcels but the moment things quiet down, my thoughts turn to my conversation with Luce last night, and the things she'd said about Guy.

Guy and I met three years ago at a mutual friend's birthday get-together at a pub in Balham. Strictly speaking he wasn't my type and I'm sure I wasn't his. He was far too conventionally handsome, too tall, and too confident for my liking and I doubted we'd have much in common, and we don't really. He likes sport, I can't stand it. He comes from a traditional nuclear family while I'm an only child of a single parent. His dad had a high-powered career in finance, and his mum, a former solicitor who had given up her career to raise her family, now devotes her time to various charitable causes and maintaining their beautiful home. Meanwhile, my mum left school at sixteen and had worked in the local supermarket ever since.

We came from different worlds and on paper shouldn't have really worked but somehow we did. Guy had a certain steadiness about him that made me feel secure in a way I never had before. In return I think I made him feel like he was being seen for the person he was rather than, as previous girlfriends had, for his status and the lifestyle he could offer them. I really liked him, he really liked me, and for the first year and a half we were happy. But then, about six months before Mum died we started arguing a lot. I couldn't understand it. We'd enjoyed a lovely summer that started with a weekend in Rome, finished with a week in Ibiza, and was punctuated by several friends' weddings. But once the summer was over and we were back to our routines, things began to become strained between us. It was stupid things at first, like arguing about my untidiness or his habit of working late, but gradually the rows became more and more frequent. It was as if he was permanently in a bad mood and so was I in return. Racking my brains to figure out why things were going wrong, I'd even asked Luce for advice and to my surprise she'd speculated that perhaps it was the summer of weddings that was to blame. "Maybe he thinks it's time you two got hitched but doesn't think you'll be up for it." Before I could put this to Guy we had another blazing row, which started about me forgetting to post his mum's birthday card for him and ended with us not speaking for three whole days. Eventually, I just felt that we were drifting further and further apart with less joy in our lives and fewer things in common. I was so miserable that I started to make plans to leave. That made me miserable too, but it also felt like the right decision. Then my mum died, my whole world turned upside down, and in the aftermath Guy became a completely different person.

Suddenly he was no longer inexplicably morose, no longer picking fights or short-tempered. Overnight he was back to being the sweet, kind, patient man I knew him to be. At first, I'd thought this change in him was because he felt sorry for me and I was sure that at some point things would revert to the way they were. Six months on, however, he was still the same. It should've been good news, proving that the rough patch we'd endured was just that, a temporary glitch in an otherwise healthy relationship, but I wasn't so sure and couldn't help wondering when, rather than if, we'd find ourselves back where we'd been before Mum died. But then following the one-year anniversary of losing Mum, I'd finally put her house on the market, and much to my surprise an offer was made almost straightaway. Before I'd had a chance to catch my breath, Guy had shown me a listing on Rightmove for a very smart, very expensive, five-bed house in Greenwich.

"What's this?" I'd asked.

"Well," he'd replied, almost shyly, "I'm rather hoping it will be our new home." Before I could react he took my hand in his and looked at me intently. "After you called and told me about the offer on your mum's place it got me thinking about a lot of things... about us... about you... and especially about this past year. It's been so tough for you, and it feels like we've sort of been stuck in a rut but I think I've found a way for us to get out of it."

"By getting a house together?"

"Think about it," he'd said. "Aren't we always saying how small this place is? I mean, I bought it when I was single, and now there's two of us here and all our stuff and it's bursting at the seams. Well, now we have the opportunity to do something about it. It'll be easy: I'll sell this place;

then we'll use my equity, plus your mum's money, plus whatever mortgage we can get and"—he waggled his phone in the air—"this house or somewhere like it could be ours." He'd looked at me expectantly. "So, what do you say, Baxter, are you in?"

It was the million-dollar question, a question I would've answered with greater confidence had I had more than a few seconds to get my head around it. My thoughts were all over the place. This time last year I'd been about to leave Guy and now here he was proposing that we make the biggest financial commitment of our lives together. Yes, things had been good between us this past year, but was it because we were permanently fixed, or had we simply been carried along by the momentum of life since losing Mum? I didn't have an answer, I couldn't say for sure, but the one thing of which I was certain was that if I said no, that would be us finished for good. This wasn't just a question about a house; this was Guy asking me if we had a future together.

In a split second I could see that saying yes to this house would be the first domino in a whole series of life-changing events. First the house, then the big summer wedding followed a year later by a big summer pregnancy, to be repeated on an annual basis until every one of those five bedrooms was full. And while I wasn't necessarily against the idea, at the same time it felt like everything was happening at light speed and I was in danger of becoming a spectator in my own life.

"Do we really need a five-bedroom house?" I'd said, hoping to pump the brakes a little. "I mean, there's only the two of us; maybe we could go for something smaller in a cheaper part of London."

Guy had been completely unfazed. "You're worrying over nothing," he'd said. "What's the point of messing about with smaller homes for a year or two here and there when we both know what we want?"

Taking a deep breath, I'd looked into his eyes and all I could see was a man who loved me and cared for me, and someone who I loved and cared for in return.

"Yeah, you're probably right," I'd said, feeling both loved and cherished, trapped and terrified. "I just need to stop worrying. Let's do this."

And right now I was still feeling good about my decision, and I didn't need Luce or anyone else for that matter reminding me of the uncertainty I'd fought so hard to overcome.

With Luce unable or unwilling to take my encyclopedias and Saturday fast approaching, I spend every spare moment for the rest of the day trying to find them a new home. I message friends but none are interested; I try libraries but they already have encyclopedias of their own. In desperation I even list them on Gumtree as "free to a good home," consoling myself with the idea that they might go on to inspire another generation, but no one is interested.

So on Friday evening while Guy is needlessly tidying the apartment in preparation for Saturday's viewings, I drag the books, bag by bag, out to the lift and take them all the way down to the bin store in the basement. Feeling like I'm letting Mum down, like I've failed her somehow, I unceremoniously dump the encyclopedias one by one into the huge recycling bin, all the while trying my very best not to feel as if I'm committing a murder.

Guy and I go to bed just after midnight and I dream vividly about Mum until I'm woken by the sound of my phone ringing. Snatching it up, I check the screen and I'm simultaneously relieved and annoyed to find that the caller is Luce. When she'd sent me a text yesterday apologizing for what she'd said about Guy the other night, I deliberately hadn't replied, hoping to make my annoyance clear. Over the years Luce and I have fallen out more times than I care to remember; it is, I suppose, the downside of being so close. I know we'll make up eventually, like we always do, but I'm not sure I'm ready to let it go just yet.

My guess is she's out and has had far too much to drink, meaning I'm about to receive either a ten-minute monologue on how much she loves me or a hysterical rant as she doubles down on her earlier offense. I think briefly about letting her call go to voice mail, but then the thought crosses my mind that she might be in trouble and need my help and so against my better judgment I pick up.

"Tell me you haven't got rid of them," she says breathlessly before I can say a single word.

"What are you talking about?" I hiss, slipping out of bed and into the living room so as not to wake Guy.

"*The encyclopedias*," she says. "Tell me you haven't got rid of them!"

In the background I can hear the sound of chatter, laughter, and music as if she's out at a bar somewhere.

"I threw them away earlier tonight," I say, wincing at the memory of my betrayal. "They're in the recycling bin in the basement."

"Well, you'd better get them out, okay?" says Luce. "Because I've just this minute found a home for them."

"What are you on about? I've tried everything; no one wants those things."

"You're wrong," says Luce. "I've just heard about a place that will take them."

"What kind of place?"

"It's at the back of a house clearance company in Peckham. One of Leon's PhD friends just told me about it."

She explains how she'd been struggling to make conversation with Leon's friends while he was at the bar getting a round in. "To be honest," she says uncharitably, "they aren't the best conversationalists and I was running low on polite chitchat, so I thought I'd tell them about the trouble you're having with your encyclopedias, thinking they might think it's a bit quirky or whatever. Anyway, as soon as I'm done talking, Leon's mate Dave pipes up that he had a similar sort of situation just a few months ago with an old sewing machine."

"A sewing machine?"

"Yeah, I know it's a bit random but apparently his great-gran had been a seamstress all her life, and get this, she'd made not only her daughter's wedding dress on this huge, big-as-a-desk sewing machine but her granddaughter's too. Anyway, when she passed away and they had to clear her house, no one wanted to throw it out, even though it had long since stopped working, but this being London, no one had the room for it either. Apparently, they went back and forth wondering what to do with it and then just as it was beginning to look like the only option left was to take it to the dump, Dave did some digging and someone somewhere—I forget who—tells him about this place in Peckham that would take in the sewing machine and look after it."

"And this place will do what? Sell it?"

"No," she replies. "That's the weird part. They don't sell the stuff; they look after it. They look after it, you know, like a museum."

"A museum?" I reply. "If it's a museum in London, how come I've never heard of it? No, I think this mate of Leon's is winding you up."

"That's what I thought at first, but he's not," insists Luce. "It's completely legit. Hang on and I'll send you something to prove it."

Moments later my phone vibrates and I check the screen to find that she's sent me a link. I click through and I'm delivered to an article from *Time Out* entitled: "London's Top 10 Quirkiest Museums." And there between Hackney's Viktor Wynd Museum of Curiosities, Fine Art and Natural History at number nine, and Chalk Farm's Vagina Museum at number seven, is the place she's talking about: The Museum of Ordinary People.

I can't believe my eyes.

It's real.

Luce isn't making this up.

Before I know what I'm doing I'm running out the front door of the apartment dressed only in one of Guy's old T-shirts, my Christmas-themed pajama bottoms, and a pair of flip-flops and clutching several empty IKEA bags on a mission to bring my beloved encyclopedias back from the dead.

3

I'm standing in front of a large brick-built Victorian warehouse wondering if perhaps I've been dropped at the wrong address. Occupying the corner plot of a quiet, semi-residential road in Peckham, the building has clearly seen better days. Its paintwork is faded and peeling, a section of guttering at the side has sprung loose, and just above the vehicle access at the front there's an alarmingly large buddleia growing out of the brickwork. In short, the place is a wreck and couldn't look less like a museum if it tried, and yet according to my phone, this is indeed the address of the Museum of Ordinary People, the supposed savior of a treasured part of my family history.

When I'd told Guy this morning about Luce's call, he didn't seem at all interested in the museum; he just seemed relieved that the encyclopedias were finally going. "Give me a shout when your Uber arrives," he'd said, "and I'll give you a hand taking them down." I, on the other hand, had been so intrigued by the idea of the museum that I'd been unable to sleep. It seemed all too unreal, a museum whose only purpose was to save objects destined for the dump.

As I stand looking at the building in front of me, it occurs to me that it doesn't look like any museum I've ever seen. To the left of the vehicle access is an old heavy wooden door that looks like it's meant to be the entrance. Pinned to it is a laminated sign that reads: "Barclay and Sons: Domestic and Commercial Clearance and Wholesale Furniture Dealers, by Appointment Only." Next to it is an intercom under which is pinned another laminated sign that reads: "Intercom BROKEN. If door is OPEN, we are in!" I try the door handle and sure enough it is indeed open. I look back at my bags of books, wondering if I should take them in with me in case they get stolen, and then smile as I recall how I couldn't even give them away when I'd tried. The encyclopedias will be safe, I am sure. And so, leaving them in situ for the time being, I push open the door and step inside.

Compared to the bright spring day, the interior of the warehouse is dark and cold. To my right, parked in front of the shuttered vehicle access, is a large, battered van with the name Barclay and Sons emblazoned across the side in peeling white lettering on a faded navy-blue background. Beyond the van, stacked along the walls, are huge piles of furniture of every description and from every era. There are nineties-style office chairs next to 1930s solid wooden wardrobes, and sixties-style armchairs stacked on top of seventies-looking dining tables.

To my left is what looks to be an office, a fact confirmed by yet another laminated sign stuck to its door: "OFFICE: KNOCK AND THEN WAIT." Keen to make a good impression, I follow the instructions, and after a moment the door opens to reveal a man who at a guess is roughly my age. He's tall, slim, with dark brown, almost black hair, and is casually dressed in a hoodie, jeans, and sneakers. But the thing I can't help noticing, even though I know I shouldn't, is that the whole of the right side of his face is covered in what look like burn scars.

"Hi there," I say, trying my best not to sound unnerved. "I'm wondering if you could help me? I'm looking for the museum."

The man subtly angles the scarred side of his face away from me before speaking.

"Museum? What museum?"

"You know . . . the er . . . the Museum of Ordinary People."

He smiles wryly and looks around the warehouse as if to say, "Does this look like a museum to you?"

I reach into my pocket and take out my phone, find the link Luce sent me last night, and show him the *Time Out* article. He gives the screen a cursory glance but then shakes his head and returns the phone to me.

"I think you've been had," he says. "Most likely some teenage hacker somewhere having a laugh at *Time Out*'s expense. I own Barclay and Sons and I can categorically assure you that we haven't got a—"

"All right, boss?"

I turn round to get a look at the owner of the voice that's interrupted him and see two men walking toward us, one older, bald and stocky, the other younger, wiry, with gelled-back hair. Each man is carrying a greasy paper bag that smells heavily of fried food.

"Weren't expecting you in today, boss," says the older man. "Everything okay?"

"Everything's fine," says the man with the scars unconvincingly. "I'm here...for a...for a meeting...you know...with a surveyor. To give the place...er...the once-over so I know how much it's going to cost to sort everything out."

"Oh right," says the older man, with just a touch of skepticism in his voice. "Well, boss, if you need building work done, you should've asked us. We've got loads of mates in the trade, haven't we, Dec?"

"Loads," says the younger man, nodding in agreement. "They'd definitely sort this place out good and proper, and at mate's rates too."

The man with the scars momentarily falls silent and the two men's attention naturally shifts to me.

"This is...I'm sorry I didn't catch your name," says the man with the scars.

"Jess. Jess Baxter."

"Well, Jess, I'm Alex." He gestures to the older man. "This is Paul," and finally he introduces the younger man, "and this is Dec."

"Lovely to meet you all," I say brightly, and in return Paul and Dec offer a polite but wary nod of acknowledgment.

"Anyway," says Alex, "it looks like Jess here has been the victim of some sort of online prank. Apparently, she read an article claiming that Barclay and Sons is a museum, of all things. I've put her right, but I suspect it might be worth looking into at some point."

A guilty look passes between Paul and Dec indicating that they know more than they're letting on, but they say nothing. I decide to press on regardless.

"Actually, I'm not just here because of the article. The thing is my friend who sent me the link last night did so because someone she knows actually donated something to the museum here only last month."

Confused, Alex runs a hand through his hair. "They actually told your friend they made a donation to the museum here at Barclay and Sons in Peckham? What sort of donation?"

"It was a 1920s sewing machine," I reply. "And yes, they definitely said they donated it to the museum here at this address."

Alex looks pointedly at Paul and Dec. "Well, that certainly sounds like a mystery. I don't suppose you guys can possibly shed any light on it?"

"We can explain," says Paul quickly. "It's nothing dodgy, like; it's just that there's something . . . well, something we haven't quite told you about Barclay and Sons."

"Okay," says Alex warily, "well, you've certainly got my full attention. Please enlighten me."

"Well, the thing is, boss," says Dec, taking over the narrative. "Mad as it sounds . . . the lady here's right."

"About what?" replies Alex. "The fact that you appear to have accepted an antique sewing machine from someone under false pretenses?"

The two men shake their heads.

"No, boss," says Paul. "About the other thing, the museum thing. The truth is, we really have got one."

The pin-drop silence seems to go on forever, giving me the opportunity to think about how weird this all is. None of it adds up at all. Who is this mysterious Alex and how did he come to have those terrible scars? And how can he as the owner of Barclay and Sons have no idea about the existence of a museum on his own premises? And more to the point, why would his employees bother to create a museum in the first place and then keep it from their boss?

It's Alex who eventually breaks the silence. "Are you actually telling me there's a museum here at Barclay and Sons?"

The two men nod but don't elaborate.

"How's that even possible? I've been all around this place and I've not seen one. Where...where is it exactly?"

Paul sniffs and uncomfortably shifts his weight from one foot to the other. "Probably best if we just show you, boss," he says. He disappears into the office and returns moments later carrying a large set of keys and then with a nod toward the rear of the building heads in that direction, closely followed by Dec, then Alex, and finally me.

As we walk, we pass elegant antique mirrors, heavy dark-wood Victorian desks, and gorgeous Art Deco wardrobes. Though it's hardly the time to be thinking of such things, it crosses my mind that were it not for Guy this would be exactly the type of furniture I'd fill the new house with, furniture that looks like it has lived a life, that looks like it has a story to tell. As it is, however, I know that Guy's taste is firmly rooted in the present and he would no sooner fill our new home with these types of vintage pieces than swap his carbon-fiber road bike for a penny farthing.

We come to a halt in front of what appears to be a rear entrance, a mirror image of the vehicle access at the front of the building, but instead of rolling shutters there's a large pair of double doors, secured with a huge chain and padlock. Paul shoves a key into the lock and with a quick twist it clicks open, allowing Dec to remove the chain. He heaves the right-hand door open, slips inside into the darkness, and after a moment's fumbling and cursing there's a click, followed by a stutter of fluorescent light, which eventually stabilizes.

"Right then," says Paul, and then he gives Alex a look that I can't quite discern and disappears inside too. Alex gives me a look, and I feel a bond between us, given that we're the only ones here who have never seen whatever lies behind this door. He ducks through the gap after Paul, and then finally, with my heart pounding in my throat, I take a deep breath and follow him.

The room is roughly a third of the size of the main warehouse but with a much lower ceiling. It's filled with row upon row of rusting industrial shelving units, all of which are crammed, like some sort of crazy church jumble sale, with all manner of objects. On the shelf nearest to me I spot a faded navy-blue Silver Cross pram minus its wheels, a stuffed grayhound with mottled brown fur and wild eyes, and a large battered metal toolbox with the words "A. Holmes" neatly painted on the side.

Oddly, every item has a small cardboard luggage label attached to it with string, written on in the same spidery, barely legible handwriting. I cock my head on one side in an effort to read the label attached to an amateurish-looking oil painting of an elderly woman with white hair, resting against the shelf near my feet. It reads: "Portrait of Olive May Findlay painted by her husband Thomas James Findlay, donated 15.11.16 by T.R. (no relation). Comment: 'Thomas was never formally trained but was very proud of this piece he painted of his beloved wife for their sixtieth wedding anniversary.'" Next to it is an old dented Cadbury's chocolate tin and this time the label attached reads: "Correspondence addressed to a Mrs. Sarah Harris mostly from her friend Mrs. Angela White, found (01.03.98) in a dumpster outside 317 Hampton Avenue NW19." Propped up against the wall at the end of the row of shelves nearest me is a rusting wheelbarrow. Its label reads: "Wheelbarrow belonging to N. Cross of Chipping Norton, donated by Mrs. P. Manion (daughter). Comment: 'My dad never really liked gardening but regardless took over the job of maintaining the garden at 415 Amberley Road SW12 after my mum, who lived for her garden, passed away suddenly.'"

I turn to look at Alex to find him already looking back at me, mouth open, eyes wide, and clearly in a state of shock. Simultaneously we look at Paul and Dec, who are standing to one side taking in our reaction to the room.

"What... what... in the world is this place?" asks Alex eventually.

Paul sighs heavily and then, clearly struggling to find the right words, he says, "I suppose... I suppose this is what you might call the late Mr. Barclay's pet project."

Taking a seat on an upturned tea box, Paul tells us about the first time he saw the museum. "It was about ten years ago. I'd only been in the job a few weeks and we were clearing a house in Kensal Green that had belonged to an old dear who'd lived there pretty much all her life. Anyway, her family had been and gone already, taking the bits they wanted, and the boss had given them a price for everything they'd left behind, the deal being that we'd leave the house completely empty. Anyway, I was in the middle of moving a chest of drawers with another lad when I knocked over a cardboard box full of rubbish and amongst loads of old bills and newspapers and the like were a couple of bundles of old photos. They were mostly holiday snaps, from the fifties and sixties, no value in them, which was probably why the old lady's family had chucked them away. I'd been about to toss them back in the box and take the whole lot out to the dumpster when the gaffer stopped me. 'We don't do that to things that need looking after,' he said. 'As long as you're working for me, if you find anything like this again, you give it to me and I'll give it a home.'"

"So, what happened next?" I ask before I have chance to stop myself. "Did he show you the museum?"

"I don't know if I'd have called it a museum myself," says Paul, sounding amused. "But yeah, as soon as we got back to the warehouse he took the photos off me, walked me down to the lock-up we're in now, opened up the doors, and showed me what was inside."

"And did it look like it does now?" I ask.

"Pretty much, I suppose," says Paul. "Although there wasn't anywhere near as much stuff in here back then, I reckon. To be honest, I didn't know what to make of it at first. It just looked like a load of old junk to me. But even so I remember that the one thing that stuck out to me was the labels he'd put on everything, like they were something special."

"And did he explain what it was all for?"

Paul shrugs. "The boss wasn't really much of a talker. The man was a complete mystery, really. He didn't talk much about himself; in fact, he didn't talk much about anything. But if I had to guess, I'd say he just genuinely liked saving stuff. Saw the value in it, even if no one else did."

4

I feel like I've walked into the middle of a very weird play and my mind is teeming with questions. Who was Barclay? What had motivated him to start such a collection when strictly speaking he was in the business of getting rid of things? But top of my list is the one question I end up asking aloud, "So how did a room full of items saved from house clearances end up getting a mention in *Time Out* of all things?"

Paul grins. "Basically, after a while word got out amongst people in the trade—furniture restorers, vintage and antique dealers, and the like—that if anyone came across anything they thought needed saving, things they knew no one would buy but which they felt wrong throwing away, then Mr. B was the man to bring it to."

"What kind of things did they bring?" I ask.

"Letters and photos mainly," said Paul, "stuff they'd come across in job lots of furniture bought at sale or auction."

"And that's how *Time Out* came across this place?"

"Not exactly. What happened was that one day we had a journalist from the *Evening Standard* knock on the door asking loads of questions about the lock-up and all the things in it. Apparently, he'd heard about it from someone in the trade and thought there might be a story in it. Anyway, he chats to the gaffer, and a photographer came round and took some photos and then they both left. We didn't think about it again until one day we're flicking through the paper and what do we see but a massive picture of the gaffer looking really awkward under the headline: 'The

Museum of Ordinary People—How one Londoner is trying to save ordinary people's pasts.'"

"So how did Mr. Barclay respond to that?"

"At first the boss thought it was just funny. But then the general public started turning up at the warehouse. Some just wanted a nose around the lock-up but others came with things they wanted him to look after."

"Like what?" says Alex.

"You name it, they brought it," says Paul. "I remember one woman turning up with a motorcycle sidecar. She told the boss it meant the world to her because it was her only connection to her late great-grandfather. Apparently, he used to take her out for day trips in it back in the fifties. Anyway, she'd kept it in a shed in her back garden for at least thirty years, but now she was moving to a smaller place, she couldn't keep it and hated the idea of taking it to the dump."

"And how about the bloke who brought in a stack of his dead mum's unpublished novels," added Dec. "He was moving abroad and he didn't quite know what to do with them. There were over thirty of them, bonkbusters I think they call them. I only read a few pages mind, but even those were quite spicy."

"Then there was a couple who brought in a suitcase full of old wedding photos and personal stuff like letters and birth certificates," says Paul. "They'd just moved into a new house and found it all in the loft and just didn't feel right throwing it away but didn't want to keep it either."

"And what about the people who came to visit?" I ask. "What were they like?"

"We had all sorts," replies Dec. "Local residents, art students, even the occasional old-age pensioner looking into their family history. Of course, once people forgot about the article it sort of died down but then a little while later it all started up again. We couldn't work out why for ages but then we found out that *Time Out* had picked up on the *Evening Standard* article and put us in a list of London's top...I think...*weird* museums or something like that."

"And that started it all off again," chips in Paul. "We even had a busload of Japanese tourists turn up off the back of that. They couldn't get enough of it. They kept taking pictures of us like we were some sort of celebrities."

What a story: a mysterious owner of a house clearance company with a penchant for looking after things no one wanted anymore. If my curiosity hadn't been piqued before, it certainly is now. I feel like something about this strange situation is speaking to the very heart of me and I just have to know more. I look briefly from Paul to Dec and then finally my gaze comes to rest on Alex.

"So, am I right in thinking the original owner, Mr. Barclay, passed away and you bought it from him, Alex?"

"Actually," says Alex, sounding somewhat embarrassed, "I didn't buy Barclay and Sons so much as inherit it."

"Oh, I see, so you're related to Mr. Barclay then?"

At this Alex looks even more uncomfortable.

"The truth is I'd never heard of Thomas Barclay until a month ago when his solicitor contacted me out of the blue and told me I was the sole beneficiary of his will."

"So, Mr. Barclay was, what? A long-lost relative?"

To my surprise Alex shakes his head.

"Not as far as I'm aware. I'm an only child and I lost my parents some years ago, and my grandmother who brought me up passed away three years ago, so there's not really anyone around left to ask."

"Oh, I'm so sorry," I say, offering a small smile of sympathy. "I'm an only child too and I lost my mum last year, so I know a little bit about what you've been through. Do you think Mr. Barclay was some sort of family friend then?"

"I don't think so," replies Alex, "and if he was, why wouldn't he have made an effort to get in touch while he was alive?"

While I know none of this is any of my business, this whole story feels like it's turning my head inside out. I feel strangely compelled to get to the bottom of this mystery.

"So, a complete stranger left you everything he owned in his will and you have absolutely no idea why?"

"That's about the long and short of it," says Alex perfunctorily. "The first thing I did after leaving the solicitor was come here hoping…I don't know…that these guys might know something that would make sense of it all, but they were just as baffled as me."

"And now to top it all," I add, "you've literally just this minute discovered that you've inherited a museum too?"

Alex raises an eyebrow. "Today's certainly not quite the day I was expecting." He turns to Dec, his face thoughtful. "I get it now. When I came here that first time, before you knew who I was, when you thought I was just a stranger who'd wandered in off the street, you said something along the lines of, 'Oh, it's closed.' I didn't understand at the time but you were talking about the museum, weren't you?"

Dec nods sheepishly. "Since the gaffer died, we just haven't had the heart to open it up."

"I get that," says Alex, a note of concern in his voice, "but what I don't understand is why you didn't tell me about the museum once you knew I was the new owner? I mean, why keep it a secret from me?"

Paul coughs nervously. "That was my fault, I'm afraid, boss. I thought it might scare you off, you know, make you want to sell the place and our jobs with it. I mean, the situation was already strange enough without adding a weird museum into the mix. We would've told you eventually, honest."

Another awkward silence descends and I'm about to use it as an opportunity to churn over everything I've learned when I look up and notice that Alex, Paul, and Dec are now all looking at me. It suddenly dawns on me that in all the time I've been here listening to their stories and asking my questions, I've barely told them anything about myself beyond my name.

"Look at me, grilling you all like I'm some sort of stakeholder in this company when I haven't even told you why I'm here," I say apologetically.

"Well, I thought you'd come to see the museum," says Paul.

"Well, I did," I reply, "but that's not actually the full story. I came because I was sort of hoping you'd look after something for me."

Without further explanation I lead the trio to the warehouse entrance and sure enough, despite my earlier worries, the bags with my books are still there.

"Oh, those are yours," says Dec as I point toward them. "I just thought we were having a problem with illegal dumping again. What's in there? Books?"

I feel myself flush with embarrassment. There's no way I'm not going to sound like an idiot to these people.

"They're not just books," I say defensively. "They're a complete set of the 1974 edition of the Encyclopedia Britannica."

The minute I stop talking I can hear how deranged I must sound. Even worse, no one says anything; instead we just stand staring at the books until finally, Paul clears his throat and, turning to Alex, says, "I think we'll leave this with you, boss. Me and Dec have got to get off and quote for a job over in Hammersmith. Maybe see you later, if you're around."

The two men then disappear back inside the building, and moments later the roller grille over the vehicle access begins to lift just as a diesel engine growls to life. Paul and Dec emerge from the building in the van, pausing briefly to give me a quick wave, and then Alex and I watch them drive away.

"My mum bought them for me when I was eleven," I say to Alex unprompted. "I know they don't look like much but they really mean a lot to me. Anyway, for one reason or another I haven't got room for them and I was sort of hoping your museum would take them for me."

"It's always difficult losing people you love," says Alex quietly. We stand, both lost in our own thoughts, and then he says, "Look, as you've probably guessed, things are a bit complicated for me at the moment. I didn't want to say in front of Paul and Dec because I haven't told them yet, but the only reason I'm here today is because I'm meeting a commercial estate agent with a view to putting this place on the market."

"Oh, I see," I say, trying my best to keep the sound of disappointment out of my voice.

"As I said earlier, I inherited it out of the blue and I don't know anything about this kind of business. I'm just a web designer, so my plan is to sell up and get on with my life. But while I won't be able to look after your books permanently, in the short term I can hold on to them for you and save you dragging them back home. Leave them here for the time being, we can exchange numbers, and when I know more, I'll let you know."

While it's not the solution I'm hoping for, it's either here or the bin, and leaving them here certainly beats risking the wrath of Guy by taking them back with me in the middle of a viewing. We swap numbers and I flash him a grateful smile.

"Thanks," I say, "it's really kind of you."

"It's the least I can do; after all, if you hadn't turned up today, who knows when or if I'd have found out that I've got a museum!" We both smile and then he picks up the handles of the bags, ready to take them inside.

"You can't take those on your own. They're really heavy."

"I'll be fine. They're not too bad."

It feels like this is our goodbye, and even though I have a million questions I still want to ask him, I decide that it's best to let him go.

"Thanks for doing this," I say. "It really is very kind of you."

He gives me a smile, and once again, my gaze is drawn to his face, his scars, and then he turns and heads back inside the building, closing the door behind him. For a moment I don't move; instead I think over everything that's just happened. It feels like I've been dreaming, and have just woken up and been thrust back to reality. Everything around me, the row of terrace houses across the road, the blackbirds chirping in the trees, and the people walking past, seems real but I can't help thinking that somehow the dreamworld of Barclay and Sons was better. I shake my head as if to clear my thoughts, then cast one last look at the building behind me and start walking back to Peckham Station.

5

THEN

In the hours before Mum died I'd been out with Luce in Notting Hill for a friend's birthday drinks. Despite the music and the dancing going on around us, she and I had been huddled in the corner of the bar, a little bit drunk, a little bit tearful, as I'd just confessed to her that after two years together I was thinking of leaving Guy.

"I know it hurts now," Luce said as she consoled me. "But in the long run it'll be for the best."

"I know," I replied. "I'm just sad it's come to this."

Just then, my phone vibrated in the back pocket of my jeans. I took it out, checked the screen, and saw a message from Mum: "Hi, sweetie, hope you're okay. Just letting you know I'm off to bed for an early night as I've got one of my migraines again, lucky me! Love you loads, Mum." Sighing, I'd set down my espresso martini on the table next to me. I loved my mum to bits but sometimes I wished I had a sibling to share the load of looking out for her, or for that matter a dad who had bothered to stick around. As it was, I was the only family she had, and though I knew it wouldn't have been the end of the world for me to ignore her text until the morning, as a dutiful daughter I felt the pressure to reply straight-away, even though I was in the middle of my own crisis.

Tapping out a quick reply, I posed the question I always asked when-ever one of Mum's migraines came on: "Have you taken the tablets the doctor gave you????" It might have seemed like an obvious response but knowing her as I did and being all too aware of her propensity to soldier on without help, it was definitely a question worth asking.

Seconds later I received a somewhat sheepish reply. "Guilty as charged!" she wrote. "I always feel a bit funny after I take them but I sup-pose I ought to give them another chance. Xxx." "Of course you should," I replied. "Take them now, make yourself a hot drink, and get an early night!!! Xxx." A short while later I got the following reply: "Think you might be right this time, sweetie! Have taken 'evil' migraine tablets and now I'm off to bed. Give my love to Guy. Night, night, xxx."

To my shame I didn't think about Mum again for the rest of the eve-ning. Instead, desperate to forget my troubles with Guy, I'd really let loose, drinking too much and ending up at a karaoke bar belting out song after song with such gusto that I made myself hoarse. It was after three in the morning by the time I decided to call it quits and poured myself into an Uber. Arriving at Canary Wharf half an hour later, I'd let myself into the apartment building and made my way up to the tenth floor. As the lift doors opened, I slipped off my heels, walked unsteadily down the corridor to the apartment, and let myself in and that was when my phone rang. My first thought was that it would be Luce, who instead of going home had carried on the night back at a friend's house, but when I checked the screen, I was surprised to see that it wasn't her at all; it was her mum, Maggie.

"Hi, Jess, I'm so sorry to call at this time. Where are you?"

"I'm at home," I said, trying my best to sound sober. "Is everything okay?"

She only paused for a moment, a split second at most, but in that instant, I knew that something had happened. I knew that something was very wrong.

"I'm at the hospital," she said. "Your mum called me a couple of hours ago. She had one of her migraines, but this one was unbearable and she asked if Dougie and I would take her to the ER to get it checked out. We didn't think to call you; we just thought we'd get her seen to and she'd be able to tell you all about it in the morning…but…" Her voice cracked, then cracked again, splintering further with every passing moment. "I'm so, so, sorry, love. The doctor said it was an aneurysm. It all happened so fast. One minute she was talking to me and the next she was unconscious and there were doctors and nurses everywhere."

"But I don't understand. What's happening? Where is she now? Are they keeping her in overnight?"

There was a pause and then Maggie said, "I'm sorry, Jess…They did everything they could but it wasn't enough. She's gone, my darling, she's gone."

"But…but…" I felt my head start to swim and reached a hand out to steady myself against the wall. "I was only texting her a few hours ago… She can't be gone…She's only fifty-six."

"I know, sweetheart, I know," Maggie said, her voice breaking. "It's just so horrible. I can barely believe it myself. Just know that Dougie and I will be with you through this every step of the way. You won't have to go through any of it alone. We're here for you, Jess."

The funeral took place a fortnight later in Northampton. It was heartening really, to see how much love there was in the room for Mum. There were people from all different parts of her life, work colleagues, friends she'd made at the weekly Zumba class she'd attended, women she'd kept in touch with from the breast cancer survivors' group, neighbors past and present, old school friends, even the couple who ran the local newsagent had shut the shop for the morning just to come and pay their respects. And as I walked past all of these people and took my seat on the front pew with Guy on one side of me and Luce on the other, Dougie and Maggie on the row behind, I remember thinking that I hoped Mum knew just how much she was loved.

The service was brief but lovely, lots of people said lots of nice things about Mum and then suddenly it was over. As I walked slowly down the central aisle toward the exit, I briefly congratulated myself on having managed to keep it together but then I got outside, and I don't know whether it was the fresh air, or the light, or the sheer weight of sorrow I'd been carrying around with me, but my resolve crumbled and I had to rely on Guy and Luce to keep me upright.

The wake was a bit of a blur, a constant stream of people hugging me and saying kind things about Mum, with me escaping when I could to the loo, to the garden, to my old bedroom, unable to bear their loss as well as my own. Even though the dining table and every inch of the kitchen counters were covered with food lovingly prepared by Mum's friends from work, I didn't eat a single thing. The wineglass in my hand, however, was never empty, no matter how much I took from it.

It wasn't my intention to get drunk, to have done so deliberately would have been disrespectful, but somehow it happened anyway. The more I drank, the less pain I felt, and the easier I found it to tune out what was going on around me. Standing in the corner by the TV while friends of Mum's talked at me ten to the dozen, I found myself looking around the room with fresh eyes: at the cream leather three-piece suite she'd bought on hire purchase after months of lusting over it, the pine coffee table she'd snagged online during Marks and Spencer's winter sale, at the pictures on the wall, the ornaments above the fireplace. All of this would have to go at some point; all of Mum's carefully collected trinkets and treasures, in fact her entire life, would have to be disposed of. It was then that it struck me that as hard as the funeral had been, there was still one last hurdle to overcome.

"I need to clear the house," I told Guy and Luce when I found them in the kitchen helping Maggie and Dougie serve food.

They both looked at me confused.

"What do you mean?" asked Guy.

"I mean when everyone's gone, when it's all over." I gestured around the room but I could see from their expressions that they weren't following me. "I mean I'm going to need to empty the house, empty the house of everything, of all Mum's things."

"Oh, mate," said Luce. "Let's not think about that right now. Let's just get today over with."

"But I want to think about it now," I said. "I need to think about it now."

Handing Guy the tray of sandwiches she was holding, Luce took me by the hand to the back door and opened it. It was raining but that didn't stop her from leading me outside, where we took shelter under the apple tree near the shed.

"I thought you might be in need of some fresh air," she explained, pulling out a packet of cigarettes from her jacket pocket. She took one out, lit it, and handed it straight to me. "Are you okay?"

"Why? Because I said I want to clear the house?"

Luce nodded. "I think you're worrying about things that don't need to be worried about yet." She lit another cigarette, this time for herself, and took a deep drag. "When you decide the time's right, Guy, Leon, and I will come back here with you and we'll get the whole thing done in a weekend."

"But that's just it," I said. "I don't want anyone to help me. I want to do it on my own."

Luce refused to countenance the idea. "That's the grief and possibly the wine talking. You'll feel different once today's over, I promise."

Although I suspected that they discussed what I'd said when I wasn't around, no one brought up the subject again that night. But in the days that followed our return to London, Luce and Guy took it upon themselves to formulate a plan between them to help me clear Mum's house. A date was chosen to make our return to Northampton, a hire car was booked, as was a medium-sized dumpster to be delivered in time for our arrival. Between them they planned for every contingency, every contingency apart from one.

"I don't understand," said Guy when I'd got him and Luce together a few days before we'd been due to leave for Northampton. "Are you actually saying you still want to clear your mum's on your own? Without us?"

"I'm sorry," I replied. "I know I should've said something sooner but the thing is, the more I think about it, I know this is something I need to do alone."

"You're still not thinking straight, Jess," said Guy gently. "If you were, you wouldn't be saying this."

"I hate to admit it but he's right," says Luce. "Why on earth would you want to do something so horrible on your own without the help of the people who love you most?"

How to explain? How to explain to my partner and my best friend that this task, the clearing of Mum's house, was my last opportunity to say goodbye? How to explain that I needed to show this final kindness to her? How to explain that I needed to sort through each of her belongings alone? That I wanted to make every last decision to do with dismantling her life from the biggest to the smallest without the help or hindrance of others? How to explain that I wanted to put as much love and care into the taking apart of my wonderful mum's home as had been poured into bringing it all together in the first place?

6

NOW

The next day, although I offer to help with the viewings, Guy, control freak that he is, ushers me out of the apartment, afraid that in a bid to be nice, I'll give potential buyers too much information, which they'll use to drive the price down. Instead, I meet Luce on the South Bank for coffee, and as we stroll along by the river I tell her all about my visit to the Museum of Ordinary People.

"Now that's proper insane," says Luce as a group of skateboarding teens whiz past us. "A secret museum in the back of a house clearance firm, owned by a mysterious handsome stranger—he was handsome, wasn't he?"

I hesitate, recalling Alex's face, his disfigurement, and then wonder why I chose to leave mention of it from my story until now.

"He had these scars," I explain, "all down one side of his face as if he'd once been badly burned."

"Excellent!" says Luce with mock glee. "Just what this story needs, a double dose of mystery! So, did you ask him about them?"

"Of course I didn't!" Luce could be so crass sometimes.

"But you wanted to know how he got them, didn't you?"

She's right, of course; I did want to know what had happened to him but there was no way in a million years I would have asked.

"Whether I did or didn't isn't the point," I say, trying to keep my hold on the moral high ground. "The point is, it's none of my business, which is exactly as it should be."

Luce laughs and adopts a posh voice. "Let the record show that Ms. Baxter didn't actually answer my initial question, which was how hot was this bloke?"

"Fine," I say wearily as I mentally conjure up his face again. "Okay, he wasn't bad looking, I suppose."

"I knew it!" says Luce triumphantly. "You fancied the pants off him, didn't you? Admit it! You fancied him and now you're going to finally leave Guy and have babies with the Phantom of the Opera!"

Sometimes Luce really is too much. "Lucy Elizabeth Smith, you are undoubtedly a terrible person, and if hell exists, then you are definitely going there."

Reaching an empty bench, we sit down and look out across the river as a pleasure boat full of tourists glides past, its occupants waving enthusiastically at anyone who even glances in their direction.

"You should've seen the place," I continue. "It was beautiful, absolutely beautiful, just like a real-life Aladdin's cave."

"An Aladdin's cave of other's people's junk."

"But that's just it," I say, "though it might have looked like junk to the untrained eye, it was anything but. Everything in there, from the smallest object to the largest, had once been loved and treasured by someone. And Thomas Barclay, for whatever reason, saw that and made it his mission to save these things, to prevent them from just ending up as landfill, to honor the memories of the people who had once owned them. I think it's such a wonderfully noble and romantic idea."

"Only you could see it like that," says Luce, taking the lid off her cup and blowing her coffee to cool it down. "But all that aside, do you reckon there's anything of proper value stashed away in there? Maybe an old master or two, or a priceless antique?"

"I doubt it; in fact, I'm not sure anything in there has any intrinsic value at all, but to be honest I like it all the more because of that. This collection isn't about great works of art, or valuable pieces; it isn't that sort of thing. It's just a room full of objects that, like my encyclopedias, either mean or once meant a great deal to someone, and until he died this guy, this Mr. Barclay, was the only thing standing between them and obliteration."

"Actually," says Luce, her tone less cynical, "now I come to think of it, when my nan passed away I remember Mum got really upset when she cleared out her house. Of all Nan's stuff the one thing Mum really wanted to keep hold of was her dressing table because she had so many wonderful memories of watching her getting ready sitting at it. But you know how small our house is; we just didn't have the room for it. In the end, I think she got Dad to sell it to a junk shop. It proper broke her heart though. I think she felt like it was an heirloom lost on her watch and it took her forever to forgive herself for it."

"That's exactly why the idea of this place is so special," I say. "It's unique, the only place in the entire world where if you were in a situation like that, you wouldn't have to sell it or take it to the dump. Instead, you'd get to leave it somewhere and know that it's safe, that it's being looked after and enjoyed by others. And should you ever want to visit it, to sit with it for a little while, letting all your cherished memories of loved ones flood back, then you can do that too. It's perfect."

"You should ask him for a job," jokes Luce. "It sounds like it was made for you."

"Wouldn't that just be amazing?" I reply wistfully. "Me finally getting my career as a museum curator off the ground after ten years of doing nothing but treading water."

I can still vividly remember the day Mum took me to a museum for the first time. I was six, it was the start of the school summer holidays, Luce was away in Spain with her family, and it had been raining solidly in Northampton since she'd left and showed no sign of stopping. We hadn't gone on holiday because holidays were expensive, but Mum being Mum had planned lots of days out here and there to make up for the fact.

On the day in question as we waited at the bus stop I'd asked her where we were going, and even though I continued to ask her throughout our entire journey, she remained tight-lipped until we reached our destination in the center of town.

"Is this where we're going?" I'd asked, looking up at the grand entrance to an old building.

Mum nodded. "It's the museum and art gallery and I think you're going to enjoy it."

What Mum couldn't have foreseen at that moment was just how much this single trip would change me. While I enjoyed the art gallery side of things, and had loved looking at all the paintings, sculptures, and photographs, it had been the museum I fell in love with.

Northampton's industrial past meant that there were countless displays dedicated to telling the story of factory life in the 1800s and detailing the history of the local shoe trade. I suppose many kids my age would have found it boring, but I was completely entranced, insisting, as I went from display case to display case, that Mum read aloud every single information label for me, even though I was more than capable of doing so myself.

As I'd pressed my nose up against the cold hard glass, I remember desperately wishing I was on the other side, able to pick up and handle these objects from a past I could never otherwise experience. I would thrill equally at the sight of a Victorian child's shoe as I would a Roman pot, as to me the important thing wasn't so much the object itself, but the fact that it had once belonged to a person with thoughts and feelings just like me. And now that they were long gone, these intriguing remnants of the lives they'd led were all the proof that remained that they had ever been here.

That afternoon as Mum cooked tea I set about turning my bedroom into a museum. I gathered together toys and shoes, borrowed some of Mum's old jewelry, necklaces, a few rings that had lost their stones, and the like, and laid these together with the old coin collection I'd inherited from my late granddad across every surface I could find. And for each and every item, I carefully wrote out an information label on paper cut out of an old exercise book and then dutifully attached it with Blu Tack to the space below each object.

From that day forward museums became my passion. Even in my teenage years, when to the outside world it appeared that I was only interested in music, clothes, and boys, I would secretly relish a school trip to a museum, a welcome break from the hormones and confusion of adolescence. My enduring love for museums was why I became the first person from my family to go to university, where I studied history, even though Luce warned me it would be dry and boring and that all the best-looking boys would be studying cool subjects like art or politics anyway.

Then, as my time as an undergraduate came to an end and friends full of doubt began to wonder about their futures, for me there was no question about my next step: I was going to get on a master's course in museum studies, and finally fulfill my childhood dream of being a curator.

I'd ended up on a highly prestigious course at Edinburgh University, where it seemed all of my fellow students were a breed apart. Unlike me, every single one of them had been privately educated and was brimming over with the kind of confidence that comes from an expensive education. Despite often feeling like a fish out of water, I persevered, focusing all of my energies into becoming the best student I could be. I relished every module, from conservation through to marketing, and after graduating was ready to do whatever it took to land my dream job. But life had other plans. The day after my course finished, Mum was diagnosed with breast cancer and my whole world was turned upside down.

Without hesitation, I'd rushed home to be by her side, turning down a three-month unpaid internship at the British Museum in order to do so. "But what if you don't get another opportunity like this again?" Mum had protested. "Of course I will," I reassured her. "You know me, I'll find a way to do this one way or another."

As it turned out, however, Mum had got a lot worse before she got better, by which time what I'd thought was going to be a six-month pit stop had turned into a three-year-long hiatus. By the time she had fully recovered, I was loaded down with so much debt that working free for a museum would've been impossible. I needed to earn money and fast.

When Luce had offered to put me up on her sofa bed in London for free, I'd leaped at the chance. I could temp, clear my debts, build up some savings, and hopefully be on the spot if ever a paid museum position came up. At least that was the plan. But then one temping job led to another and despite working full time and doing shifts at a bar most evenings and weekends, I just couldn't seem to make a dent in the money I owed.

Looking back, I don't think there was ever a point where I officially gave up on my dreams; instead I think it happened gradually, as these things do, so that I barely noticed the shift in my thinking. First, I cut back on the bar work because I was so exhausted from my day job as a receptionist; then I stopped looking for job openings at museums because, well, what was the point when I was never going to get them without experience? Though I continued to love and enjoy museums, the thought of becoming a curator seemed so impossible, so far removed from the life I was living, that I felt like I had more chance of becoming an astronaut than I ever would of actually getting my dream career off the ground.

After parting with Luce, I head home and that evening while Guy is drawing up a shortlist of properties for us to view once he's got an offer on the apartment, I find myself looking up the names of some of the people from my museum studies course. I discover that Allegra Cavendish, who'd barely attended any lectures, is now an assistant curator at the Museum of London; Bryony Campbell-Nicholls, who never spoke to me once the entire time we studied together, is now Collections Manager at the House of Commons; and Verity Afferson, who I'd constantly vied with to get the best marks on the course, is now Project Curator of Medieval Collections at the British Museum.

As I stare down at the black-and-white photo of Verity on the museum's website, looking so cool, collected, and accomplished, I find myself whispering an apology to the person I used to be. This could have been me, it should have been me, and would have too had things been different. But then I remember something Luce said earlier and a thought occurs to me, and before I can talk myself out of it I decide to take action. I scroll through my contacts, locate Alex's number, and then, taking a deep breath, tap out a quick message: "Hi, Alex, it's Jess (Encyclopedia Woman!) from yesterday. So sorry to bother you again but I was wondering if you might be free to meet up with me sometime soon? I've got a proposition I think you might find interesting."

7

So, I'll see you at the Greenwich house at three?" says Guy as I scoop up my keys from the kitchen counter.

"Yeah," I reply, and plant a kiss on his cheek. "See you later."

"Who is it you're seeing again?"

At this I can't help but wince slightly. I hate lying to Guy, I really do. But I don't want him to talk me out of my plan before I've even had a chance to put it to Alex. I feel nervous enough about this morning as it is without anyone pointing out the many and obvious flaws in my thinking. Several times over the past few days I'd been on the verge of calling Alex to cancel today's meeting and although I'd managed to talk myself round, I was still an absolute mess of nerves. So, when I'd told Guy I'd be busy this morning, I'd been deliberately vague, wanting to avoid any questions he might have, and yet now here he is drilling down on the specifics and making me feel worse about my actions with every question.

"Faye Webster," I reply. "We used to be friends in school."

He nods, feigning recollection of the many times I've spoken about my nonexistent friend Faye.

"What are you going to do? Brunch and a bit of shopping?"

"Something like that."

"I'm going for a quick ride this morning, nothing too strenuous, but maybe once I'm done I could come into town—after I've showered of course—and meet you and..."

"Faye."

"That's the one! For a quick drink and then you and I could go over to Greenwich together. How does that sound? It would be nice to chat to an old friend of yours who isn't Luce for a change. Might get a few interesting stories."

"Well...she's only in town a few hours," I say, thinking on my feet. "And I've not seen her for ages and we've got a lot of catching up to do. So, maybe it's best that we just stick to the plan."

He comes over and plants a kiss on my cheek. "Of course," he says. "The last thing you want is me being a boring old third wheel. See you later."

The reason Guy and I are meeting in Greenwich is because yesterday he had an offer on the apartment. "It's a young woman relocating from New York," he'd explained when he'd called me at work to tell me the news. "And she must be loaded too because she didn't mess about. She offered the asking price off the bat."

"And you've accepted?" I asked, suddenly feeling almost dizzy with the speed of everything.

"Of course I did," he said. "As well as offering the asking, she's chain-free and keen to move quickly, so it was a no-brainer. And that's not even the best news of the day."

"There's more?"

"Remember that fantastic house in Greenwich I showed you online? Well, it hasn't sold yet and so I've booked us in to see it tomorrow."

So that was that; after all the ups and downs of the past few weeks, Guy and I were finally in a position to start making offers, which felt surreal in the extreme. On my way home that evening I'd thought about my late grandparents who'd come over from Antigua in the sixties for work. I'd thought about how they'd spent all their working lives in backbreaking factory jobs to pay off the mortgage on the tiny terrace they'd bought under the Right to Buy scheme. How after they'd passed away the only way Mum could afford to keep the house on and maintain it was because of the long hours she'd put in at the supermarket. And now here I was, benefiting from money I hadn't earned, looking at houses they wouldn't have been able to even dream of owning. It seemed wrong somehow, like everything was upside down.

Emerging from Hyde Park Corner Station, I scan the area near the top of the steps and immediately spot Alex standing, as we'd arranged, to the left of an empty information booth. He's looking at his phone but as I approach, he lifts his gaze and as our eyes meet, my attention is once again drawn to his face, his scars.

"Thanks so much for agreeing to meet me today."

"It's no problem. I mean, it's not like I could pass up such a mysterious invitation, is it?"

I feel myself flush with embarrassment. "You must think I'm being needlessly secretive, but I promise it's all for a good cause. Everything will become clear soon. Our destination's just down here."

As we walk, it's impossible not to notice people staring at Alex, or more accurately his scars. Some look, then turn away the moment they're caught looking; others stare pointedly, seeming not to care when I catch their eye. Surprisingly, given that I barely know him, I feel angry on his behalf at these people. I can't help thinking how exhausting it must be to be looked at and judged like this all the time. Part of me wishes I had what it took to tell them to mind their own business and keep their eyes to themselves, but then I recall my own reaction when I saw his face for the first time and I feel like a hypocrite.

"So, do you live near Barclay and Sons?" I ask as we reach Wellington Arch. Though I am genuinely curious about the answer to this question, what I really want to know is whether Alex has found out anything more about Mr. Barclay and his secret museum, but I decide that maybe this is a question for later.

"Oh, no, not at all," says Alex. "Walthamstow, actually. I've been there for about ten years now. It's a nice enough area and there are plenty of green spaces nearby to escape to, so I can't complain."

"And do you work over that way too?"

Alex smiles. "I work from home. I'm freelance. On the plus side it's a short commute but the watercooler banter isn't up to much. How about you? How's your commute?"

"Not too bad. Canary Wharf to Holborn. I suppose I should walk, or at the very least cycle, you know, get a bit of exercise and save the planet and all that, but most of the time I'm running so late that it's not even an option."

"And what is it you do in Holborn?"

"I'm a receptionist at a big office building. It's not exactly my dream job but it pays the bills."

"So, what is your dream job?"

"It's a long story."

He opens his mouth as if to ask another question but then stops as I come to a halt in front of a honey-colored stone building that looks a lot like a more compact version of Buckingham Palace surrounded by green wrought-iron railings.

"Is this where we're going?"

I nod, and he reads aloud from the sign attached to the pillar next to us: "The Wellington Collection: Apsley House." He raises an eyebrow and smiles. "Now I really am confused."

At security we join a queue made up largely of tourists to have our bags checked, after which we head up the grand staircase and make our way toward the Piccadilly Room. Here I take on the role of tour guide, telling Alex all I know about the house and its priceless collection of artworks and antiquities.

Later, as we stand admiring the thousand-piece silverware service set out across the table in the impressive state dining room, Alex jokes, "I wouldn't like to be the guy on silver-polishing duty," and the elderly couple standing next to us both laugh, as do I. Finally, we double back on ourselves, return downstairs to visit the Museum Room, home to all the gifts given to the first Duke of Wellington by grateful monarchs after he saved their thrones from Napoleon, and it's there, once we've seen all the room has to offer, that I try to steer the conversation round to my reason for bringing him here.

"So, what did you think?"

"Of this place? It's…it's okay, I suppose." His voice is uncertain. "It's a grand house, isn't it? It's what they all look like: opulent, ornate, all that gilding and those priceless treasures. A nice enough place for a day out." He pauses, half wincing. "I've said the wrong thing, haven't I?"

"No, of course not," I reply. "I think you're right. Most people's view of museums and grand houses is the same. Nice places to visit on a first date, or a bank holiday, but that's about it."

"So, it's not a bank holiday and unless I've misread the situation this isn't a first date, so what are we doing here?"

I find myself blushing again.

"Because…because…as you might have guessed by now, I love museums and I love places like this that are full of beautiful objects with a rich history. I think it's important that objects with an important cultural significance have a home and that they are properly looked after for future generations."

Alex frowns. "Okay…"

"What I don't like about places like this is the fact that this level of care and attention is only ever afforded to the belongings of the rich and famous. And this is where I think you can make a real difference."

"A difference," repeats Alex. "How?"

Not for the first time I feel my resolve start to crumble. My idea is so out there, not to mention brazen, that I can't actually believe I'm about to say it out loud. But I've come this far and I've got nothing to lose apart from my dignity, and so I ball up my fists and go for it.

"I know you must think I'm some kind of crazy woman with my encyclopedias and useless facts and dragging you here on a Saturday morning, and well, I don't know, maybe I am a bit crazy. But what I do know for sure is that since the moment I left Barclay and Sons last week, all I've done is think about the Museum of Ordinary People. It moved me, Alex, really moved me. And it got me thinking too…and well…

I was wondering...I know you said you were going to sell it...but do you think...I don't know...your little place...it's just got so much potential...all those treasures...all those stories...I was wondering... whether you might agree not to sell it...at least not for the time being and allow me to curate the collection and turn it into a proper museum?"

Alex is momentarily lost for words but eventually recovers himself.

"You want to turn that room at Barclay and Sons into a place like this?"

"Well, maybe not exactly like this, but a proper museum yes."

He gestures around the room. "But this place looks like a palace; the lock-up at Barclay's is just a dirty old storeroom full of other people's junk."

I know I should just keep quiet but I can't help myself; the words seem to tumble out before I can get my brain into gear.

"But that's just it. I think it's so much more than that. Or at least it could be. I know this must feel like it's coming out of the blue, but let me explain. I'm not just some random weirdo talking out of the top of my head. I've got a degree in history, a master's in museum studies, and I know my stuff. I've had work placements in some of the best museums in the UK and I just know that if you let me, with a bit of care and attention I could put your museum on the map."

"But it's not really a museum, is it?" He points to the painting on the wall opposite that just happens to be the world-renowned *Waterseller of Seville* by Velázquez. "This is the kind of thing people come to museums to look at. Priceless treasures, important artifacts, not the rubbish in that old lock-up."

"You're forgetting people have already been coming," I counter. "Regular, everyday people who could have been visiting places like this chose instead to go to Peckham and see the Museum of Ordinary People. If that doesn't prove there's a market for a museum that's a little bit different, I don't know what does."

Alex stares at me uncomprehendingly but I plow on regardless. "I just think there's room for a museum celebrating the lives of ordinary people, revering their possessions, their legacies, their stories. That's why I loved the name of your museum: the Museum of Ordinary People. It's like a mission statement and title all rolled into one. And of course, I'd do it for free. I'd curate it, organize and present it in a way that would do the collection justice."

Alex's expression changes from confusion to curiosity. "You'd do all that for free? Why?"

It's a good question. And while there are any number of things I could say in response, something about Alex makes me tell him the truth, or at least something truth-adjacent.

"Because I've been drifting," I reply. "I've been drifting for a long time. I've just been going with the flow, putting up as little resistance as possible, and daft as it might sound, your museum makes me want to stop doing that, and really do something deliberate, something with a purpose." I pause, my eyes searching his to see whether I might possibly have won him over. "So, what do you say? Will you let me give it a go?"

There's a long silence and then Alex shakes his head. "I can't," he says. "It's too late. Barclay and Sons is as good as sold."

"Already?"

Alex nods. "The property agent I saw last week showed it to a developer he knew and they made an offer on the spot, which I accepted."

"Oh, I see."

"I'm so sorry, Jess, really I am, because I can see how much this means to you. But I'm afraid the answer's no."

While I'd known this was a long shot, I'd assumed the difficult part would be talking Alex into taking a chance on me; it hadn't once crossed my mind that I might be too late.

"But what will happen to the museum? To the collection? To everything Mr. Barclay saved?"

"I don't know, I doubt they'll want it, so you're more than welcome to it."

The irony of this suggestion isn't lost on me. I'd gone to the Museum of Ordinary People looking for a home for a set of encyclopedias I didn't have room for, and now here I am being offered the vast collection at Barclay and Sons. It would be funny if it wasn't so sad.

"I think I'll have to take a pass on that one," I say, and he gives me an awkward smile and we turn and start walking toward the exit. With the uncomfortable silence between us, it feels like the longest walk of my life and it's only when we step outside that either of us seems able to speak again.

I want to run away and hide, but I just about manage to hold on to my composure.

"Thanks so much for coming today," I say, putting on my best brave face. "I really do appreciate it. I'll be in touch about collecting my encyclopedias soon."

"Are you not walking back to the Tube?" asks Alex.

"I've got a few errands to run," I lie, desperate to save him from having to see me cry.

"Of course," he says, and goes to leave but then he stops and turns. "I really am sorry I couldn't have been more help."

"No need to be sorry; some things just aren't meant to be."

With that, I turn and walk quickly away in the opposite direction and once I'm sure I've put enough distance between us I sit down on a wall and finally give in to my tears.

8

It's quarter to three as I arrive at the Greenwich house, having spent the past three hours walking aimlessly around central London cursing myself for being such an idiot. I can't believe I'd ever thought Alex might go for my crackpot idea. I can't believe I'd ever thought he might agree to be part of such a scheme when he'd already told me he wanted to get rid of the place. I was lucky he hadn't laughed in my face, it was the least I deserved, and now to compound my shame I was going to have to come clean with Guy.

"Hey you," he says, wrapping me in an embrace. "Ready to look around our forever home?"

"You bet," I say, trying to sound upbeat. "But before we go in, there's something I need to tell you."

"Oh, okay," he says carefully. "What?"

Suddenly I feel like a naughty child, like I'm a kid at school owning up to a teacher.

"You know how I told you I was meeting up with an old friend this morning? Well, I wasn't being entirely truthful...Actually I wasn't being truthful at all. Remember that place I told you about over in Peckham? You know, the one that agreed to look after my encyclopedias?" Guy nods solemnly. "Well, this morning I went to meet Alex, the man who owns it."

He looks at me confused. "What for?"

"To ask him a favor."

"What kind of favor?"

I flush with embarrassment at the thought of how much of an idiot I'm going to sound.

"Remember how I told you there was a museum at Barclay and Sons?" Guy nods vaguely. "Go on."

"Well, the thing is... ever since I saw it I've been thinking about how I never really got my career off the ground and well, I got it into my head that maybe... I don't know... maybe I could ask Alex if I could run his museum for him."

"But I thought you said it wasn't a proper museum."

"It isn't, not really. But with some work I really did think it could be. I had this crazy idea that maybe I could rework the whole thing and turn it into something special. Anyway, I pitched the idea to him this morning, and long story short, I was too late; he's already sold the building."

Guy is silent for a moment and then finally he says, "But I don't understand. Why didn't you just tell me?"

"I don't think I was really thinking properly. I suppose I just wanted to be able to present it to you as a done deal. But it was a stupid idea and it's come to nothing. So that's that really."

"Oh, Jess," he says. "You should have just told me; I'm not a monster. We could've talked your idea through together and come to some sort of conclusion. Still, I suppose what's done is done. I'm sorry it didn't work out but it's probably for the best, don't you think? I mean, I can't see how it would've worked. I've seen the post you get, even high-profile museums are always begging for money, so how could a little independent thing like you had in mind have been financially viable?"

"I know, you're right. It was just a pipe dream, I suppose."

"Glad we're on the same page," he says, visibly relaxing. Circling a hand around my waist, he gently pulls me toward him. "And, anyway," he adds with a smile, "I don't mind admitting that I would've been more than a little suspicious if this Alex character had taken you up on the idea. Judging from how you described it to me, he'll be getting quite the lorry load of money from the sale of that place, so I'd have had serious doubts about his motivations if he'd given it all up just to open some weird little museum." He plants a kiss on my cheek as if to show that he's only joking and then adds, "Anyway, if things work out with this place or one like it"—he pauses and looks up at the house we're about to view— "we're going to have our hands full. There's going to be so much to do with this move, and you know how slammed I am at work, there's no way I'll be able to keep on top of everything that needs doing."

Suddenly the presumption in his voice makes my blood boil.

"So, what, that'll be my job then?"

He at least has the decency to look shamefaced, given that he's effectively just appointed me as his personal assistant. But he's right of course; his work is always insane and mine isn't, and with the move and sorting out the new house there's going to be a lot to do and it makes sense for me to take on the bulk of it. Besides which he's right, I shouldn't have lied to him and if doing this will get me back in his good books, then do it I will.

"I'm sorry," I say. "You're right. Do you forgive me?"

Guy puts his arms around me. "Of course I do."

"Good," I say. "Then let's go and see this house."

We knock on the door and are greeted by the estate agent, a tall, slim, glamorous blonde who introduces herself as "Izzy from Lovegrove Estates." She looks exactly like the kind of woman Guy used to date before he met me, and as she welcomes us into the house the thought crosses my mind that in an alternate universe Guy would be living in a place like this with someone like her.

As she gives us the guided tour, it quickly becomes apparent that all the clichés of expensive modern London homes are present and correct: the downstairs reception rooms have been knocked into one, the state-of-the-art kitchen-diner has been extended into the garden accessed through bifold doors. And of course, the walls are gleaming white, the deep luxurious carpets pale cream, and the original floorboards beautifully sanded. Lovely as it is though, I can't help feeling it's all a bit soulless, a bit posh house by numbers.

Once Izzy has shown us around, she leaves us to make a second circuit without her, and with every room we enter Guy's smile seems to grow wider. Finally, we make our way back to the kitchen, where the estate agent is waiting for us.

"So, what do you think, guys?" she asks all faux chummy. "Fabulous, isn't it?"

"It's certainly got a lot to recommend it," says Guy, leaning casually against the expansive marble-topped kitchen island, "apart from the price, that is. I have to say it's a little expensive for what it is."

"In this area it's a seller's market, I'm afraid," says the estate agent, without missing a beat. "Because of the local schools, most people are more than happy to pay a premium, especially for a property that's been so wonderfully finished. Still, here's a brochure with my card attached, so even if you do decide this property isn't for you, feel free to give me a call and I'm sure I'll be able to find you something that suits."

The ability to be simultaneously condescending and polite is a skill I've yet to master but the estate agent does it so well that I feel a degree of admiration for her. I can see from Guy's face, however, that he's completely unfazed by the encounter, having other things on his mind.

"You like it, don't you?" I say, voice lowered, as we watch Izzy getting into a Mini emblazoned with the Lovegrove Estates logo.

"Is it that obvious?"

"To me it is," I say, taking in his green-gray eyes, which are practically alight with excitement.

"You have to play it cool with these people; otherwise, they'll use your enthusiasm against you. But you're right, I do love it. I can really imagine us being happy there. I can really imagine it being our forever home. So, what do you think, should we make an offer?"

His question makes my head swim. I'd thought this would be the first of many viewings, not the last. I'd thought there would be more time.

"But, Guy," I say, "we've only seen it once. Shouldn't we at least see some other places first?"

"And risk losing this one? No, thanks. This is London; places like this don't hang around."

It crosses my mind to point out that it's been weeks since Guy first showed me the listing for this house online and so far it hasn't sold, but to do so would be missing the point, which is that he really wants this and reason has got nothing to do with it.

"So, what do you think?" he asks again. "Shall we make an offer?"

I pause, more uncertain now than ever that this is the right thing to do. This house is too big, too expensive, too everything for my liking. In my ideal world nothing would change, we'd stay exactly as we are, I'd tuck Mum's hard-earned money safely away in the bank and just carry on with life as it is. But staying as we are isn't an option, not really. This is crunch time for us; this is Guy asking me again if I'm in or out. And after all we've been through I want desperately to say that I'm in. I want desperately to say that I want us to work.

"Let's do it," I say. "Let's make an offer."

His face lights up. "This is going to be the best decision you will ever make, Jess Baxter, you see if it isn't. I'm going to call Lovegrove's office right now."

Overcome with nerves I begin pacing up and down the road as Guy talks on the phone. This seems like madness, making such a massive decision on the basis of one viewing. I'd feel better if we at least had something to compare it to, if we'd explored other options before going all in on this one. But Guy's the sort of person who knows exactly what he wants and goes for it, unlike me who can't even buy a new shade of lipstick without agonizing over it. I tell myself I have to trust him, I tell myself everything will be okay in the end, but then just as I'm making my fourth circuit my phone rings.

My first thought is that it's Luce hoping to catch up, but when I check the screen I'm surprised to see Alex's name. What possible reason could he have for calling? I think about letting it go to voice mail but then curiosity gets the better of me and I take the call.

"Hi, Jess, sorry to bother you," he says, sounding just as awkward as when I last saw him.

"No, it's fine. Is it something to do with my encyclopedias?"

"No, they're okay. I'm actually calling about your idea."

Now I really am confused.

"What about it?"

"Well, I've been doing a lot of thinking over the last few hours and . . . I don't know . . . well . . . long story short . . . you can have the museum."

I feel sick and dizzy, unable to quite believe what I'm hearing. Has he really said what I think he's said?

"I . . . I . . . can have the museum?"

"If you still want it, that is."

"But I thought you said the sale was a done deal."

"It is, but I've managed to delay it. I should stress it would only be for six months and after that, the sale would go through just as before, but I don't know, maybe by then you'd be in a position to find a new home for it all."

Six months of me running my own museum? It's the easiest decision I've ever made.

"Oh, Alex," I reply, wondering but not daring to ask why he's changed his mind. "I really can't begin to thank you. You won't regret it, I promise."

I don't remember much about the rest of our conversation but the next thing I know, Guy is standing in front of me looking at me strangely.

"Are you okay?"

"I'm . . . I'm . . . I'm going to open a museum," I say, shell-shocked.

He pulls a face, confused. "What, you've been offered a job?"

"Not exactly. That was Alex on the phone. He's had a change of heart and delayed the sale for six months, and he's giving me free rein to do what I want with the museum at Barclay and Sons. I'd be completely in charge, able to organize it however I see fit. Isn't that the best news ever?"

"Well, it depends how you view the fact that we've just had our offer accepted on our dream house."

"What? Already? How's that even possible?"

"When I made the offer, the estate agent kept me on the line while they spoke to the developer and after a bit of back and forth, I upped the offer by five thousand and he accepted on the spot."

"So, we've just bought a house?"

"Yeah, isn't it great news?"

"Yes, of course it is," I say, even though my stomach is churning with anxiety at the thought of it. "It's fantastic. We should go out tonight and celebrate."

"Great idea. How about I book somewhere while you call this Alex chap back and let him know you won't be doing the museum after all. Like we said earlier, we're going to have our hands full from now on."

"It'll be fine," I reply as Guy starts looking at his phone. There's no way I'm going to let this opportunity go now, or I'll lose it forever. "I can do both. It won't be a problem."

He stops what he's doing and looks at me. "Seriously, Jess, you're underestimating how much work moving house can be. Plus, is this chap even paying for all the work you'll be doing?"

"I'll be doing it for free in my spare time."

"What spare time, exactly?"

It's a challenge of sorts, but I refuse to back down. "I don't know, I'll make some. I'll do evenings and weekends, whatever it takes." I kiss him tenderly and hold his gaze. "I promise I'll make it work somehow, you'll see, but this is just too good an opportunity to turn down."

9

While I get the sense Guy is far from happy with my decision to juggle the Museum of Ordinary People and the house move, he must see how much it means to me because eventually he lets the matter drop. That evening, having managed to snag a last-minute booking at a hot new Indonesian restaurant in Spitalfields, we raise a toast to both pieces of good news and spend the night talking excitedly about our plans for the future.

When Monday evening comes around, instead of heading home, meeting up with friends, going to a spin class, or any of the other things I could've done, I make my way over to Peckham to pick up the keys to the Museum of Ordinary People.

As I approach the Barclay and Sons building, I can't help but smile at the thought of being here again, even more so when I think about the collection, and the fact that very soon I'll be able to explore it all in detail.

I try the door, and find it's open and there's no sign of anyone about, but then I try the office and find Alex sitting behind the desk, sifting through a huge pile of paperwork.

"You look busy," I say from the doorway.

"Oh, hi, Jess," he says, startled, once again angling the scarred side of his face away from me. "I thought I'd have another go looking through Mr. Barclay's stuff and see if I could pick up any clues to the big mystery."

"Any joy?"

He shakes his head. "I can tell you all about his last tax return if you're interested?"

He gives me a shy grin, then reaches into a drawer, takes out a set of keys, and hands them to me. "There's one for the main door, one for the office in case you want to make yourself a cup of tea, and one for the lock-up...sorry...museum. Feel free to come and go as you like. Unless they're on a clearance or delivering furniture, Paul and Dec tend to be around from about ten until six Monday to Friday and they do half days on Saturday. I've told them you'll be working on the museum from now on so they'll know not to bother you."

"And what did they say when you told them what I was planning?"

Alex winces. "Honestly? They both laughed and told me to wish you the best of luck. But I shouldn't put any store by them. You'll be fine."

I stare at the keys for a moment. This is really happening. Alex is really going to let me do this. After all this time I'm finally going to have a shot at being a museum curator, albeit of a very quirky collection.

I look up and smile at Alex. "This is really so very kind of you."

He shrugs nonchalantly. "I'm just glad to be able to help, that's all."

"Well, I'm really grateful. I'm hoping to make a start on Saturday. Will you be here plowing through yet more paperwork when I come?"

"I doubt it. Though I'll most likely take some home to work through at my leisure. I might drop in from time to time, if that's okay, but you can consider me a silent partner in this particular venture."

I smile but can't help feeling a little disappointed. I'd been looking forward to the opportunity to get to know Alex a bit better, and perhaps find out more about his story.

"Well, if I'm not likely to see much of you, how about you at least let me take you for a quick drink to say thank you?"

He pulls a face. "Actually, I hate drinking on an empty stomach, but would you fancy grabbing a bite to eat instead? Paul and Dec were raving earlier about the Indian takeaway up the road so we could try that and maybe bring it back here?"

"That sounds great. I haven't eaten either and I'm starving."

Leaving Alex in the office, I disappear to get the food and have no problem finding the takeaway he told me about. Not being sure what he likes, I order a selection of dishes and a small box of beers, and as I wait for it to be prepared, in the spirit of openness I call Guy and tell him about the change of plan.

"Oh right," he says, clearly trying his best to sound neutral. "You won't be too late, will you?"

"No, not at all."

"Okay, well, I guess I'll see you later. Text me when you're on your way."

I can tell it had taken a lot for him to be so restrained but I'm glad that at least he's trying. He's wrong about Alex. I don't think for a moment he has any ulterior motive for helping me out, but I can see how it might look. Perhaps when the museum is up and running and Guy finally meets Alex, he'll relax and stop fretting over nothing. And who knows, maybe they'll even become friends.

Returning to Barclay and Sons with the food, I'm surprised to find that not only are the shutters open but Alex has set up an impromptu outside dining area using some of the Barclay and Sons furniture stock. Out on the pavement is a small 1950s drop-leaf dining table with two ornately carved turn-of-the-century chairs positioned on either side.

"It seemed like madness eating in the office when we've got so much furniture," he says by way of explanation. "Plus, it's too nice an evening to be stuck inside."

"It's perfect," I reply, and begin unpacking the food while Alex goes in search of a bottle opener.

"So, tell me," he says a little while later while we're eating, "knowing nothing about this world, I'm really intrigued to find out how you plan to go about transforming the Barclay and Sons lock-up into a real museum. I put my head in there again this evening and it struck me I wouldn't even know where to begin. But you're the expert, so I suppose you've got a plan all worked out?"

I take a swig of my beer in order to cover my nerves. All week I've had ideas, millions of them, but a distinct plan, I'm not so sure. But the last thing I want is to make Alex doubt the faith he's put in me, and so feigning a confidence I don't feel, I try my best to sound like I know what I'm talking about.

"Well, obviously I'll need to get everything out so that I can assess the extent of the collection and document each item so that there's a clear record of what's in the archive. I'll also have to gauge what sort of condition items are in and see what, if any, conservation work needs to be undertaken. And at the same time I'll tidy up and rethink the space so that when all the objects are returned they'll be organized in such a way that they make sense."

"Make sense how?" asks Alex. "It's just a room full of unconnected bits and pieces as far as I can tell."

"Well, I suppose that's how any museum would look if you just bundled everything into one room. Think back to Apsley House and imagine everything from there stacked up in Barclay and Sons; it would be chaos. So just as they've done, putting together items from particular periods, or by particular artists, I'd try and group objects by some sort of theme too."

"Wow," says Alex, "that sounds like six months' work right there."

He's right, it does, maybe even longer, but I'll get it done somehow.

"It does sound like a lot," I admit, "and I suppose I will have to cut a few corners given the time frame. I mean ideally I'd like it to be open to the public within a month."

"A month," says Alex. "That's going to be quite some feat."

"Like I said," I reply, "I'll make it work."

"And so how will you get the word out about the museum?"

"Obviously, I'll do all the usual stuff: you know, contact newspapers, magazines, and websites. I was thinking of maybe getting in touch with a few well-known curators and see if they might push the museum on their social media channels. You know, get a buzz going."

"And how about opening hours?"

"Well, I was thinking perhaps to begin with we'd open just on the weekends, but if it turns out that there's a demand, we could open on some weekdays, perhaps by appointment if say a school group or a large organization wanted a tour. We wouldn't charge visitors at first but perhaps suggest a five-pound-per-person donation on the way out. I've seen a lot of places where that sort of model works well, and people tend to be a lot more generous if they feel like they're in control of the giving. And of course, any money we raise we'd use to cover costs and improve the infrastructure to keep it self-funding."

Alex nods. "Sounds like you know exactly what you're doing. I've only got one more question but it's a big one: do we need planning permission or a license for any of this? I'm no expert but even I know you can't invite the general public to come and traipse around Barclay's in the condition it's in. I know they got away with it in the past but that was when it wasn't official. I mean, what about toilet facilities and parking, let alone things like health and safety and public liability insurance?"

My heart sinks. Of all the questions he could've asked, this is the one I'd been dreading most.

"You're absolutely right, and I was going to talk to you about this. Yes, legally speaking we do need all the things you've mentioned."

Alex smiles wryly. "But you're not going to get them, are you?"

"Of course, I would if these were ordinary circumstances, but the fact is they aren't. It could take me at least six months just to get the plans in front of the people who mattered, and even then there's no guarantee they'd say yes. Obviously I'd do everything in my power to keep everyone safe and abide by what rules I can but there's no way on earth I could jump through all the hoops required and get the museum open on time." I set down my fork. "I understand that this is a big deal, and though I'd be disappointed I'd completely understand it if you were getting cold feet right now."

"So, you're saying the museum would be completely unofficial?"

I nod. "I suppose you could see it as more of an underground thing, like raves and warehouse parties were in the eighties."

Alex laughs. "Like a guerrilla museum?"

"If you like. There's certainly crazier stuff happening in the art world all the time; why shouldn't museums get a piece of the action?" I pause and take another sip of my beer. "So now that I've come clean, are you still up for the idea?"

There's a long silence, during which I close my eyes and hold my breath, waiting for his answer. The next few seconds feel like they have the power to make or break my future.

"Do you know what?" says Alex wryly. "I actually think I'm even more up for this now than I was when I called you. It's such a mad idea but then again so many mad things have happened to me lately that I'm starting to think I should just go with it. In fact, if you'll have me, I'd like to help you out with the museum."

"You'd do that?"

"Yes, I think it'll be fun."

"That's amazing, of course I'd love your help."

"Good," says Alex, "and while I'm at it I'd like to volunteer Paul and Dec's services too."

"Won't they mind?"

Alex grins. "Well, let's just say it's become apparent that since Mr. Barclay passed away, not a lot of work has gone on at Barclay and Sons, even though they've been collecting their wages. Long story short, we've had a conversation about time owing and trust me, they won't object."

"Alex, that's amazing, I don't know what to say."

"In that case," he says, picking up his beer, "let's raise a toast: here's to the Museum of Ordinary People 2.0! And let's hope it doesn't end with us all getting arrested!"

10

THEN

It was a little after midday as I pulled up in the rental car outside Mum's house on Arnold Street. Switching off the engine, I sat for a moment taking in my surroundings. This street was well beyond the grasp of gentrification, with its rows of near-identical back-to-back terraces and front doors that opened straight onto the pavement; it had given birth to me and made me everything I was today.

This street was lined with the homes of gas fitters and shop assistants, of delivery drivers and care support workers, of retired widows and young single mums. Behind some of the doors were people I'd known all my life, some of whom could still even remember when the house had belonged to my grandparents.

I cast my eyes to the spot where as kids Luce and I would play endless games of kerbies, to the bedroom window of number thirty-four that one of the boys from the road accidentally smashed with a stone fired from his older brother's fishing catapult, and to the telegraph pole outside number twenty-two, onto which my ten-year-old self had carved my undying love for Nick Carter from the Backstreet Boys with Luce's cousin's penknife.

So much time, so many memories. My roots to this place ran so deep that it seemed almost impossible that a day would come when my connection to it would be broken. And yet this was exactly the reason I was there: to sever the cord, to empty Mum's house of all of its contents and bring this chapter of my life to a close.

As I reached to open the car door, my phone rang. It was Guy.

"Hey you," he said. "Just seeing how you're holding up."

"I've literally just arrived. Haven't even got out of the car yet. But I'm fine. Or at least I will be when I get started."

There was an awkward pause and I felt guilty as I thought about everything he and Luce had done to try to help me and how disappointed they'd been when I'd announced that I was going to do this without them.

"I'm sorry," I said. "Messing you around like that. It wasn't fair. I should've said something sooner."

"You shouldn't have said it at all," he replied. "I'm not happy about this, Jess. It isn't right. You shouldn't be doing something like this alone. Why don't you let me come up? I could get the train."

"I promise I'll be fine, really I will. This is something I just need to do. I can't really explain it, and I don't know for sure but I think doing it might really help me."

We talked for a little while longer and he told me about his plans for a weekend without me, which involved a potential bike ride with a couple of friends out to Brighton. I listened to everything he had to say and asked a few questions until somehow there was a renewed sense of peace between us even if it felt like a fragile one.

Taking my bags from the trunk, I let myself into Mum's. These sorts of houses are so small there's no hallway; you walk straight from the street into the house. And so standing there on the welcome mat, I looked around the room: the cream leather sofa, the TV in the corner, the photos above the fireplace, and the pictures on the wall. Everything about it seemed so utterly familiar, so exactly as it had always been, that for a moment I couldn't help wondering if the past few weeks hadn't all been part of some elaborate and terrible dream.

I longed for the noise of the vacuum cleaner being run over the carpet upstairs, the sound of Mum singing along to songs from the Golden Oldie hour on Magic FM as she ironed in the back room—even something as mundane as the churn of the washing machine in the kitchen reaching its spin cycle would've provided some comfort. But instead, the only sounds I heard were the gentle ticking of the clock on the wall in the living room, the faint hum of the fridge, and the creak and groan that 132-year-old roof timbers make whenever the sun warms up their tired joints.

Determined to make a start as quickly as possible, to rip the metaphorical Band-Aid off the wound, I took my things upstairs and deposited them in my old room but then as I turned round to leave, it suddenly dawned on me that I had no idea where to begin. Standing on the landing, I looked across to the bathroom and considered that as a starting point but somehow it felt weird. Next, I glanced across to Mum's room but even without putting my head round the door, I knew I wasn't ready for that yet. Going back downstairs, I immediately decided against the living room, reasoning that it might be better to wait until the bigger furniture had gone; then I moved into the back room with the dining table that we only ever used at Christmas, but this too felt like a job for later.

Finally, I ended up in the kitchen and as I looked around the room, weighing up all the different options, I spied the fridge. "I can empty that," I thought. "That is something I can definitely do." I told myself it would be a soft start, an easy win, a way to build myself up to the more difficult decisions that would inevitably need to be made.

Grabbing a roll of bin liners from the cupboard under the sink, I strode purposefully toward the fridge but as I reached out to open it, there was a sharp knock at the front door. Setting down the bags on the kitchen counter, I went to answer it and found Maggie and Dougie on the doorstep, their plaintive faces looking back at me.

I couldn't remember a time when Luce's parents weren't part of my life. Dougie had been two years above Mum at school and Maggie two years below her. When they got married, they'd moved into number sixteen, completely unaware that Mum lived in the house directly opposite. When the two of them bumped into Mum heading out to work one morning, they'd got talking and in no time at all became firm friends, their friendship only deepening when Mum and Maggie had me and Luce, three months apart. It's partly why Luce and I were so close. They were like family to me. And even though I hadn't been able to be with Mum when she died, it was a huge comfort to know Maggie had been.

"We saw you arrive, love," said Dougie. "Thought we'd give you a few minutes to settle in before we popped over. Hope that's all right?"

"Of course," I said, giving them both a hug. In that instant I recalled all the times I'd eaten tea at their table, played in their garden, and celebrated birthdays and New Year's in their front room.

Maggie picked up a carrier bag by her feet and presented it to me. "For you, love," she said. "Just a little something to save you cooking. It's vegetarian chili with rice. I'm not sure if it's vegan though. To be honest, I'm not sure I'd know the difference. But you can always fish the bits that aren't vegan out, if you like. I won't be offended."

Reassuring her that unlike Luce I was still very much an enthusiastic carnivore, I tried not to laugh as I recalled Luce's brilliant impression of her mum's bafflement about veganism. "I don't know what all the bloody fuss is about," she'd said, wide-eyed. "It's just a bunch of vegetables but the way all these bloody Londoners bang on about it you'd think they'd fought in a world war!"

I invited them in and we stood in the living room, and though no one said it, I think we were all waiting for Mum to pop her head round the door and tell us that she'd just put the kettle on.

"Dougie's been watering your mum's plants and sorting out the post every day before he goes to work," said Maggie, filling in the silence.

"And I cut back the lawn last weekend because it was getting a bit long," added Dougie.

"I gave the house a run-through with the vacuum so it wouldn't be too dusty for you," added Maggie. "And we left all the post in the kitchen on top of the microwave."

I was so moved by their kindness that I hugged them again, even though they insisted that under the circumstances it was the least they could do.

"We both adored your mum and miss her something rotten," said Maggie. "We only wish we could do more."

There was another silence and they looked at me pointedly and then finally Dougie said, "Luce told us all about your plans to...you know... do this alone. And of course, we completely respect your wishes, but are you absolutely sure? It's okay to change your mind, you know. We could do a bit of cleaning if you like. Or help move some of the heavy furniture. We promise not to get in your way. We just want to help."

"It's really lovely of you to offer," I said. "But I'll be fine, honest."

Although they did their best to hide their disappointment, I could tell from their expressions they weren't happy.

"All right then, love," said Maggie finally. "We'll leave you be. But only if you promise to call us if you need anything, anything at all."

"I promise," I replied, and then seemingly satisfied with this response they headed back to the door and stepped outside.

"We just want you to know you're not alone in this, Jess," said Dougie as they stood on the pavement looking back at me. "So, if you need us, just say the word, okay?"

Returning to the kitchen, I picked up the bin bags and glanced over at the fridge. I could make a start, I thought, but instead I filled the kettle, flicked it on, and opened the cupboard, the one full of Mum's herbal and fruit teas, and after a short deliberation, opted for Camomile and Rosehip, which the packaging told me was a calming blend. I could do with being calmed.

I made the tea and as I waited for it to brew my phone rang. This time it was Luce.

"Please tell me Mum and Dad weren't too full-on," she said. "I told them not to bother you but they just wouldn't listen."

"They were fine actually," I replied. "Really sweet, in fact. I don't think they get it, but I wouldn't really expect them to."

"They think you've lost the plot. And to be honest so do I. Why are you doing this alone? Forget Guy and Leon, why wouldn't you at least let me come up with you?"

"You know why," I said.

Luce sighed. "I get it, I get it, and I think you're so insanely brave for doing it but I'm telling you now, when my folks pop their clogs, don't think for a minute I'm not going to drag you back to Northampton with me. There's no way I'm emptying their house alone—who knows what I might find!"

We talked for a little longer, mostly about Luce's plans for the weekend. She and Leon were going out in Balham for something to eat and meeting up with friends in Hackney the following day for brunch and then a visit to Chatsworth Road market. As weekend plans went, it all sounded so wonderful, so utterly normal, that for a short while at least I forgot that my weekend would be the complete opposite.

Once the call was over I picked up the roll of bin bags again, headed straight for the fridge, and opened it. Instantly I was hit by a wave of emotion as I gazed at the contents. This was food Mum had bought to eat. Food that, at the time of its purchase she would've thought insignificant and yet now, all these weeks later, was heavy with symbolism.

"This is the last bottle of salad dressing Mum ever bought," I thought as I stared at the shelf before me. I pulled open the vegetable drawer that now only contained an out-of-date box of eggs. "And these eggs are the last she bought too."

Nothing, not salad dressing, not even rotting eggs, was insignificant any more. Because of Mum's absence, everything now had weight and gravity; nothing felt disposable. Every single thing in the house, no matter how commonplace, now represented something important and precious.

Defeated, I abandoned my mission and retreated upstairs to my old room. I climbed into bed, pulled the duvet over my head, and then proceeded to sob my heart out. And with each moment that passed, the impossibility of my mission was gradually revealed to me. How could I complete what I'd come to do when every fiber of my being wanted to keep everything the way it was? How could I possibly empty the contents of Mum's house, when just like King Midas I felt like everything she owned, no matter how ordinary, had been turned into gold by her touch?

11

ᴥ

NOW

So, you promise you'll message me when you get there?" asks Guy as I stand at the front door on Saturday morning, bag in hand, ready to leave for my first day as curator of the Museum of Ordinary People.

"Scout's honor," I reply, and give him a kiss on the cheek. "Thanks so much for my special breakfast; it was really sweet of you to get up early and make it for me."

"No problem. Although, I'm guessing you could've done without the burnt croissants."

"They were the best bit. Who knew that I like my French pastries well done?" I give him another kiss and, holding his hands, I look up into his eyes. "I really do appreciate you being supportive about this."

"It's not like I've got much of a choice," he replies, and then he pulls a face like he immediately regrets it. "Sorry, I shouldn't have said that. You've been great getting together all of the stuff the mortgage guy asked for and sorting out the solicitor. This is your big day and I really do want it to go well. With you in charge I think it's going to be the best weird museum full of other people's creepy stuff in town."

Since picking up the keys from Alex on Monday, every night my mind has been so overflowing with ideas I've barely been able to get to sleep and every morning when I've opened my eyes the first thing I've done is pick up my notepad and scribble down yet more thoughts. Even at work it's been hard to focus on anything but the museum, and I've had a couple of narrow escapes with Christine, where she's almost caught me sketching out floor plans or pricing up display cabinets on eBay.

Leaving the apartment, I take the DLR to Shadwell and when I reach the station to get my connection to Peckham my phone rings.

"Speak of the Devil," I say when I see it's Luce calling. "I've just been flicking through your Instagram from last night. I wouldn't have thought you'd be surfacing until well after lunch."

"That would be true if I'd actually been to bed yet," says Luce. "But just because I'm dead on my feet doesn't mean I'm not going to call my bestie and wish her good luck on her first day as an actual museum curator! So, are you all ready for your big day?"

"As I'll ever be. To be honest, I'm a bit scared. I mean, what if I'm not up to this? What if I fall flat on my face?"

"Are you kidding? You're going to absolutely smash it. You were born to do this. Think about it: you're the only woman our age I know with a National Trust *and* an English Heritage membership. And I can't think of anyone else in the world who gets as excited about nabbing tickets for exhibitions at the British Museum as they do for Glastonbury. You, my girl, are going to knock 'em dead."

"You really think so?"

"I know so," says Luce. "Now go and show them what you can do."

It's a little after nine when I arrive at Barclay and Sons. Dipping my hand into my bag, I take out the keys Alex had given me, only to find that the door is already open and the lights in the office are on.

"Morning," I say, entering the office to find Alex once again sitting at the desk trawling through paperwork. "Still no luck?"

"Morning," he replies. "None as yet, but I've only been at it a few minutes, just killing time before you arrived really. Fancy a drink before we start?"

As he fills the kettle and sorts out mugs and teabags, I find myself wondering about his scars again. Had he been in a car accident or even worse, a victim of one of those horrific acid attacks? I know it's not the sort of question I can ever ask directly and I wonder if one day we'll know each other well enough that he'll want to tell me. As this thought crosses my mind, Alex turns unexpectedly. Desperate not to be caught staring, I quickly pretend to study the year planner on the wall, which I realize just a moment too late is not just one, but two years out of date.

"Milk and sugar?"

I turn to face him. "Sorry?"

"In your tea?"

"Milk, no sugar, thanks."

Alex nods at the year planner. "I was confused by that too. It's a wonder this place is still in business given their casual approach to organization. They haven't even got an answering machine let alone a computer. I'm beginning to think that Mr. Barclay was something of a technophobe."

He gets back to making the tea and when he's done he hands me a mug and we both sit down. "Thanks again for letting me do this. It really is so very generous of you."

Alex smiles. "You really are going to have to stop thanking me at some point. Honestly, it's like I said, I'm intrigued."

A wiser woman than me would have left it at that but I just can't let it go. "Stupidly, it hadn't occurred to me until my boyfriend pointed it out that you're actually sitting on a bit of a gold mine here. I'd hate to think I was standing between you and the equivalent of a lottery win."

"No one put a gun to my head," says Alex. "This is my decision and I'm happy with it, plus to be honest you're not standing in the way of anything. Like I said, the sale is still going ahead; it's just been postponed for a bit. Besides, it's not as though I've got any big plans for the money. I've no real desire to travel the world or buy a sports car if that's what you're—"

Just then the office door opens, revealing Paul and Dec.

"Morning all!" says Paul. He looks at me and grins. "According to the boss, we're museum workers today; is that right?"

"Yes," I reply, trying my best not to sound nervous. "And I'm so grateful for your help."

"It's our pleasure, isn't it, Dec lad?" says Paul.

"Yeah," says Dec. "Couldn't be happier."

"So, what's the plan of attack then?" asks Paul, rubbing his hands together like he means business, and it takes me a moment to realize that all three men are looking at me expectantly waiting for my direction.

"Today's job is going to be a dirty one, I'm afraid," I begin. "Today, we need to empty the lock-up and lay everything out across the warehouse floor so that we can really see what we're dealing with."

After we finish our drinks, we head down to the museum and once again I'm filled with the same sense of anticipation and excitement as I was the first time I made this short journey. As Dec removes the padlock and I follow him into the lock-up with Alex and Paul behind me, the stale, musty air inside transports me back to the moment I saw the collection for the first time, and the sight of it still takes my breath away.

Paul flicks on the radio he's brought down with him and to the soundtrack of top-forty hits, we start clearing the room. First, Dec grabs a moth-eaten rocking horse with a matted mane and patchy fur; then Paul picks up a beautifully worn dining chair that wouldn't have been out of place in an antique shop had it not been for the fact that it's missing three of its spindles. Next, Alex and I maneuver a large rusting railway clock from its resting place and into the main warehouse, where we begin setting everything out neatly in rows.

As we work, we chat about the objects and even take turns reading out some of the labels Mr. Barclay had attached to them. Some make us smile, like the one accompanying a glockenspiel, which reads: "Purchased by Pyotr Nemtsov for his son Dimitri and donated by Dimitri (5.5.10), who comments: 'I always hated the sound of this glockenspiel and so did both my parents but that didn't stop me from keeping it for fifty years.'" Others, however, are touching, like the label attached to a dusty tea caddy: "Found (16.5.01) in a wardrobe following a house clearance at 35 Loftway Avenue, Herne Hill: Tea caddy containing the baby identification labels of five children." Others just leave us confused: "Collection of dog hair (???) found in a dumpster outside a house clearance in Hornsey," says the label attached to a cigar box. "Note inside reads: 'My Benji, he was the best friend I ever had.'"

We carry on like this, removing object after object, carefully laying each item down on the warehouse floor for a good hour or so before we take our first break. Alex volunteers to do a take-out coffee run and when I insist that it should be me buying the drinks, he just smiles and says, "It's all for the cause," and heads out of the warehouse, leaving me alone with Paul and Dec.

They ask me about what I do for a living and how I got into museum curating and in turn I ask them about themselves and how they ended up at Barclay and Sons. Paul, I learn, lives in Lewisham with Julie, his partner of twelve years. Having started off his working life as a laborer in the building trade, he'd made the switch to house clearance after seeing the position at Barclay and Sons advertised in his local job center.

"I thought to myself, I'll do it for a while and then look for something else," he says, "and here I am all these years later practically part of the furniture!"

Dec, meanwhile, is single, lives with his mum in a tiny two-bed flat on an estate, and is Peckham born and bred. "I heard about the job through Paul's Julie, because she and my mum are like best mates. I didn't like it to begin with. A bit too dirty and grubby, but I'm used to that now and anyway, it's never boring looking round other people's houses."

Paul looks toward the door as if checking that the coast is clear and then, leaning toward me, he says conspiratorially, "So, what do you make of the boss then?"

"How do you mean?"

"Well, apart from anything, what do you make of those scars of his? He terrified the life out of me when I first saw him. I didn't know what to make of it, did I, Dec lad?"

Dec laughs. "You thought it was makeup or something and that one of the furniture dealers had sent him over to wind us up."

"Well, how was I supposed to know he was the new owner?" says Paul ruefully. "I'd never laid eyes on him in my life! So, we called the solicitor and he told us, yeah, you've got a new boss."

"Honestly," said Dec, "you've never seen two people eat humble pie so fast. We couldn't believe it. First meeting with the new gaffer and we insulted him to his face."

"He gave us a right roasting over that," says Paul. "What was it he said?"

"He said if he ever heard us talking that way to anyone again, he'd sack us on the spot," replies Dec. "To be fair to him, he was in the right." Dec looks at me. "So, do you know what happened to his face?"

Though I know they don't mean anything by their question, it feels wrong even contemplating it, as if I'm somehow betraying Alex by gossiping about him behind his back.

"I don't think we should be talking about him like this," I reply, even though the truth is I want to know the answer to that question just as much as they do.

Thankfully, before there's any more debate, Alex returns, carrying a tray of coffees and a bag of pastries. Twenty minutes later it's back to work, and over the next few hours we remove everything from a wedding dress and shoes crammed into a seventies-style sports bag through to a battered vintage cigarette tin containing half a dozen children's baby teeth. As before, each and every item has a label attached to it written in Barclay's distinctive hand. Finally, just as I'm about to duck back inside the lock-up a little after five to pick up my next item from the collection, Alex stops me. "All done," he says, and holds up a battered old accordion still in its case. "Apart from the shelving units this was the last thing in there."

I return to the warehouse and, along with Alex, Paul, and Dec, take in the collection in its entirety now spread across the floor.

"Wow," says Alex. "Just wow."

"Whatever was the gaffer thinking, saving all this lot?" says Dec.

"I always knew there was a lot in there," says Paul. "But this is ridiculous."

As we all stand taking in the scale of the collection, I feel like I ought to say something, but I'm momentarily speechless. Paul's right, there's so much here—far more than I imagined—and it's quite overwhelming.

"It'll all be fine," I say, not wanting to show them just how unequal to the task I feel. "But why don't we call it a day; go home and get some rest and we'll pick things up again tomorrow."

I prepare to leave just like everyone else but at the last moment I realize that I've left my phone in the office. Telling them to carry on without me, I head back inside and grab my phone, but as I turn to leave I catch sight of the collection spread out across the warehouse floor and can't resist spending a few more minutes drinking it all in.

As I walk slowly up and down each row, I cast an appraising eye over the items now in my care, take a mental picture of every single object, briefly assess its condition, and even find myself wondering how it might fit into the opening exhibition.

Some things, like the wedding album I'm standing in front of right now, its cover and pages singed by flames, I just know will make the cut straightaway because they're so visually striking. Others, like the carrier bag of correspondence between two old friends, will need me to unearth more context about them before they can be included.

As I reach the middle of the third row, I find myself drawn to a battered violin case sandwiched between a plastic hood hair dryer and a 1970s telephone table. Stooping down to get a better look, I carefully open it up. The instrument inside is unlike any I've ever seen before. It's bruised, battered, and stringless, the neck looks like it might belong to an entirely different violin, and in addition it appears to have undergone a number of rudimentary repairs over the course of its life. Judging by the lengths its former owner had gone to keep it going, this instrument, unappealing as it might look at first, had clearly meant a great deal to someone once.

Barclay's label doesn't give any clues to its origin beyond the fact that it was found in a dumpster outside a house in Balham, in January 2014. But in spite of this, for some reason, of all the wonderful objects in the collection I can hear this one speaking to me. I can hear it trying to tell me its story but I just can't quite make out the words. There's something special about it, something out of the ordinary, I can feel it in my bones. This violin has a story to tell and I am going to find out what it is. And so, carefully picking it up, I put it into a bag, and decide to take it home with me.

12

So, are you saying you think this is a Stradivarius or something?" asks Guy at home later that evening when I show him the violin.

"Of course not," I reply, wishing for once that he would just listen and nod encouragingly rather than asking me a million and one questions. "Apart from anything, I wouldn't know a Stradivarius if it slapped me in the face."

He takes two bottles of beer from the fridge, opens both, and hands one to me.

"So, what exactly is it you're saying?"

"I don't know," I reply, feeling my enthusiasm for this conversation taking a nosedive. I take a sip from my beer. "I suppose I'm saying that I think it's special, that I've got a feeling in my gut about it, that's all."

"Doesn't sound very scientific to me," he says. "Can't you just google it or get a book about it or find something that will tell you for sure?"

"Sometimes there are no books; sometimes as a curator all you've got to guide you about an object is that little voice in your head telling you you've come across something special." Setting down my beer, I put the violin back in its case, take it to the bedroom, and tuck it safely inside the wardrobe. Returning to the kitchen, I pick up my phone, open up a take-away delivery app, and look at Guy. "Indian, Thai, or Chinese?"

He thinks about it for several moments and then says, "Thai...no, Indian...no, Thai, definitely, and can you order a few more beers too? I think we're running low."

I make the order and as we wait for it to arrive, he tells me about his day, which turns out to have been mostly taken up by a 40 km ride with his cycling friends. As he takes me on a detailed journey through the highs and lows of the ride, I nod, smile, and try my very best to look interested. In fact, I do such a good job that he's still talking about it as our food arrives, and as he finally brings the conversation to a close while I unpack the containers on the kitchen counter, I find myself wondering, "Why can't you listen to my boring stories the way I listen to yours?"

My day of physically demanding work has clearly taken its toll because instead of the small plateful of food I normally consume as my share of the takeaway, much to Guy's surprise I end up eating half of it, so unusually there's nothing left over. Afterward he suggests watching a film, some big blockbuster, with an incomprehensible plot and lots of explosions. But with a full stomach and bones aching from a day of lifting, I'm so tired that all I want to do is go to bed, especially as I've got another long day ahead of me tomorrow.

I feel bad though, so I tell Guy a film sounds like a great idea and curl up next to him on the sofa, promising myself that I'm going to stay awake. With the lights off and the cashmere blanket from the back of the sofa draped over me, however, I really don't stand a chance. It feels like one moment I'm watching the film's high-octane opening, a car chase through the streets of Milan, and the next I open my eyes to find the credits rolling.

That night I dream I'm back at the museum sorting through the objects, one by one. As I handle them, they seem to tell me their stories, which I carefully note down for later reference. Alex is in there too, working side by side with me, but though the scars on his face are still there, they seem to have faded somehow and, still dreaming, the thought crosses my mind that perhaps it's not the scars that are changing but rather my perception of them as I get to know more about the man behind them.

The following morning, my alarm goes off at just after six thirty. Ordinarily I wouldn't even be thinking about leaving my bed on a Sunday morning until midday, but today it doesn't even cross my mind to hit the snooze button. Today is another day I get to be at the museum, and so it's with a smile on my face rather than a scowl that I get out of bed. Once I'm showered, dressed, and vaguely presentable, I head to the kitchen to grab some fruit to eat on the way before scribbling out a quick note to Guy. "Morning, sorry to sneak out without saying goodbye but I didn't want to wake you. See you later, love you, J xxx."

Reaching Barclay and Sons a short while later, I let myself in to find the whole building in total darkness. In an effort to keep Paul and Dec on my side, at the end of yesterday I'd suggested that we start a little bit later today, perhaps around ten. Paul had patted me on the back and called me a "good sort," but I knew I'd still be in early because there's simply too much to do.

Opening up the office, I make myself a tea and then, mug in hand, take another tour of the collection still spread out across the floor of the warehouse. As I walk along the rows past paintings and prints, suitcases and bin bags, I'm reminded of the first time I went down to the stores at the Victoria and Albert Museum as a student on work placement. It had been such a thrill to see all of the wonderful objects kept there usually hidden from the public, waiting for their turn to take center stage at an exhibition. And although the objects here are obviously of a very different nature, the excitement I feel is just the same.

As I reach the very last item, I lift my head, look up across the warehouse floor, and take in the collection as a whole. It's huge, far bigger than I'd anticipated, and once again I wonder if I might have actually bitten off more than I can chew. Restoration and conservation work alone could take the entire six months Alex has given me, and that's without taking into account all the work the lock-up will need to get into shape. It's enough to make me want to run and hide, but I tell myself I have to make this work, and even though it might tip me over the edge, I decide that now is as good a time as any to assess the state of the lock-up and work out how exactly we should tackle it.

As I open the doors, I'm taken aback by how big the space looks with everything, even the rusty old shelving units, removed from the room. Despite the peeling paintwork, patches of damp, and lingering smell of dust and grime that's to be expected from a room that's been shut up for so long, I can see in my mind's eye exactly how I want it to be. I imagine all the damp patches banished, the walls and floor painted a brilliant white that bounces light into every corner, the ugly fluorescent light fitting above my head exchanged for something more aesthetically pleasing. I imagine the layout of the first exhibition, a carefully curated selection of perhaps a quarter of the whole collection. I imagine the exhibits being shown off in their best light, perhaps housed in vintage museum display cases or mid-century shop cabinets with maybe a few items proudly displayed on the surrounding walls.

Finally, I imagine the room full of people, families on a day out, older couples keen to see what all the fuss is about, groups of young people excited by the idea of a museum that breaks all the rules. And everyone, whether young or old, is engaged, really captivated by the exhibits, keen to learn not only about the story of each object but also that of the museum and Mr. Barclay too.

"Penny for your thoughts."

I spin round to see Alex standing in the doorway holding two coffees. "Alex, you scared the life out of me. What are you doing here so early?"

"Couldn't sleep, so I thought, I know what, instead of stewing in bed all morning watching TV, why don't I get up and give Jess a hand." He hands me one of the coffees, which I gratefully accept. "Hope that's okay?"

"It's more than okay. But I do feel bad that you're spending your whole weekend including your Sunday morning lie-in here."

He shrugs. "Believe me, it's no loss."

There's something about the way he says this that makes me feel sad, as if this is no joke, as if his life is empty. I don't want to pry but this feels like a good opportunity to find out more about him.

"So, what would your weekend have looked like if you weren't spending it here?" I ask before taking a sip of my drink. "Would you be out and about or are you more of a home bird?"

"I'd probably be at home," he replies. "I'm not one for going out really. How about you?"

"Nothing really," I reply. "Or at least nothing that seems as important as what I'm doing right now."

Alex smiles. "You really are smitten with this place, aren't you?"

"To be honest," I reply, "it was love at first sight."

After finishing off our drinks we agree to make a start on today's task: photographing and cataloging the collection. My plan, such as it is, is to log every item on a spreadsheet and photograph them, armed with only my ancient laptop and the camera on my phone. It's not exactly the way they'd do things at the Smithsonian but then again it's not as if I have a Smithsonian-sized budget.

"I was thinking," says Alex as we head out of the lock-up. "I could take the photos if you like."

"That would be great," I say. "You're not a professional photographer as well as a web designer, are you?"

"Not exactly," he replies. "But I did photography in school and I've always liked to keep my hand in." He slips off his rucksack from his shoulder, opens it, and takes out one of those professional-looking cameras that real photographers use.

"Wow," I say, "your photos will be a million times better than the ones I was going to take with my rubbish phone. Thanks so much."

"It's nothing really," he replies, and then he's quiet for a moment, as if he's thinking, and then he adds, "Obviously, this is your thing, and you're the boss. But I was also thinking that as well as using the photographs to catalog the collection, we could use them for the basis of an Instagram feed. You know, maybe put up a new photo every day for people to have a look at and get excited about."

I only just about resist the temptation to hug him. I'd been meaning to pin down my ideas about a social media campaign for days but hadn't managed it yet. But Alex is right, it's just the sort of thing we need.

"That's an absolutely brilliant idea. And the perfect way to get people excited about visiting us."

I don't think I'd realized until now how important it might be to have someone other than me contributing ideas to this project. It makes me feel less alone, like we're in it together, like this is something we both want.

"Well, if you like that," he says, "how about this? I could shoot a video of the whole project, starting from today, and going through all the way until we're ready to reopen. Then when it's done, we could maybe show it on the opening night or even have it playing on a screen in the museum so people can see what it's taken to make all this happen."

Now I really do want to hug him. "Oh, Alex, that's an amazing idea. Absolutely perfect. And such a brilliant way to demystify what goes on behind the scenes of a museum. But are you sure you want to do all that work? You've already got a full-time job; surely you don't need another."

"To be honest, none of this feels like work, and that's what I like about it."

Alex's words are exactly what I need to hear right now, and this time round I don't stop myself from hugging him.

"I'm sorry," I say, feeling suddenly awkward. I don't know whether Alex is a hugger or more of a handshake sort of person, and the last thing I want is to make him feel uncomfortable. "Was that weird?"

Alex laughs. "It's fine, don't worry about it. Anyway, no need to hug me again but I have got one more idea. I was thinking, now that we've seen the full scale of what came out of the lock-up, there's going to be an awful lot of work to do. And while me, Paul, and Dec can help with some of it, when it comes to expertise, you know, there's just you."

"You're right," I say. "It's going to hold things up massively."

"So, what if you contacted one of your old university mates or something and asked them if they knew of anyone who would be interested in volunteering with us. I mean, it would be an amazing opportunity for a student, someone who wanted to be a curator and needed experience, wouldn't it?"

He's right, of course. Skilled volunteers, people who actually know something about conservation and restoration work, would make a huge difference.

"That's a genius idea. I can't believe I didn't think of it myself."

"It's because you're trying to think of everything," says Alex. "I'm the same at work sometimes. If I try and do too much, too quickly, I end up overlooking solutions that would've been obvious had I not been running around like a headless chicken."

I smile; that's exactly how I've been feeling since I took on the museum.

"You're right," I say. "Not just about the headless-chicken thing but about the need for more expertise, and I know just who to ask."

13

So, come on then," says the flame-haired, smartly dressed older woman sitting opposite me with good-natured impatience. "What's this all about? You didn't exactly give a lot away in your email other than you were in need of some advice."

It's early evening and I'm sitting in the Museum Tavern, a stone's throw away from the British Museum, opposite Audrey Bannister, my favorite lecturer from my museum studies course. Despite not having seen her for years, she's exactly as I remember: tall, well-groomed, and perfectly stylish.

After Alex had suggested asking around for help, Audrey's name had been the first to spring to mind. She was an expert in her field, having worked at some of the best museums both here and abroad, and yet always made time for her students, unlike other lecturers who had sometimes seen us as an inconvenience.

It hadn't taken long to track Audrey down. A quick search online had led me to discover that having left Edinburgh, she was now heading up the postgraduate program at University College London. I'd messaged her, hopeful that she'd remember me, and thankfully just a few hours later I'd received the following reply: "Jess Baxter! Now there's a name I haven't heard for a while! Would be absolutely wonderful to catch up with you. Am quite busy this week but could squeeze you in on Tuesday evening if you can manage that. Let me know, and we'll make arrangements to meet at the pub! All best, Audrey. PS. Mine's a double gin and tonic!"

"I do need advice," I say finally, "but it's a bit left field."

"Well, I certainly like the sound of that, very intriguing. Tell me more."

And so that's what I do. Over drinks I tell her everything that's happened, from losing Mum and clearing her house through to taking my encyclopedias to Barclay and Sons and then finding myself in charge of my own museum.

"Goodness," she exclaims. "And there was me thinking you were simply in need of a character reference for a job! That'll teach me to make assumptions!" She takes a sip of her drink, mulling over everything I've told her. "I'm so sorry to hear about your mother," she says eventually. "I lost mine to cancer back when I was in my forties. It completely knocked me off course for a while."

"It was the same for me. In fact, if it wasn't for the museum, I think I'd still be feeling lost."

"Well," says Audrey. "I have to say that this certainly sounds like a most unusual project you're taking on."

"Unusual but fascinating. As soon as I saw the collection, it reminded me of something you once said in a lecture, how given the right context anything can be a museum piece."

Audrey grins widely. "Look at you, you little minx, appealing to my vanity by quoting me back to me! Luckily, I've got a huge ego that needs regular stroking, so thank you for that! But before we delve into the details of this project, tell me, where exactly are you working now? I think last time we were in touch was a quite a few years ago when you needed a reference for a job at the Imperial War Museum."

"That's right," I reply, immediately feeling like a failure. "It didn't pan out, I'm afraid. I heard they had over a thousand applicants for what was essentially a tea-making job. In fact, if I'm honest, nothing's turned out quite the way I'd hoped…Right now I'm working as a receptionist at a big office block over in Holborn—I have been for the past few years."

"Nothing wrong with that," says Audrey kindly. "And at least you get to sidestep all of the politics that come with this world. But anyway, I take it you've never lost your love for museums?"

I smile, thinking about the hundreds of exhibitions I've been to over the years.

"Not for a second. It's more the career side of things that I've struggled with. I suppose I sort of lost my way."

"That is until you needed to find a home for your encyclopedias?" says Audrey wryly.

"I know it sounds ridiculous. And it's probably completely beneath the sort of thing you're usually involved with but I really believe in this, and truly think I can make it work."

Audrey smiles. "I was just pulling your leg. You know what, I don't remember all of my students, but I do remember you. I don't think I've ever had a student wanting to be in one of my lectures more than you did. It's such a shame things didn't go right for you, but I'm a big believer in second chances, and I think this might be yours. Far from it being beneath me, I think it's a wonderfully compelling idea. I remember hearing of a similar sort of project in Milan back in the eighties and was fascinated by it then. Yours sounds even better."

"Thank you," I say, suddenly brimming with emotion. "That's lovely to hear from you of all people."

"I only say what's true," says Audrey, and then, leaning forward in her chair, she says, "So, how exactly do you think I can help?"

For the next hour, I talk nonstop about all the ideas I have for the museum. And rather than picking them apart as I'd feared, instead Audrey listens carefully to everything I have to say, gently critiquing my plans and even throwing in a few suggestions of her own. By the end of the evening, I've filled half a dozen pages of my notebook and am buzzing with excitement and positivity.

"I can't thank you enough," I say as we draw the conversation to a close. "You've been absolutely amazing."

"My dear girl," says Audrey. "I've barely done a thing. It's all been you. But if you really must thank me, send me an invitation to your launch party. If there's one thing I enjoy more than catching up with former students, it's a free glass of wine and a good old-fashioned shindig."

"You'll be top of the guest list, I promise," I say as she stands up and gathers her things together.

"And do feel free to drop me a line if you have any more questions or need to bounce ideas off someone."

"I will...and look, I know I've already asked a lot of you but I need one more favor...well...actually...two."

Audrey smiles. "Go on then, what is it?"

I reach into my bag and take out the violin case I'd picked up from home, open it, and hold it out to her.

"I know musical instruments aren't your field of expertise," I say as she peers at it, "but I was wondering if you might know someone, or at least someone who knows someone who might be able to tell me something about this. There's something special about it, I just know it, I can feel it in my gut, but I just don't know where to begin."

"It just looks like a violin to me," says Audrey. "And not a particularly attractive one at that. But then again, whenever I played mine in my youth it sounded like cats' claws being dragged down a blackboard, so what do I know? Leave it with me; I'm sure I'll be able to find someone who can shed some light on it, if indeed there's light to be found."

Taking it from me, she closes the lid and slides the case carefully into a large tote bag on her shoulder and then fixes me with a sly smile.

"Okay, so that was favor number one..."

"Well...favor number two is a bit of a reach," I admit. "But if I'm going to get the museum open on time, I really will need some help. I know it's going to be a hard sell but I was wondering whether you might ask your students if they'd fancy volunteering with me?"

Audrey laughs. "You don't ask for much, do you? Still, if you don't ask, you don't get. I can't make any promises, students on the MA course can be quite picky these days, and though I love your project, I imagine most of them will be too blinkered to get it, but I'll certainly ask the question."

In the days that follow my meeting with Audrey, my life is reduced to just three locations: home, work, and the museum. Every morning I leave just after seven thirty to go to work; then at five thirty I leave for Barclay and Sons, where I stay until around ten thirty. Afterward I head home, catch up with Guy, update him with progress on the house move, and then make myself something to eat before falling into bed. By rights I should be exhausted, ready to fall down flat on my face, but the fact of the matter is I've never felt more energized, more alive. After all this time, all these years, I'm doing the thing I love and no amount of tiredness can take the edge off the elation I feel.

When the weekend rolls around, rather than sleeping in and recharging my batteries, once again I set out early for Barclay and Sons, arriving not long after eight. I'm not expecting anyone else in until ten at the earliest. And so, eager to begin the next stage of my work with the collection, I get changed and slip on my overalls.

As a student, conservation and restoration were some of my favorite aspects of the course. I'd loved learning about all of the techniques employed to address the damage caused to an object by everything from the sun, to the simple passing of time. Once on a work placement, I got to assist, albeit in a minor way, on the restoration of a priceless statue, and on another I helped with the preservation of a seventeenth-century map. And while I was by no means an expert on any of it, I'd learned some key skills that I knew would help me with the archive of the Museum of Ordinary People.

While Mr. Barclay had almost certainly saved the pieces in the museum from certain destruction, what he hadn't done was anything to conserve them besides putting them in his lock-up. Nothing had been done to protect the collection from extremes of temperature or moisture, from the effect of light or, for that matter, anything that might damage their material well-being. Some of the objects appeared to have been water-stained from a possible leak, others were thick with dirt and grime, and pretty much everything smelled of damp and dust.

I walk over to the collection, still spread out across the warehouse floor, and try to work out which of the objects is most in need of help.

As I move up and down each aisle, I come across books with yellowing pages, handwritten letters where the ink is fading, photos that are beginning to discolor, furniture that's started to warp and bend, and clothing that's clearly suffered from moth infestations. It's so disheartening seeing the state some of the objects are in and it breaks my heart that I can't fix all of them. I'm so torn I barely know where to begin and could easily waste the entire morning trying to make up my mind.

Finally, I spy a wing-back chair covered in a worn pale green patterned fabric and decide this will be my first project. The label attached reads: "Chair donated by P. Freeman, 23.10.11, 'This was my granddad Tony's favorite chair that he bought secondhand in 1966. He loved it so much that even when it started to fall apart and the family tried to get him a new one, he refused to give it up. Every time I see it, I think of Granddad, and imagine him perched on it, mug of tea in hand, happy as Larry.'"

It's a lovely little story, and no matter what the circumstances, I can only imagine how difficult it must have been for P. Freeman to part with it, just as I'd agonized over letting go of my encyclopedias.

I cast an appraising eye over the chair, and it soon becomes clear that I've got my work cut out. The seat is so worn that at some point in the past it has been repaired with silver gaffer tape, as have the arms and part of the headrest. While I love all the signs of natural wear and tear that help to tell the chair's story, what I can't abide is how dirty it has become after being in the lock-up all these years.

I fill a bowl with warm water, add the tiniest amount of washing-up liquid, and, after moving the chair away from the rest of the archive, I begin, as gently as I can, to clean the fabric. It's painstaking work, but strangely satisfying too. I feel like it's an act of kindness toward P. Freeman and his grandfather, as if with each square inch of grime that's removed I'm honoring an ordinary life that otherwise would've been forgotten.

"Hello there," says a cheery voice from behind me.

I spin round to see a young woman dressed from head to toe in black.

Her long hair is dyed jet-black too, the contrast of her pale, artistically applied makeup giving her the appearance of the bride of Dracula or at the very least some sort of goth princess.

"Sorry to startle you," she says quickly in a thick Geordie accent. "I knocked on the door but there was no answer, so I thought I'd come in and see if I could find anybody. I don't know whether you can help me but I'm looking for something called the Museum of Ordinary People."

14

$\mathscr{S}$

My initial assumption is that the woman is a prospective visitor to the museum. "I'm afraid we're closed at the minute, sorry," I tell her. "But we're hoping to reopen at the end of the month, so if you leave your details I'd be more than happy to put you on our mailing list and contact you nearer the time."

The young woman looks confused. "Oh, that's strange. I was told you needed help straightaway. Or at least that's what Audrey said."

Finally, the penny drops.

"Oh, Audrey sent you? You must be one of her postgraduate students. Sorry, I should have realized. To be honest, when I didn't hear anything earlier in the week I'd just assumed nobody was interested."

"I probably should've emailed you first but I thought I'd just come down and see you in person."

"Well, I'm so glad you're here. I need all the help I can get. There's just so much to do. What's your name?"

"Angel, Angel Evans."

"Well, Angel," I say, taking off my rubber gloves and offering her my hand. "I'm Jess, head curator, marketing manager, and chief bottle washer, and this," I say, gesturing to the archive laid out across the floor, "is the contents of the Museum of Ordinary People."

Without further ado, I walk Angel around the room, pointing out some of my favorite pieces and telling her a bit about Barclay and the museum's history. The longer I talk, however, the more self-conscious I become as it gradually dawns on me that Angel is the first person who actually knows anything about museum curation to see the collection up close and I can't help but feel exposed. Does she think it's a great idea or a stupid one? Is she really getting what I'm trying do with the museum or is she calculating precisely how long she needs to indulge me before she can politely make her excuses and escape?

"So, what do you think?" I ask, bracing myself for rejection.

There's a short pause and then to my relief she grins. "I love it. I really love it. I've never seen anything like it but I think it's a fantastic idea."

"And you're not just saying that?"

Angel laughs. "I swear, hand on heart, I love every single thing in the collection, even the creepy cigarette tin with the children's baby teeth and the thing with the dog hair! It's all so intriguing. The very idea of it. I mean, who hasn't walked past a dumpster and seen something chucked there that obviously once meant something to someone? I mean it's tragic really. And who hasn't had something special that used to belong to someone they loved and had no choice but to get rid of it because they didn't have the room to keep it?"

"Yes, that's exactly it," I say as a wave of relief sweeps over me. "I'm so glad you get it. Sometimes I feel a bit like I've been in my head with this so long that I've lost all perspective about it."

"Absolutely not," says Angel. "I think your judgment is spot on here. I think everyone's got something they would've wanted the Museum of Ordinary People to look after if they'd known about it."

I lean against an old filing cabinet and look at her. "What would yours have been?"

Angel smiles. "You're going to think I'm mad, but I think it would've been my granddad Bill's shed."

She tells me how when she was fifteen her granddad passed away. At the time, her mum asked if there was anything from his house that she wanted to keep to remember him by and the only thing she could think of was the shed in his back garden. "He'd been a mechanic by trade," she explains. "But he loved working with wood and used to make all sorts of things in that shed. He made me a dollhouse once, and he used to make bits of furniture for Mum and all my aunties too. When I was little, there was nothing I loved more than standing on a stool next to him watching him make things."

"So that's why you wanted the shed?"

Angel nods. "We'd had so many happy times in there, it almost felt like an extension of him. Of course, my mum thought I was just being an awkward teenager, so in the end I had to settle for his old woodworking tools. But I remember after his house sold I walked by it one day to find a whole load of builders gutting the house, the shed smashed to pieces in a dumpster. It proper broke my heart seeing what had happened to it. It was like they didn't care about my granddad, or how lovely and kind he'd been. So, I grabbed a little piece of it out of the dumpster and took it home, and I've still got it to this day." She stops and looks at me, suddenly shy. "I've never told anyone that story before."

"Well, I'm so glad you did," I reply, "because it shows me that you get it. You understand what this whole project is about."

This moment seems to be the tipping point for us, and in no time at all we're talking nonstop. She tells me about how, just like me, she is from a single-parent family and she too was the first of her family to go to university. She tells me about a school trip to the Discovery Museum in Newcastle upon Tyne when she was seven, and how it changed her. "I just couldn't believe that they kept all this amazing stuff together under one roof," she says animatedly. "All the time I was there I kept thinking I was dreaming and that I'd wake up any minute."

She tells me how she went to one of the worst schools in Newcastle and how her career counselor had laughed when she'd told her that she wanted to be a museum curator and said she might be wise to set her sights a bit lower, perhaps working the till in the gift shop.

"Cheeky cow!" says Angel, laughing. "I thought to myself, 'I'll show you!' and so I knuckled down, aced my GCSEs, and got myself into the best school in Newcastle. I ended up at Oxford reading medieval history and from there I volunteered at the Ashmolean until I could get on Audrey's course at University College London. And now, here I am."

Just then, Alex arrives, closely followed by Paul and Dec, and over tea and coffee I make the introductions. Although I can see from the look on Paul's face that he's dying to make a quip about Angel's unique look, thankfully he keeps his opinions to himself and in no time at all he and Dec are chatting and laughing with her like old friends.

"She seems great," says Alex, producing a packet of biscuits from a cupboard and offering me one.

"She's lovely," I reply. "I just wish there were about fifty more like her . . . at least then we'd have a chance of opening on time. As it is, even with Angel's help, I think we're really going to struggle."

"Well, I can't magic up another Angel," says Alex. "But I do have something that might cheer you up."

Reaching into his pocket, he pulls out his phone and shows me the screen and I immediately let out a little yelp of delight.

"Everything all right?" asks Paul, looking over.

"Couldn't be better," I reply. "Come and see what Alex has done."

Everyone huddles around Alex's phone, staring at the web page open on the screen headed in stylish black lettering: "Welcome to the Museum of Ordinary People."

"Is this the museum's website?" asks Angel.

"It's just a rough draft," says Alex. "I only started it last night but even though I say so myself, I think it's coming together pretty well."

"He's being modest," I tell Angel. "It's amazing."

It's everything I would've asked for had I been peering over Alex's shoulder while he designed it. It's clean and functional and yet intriguing and beautiful to look at. And I don't doubt for a moment that had I had to pay for it, it would have cost a small fortune.

"I remember you saying last week about museum websites and how good some of them were," says Alex sheepishly. "So, I spent a couple of hours taking a tour of the best of them to get a few ideas together and then knocked this up yesterday. It's a bit rough around the edges but the real thing will be a million times better. I was even thinking at some point it might be fun to create a sort of virtual museum tour for people who can't make it here, but that's for a little bit further down the road."

"I think it could probably do with some music," says Dec, unprompted. "Might give it a bit of life. Maybe a dance track of some kind, something to grab people's attention."

I look at Alex and can see from his expression that he hates the idea as much as I do.

"Well, thanks for the feedback," I say. "Alex and I will definitely keep it in mind."

Angel comes in whenever she can and proves herself a valuable member of the team. Her skills as a conservator are about a million times better than my own and she's as adept at working with dresses and photographs as she is with letters and paintings. Even better, she's also got a good eye for the exhibits and is invaluable as a sounding board as I start to make preliminary decisions about which items will make the cut for the first exhibition.

"Sorry to bother you," says Alex as Angel and I huddle over the desk in the office discussing the best to way to conserve a 1960s christening gown that has seen better days. "Have you got a second? Me and the boys need you to come and take a look at something."

"Of course," I reply, immediately wondering what's gone wrong and how much it's going to cost to fix it. As it is, I've already maxed out one credit card and am close to reaching my limit on a second.

"Do you need me as well?" asks Angel. "Or shall I carry on here?"

"Actually," says Alex, "I think you'd better come too."

As we follow Alex down to the lock-up, it occurs to me I've been so focused on the archive of late that I can't remember the last time I'd even poked my head through the door.

At the entrance Alex stops and looks at me. "Are you ready?"

"For what?" I ask, but he doesn't reply; instead he trumpets a jokey fanfare and then opens the doors, revealing a completely transformed room. The horrible flaking walls have been covered in a brilliant white paint, making the room seem not only brighter and cheerier but bigger too. And if that isn't enough, the ancient rusting fluorescent lights that used to hang at angles from the ceiling have been replaced by a set of eight reclaimed polished-brass light fittings.

"Are those the ones I ordered off eBay?" I ask. "I didn't even know they'd arrived."

"Dec signed for them a couple of days ago," says Paul, "but we didn't tell you because we wanted to see the look on your face when you saw them in place."

"So, what do you think?" asks Alex. "It's pretty impressive compared to what it used to be, isn't it?"

Impressive doesn't even begin to cover it. What had been little more than a dingy cave now looks more like a cool, contemporary modern art gallery.

"This is amazing," I say, hugging Alex, Paul, and Dec in turn. "It's a thousand times better than I ever dared hope it would be."

"And that's not all," says Alex, pointing in the direction of the stairs leading to the attic space. The last time I'd been up there it had been full of junk, everything from old canvas tents through to filing cabinets, the result of years spent as a dumping ground for things Barclay wanted to keep but needed out of the way. Now, however, the space had been emptied, the roof and walls had been rubbed down, and there was a long line of shelving units on either side.

"When did you do all this?" I ask, completely stunned.

"The last few days," Alex replies. "We were talking with Angel and she mentioned that you'll need somewhere to store the parts of the collection that aren't on show and I just thought upstairs would be perfect."

"And it is," I reply. "It's absolutely perfect."

We join the rest of the team and as Alex, Paul, and Dec take turns remarking on how well the room has scrubbed up, I look from them to Angel, who has made such a huge difference to my workload here, and then finally I look around the room once again. And for the first time since we started, I find myself thinking, "We really are going to do this. We're really going to open a museum."

15

THEN

For the first few moments after I woke on the Sunday morning, I didn't know where I was. A quick glance around the room told me I wasn't at home in London but it was only when my brain registered the pastel floral wallpaper that I realized I was back at Mum's in the spare room that had once been my bedroom. Immediately, the memory of my embarrassing defeat in the battle to empty Mum's fridge flooded back and straightaway all I wanted to do was pull the duvet over my head and go back to sleep. In the end, however, hunger forced me out of bed and I went downstairs to make myself breakfast.

I hadn't wanted much, just a cup of tea and some toast, but with no bread or milk in the house I had no choice but to throw on some clothes and nip down to the corner shop. As I walked back, I found myself stuck behind a dad and his two kids on their way to the park. The younger child, a little girl, was holding her father's hand and talking to him animatedly about something while the older one, a boy, wheeled along next to them on a bright red scooter.

It was nice seeing a dad so involved with his kids but I found myself feeling strangely envious of them. If my dad had been around like he should have been, I would've had memories of trips to the park with him, just like the ones they were busy creating. If my dad had been around like he should have been, I wouldn't be emptying Mum's house. Instead, I'd be comforting him and he'd be comforting me, and we'd be working out together how to live life without her. As it was, he was nowhere to be seen. I didn't know if he was alive or dead, living in America, where he was from, or somewhere else entirely. All I knew for sure was that he'd never been a part of my life; all I knew for sure was that it had always just been Mum and me.

Over the years, Mum had told me a few key pieces of information about my father. He'd been an American serviceman briefly stationed at RAF Croughton and they'd met on a night out in Northampton and had dated for a while before he was redeployed to an airbase in West Germany. A few weeks after he'd left, Mum had discovered she was pregnant with me and that was that.

What I didn't really know was if she'd ever told him about me. She was always sort of vague about the details, but I couldn't imagine she wouldn't have at least given him the opportunity to play a part in my life. Therefore, the fact that I'd never met him could only mean one thing: he wasn't interested in me as a child or an adult.

After breakfast I washed up and as I dried my hands on one of Mum's novelty tea towels, printed to look like a fried egg, I made the decision to stop feeling sorry for myself. No amount of anger over a man I'd never met was going to change this situation. I'd come here to do a job and I wasn't about to leave without it being done. With that in mind I drove to the big supermarket on the other side of town, where I picked up a few more groceries along with half a dozen empty boxes I found stacked up near the tills. Back at the house I set the boxes down on the kitchen counter and then, gritting my teeth, began emptying the kitchen in earnest.

Starting with the food cupboards, I put aside what I thought I might use during the week and then emptied all the open packets and containers straight into bin bags and put them in the wheelie bin outside. Next, all Mum's tins of beans and soup, packets of pour-over sauce mixes and custard, along with everything else that was intact and unopened, went into boxes ready to take to the local food bank.

By late afternoon all the cupboards were empty, the surfaces cleared of everything apart from the kettle and toaster, and all the pots and pans were stacked up by the front door, ready for the scrap-metal man. I looked around the room. It seemed sad and lonely, somehow empty of life and love, but I'd done it; I'd finally managed to clear a room.

The next day I worked hard to keep my momentum going. I emptied my bedroom, the bathroom, and even the garden shed. I put a few things aside I thought Dougie and Maggie might want as keepsakes, then arranged for a charity shop to come round and collect all the big bits of furniture that remained. I was doing well, far better than I'd anticipated, and so when Tuesday morning came round I made up my mind to finally tackle the room I'd been dreading the most.

Pushing open the door to Mum's bedroom, I stood on the threshold, watching the early-morning light casting shadows across the walls. I took in the room as a whole: the feature wall decorated in a subtle pale blue bird-print wallpaper, a rich yellowish-cream painted on the remaining walls. The double divan bed, triple-door wardrobe, chest of drawers, and two matching bedside tables. All of it spoke of Mum's style, of her desire to make this room her safe space, her sanctuary.

I tried to remember the last time I'd been in there when Mum was alive. It must have been back in March for Mother's Day. Usually, I sent flowers and chocolates and would call her up for a long chat but this time round, feeling bad as I hadn't been up to see her since Christmas, I'd surprised her by taking the train up to Northampton on the Saturday afternoon. We'd ordered a takeaway from the Sunrise Garden and washed it down with a bottle of Cava and some cheesy Saturday-night TV. Then the following morning I'd woken up extra early, loaded the oven with pastries I'd brought with me from a posh bakery in London, and then taken Mum breakfast in bed.

"Oh, Jess! You shouldn't have," she'd protested. "You work hard enough as it is with all that dashing around London you do and now you've spent valuable time waiting on me when you should've been resting!"

Sitting down on the bed in the same spot where I'd sat chatting to Mum that Mother's Day morning, I found myself instinctively reaching out to pat the space where she should have been. The empty space, the shocking absence of her was so intense I could barely breathe.

What was I doing thinking I could empty this room alone? Of all the rooms in the house this one was the most her, the one where I was guaranteed to encounter the ghost of Mum, not in any supernatural way, but rather in terms of her essence. I took out my phone, ready to give in and call Guy or Luce and beg them to jump on a train to come and help me, but then I caught sight of the silver-framed photograph on Mum's bedside table and I knew I had to carry on.

The picture, taken during a session at a professional studio, had been part of my fiftieth birthday gift to her. We were both dressed up, with perfect hair and makeup, and were laughing, really giggling at a terrible joke the photographer had just made. In and of itself it was a lovely photo, but knowing what I did about our lives, about how much Mum had struggled, about the obstacles we'd had to overcome, it represented so much more. It was me and Mum as victors, the two of us united against the world. And of course, it was also a reminder, just when I needed it most, of exactly why I'd chosen to do things this way.

Getting to my feet, I turned to the large wardrobe that took up almost an entire wall of the room, and drawing a deep breath, I opened the doors. As much as I'd braced myself it was still a shock to come face-to-face with so many things that were so quintessentially her. From posh formal dresses to warm winter coats, each and every item seemed to have something to say about who Mum was, about the life she'd led and the person she'd been.

The brightly colored dresses were a reminder of how, when the mood took her, Mum could be the life and soul of any party. The tidy stacks of thick, warm jumpers and neatly ironed jeans were evidence of her ever-present practicality.

I decided the way forward was to make two piles: one of clothes to keep and the other to bag up, ready to take to the charity shop. The clothes I couldn't even remember seeing Mum wear were relatively easy to get rid of. But where I really struggled was with the pieces that had memories attached to them: a black cardigan with funny silver bobbles she'd bought the winter I'd spent revising for final exam mocks; the pale blue dress and floral jacket she'd worn to my graduation; the tailored dove-gray trouser suit she'd bought for her long-service award ceremony at the supermarket, to name but a few. As a result, by the time I'd finally emptied the wardrobe, the pile of clothes I'd put aside to keep was three times bigger than the one to give away.

In the end, for reasons of practicality, I decided against keeping any of Mum's clothes despite the memories attached to them. The plain truth was, back in London I barely had room for my own let alone ones I already knew I'd never wear. As a compromise, I put aside my favorites from her collection of scarves—ranging from pale pastels to bright, vibrant patterns—and placed them to one side ready to take home with me.

After lunch I took the bags of clothing downstairs to the dining room and then returned to make a start on the dressing table. As I sat down ready to go through the drawers, I thought back to all the times as a little girl when I would watch Mum getting ready: styling her hair, applying her makeup, examining her features. This had been the location of my first exposure to the secret world of women, and one of my favorite things to do as a child was to sit on this very stool and pretend to be her.

As I emptied the drawers of countless packets of tissues, cotton balls, hair-removal strips, brushes and combs, bottles of nail polish and half-used pots of moisturizer, I was reminded of the chaos of my own armory of beauty products back in London, stuffed into a drawstring rucksack underneath the bed.

If Guy and I had the space, I would have the dressing table brought to London and fill it with my own things and think of Mum every single time I sat down at it. As it was, however, we simply hadn't the room and so this and all the fond memories attached to it would soon be gone too.

I did keep her makeup bag though. It was a pink floral number I'd bought her for Christmas a few years earlier when I'd noticed her old one was on its last legs. Unzipping it, I gently shook out the contents, assuming there would be nothing in there I'd keep, but once it was all spread out before me I knew all of it would be coming home.

There were lipsticks still bearing the impression of her lips, a compact of her favorite face powder, its warm floral fragrance immediately conjuring the familiar comforting smell of her. The blusher brush, with its baby-soft bristles still tinged peach. All of it was so evocative, so familiar, that when I closed my eyes I could almost imagine Mum was leaning in to kiss me.

Moving quickly on to the bedside table, I tipped out the drawers one by one until there was a huge pile of the contents in the middle of the bed. Much like my own at home, Mum's bedside table was a repository for things she had clearly wanted to keep and things she hadn't had the time to throw away. Amongst the countless packets of tissues, headache tablets, and half-empty boxes of throat lozenges were broken watches, defunct mobile-phone chargers, tangled necklaces, old letters, wedding invitations, and even a couple of orders of service brought home from funerals of friends and colleagues.

Once I'd sorted through the pile on the bed, I turned my attention to the last piece of furniture left to empty: the chest of drawers. I remembered it being delivered not long after my sixteenth birthday. Along with the bedside tables, it had come from a pine-furniture warehouse that was having a huge sale. Mum had been thrilled to bits with the bargain and even more so when they'd thrown in free delivery too.

The top drawer was full of her typically practical fuss-free underwear, sensible black-and-white sets from Marks and Spencer along with neatly folded pairs of socks and tights. The second and third drawers contained an array of thermal vests for cold weather, shapewear for special occasions, and various forms of night attire. The bottom drawer was home to a motley collection of beauty tools: a pair of straighteners from when her hair was long, a depilator still in its packaging, and one of those battery-powered foot files that had been all the rage a few years ago.

Underneath all of this, covered by an old pillowcase, I found a satin-covered gift box that looked like it had once contained some sort of confectionery. Inside was a collection of mementos of my late grandparents: a color-tinted photograph taken on their wedding day, my great-granddad's pocket watch, half a dozen letters from Granddad to Grandma, and finally, wrapped in tissue paper, my grandmother's wedding ring.

I picked up the ring and gently held it in the palm of my hand. I didn't have many memories of my grandparents—they had both passed away when I was fairly young—but I was really moved by these physical reminders of their existence. I loved the fact that Mum had carefully treasured these few things all these years, and I felt emboldened by the idea that it was now my turn to become their custodian.

Scooping up the box of mementos, I carefully placed them in a bag and as I took them downstairs wondered who would become keeper of my treasures when my time came? Would it be Guy, Luce, or some child or children I was yet to have? And having inherited my things, would they even want them, or would they end up in a dumpster somewhere, cast aside, considered worthless?

16

⤙⤚

NOW

So, is that everything?" asks Paul as we look around the transformed lock-up, taking in the changes we've all worked so hard to achieve.

"Yes," I declare. "I think that's it. I think we're finally done."

There's a collective sigh of relief and I check my watch to discover that it's after midnight. As Paul searches around for his coat and Dec and Angel start collecting various mugs and plates of half-eaten sandwiches from around the room before heading home, I take a moment to enjoy the space.

While the layout for the museum might not match the vision I'd had originally (antique museum displays and Victorian shop fittings had proved way beyond our meager budget), it has still come together brilliantly. We've had to make do and mend with a lot of things but that seems fitting somehow. The objects in the first exhibition are now displayed on the trestle tables Paul and Dec found in the warehouse (now sanded down and painted a dove-white), spread across the numerous shelves positioned around the room, hung directly on the walls, or in the case of the larger items like the motorcycle sidecar, set directly on the floor.

The collection as a whole is divided by theme. There are sections dedicated to all things wedding-related, others to treasured pieces of furniture. There's an area devoted to beloved family pets, and another detailing precious holiday memories. There are well-loved sets of gardening tools and cooking utensils, next to a display I've entitled "Creative Endeavors," featuring everything from carefully painted portraits to collections of poetry. There's a table given over to personal correspondence and another featuring a small sample of the many suitcases we have that had been stuffed full of things saved for posterity only to be dumped when the owners passed away. And all of it, every single item brought into the room, has Barclay's original, handwritten label attached to it, detailing where and when it was found or donated to the museum.

"Hold on," says Alex suddenly, and everyone stops what they're doing. "Actually, we're not quite done yet." He pauses and smiles at me. "I think you've overlooked something, haven't you?"

"Have I? What?"

He points to a shelf behind me, the only empty one in the room.

"I can't believe it," I say. "In all the rush I completely forgot."

I move toward the stairs leading to the newly refurbished storage area but Angel and Dec beat me to it, returning moments later carrying three familiar-looking IKEA bags, which they place on the table next to me. Paul grabs the stepladders and positions them in front of the shelf.

"Right then," I say, trying my best to sound businesslike but feeling as if I might cry. Taking a deep breath to steady myself, I climb the ladder, take a book from Angel's outstretched hand and, as everyone bursts into spontaneous applause, place the first volume of my encyclopedia carefully on the shelf. This simple act feels momentous, the culmination of weeks of hard slog, late nights, and dedication. I wish Mum were here to see what I'd achieved. I know in my heart she'd be proud of me—she always was my biggest fan—but what I wouldn't give to be able to share this moment with her now. Overcome with emotion, I bite my lip and turn to this group of people, once strangers, now friends.

"Thank you, thank you all, so much, not just for today but for everything. There's no way any of this would have happened without you."

When the last volume is in place, Alex hands me the label that I'd written out earlier in the day in preparation and I attach it to the wall with Blu Tack beneath the shelf. Leaning back, I read it aloud: "Object: Set of Encyclopedias donated by J. Baxter. Comments: 'These were given to me by my late mum, Maria Baxter, in the hope that they would inspire me to do great things.'"

That night I head home in the back of an Uber to find Guy already fast asleep in bed. I crawl in next to him and the moment I close my eyes I drift off straightaway. When my alarm goes off the following morning, I find that I'm alone in bed. I call out to Guy, but there's no answer; he must have left for work early. I check my phone to see if he's left me a message, perhaps a few words wishing me well for the launch party tonight, but there's nothing and though I scan the kitchen, there's no note there either.

Disappointed, I console myself with the idea that he's probably got something planned for this evening, and after a quick shower I grab some breakfast, pack a bag with clothes and heels for later, and head straight back to Barclay and Sons to prepare for the launch party.

One of the things I've been doing since the day Alex gave me his permission to run the museum is lobbying journalists, historians, and even a few celebrities on Twitter to come along to the launch. My hope was that enough of them might be sufficiently intrigued by the quirkiness of the place to accept an invitation or at the very least mention it to their legions of followers on social media. Disappointingly, most, even if they were polite enough to respond to my invitation, had turned it down. Consequently, the crowd I'm expecting tonight is mostly made up of friends, and friends of friends, rather than the cultural influencers I was hoping for. Regardless, I'm determined to put on a good show, the best I possibly can.

From the moment I arrive, there's no time to spare, especially as Alex messaged me on my way in to say that a work thing has come up and he won't be able to make it in until later this afternoon. I dole out the tasks for the day to the rest of the team—everything from decorating the museum with balloons and bunting, through to making sure that all the piles of Barclay and Sons furniture stock, dotted around the warehouse, are safely cordoned off.

As a hands-on boss, I've saved the least attractive job for myself, and so, filling a bucket with soapy water, I don a pair of cleaning gloves, get down on my hands and knees, and try my best to make the Barclay and Sons loos presentable.

"Oh, the glamour!" exclaims a familiar voice, and I turn round to see a grinning Luce standing in the doorway.

"You nearly gave me a heart attack," I say, getting to my feet to welcome my friend, who has booked the day off work just to help me. Carefully angling my gloves away from her, I wrap her in a huge hug. "I thought you weren't getting here until midday."

"I woke up earlier than I'd planned and thought that you could probably do with the help," she explains. "Anyway, what are you doing cleaning the loos? Aren't you supposed to be the head curator of this place?"

"Indeed, I am," I reply, giving her a little curtsey, "but when the budget's as tight as the one I've got, it means there's no job I won't do."

We head down to the museum and on the way bump into Paul, Dec, and Angel, all busy getting things ready for the launch, and I introduce them to Luce before moving on.

"They seem like a nice bunch," she says, once we're out of earshot. "But where's the mysterious Mr. Alex? I was sort of hoping for an introduction." She gives me a cheeky wink as if the suggestion in her voice alone hadn't been enough for me to understand her meaning.

"He's got a work thing today," I explain, choosing to ignore her, "but if you're good I'll introduce you to him when he gets here later."

"Well, if he's half as interesting as you've made him out to be, I'm sure he'll be well worth the wait."

At the museum I open the door and let Luce step in first, and I can't help but feel proud when she lets out a gasp of delight.

"Oh, Jess!" she says, genuinely awestruck. "This looks absolutely amazing. I mean it, I'm blown away. You've done such a fantastic job here. Oh, mate, I can't tell you how proud I am of you."

"So, you approve?"

"I love it so much that I can *almost* forgive you for having dropped off the face of the earth this past month."

"Yeah, I'm sorry about that," I reply, and then pull a face as I think about all the messages she's left that have gone largely unreturned. "Do you forgive me?"

"Of course I do, you idiot. I wouldn't be here otherwise, would I?" She looks around the room again admiringly. "I really love it. And I especially love how you've laid the exhibits out on these tables; it looks really chic."

"You don't think it looks too much like one of those trendy homeware stores?"

"Now that you say it, it does a bit...but that's good, isn't it? You've said from the start that you didn't want this place to look like a stuffy old museum and it doesn't. It's perfect." She bends down to examine a colorful handmade quilt from the sixties on the table next to her. "So, is this everything that was here originally?"

"No, there's tons more stuff that we'll bring out over the coming weeks so that we can change things up and keep things looking fresh. For instance, there's an old doctor's bag that's got a lovely story attached to it that didn't make the cut this time round and a hideous 1970s wedding dress that is so bad it's good that we didn't have room for either."

Luce continues looking around the room, coming to a halt in front of an ivory-silk-covered wedding album from the 1920s featuring a handsome-looking young couple.

"Someone actually threw this out?" she exclaims. "It's beautiful."

"I know, right? Even though I have no idea who these people were, what happened to them, or why it was thrown away, it just seems tragic to think that their wonderful day might have been consigned to rot in the dump if it hadn't been for—"

There's a knock and Dec pokes his head round the door.

"Sorry to bother you, Jess, but there's a bloke here with a load of wine-glasses. Where do you want them?"

I flash Luce an apologetic smile. "I think that's our cue to get to work."

*   *   *

The rest of the day flies by in a flurry of activity. Luce helps me deal with the wineglasses, then set up tables for the food and drink before helping Angel decorate the main warehouse space. In the middle of the afternoon, I discover that the friend of Luce's I'd asked to DJ can't make it and so she and I spend the next hour phoning around everyone we know to get a replacement.

In typical fashion, the moment that problem is sorted my phone buzzes with a reminder to pick up the food and drink for tonight and so Luce and I borrow the Barclay and Sons van to go and collect it.

"Is Alex here yet?" I ask Angel later as she helps us unload.

"I don't think so," she replies. "But I've been down in the museum making those last-minute adjustments we talked about, so he could easily be in the office."

When I head to the office, there's no sign of him and when I check in with Paul and Dec, who are busy constructing a small stage for tonight out of scaffolding, they haven't seen him either. I take out my phone to call him but then the replacement DJ arrives and the next thing I know, Luce is telling me that there's just half an hour to go until guests start arriving and unless I want to greet them looking like the bride of Frankenstein I need to go and get ready.

Swinging by the office, I grab my bag and go to the now spotlessly clean toilets to get changed. Slipping out of my sweatshirt, jeans, and sneakers, I pull on a pale green vintage evening dress that I'd last worn two summers ago to a friend's wedding. Thankfully, not only does it still fit but as far as I can tell from my reflection in the cracked and mottled mirror, it looks pretty great too. With what time I have left I quickly do my makeup and hair.

As I stand back to check my reflection again, I feel my stomach flutter with nerves. I so want tonight to go well; I so want people to see just how special the museum is, and to tell everyone they know about it. Taking a deep breath, I dump my bags in the office and after giving myself one last pep talk, I head back into the warehouse.

Desperate to make sure everything is in order, I take one final tour of the museum before guests arrive. As I wander along the aisles, I feel a little thrill of pride as I imagine people seeing this place for the first time. It's perfect, absolutely perfect, and I suddenly wish Alex was here to share this moment with me. There's so much I want to say to him, so much I need to thank him for. I dial his number but even though I try several times, he doesn't pick up. I tell myself he must be on his way over and so don't leave a message. Instead, I blow a kiss in the direction of my encyclopedias and, fixing a smile on my face, head back to the warehouse and prepare to greet my first guests.

17

I'm in the middle of catching up with a very excited Zofia and Maria from work when I feel a hand on my shoulder, and I turn round expecting to see Alex but instead find Guy looking back at me clutching a bouquet of flowers.

"So, you weren't joking when you said this place was in a house clearance company," he says, nodding toward the stack of furniture cordoned off behind me. "If that lot topples over, we'll all be crushed to death."

"And a good evening to you too," I reply a little caustically, and then, immediately regretting my tone, take a deep breath and give him a peck on the cheek.

"Sorry, didn't mean anything by it," he says quickly, handing me the flowers.

"They're gorgeous, thank you," I say, and give him another kiss.

"You look amazing, by the way," he says. "And you've certainly managed to pack this place out too. Well done, you." He scans the room briefly. "So, where's your fairy godmother then, the mysterious Alex?"

"He's not here yet. But I'm sure he's on his way."

"Cool," says Guy a little tersely, swiping a glass of wine from the tray of a passing waitress. "Can't wait to meet him."

Before I can respond I spot someone waving frantically in my direction as they move through the throng toward me, and a moment later I realize that it's Audrey wearing a huge smile on her face.

"Here's the woman of the hour!" she says, hugging me. "Congratulations, you. You've certainly drawn the crowds tonight."

"Thank you so much for coming," I reply. "You don't know how much it means to me."

"I wouldn't have missed it for the world," says Audrey. "Thank you so much for inviting me."

Guy theatrically clears his throat and I suddenly remember my manners and make the introductions.

"You must be a very proud man right now," says Audrey.

"Absolutely," he replies, putting an arm around my shoulder. "Such a clever girl."

Part of me wants to kick him in the shins and remind him of all the times he's doubted both me and this project, but the last thing I want to do is make a scene in front of Audrey, so I just go with it and smile.

"He's my biggest supporter," I say pointedly. "I wouldn't have been able to have done any of this without him."

Guy has the decency to at least look a little bit embarrassed by this blatant untruth before mumbling something about leaving Audrey and me to catch up, and disappearing into the crowd.

"Would you like me to show you around the museum?" I ask Audrey nervously. "It won't be the full guided tour but I can at least talk you through what I was trying to achieve."

"You're doing yourself down, my dear," says Audrey. "That was always one of your worst habits. I've already been around the museum, thank you, and it's quite plain to me that you've more than accomplished what you set out to do. It's a triumph, my dear, an absolute triumph."

I feel myself flush with pleasure. It's one thing to have compliments from friends and well-meaning acquaintances, but to hear Audrey, who I know from experience isn't given to empty praise, say something so positive about this project that I've poured my heart and soul into, means the world.

"Thank you," I reply, trying my best not to cry, "thank you so much."

For the next few minutes I unashamedly grill Audrey for her thoughts about the exhibition, desperate to know what she felt I'd got right, and what she felt could be improved upon. Her insight is so incisive that I could've listened to her talking all night, but then Angel appears at my side and discreetly whispers in my ear that it's time for my speech. Shocked at how quickly the time has gone, I check my watch and sure enough she's right.

"I'm sorry, Audrey, but I'm going to have to go," I explain. "I'll catch up with you later."

As we make our way toward the stage, I hand Guy's bouquet to Angel to look after and ask her if Alex has arrived yet. "No one's seen him at all," she replies. "And Paul and Dec have both tried his mobile but he hasn't picked up. Could be that he's just on the train and got no signal. I can't imagine he's not coming, can you?"

"No," I reply, "he's as much invested in all this as I am. I know he won't miss it, if he can help it. How about we give him ten more minutes to get here and take it from there?"

Ten minutes come and go but still no Alex, and so finally I have no choice but to take to the stage and, picking up a school bell that's also one of the exhibits, I ring it several times until the music is turned off and a hush settles around the room.

"Hi, everyone, thanks so much for coming tonight," I begin nervously, my mouth suddenly dry and my hands shaking slightly. "It really does mean the world to me that you've all made the effort to be here on a rainy Friday evening. I promised myself I'd keep my speech short and sweet. Many of you already know how I stumbled across the Museum of Ordinary People. Like so many others who have come through its doors, I was struggling with the grief of losing someone I loved and trying to find a home for an object that was so much more than the sum of its parts. In my case it was a set of battered, out-of-date encyclopedias. But others have come looking for a safe haven for items as diverse as a Utility Furniture chest of drawers, bought just after the Second World War by a young couple setting up their first home, to a 1980s Kirby vacuum cleaner, which the donor described as being 'one of his late mother's most treasured possessions.'"

There's a ripple of faint laughter and I look around the room and smile before continuing.

"Other objects have made their way here through the efforts of the late Mr. Thomas Barclay, who first formed the collection in the mid-nineties for reasons that to this day remain a mystery. I like to think that, like me, he hated the thought of these everyday objects and the memories they represent being thrown away like rubbish. I like to think that, like me, he believed they have as much right to exist and be cared for as those belonging to the famous or celebrated, whose possessions are so often preserved and venerated for posterity. The Museum of Ordinary People is, then, exactly what it says it is: a museum about and for ordinary men and women like you and me, and the extraordinarily ordinary lives they lead. Perhaps none of us is in line to the throne, perhaps none of us will ever win an Academy Award or walk on the moon, but that doesn't mean we haven't made a difference while we're here to the people who love us.

"The things on display here at the Museum of Ordinary People are a testament to the memories of the people they once belonged to and as such are priceless. If you haven't looked around the museum yet, please do so, and for those of you who already have, please tell your friends. Finally, I'd just like to thank everyone who has helped make this project happen: Paul, Dec, and Angel, the dream team who have poured so much time and energy into transforming what was once a humble lock-up and its contents into what we see tonight; Audrey Bannister, for all of her invaluable help, advice, and gin and tonics; my long-suffering best friend, Luce, who has counseled me through countless crises in the run-up to tonight; and of course, my incredibly patient partner, Guy, who has barely seen me this past month; and last, but by no means least, I'd like to thank the man who made this all possible…" I pause here and look over to Paul, who I'd left in charge of scouting for Alex, but he just shrugs and shakes his head, leaving me no option but to continue. "It appears he's far too modest to make himself known, so in his absence please join me in raising a toast to the current owner of Barclay and Sons, Alex Brody, without whose generosity and kindness tonight would not have been possible."

The moment I leave the stage I'm immediately surrounded by well-wishers keen not only to congratulate me on my speech and the exhibition but also to tell me about objects from their own pasts they wished could have been saved by the museum. A friend of Audrey's tells me how she wished she had kept her granddad's old pushbike that he rode every day of his life until he was hospitalized following a stroke. Another, a heavily tattooed builder friend of Paul's, first tells me that he's never been to an event like this and then goes on to describe the bumper car that used to live in his parents' back garden, a relic of his dad's former life as a fairground worker, and how they'd had no choice but to dump it when his parents moved into sheltered accommodation. A friend of Angel's tells me about how she and her friends, on their way home from a night out in Sheffield, had discovered an old suitcase in a dumpster, full of twenty years' worth of personal handwritten letters dating from the late 1980s. "We were all completely torn," she says. "It seemed wrong to leave them there but at the same time we didn't really know what to do with them either. If only we'd had somewhere like this to bring them to."

It's so wonderful to hear how people connect with the idea behind the Museum of Ordinary People but as the evening wears on, I find myself struggling to concentrate. I'm really worried about Alex. Has something happened to him? Is he ill? Or has he had an accident? I don't want to mother him, or make a fuss, but I just can't help feeling there's no way he wouldn't turn up without letting me know. He's been so invested in the project, I just can't believe he wouldn't want to be here to celebrate the launch.

Eventually, I manage to slip away to the office to try to contact him one last time before getting Paul to drive over to his flat to check he's okay. As I pick up my phone, however, I see there's a text: "Hi, Jess, so sorry to have missed tonight. Something came up at the last minute and I just couldn't get out of it. Hope it all went well. I know it will have after all your hard work. See you tomorrow, for the grand opening of the museum. Alex x." While I'm glad he's okay, something about this doesn't feel right. I don't believe something just came up. I don't believe it for a second. I look at my watch; the text came in when he knew I'd be making my speech so wouldn't hear it. It was almost like he didn't want me to get it until it was too late to do anything about it. I'm starting to think Alex never had any intention of coming at all, and worse still, I've got a horrible feeling that I might know why.

Taking out my phone, I begin scrolling through my emails. When Alex emails me, it's from his Gmail account, but there have been a couple of times when he's messaged me from his work account and those messages have his home address at the bottom. Without thinking I book an Uber, type in Alex's address, and then head outside to wait for it to arrive, telling myself that with a bit of luck I'll be back before anyone notices I've gone.

18

As I get out of the Uber, my phone vibrates. I check the screen and see a message from Guy: "Looking for you everywhere. Where are you?" Though I feel terrible about it, I don't reply, reasoning that he wouldn't understand. Anyway, I'm not planning to be here long, so I'll message him on the way back. As the car pulls away, I return my phone to my bag and then stand for a moment taking in the purpose-built low-rise block of flats in front of me. I switch my attention to the panel of buzzers to the left of the entrance. I press Alex's once and wait, but there's no response and so I try again and again until finally on the fourth attempt I hear a click followed by an uncertain voice saying, "Hello?"

"Hi, Alex, it's me, Jess."

There's a long silence and then he says, "Jess? What are you doing here?"

"I just need to tell you something. Do you mind if I come up for a minute?"

There's another pause and then finally, "Er...yes...I suppose...I'll buzz you in."

The door releases and I make my way through a neat, well-maintained lobby up three flights of stairs to the third floor to find Alex standing in his doorway wearing a confused expression on his face. He's dressed in a band T-shirt and tracksuit bottoms and has nothing on his feet aside from a pair of tartan-patterned socks. He briefly looks me up and down, taking in my evening gown.

"What... what... are you doing here?" he asks. "Aren't you meant to be at the party? Is everything okay?"

"Funnily enough," I say, "I was about to ask you the same question."

His face falls. "Sorry I didn't make it. Like I said, something came up."

"Really?"

He considers me for a moment and then, sighing, shakes his head. "Come in," he says, "and I'll make us both a drink."

While until this moment I hadn't given a great deal of thought to what Alex's flat might be like, I'm surprised by what I find. Though the outside of the building is modern and boxy, the living room in which Alex deposits me feels light and airy, with large windows and higher ceilings than I imagined there would be. The walls are painted in an uplifting shade of sky blue and are covered with prints and photographs, line drawings and paintings. There are plants of every description displayed along the windowsills and also in baskets hanging from the ceiling and dotted on top of bookcases that are full to bursting. It's a comfortable, homely-looking sort of place, far less functional than a stereotypical single man's flat might be.

"Nice place," I say as Alex returns to the room carrying two mugs of tea. "It's much bigger than it looks from the outside and I love what you've done with it. How long did you say you've been here?"

"Ten years now," he replies as he hands me my drink. "I viewed tons of different places when I was looking to buy, and a few were quite a bit bigger than this but I just like the feel of this place."

"I can see why," I say, looking around the room again. We fall into an uneasy silence, and I find myself focusing on the mug in my hand as I try to pluck up the courage to say what I came here to say.

"About tonight..." says Alex suddenly, but then his voice trails off and so I decide it's my turn to speak.

"Actually," I begin, "would you mind if I say something? The reason I'm here is because I want to apologize. I've been so wrapped up in everything to do with the museum and getting ready for tonight that I'm afraid it didn't even cross my mind that you might... I don't know... feel uncomfortable... and not want to come to the launch party. When I got your message... well... I was worried about you. Worried that I'd put you in a difficult position and I just wanted to see if you're okay and to tell you how sorry I am. I mean, when we first met, you wanted to be rid of Barclay and Sons and now because of me you've still got it and you've been up to your neck in paint stripper and renovations. I really am sorry."

"There's no reason to apologize," he says after a moment. He puts down his mug on the coffee table and stares at it, as though deep in thought. "The truth is I fully intended to be there tonight and even bought a new suit for the occasion. The last few weeks have been fun, I really enjoyed being swept along by the excitement of it all, but when I went to get ready tonight... I don't know... I thought about how it would feel to be in a room full of strangers... people who I know from experience would all be looking at my scars and wondering how I got them and... I don't know... I just felt exhausted at the thought of it."

"Oh, Alex," I say, "I'm so sorry you feel that way. But I'm sure if you had turned up, people would've been lovely. They're mostly friends of mine, or at least friends of friends. They wouldn't have been horrible."

He looks over at me. "Wouldn't they? I'm not so sure that's true. Wherever I go, whatever I do, people always stare; they can't help themselves. I'm getting better at dealing with it but, I suppose, sometimes I just can't."

I think back to my own reaction the first time we met, how despite my best intentions I too had stared at his scars; I too had wondered how they'd come about. And as easy as it might be to simply write it off as natural curiosity, to be stared at, to be constantly scrutinized must feel horrible.

"Ever since it happened," continues Alex, without specifying what "it" is, "people have looked at me differently. At school, at college, at uni, and for the short while when I first moved to London and wasn't self-employed, at work too. Eventually, I just got so sick of it that little by little, I built a life for myself that didn't involve seeing people face-to-face unless I wanted to. I bought my flat, meaning that I no longer had to share. I went freelance, meaning that I no longer had to commute. I made sure I never had to meet a single client face-to-face, only ever using email or phone, and the way the modern world works meant that building a life away from people became easier and easier. Thanks to Ocado I never had to cross the threshold of a single supermarket, thanks to Deliveroo I never had to miss out on a weekend takeaway, and thanks to Amazon, I never had to venture into town on a Saturday afternoon in search of things to spend my money on."

My phone buzzes from inside my bag and he looks over at me as if to say that he doesn't mind if I answer it, but I shake my head and so he continues.

"Every now and again, of course, the isolation would get to me. I'd think about the lives being lived by people my age: the fun they were having, the relationships they were forming, and the futures they were building, but for the most part, I was happy and secure. Here in my flat no one stared at me in horror, pointed at me in amusement, or patronized me with pity. Here in my flat I could simply be me. But then about a year ago I read about someone, a therapist who helps people like me, and so before I could talk myself out of it, I booked myself in for an online session with her: me in Walthamstow, she in her consulting room in Fitzrovia. It turned out to be exactly what I needed: she was sympathetic without being a pushover and challenging without being overbearing."

He tells me how over time, little by little, session by session, his therapist began setting him real-world challenges. Things like going out to the supermarket, going for a walk in the park on a sunny day, and taking short Tube rides.

"I know to an ordinary person these challenges wouldn't even have registered as such, but to me back then they were about as easy as being shown a photo of Mount Everest and then being told, 'Okay, now you've seen it, go climb it.'"

He tells me how much he hated these challenges to begin with and at times considered giving up therapy altogether just to be free of the stress of being so vulnerable, so out in the open. But then just as his therapist had predicted, the more he did, the more he refused to give in to fear and the stronger he grew. Soon he was seeing his therapist in person rather than over the Internet and even making sojourns out into the world when she hadn't tasked him to do so. Things normal people did without thinking, like picking up a coffee from the local café, buying a weekend newspaper from the corner shop, or going to the pub if there was a big match on.

"I suppose what I'm trying to tell you," he says in conclusion, "is that while I'm a lot better than I used to be, I'm still not exactly where I want to be, not yet, not all the time anyway. I mean, inheriting Barclay and Sons has pushed me even further out of my comfort zone than I thought possible and then I met you and said yes to the museum but…well, tonight was…I don't know…just a little bit too much, too soon."

"Of course," I say, resisting the urge to say I understand because I know that I can't. I have no idea what it's like to be Alex; I have no idea what it's like to be him at all. "I'm just sorry I didn't think things through more, sorry that I put you in this position. I give you my word it won't happen again."

Alex smiles. "You don't need to treat me with kid gloves. Like I said, I'm fine most of the time."

"Well, in the future if you're not, will you promise you'll say something?"

"I promise," he says, and then he gives me a wink. "Scout's honor. Now tell me how the party went."

I tell him all about the evening and he listens intently to every word I say. As I speak, I begin to wonder once more about this man sitting across from me, his past, the deep sorrow he seems to carry with him, and his connection to Barclay. Part of me is desperate to know his secrets, to become his confidante, because he seems so alone, and I'm almost tempted to ask him to share more of his story with me but know I can't. I know Alex will tell me what he wants me to know in his own good time, and in the meantime, I'll just have to be as good a friend as I can be.

"So, will I see you in the morning?" I ask as we stand at his front door.

"Obviously, you don't have to come if you think it'll be too busy for you," I add hastily. "But if you do swing by…maybe when it's quieter, I'd… we'd really love to have you there."

"Thanks," he replies, and then without thinking I hug him tightly, burying my face in his chest, and he hugs me back, and it's only when we've parted and I'm on my way down the stairs that I realize I'm crying.

19

Despite the bittersweetness of the night before, there's a real spring in my step as I emerge from Peckham Rye Station and start making my way toward Barclay and Sons. I've got a good feeling about today, a really good feeling, which not even Guy's sourness this morning at having to spend yet another Saturday alone could spoil.

As Guy moodily asked over breakfast how many more of our weekends would be sacrificed at the altar of the museum, it had taken all the patience I could muster not to retaliate. After all, over the years we'd been together, how many weekends had I spent alone because of some big project with a ridiculously tight deadline that he couldn't get out of? How many weeknights had there been when he hadn't made it home until long after I'd gone to bed, only to head back out to work first thing in the morning before I was even awake? And then of course, there were the countless cycling weekends (including a few bank holidays) spent everywhere from the Lake District through to the Andalusian countryside.

Not once have I ever complained about any of this, understanding that this is part of who Guy is and what he needs to be happy. But the one time I have something I'm dedicated to, the one time I could have done with his support, is of course the moment he chooses to behave like a spoilt brat and accuse me of not giving him enough attention. Though we'd eventually parted on reasonably good terms, I couldn't help but feel annoyed. Annoyed that he didn't seem to understand how important the museum is to me, and annoyed that it has never even crossed his mind that if he really is all that desperate to spend time with me, he could have volunteered to come with me to the museum this morning and help out.

As I pass a local café proudly displaying a poster for the museum in the window, my phone buzzes with a text from Luce: "Hope it all goes well today! I'm sure it will. Love you loads, you museum mogul!" I'd received so many lovely messages like this from friends saying how much they'd enjoyed last night, promising to spread the word about the museum and wishing me luck for today's official opening. It's so lovely to know people are willing me on. It makes me feel like I'm not alone in this, that my success will be theirs too.

I tap out a quick reply thanking Luce and remind her to pass on my love to her parents. It's Dougie's birthday today and she and Leon are heading up to Northampton for the weekend to help celebrate. "Forty-eight hours under the same roof," she'd said when she'd told me about it. "How am I going to stop myself from throttling them?" She'd meant it as a joke of course, but even so I'd had to bite my tongue in order to avoid lecturing her about the dangers of taking her parents for granted. "They won't always be around," I heard myself saying. "You should make the most of them while you can." Still, the last thing Luce needed was me making her feel guilty. After all, there had been many times in the past when I'd felt exactly the same about my own mum. It's just what you do when you can't conceive of a time when the people you love most will no longer be around. It's human nature, our way of coping with mortality.

Arriving at Barclay and Sons, I let myself in and switch on the kettle and before it's boiled Alex arrives. Given our conversation from the night before I'm surprised to see him and there's a moment of awkwardness between us but then the kettle flicks off, and that seems to be just enough to jolt us back to normal. As I make us both a cup of tea, we chat about the jobs that need doing and I'm just thinking about how best to tell Alex that there are plenty of things to do behind the scenes if he wants to avoid the crowds when we're interrupted by the arrival of Paul, Dec, and Angel.

As I refill the kettle, the office is abuzz with lively conversation about the party and excited speculation about how many visitors we'll have today. "I reckon there could be a good couple of hundred, judging from how many people were at the party last night," says Paul.

"Could be even more than that," says Dec. "I walked down the high street this morning and there was barely a single shop without one of our posters in the window."

We spend the hour left before opening filling helium balloons emblazoned with the museum's logo (as designed by Alex), arranging half of them around the entrance to attract visitors and tying string to the rest to give away to children. After one final check of the museum, I gather everyone around the entrance, feeling the need to say something monumental but not quite sure what.

"Okay," I begin nervously as I check my watch, "there's just a minute to go until we officially open and before we get busy I just want to say a huge thank you again for everything you've done over these past few weeks. You've all been fantastic, constantly going above and beyond, and today would've been impossible without you. And though, sadly, I never got to meet Mr. Barclay, I feel sure he'd be proud of what we've managed to achieve."

"I doubt it," says Paul. "He could be a miserable old sod when he wanted to be, but I get what you're saying."

I look down at my watch, and with just ten seconds to go I begin the countdown and everyone joins in until finally, at exactly ten o'clock, we let out a cheer and throw open the doors.

The first sign that perhaps something is wrong is the distinct lack of people waiting outside keen to be first over the threshold. Instead, the only thing that makes its way inside is an empty crisp packet and a waft of cold air. Still, it's only just ten o'clock, and even with the best will in the world it's unlikely most people have even had their breakfast this early on a Saturday, let alone been dressed and ready for a day at Peckham's newest museum.

"Where is everyone then?" says Dec.

"Try looking round the corner," says Paul. "Maybe they're all queuing at the main door."

"They shouldn't be," says Angel. "I triple-checked all the signs this morning and they all clearly say to come to the side entrance."

Dec goes out through the doors and returns moments later shaking his head. "Nope," he says. "There's no one at the main door or anywhere else, from what I can see. It's completely dead out there."

"It's still early," says Alex confidently as I throw a look of panic in his direction. "Give it half an hour and I'm sure this place will be filling up nicely."

So that's what I do. I give it half an hour, then another, and then another. Finally, when midday comes and goes without even a hint of a visitor, a horrible feeling begins to rise in my stomach as I think about the hundreds of posters, flyers, and specially designed invitations Angel and I have distributed over the past fortnight. I know for a fact that I'd checked the information on them several times before sending Alex's artwork off to the printer's, and I know that he and Angel had checked them when they'd picked them up. But what if some vital piece of information has been missed off and we've somehow failed to spot it, not only wasting four hundred pounds in printing costs but confusing potential visitors too? While the others stand by the door exchanging awkward looks, I grab a leaflet from the pile next to me and frantically scan the wording, checking for mistakes. But there are none. Everything is just as it should be.

I take out my phone and check the museum's website and social media accounts but all the information there is complete and correct too. Finally, it dawns on me that there hasn't been any mistake. The reason people haven't come is simple.

"They're not interested," I say, finally voicing the thoughts I'm sure everyone else has had by now. "I really don't think anyone's going to come."

"Maybe there's something else on today," suggests Angel as everyone surrounds me. "A fair or a festival or something like that."

"Well, I haven't seen anything advertised and I only live up the road," says Dec, only to receive a dig in the side from Paul's elbow.

"Don't listen to him, love," says Paul. "He hasn't got the sense he was born with."

"He's only being honest," I reply. "I think we've got to face facts; today just isn't happening."

Despite their protests, I send Paul, Dec, and Angel home early and they reluctantly leave, promising to return in the morning when they are convinced things will be different.

"I'm sorry, Alex," I say once they've gone. "What a disaster. I can't imagine how things could've gone any worse."

"It's not your fault. I know it's disappointing but sometimes these things just take time. Over the years, I've been involved in more than my fair share of marketing campaigns, really good ideas that should have been an easy sell, and for one reason or another they ended up taking quite a while to get off the ground."

"I just feel so stupid. Can you believe I actually thought there'd be huge queues of people chomping at the bit to come in?"

"And there still might be. Like I said, it's early days. Certainly too soon to be calling it a failure."

"But I just don't understand why no one's come. People came to see the museum when Barclay ran it and he wasn't even trying. Some expert I am. I don't know what I was doing thinking I could pull this off." I bite my lip, trying my best not to cry. "I just feel like I've let you down. You put all of that faith and trust in me and I've made a mess of everything."

"You've done nothing of the sort," says Alex. "I'm telling you, this is just a blip, a bump in the road. It will be a success, you'll see. You've just got to give it some more time, that's all. People will eventually get the message. Trust me, it's too much of a good idea to fail."

Any hope that the opening-day disaster is just a one-off, a blip, is extinguished the following day when once again we open our doors to find no one waiting. There's a slight flurry of excitement around lunchtime when a small, middle-aged man wanders in and much to my surprise begins speaking to Angel in French. With the help of Google Translate, however, we soon learn that he hasn't come to see the museum but is in fact a lorry driver with a cargo of sheet metal, looking for directions to a nearby industrial estate.

After all the effort the team has put into getting the museum ready, and the success of the launch party, it's hard not to be disappointed. I'd been so convinced people would pour through the doors this first weekend, curious to see what all the fuss is about, that I hadn't once considered it might be a total flop.

When after lunch we still have no visitors, I resort to messaging everyone in my contacts begging them to come down. Some send apologies, promising to visit soon, but most don't reply, clearly busy with other things. Eventually, I send the rest of the team home, including Alex, even though he's reluctant to leave me on my own. In desperation, I even spend money I don't have setting up a social media advertising campaign and ordering yet more flyers. If I'm going down, I tell myself as I lock up that evening and head home, I'm at least going to go down fighting.

20

THEN

As I squashed the last of the black bin liners full of Mum's clothes into the back of the car to take them to the charity shop, I felt like the absolute worst daughter in the world. Getting rid of her beautiful clothes like this, things she'd so carefully chosen and taken care of over the years, felt disrespectful somehow but really, what choice did I have? Anyway, far better that someone else got the use of them, someone who perhaps might love them as much as Mum had.

Sensing someone standing behind me, I turned to see a smiling elderly woman in a pink raincoat who I recognized immediately.

"Mrs. O'Connor," I said, "how are you? I haven't seen you in ages."

Mrs. O'Connor was Mum's next-door-but-one neighbor and had lived in the street for as long as I could remember. Even though she must have only been middle-aged when I was born, I can't seem to remember a time when she hadn't looked like a quintessential old lady.

"Oh, a lot better than I was," she said, gesturing to her walking stick. "I got a new hip at the start of the year and it's taken a devil of a long time to get used to it."

"I'm sorry to hear that," I said. "At least you're on the mend now."

"It's why I couldn't make it to your poor mum's funeral," she explained. "I did send a card but I don't expect you'd remember with all that you had to contend with. She was a good woman, your mother, always looked in on me when she could. Gone far too soon, if you ask me."

Right on cue, as if propelled by my mother's angry spirit, one of the bin bags tumbled out of the trunk onto the road between us and for a moment I didn't know whether to laugh or cry as I bent down to pick it up.

"You really do look like her," continued Mrs. O'Connor. "Such a beautiful little thing you are and so was she. You're living in London now, I hear. I daresay you're here to take care of your mum's affairs?"

I nodded, but didn't embellish.

"It's such a heartbreaking job to do," she said flatly. "I did the same for my parents and my husband too. It was easier doing my in-laws mind, I was never that keen on them to begin with, but when it's someone you really love...well, that's a different matter."

Unsure of my ability to continue the conversation without becoming an emotional wreck, I smiled at her politely and closed the trunk of the car. She didn't move, however, seemingly determined to make the most of our interaction.

"She was ever so proud of you, your mum. Going off to university and everything. My youngest grandson is at university. He's studying medicine, wants to be a one of those...what do you call them, the people who operate on brains?"

"A neurosurgeon?"

"That's the one. So, what is it you do again?"

"I'm a receptionist," I replied, and then out of guilt, knowing that people expected such great things of me after going off to university, I added, "It's a good, steady job and I don't have to take work home with me."

Mrs. O'Connor nodded thoughtfully. "And you're living with your young man, so your mum told me?"

"Yes, his name's Guy."

"And is marriage on the cards?"

I felt myself redden as though I was a self-conscious teenager. "Maybe," I replied, "one day. Anyway, I don't mean to rush off but..."

"Of course," she said. "Can't stand around gabbing with me all day. You've got things to do. Take care, love."

As I drove away, I couldn't help thinking how sad it was that Mum would never get to be a nosey old lady like Mrs. O'Connor. She'd never get to grill unsuspecting young people in the street about their life plans as should have been her right. Instead, she'd be forever fifty-six, not properly old and yet not properly young either, frozen in time and stuck in midlife. This sobering thought carried me all the way to my destination, the small row of shops on St. Leonard's Road. Pulling up outside the shuttered Chinese takeaway, I unloaded as many bags as I could carry, and then drawing a deep breath, I pushed open the door to the charity shop.

Back in my youth, Luce and I had been regulars at this and every other charity shop in Northampton. We'd bought clothes, books, records and CDs, and on one memorable occasion a stuffed-and-mounted fox, which we'd given to the head teacher as a joke leaving present. Back then when we had so little, it seemed remarkable to us that we could buy so much from places like this so cheaply. What person in their right mind would want to give away beautiful silk scarves, gorgeous costume jewelry, and cool vintage suitcases? Were they mad? It was only now, as I stood looking at the artfully displayed clothes, handbags, ornaments, and knick-knacks, that it occurred to me that very likely they were brought here by someone like me, someone whose heart was breaking as they tried their best to empty a loved one's home after their passing.

A middle-aged woman behind the till looked up from the magazine she was reading. She had bright red dyed hair and immaculately manicured exotic-looking fingernails.

"Hi there," I said, dumping the three heavy sacks of clothes in my hands onto the floor. "I'd like to—"

"They need to go to the back of the shop," she said, rudely cutting me off. "We don't take donations at the till."

For a moment I thought about losing my temper, telling her all about

Mum and that I was finding this hard enough as it was without her attitude, but then I estimated how much energy this would take and how little I had in reserve. Biting my tongue, I picked up the bags again, navigated my way through the slalom of clothes rails and shelving units to the back of the shop, where I was met by another volunteer, a cheery-looking white-haired woman.

"Donation, is it?" she said brightly.

"Yes," I said. "And I've got some more bags in the car."

"Have you signed up for Gift Aid?"

Before I could reply, she proceeded to rattle off a well-rehearsed spiel about the benefits of Gift Aid and then handed me a pen as if I'd already agreed to do it. I didn't put up a fight; I just completed the form, handed it to her, and then headed back outside to get the rest of the bags. By the time I returned, Mum's neatly washed and ironed clothes, the clothes she'd picked out and paid for, the clothes I saw her wearing when I pictured her in my mind's eye, were strewn across the floor of the stockroom, the volunteer on her hands and knees sorting through them.

"If you just leave those by the door, I'll get to them in just a minute," she said over her shoulder as she continued to sort. "Thank you so much for your donation."

I turned, rushed out of the shop, and as I sat in the car, tears streaming down my face, I thought to myself that if only I had the space, I wouldn't have to give Mum's things away. I could hold on to them, look after them, and treasure them just like she had.

Back at the house I calmed myself down by making what was either a late breakfast or an early lunch. Then, after considering several options, I decided I would spend the rest of the day emptying the loft.

Getting out the stepladders, I gingerly pushed open the hatch, wary of the potential for falling dead mice as had happened one Christmas when Mum asked me to retrieve the decorations, and from which I'd never quite recovered. I pulled the light switch and discovered that, much like the shed, the loft had also become a limbo for things that no longer worked. I found an old desktop computer that I couldn't remember

Mum ever using and that refused to boot up. I found an old portable combined TV and video recorder, our old hi-fi that I could've sworn she'd given away to one of our neighbors, and the aforementioned box of Christmas decorations complete with several decades' worth of broken tree lights.

As I picked up the TV/video recorder, surprised by how heavy it was, my phone rang and, glad of the excuse, I set it down and took the call.

"Hi, am I speaking to…Ms. J. Baxter?"

"Yes," I replied, assuming that it was one of the many people I'd called that week trying to sort out Mum's affairs. "Who's this?"

"I'm Elaine, manager of the Age UK shop on St. Leonard's Road. I hope you don't mind me calling. I got your number from the Gift Aid form you filled in this morning."

"That's fine, is there a problem?"

"No, not really. It's just that one of my volunteers found something amongst the clothing that I'm not sure you meant to donate."

"Oh, what sort of thing?"

"A diary."

"A diary?" I echoed. "What, like an appointment diary?"

"No, to my eyes at least it looks more like a personal one, you know, like one you write in every day. We haven't read it and we're more than happy to dispose of it if you'd like us to but I just thought you ought to know."

I racked my brain trying to make sense of what she'd said. As far as I knew, Mum never kept a diary and even if she had, I hadn't seen one amongst the clothes. More than likely, some of Mum's stuff had got mixed up with someone else's in the sorting room.

"And it was definitely in the bags of clothes I brought in?"

"Definitely. The volunteer was quite certain about it."

"Okay," I said, confused. "I'll come over now and get it."

"Well, we're closing now as it's our half day. But we'll put it to one side for you and you're more than welcome to pick it up tomorrow whenever is convenient."

21

NOW

Morning," says Alex brightly as he walks into the office at Barclay and Sons. "How are you today?"

"Okay," I reply, feeling very much the opposite. "Although I've got a blister on my heel the size of a fifty-pence coin."

"How come?"

"I spent three hours last night trudging around the streets of Peckham in the rain delivering leaflets."

"You didn't do it on your own, did you? You should've said, I would've helped."

"You've already done more than enough. And anyway, blister or not, it was good exercise. I just hope it was worth the effort."

It's our second weekend here at the museum, and it's just me and Alex on today. After a review meeting on Monday evening following our disastrous opening weekend, we took the decision to split the team to cover the two days we're open to the public. While Alex makes us both a drink I go down to the museum and make a quick tour of the exhibits to check that everything is in order. A few minutes later he arrives with my tea and then just before ten o'clock I take a deep breath and, desperately hoping that I've finally done enough to get people interested, I open the doors.

"Now don't forget," says Alex as he sees my face fall at the sight of the empty doorway. "It's still early; there's plenty of time yet for people to come."

"I know," I say, attempting to inject a note of brightness into my voice, "but here's hoping they don't leave it too long this time round."

For the first hour, there are no visitors at all and I use the time to show Alex some of the brilliant conservation work Angel has been doing on a beautiful handmade children's patchwork quilt. It's barely recognizable from how it had been last week. Gone are the spots of mildew and moth damage and it now looks much brighter and more cheerful, a testament to whoever had made it with such love and care.

I'm about to take it back upstairs to the stores when the museum door opens, and in walks a tall gray-haired man who looks to be in his late fifties. He's wearing a leather jacket and jeans, and his skin is deeply tanned as though he's been living in far warmer climes. For a moment I'm so surprised we have an actual visitor that I'm frozen to the spot and the expression on Alex's face tells me he feels the same.

The man smiles at the two of us. "Hi, am I in the right place for the Museum of Ordinary People?"

"Yes," I reply, finally finding my voice. "Yes, you are. Please feel free to look around. And don't hesitate to ask if you have any questions."

The man smiles again and begins walking slowly around the trestle tables, reading the labels and taking in the objects. I'm really torn—as much as I want him to enjoy the experience at his own pace, I'm longing to ask him all of the hundreds of questions that are rolling around in my head right now. How had he heard about the museum? What had made him come? What did he think of the exhibits? What could we do to attract more people?

I don't say anything of course, for fear of scaring him, the museum's one and only visitor, away. Instead, as Alex disappears to put the kettle on, I pretend to make minor adjustments to the exhibits in my immediate vicinity, all the while tracking his progress around the room. I'm heartened when he lingers by the table full of holiday photos but disappointed when he barely glances at the stack of unpublished novels I've collected together from the archive. Is he just not interested in literature or is it something about the way I've displayed them that's put him off?

On the whole, I feel sure he's enjoying himself. He's not just whizzing past the exhibits; he's taking his time and really drinking them in. He spends longest looking at the model railway display, a smile playing on his lips as he watches the train progress around the track. He also seems to enjoy Alex's montage of found cine film that's being projected on the wall beneath my encyclopedias and watches the whole thing twice before moving on.

Finally, he approaches me, wearing a distinctly nervous expression.

"This is such a wonderful place you've got here, it really is. Can I ask you a question?"

"How can I help?"

"Well, I'm quite a fan of quirky history-type things, so when a friend of mine told me about your Instagram page I followed it immediately. You've got so many interesting items here and I love the idea of you rescuing all of these wonderful objects. The thing is though...a few days ago something on your feed caught my attention, which is why I'm here today, but I can't seem to see it on display."

"It's a small space," I explain, "and we have such a huge archive that it's impossible to display everything at once. The idea is that over time there'll be a regular turnover of exhibits to keep everything fresh and interesting. In the meantime, we're using Instagram to give a flavor of what might be in store."

"Ah, I see. So, does that mean I wouldn't be able to see the item in question?"

I think for a moment. While this isn't exactly how I'd hoped the museum would work, the last thing I want to do is disappoint our one and only patron.

"What's the item you have in mind?" I ask, wondering how long it will take to locate it.

"It's a suitcase," says the man. "A medium-sized brown leather suitcase with the initials T.W.G. painted on the side."

Although we have an awful lot of suitcases, I know the one he's talking about straightaway because I've been wanting to properly catalog its contents for a while but so far haven't had the time.

"I think I know the one you mean. Why don't you take another turn around the museum and I'll ask my colleague to get it out of storage for us?"

As the man heads over to the trestle table nearest the entrance, I hurry over to Alex, who I can tell has been listening to everything that's been said.

"Why do you think he wants to see that?" he whispers.

"Your guess is as good as mine. He didn't volunteer anything and it seemed weird to ask."

Under the guise of straightening the folds on the 1930s wedding dress on the mannequin next to me, I take a surreptitious look at the man while Alex goes upstairs to the store to find the suitcase. Though I want to believe the man's intentions are innocent, I can't help wondering if he's got some sort of ulterior motive. Is he an antique dealer who has spotted something about the suitcase I haven't noticed? Or is it simply a ruse to distract us while he steals something else he's got his eye on? Worse still, is he an undercover council worker covertly filming us to get enough evidence to shut us down? I feel sick just thinking about it but before I can kick myself for not being more cautious, Alex returns with the suitcase. I clear a space on the table and Alex sets it down.

"Is this the one you mean?"

Staring at it almost reverentially, the man nods and slowly reaches out a hand to touch its surface but then pulls it back at the last moment.

"Would it be too much trouble...I mean, may I look inside?"

I hesitate for a moment. "Can I ask why?"

"I'm sorry, you must think I'm really odd. It's just that this suitcase... well...I'm almost certain it belonged to my late father."

Alex and I look at one another but say nothing, allowing the man to tell his story.

"My mother died when I was in my teens and my father and I never had what you might call an easy relationship. I suppose I'm just like him in a lot of ways. Maybe that's why we butted heads so often. Anyway, following a big argument in my twenties, I washed my hands of him for good, moving abroad, first to Berlin, then Malta, before finally ending up in Morocco, where I lived happily with my wife until she passed away last year. I suppose that made me think about family and so I decided to come home, determined to straighten things out with Dad. When I learned he'd died, I was heartbroken. I'd missed the chance to patch things up, to say goodbye. But then I saw the suitcase on your Instagram feed and I recognized it straightaway."

I turn the case so that it's facing away from the man and open it. Inside is a motley collection of old birthday cards, family photographs, bank statements, wage slips, household bills, and the like, paraphernalia accumulated over the course of a lifetime. I open one of the birthday cards and read the inscription inside written in a child's hand: "To Dad, hope you have a great day, lots of love, Stephen."

"What did you say your name was?"

"Stephen, Stephen Grant."

I take out an old gas bill dated October 1995 and read the name of the addressee.

"And your father's name?"

"Ronald. Ronald Patrick Grant."

Sure enough that's the name on the bill but as I close the lid of the suitcase to check the initials, the man smiles and says, "The suitcase originally belonged to my grandfather, Terence William Grant."

"I'm sorry," I say, turning the case back around so that he can look through the contents. "I didn't mean to give you the third degree. It's just that I feel a responsibility for the objects in our care. I wouldn't have been doing my job if I hadn't checked."

"I understand. I'm just glad that it's managed to survive all this time. How did you come to have it?"

I tell him all about Barclay's habit of collecting things and then read out the label attached to it: "Suitcase belonging to a Mr. Ron Grant brought in by a Mrs. S. Wakefield, care assistant at Horncliffe House residential care home, Mitcham. Comments: Mrs. Wakefield said: 'I liked Ron a lot, he was good fun to be around and it was sad that he never had any visitors. When he passed away, I just didn't have the heart to get rid of his things like we normally do when no one comes to claim them.'"

Stephen suddenly turns away, momentarily unable to control his emotions, leaving Alex and me to maintain a respectful silence while we wait for him to recover.

"I'm sorry," he says, turning back to face us. "I just wish I'd made my peace with him while I had the chance. I suppose we all think there will always be more time, don't we?"

Alex makes Stephen a drink, and as he leafs through the things in the suitcase, he shares some of the countless memories sparked by the contents. Stories about his childhood and family holidays, memories of his grandparents and the times he'd enjoyed with them. Finally, with our blessing, he leaves, carrying the suitcase underneath his arm, but not before depositing five twenty-pound notes in the donation box.

"Well, I wasn't expecting that," says Alex.

"I know, and I'm glad the suitcase is back with its rightful owner."

"But?"

I sigh heavily. "But what sort of museum are we?"

"How do you mean?"

"Well, what other museum do you know that counts it as a good day when they end up closing with fewer exhibits than they started with?"

Alex smiles. "You always said you wanted this place to be different."

"True, and anyway, if nothing else, today has given me an idea."

"Oh, what's that?"

"I've been calling newspapers and magazines for weeks trying to get someone to write something about the museum. But I haven't been able to drum up any interest. But today has made me see that what we need is an angle, a story a bit like Stephen's, something personal, something affecting, something that will make a newspaper or magazine want to write about us. The question is, what?"

22

So, have you read them all? You know, the love letters?"

"Every last single one," I say, flicking on my turn signal to overtake the tiny Fiat we've been stuck behind for the past twenty minutes. "To be honest, it felt strange at first, quite intrusive, but then I told myself it's all for a good cause and so I plowed on through."

"Were they a bit racy then?" asks Alex.

"Quite the opposite. It was all very prim and proper, which to be honest only served to make the reading of them that much more intense. So much of what they wrote was about memories of their time together at university and I just couldn't help feeling that all the detail they went into, the level of recall they had was an expression of...I don't know...I suppose their longing. In one of the letters, 'B' wrote of a summer afternoon they'd spent together walking in the rain and the writing was so powerful, so intimate, that I almost felt myself blushing as I read the words. Whether they got together or not, there's no doubting how much 'B' adored Sylvia. And that is going to make an absolutely irresistible story for the press."

Following my idea the previous weekend, I'd made it my mission to find a juicy human-interest story, something to entice the press into writing about the museum. To this end, Angel and I had scoured the archive searching for suitable objects that I could present as a complete story, something that would stand alone as a little vignette, a mini portrait of what the museum stood for. In the end we'd shortlisted a collection of Mother's Day cards dating from the 1940s, a turn-of-the-century notebook of handwritten poetry, and a Huntley and Palmers biscuit tin stuffed full of love letters.

With Angel working on trying to find out more about the cards and the poetry, I'd taken the letters home to read and quickly became fascinated by them. The story that had emerged from their pages, written on paper that had yellowed and crinkled with age, was of a couple, Sylvia and a man who signed his name as "B," who had met and fallen in love at university in Sussex in the early sixties but had been unable to be together because of some sort of opposition from her parents.

The two had eventually gone their separate ways, only to reconnect some years later following a chance encounter in a department store on Oxford Street and this had been when their correspondence had begun. The early letters, dated in the spring of 1974, were mostly reminiscences about their time together at university but gradually their focus had shifted to their increasing desire to see each other again, culminating in a final letter dated 6th June 1975 where they made arrangements to meet up for an afternoon at the National Portrait Gallery, and there, frustratingly, the trail went dead.

I'd used all the spare time I had researching every clue I could find in an effort to trace the letter writers. I'd trawled through the land registry and census data, local newspapers, and death notices but it all came to nothing. On the verge of giving up, I'd even contacted Stephen Grant, hoping he might be willing to share his story about the suitcase for the sake of the museum; though he was sympathetic to our plight, understandably he declined, reluctant to make public such a private matter that was still so painful for him.

With Angel also drawing a blank with her research, I'd been about to suggest that we take another look at the archive when I'd had an unexpected breakthrough. A message I'd left on a Facebook group for residents of Colliers Wood at the start of my investigation proved fruitful. I got a response from somebody who said they might be able to help and to my amazement this somebody turned out to be Denise Gastrell, the daughter of Sylvia, from the love letters. I messaged her straightaway and after a little bit of back and forth she'd agreed to meet with me.

The very first person I'd told was Alex, who had seemed almost as excited at the news as me. So much so that, without thinking about the logistics of the journey, I'd invited him to accompany me.

"I could get a cheap hire car," I'd added quickly, worrying that he might find the prospect of public transport off-putting. "There are some really dirt-cheap deals around, especially if you book in advance, and it'd probably cost us less than getting the train. So, what do you think?"

"You had me at hire car," he'd said, and so we'd arranged to swap shifts with Angel, Dec, and Paul and then this morning I'd picked him up from Barclay and Sons and we'd headed out toward the A2 with Maidstone as our goal.

It's a little after eleven as we pull up outside a smart 1950s bungalow in a quiet cul-de-sac on the outskirts of Maidstone. Switching off the engine, I turn to the back seat to get the biscuit tin and to my surprise Alex unclips his seat belt and reaches for the door handle.

"Are you coming in?"

"If that's okay with you."

"Of course it is," I say, relieved that at least I won't be doing this on my own. "But what about...you know...I just don't want you to feel uncomfortable, that's all."

Alex shrugs. "It'll be fine, and if it's not, I'll deal with it."

I know it's not my place to baby Alex but the more I get to know him, the more protective I feel toward him and I'd just hate it if this woman reacted badly to his scars.

"Are you absolutely sure?"

He nods. "I'm positive. I promise you there's no need to worry. To be honest, I've been feeling a lot better lately, and anyway, meeting new people is good practice."

I wonder once again what it must be like to be Alex, to have to carefully consider every new encounter with a stranger, to never be fully relaxed, to always be on your guard.

"Come on then," he says, opening the door on his side. "Let's go and bag ourselves the rights to the love story of the century."

Though there's no mistaking the quick double take that Denise Gastrell makes when she sees Alex, thankfully she quickly recovers herself and proceeds to welcome us both into her home with the minimum of fuss. The front room she guides us to, before disappearing to the kitchen to put on the kettle, reminds me a little of my mum's house back when Gran was alive and still in charge of the décor. There's a collection of ceramic cat figurines on the mantel, below which is an old-fashioned three-bar electric fire, the likes of which I haven't seen in years, and on the wall above the sofa is a set of well-polished ornamental horse brasses.

Denise returns carrying a tray, which she sets down on the table in front of us. "Help yourself to sugar," she says, handing one mug to me and another to Alex.

"You must've been completely thrown when you got my message," I say once we're settled.

"A little," she says. "You hear about all sorts of scams and schemes people get up to and I'll admit my first thought was this might be one of those. But then when we spoke and you gave me the address mentioned on the letters, I knew it was real. So how exactly did my mother's correspondence come into your possession?"

I tell her the whole story of Barclay and the museum and as I speak I observe her closely, hoping for a small nod of comprehension, a smile, or indeed any reaction at all. Instead, she just looks at me strangely as if I'm talking gibberish.

"Well, I must say it all sounds very odd indeed," she says finally. "What sort of letters are they exactly?"

Alex and I exchange a brief look.

"Maybe you should see for yourself," says Alex tactfully, handing her the biscuit tin.

Denise's demeanor changes as she studies it, and there's an almost but not quite smile on her lips. "Mum always did like Huntley and Palmers. They were her favorite."

Slipping on a pair of reading glasses, she opens the tin, plucks out a letter, and begins reading. At first her expression is impassive, but quickly it becomes concerned and then pink spots of color appear on her cheeks and she stops reading and fixes me with a hard stare.

"You say these were found in a dumpster?"

"Yes, in Colliers Wood back in 1998."

Denise nods, and exhales heavily. "That must have been Dad's doing."

"Oh," I say, taken aback. "I thought…I thought…well, aren't these letters from your dad to your mum?"

There's a long silence, during which Denise gets up and stands staring out of the bay window, arms folded tightly. "My dad was called Keith," she says eventually, "and while he was a lot of things, he certainly wasn't a letter writer. Not his sort of thing at all, but I suspect I know who did write them." Pausing, she briefly turns to face us again and then, as though thinking better of it, she looks away. "Mum had an affair when I was very small and for a while it blew our family apart. She left us to be with him. Dad would never talk about the details. She was gone for the best part of five years but then one day I came home from school and she was back, and things just carried on as if she'd never left."

I was mortified. So much for this being the love story that would turn around the museum's fortunes.

"While they were never exactly what you might call happy," continues Denise, "they weren't miserable either and when Mum passed away suddenly in '88, Dad was so lost without her that for years he refused to get rid of any of her things. When he retired, I suggested he sell up and move in with me here in Maidstone. He had to have a massive clear-out of course and get rid of a load of stuff and in the process he must have come across these. I've no idea where Mum had kept them hidden all those years and I can't imagine the pain he must have felt knowing she'd hung on to them. He never mentioned a word about them to me, he wouldn't have. Dad was a proud man and a very protective father. Anyway, the move and clearing the house all happened back in 1998, the year your Mr. Whatsit found the letters, so it all fits."

Taking off her glasses, she crosses the room, returns the letter she'd read to the biscuit tin, and hands the whole lot back to Alex. Her expression leaves me in no doubt that she wants nothing more to do with either the letters or indeed us.

"I don't quite know why you feel the need to bring all sorts of upset to people's doors," she says firmly. "But I'd like you to leave now."

"I'm so sorry," I say quickly. "I had no idea about this at all. I was just hoping it was going to be some lovely love story."

"Well, it wasn't," she replies. "It was a horrible time in all of our lives and something we all wanted to forget."

Alex and I quickly get to our feet, and for a moment I'm not sure whether to take the letters with me or leave them behind. Sensing my dilemma, Denise says, "Yes, take them with you. I don't want them." But then after a pause she adds, "I know you might think you're doing the right thing with this museum thing of yours, but you'd do well to remember that not everything needs to be saved. Sometimes people throw things away with good reason and who are you to say otherwise?"

Alex and I barely say a word to each other on the way back to London, both lost in our own thoughts, and it's only when we reach Walthamstow and I pull up outside his flat that we break the silence.

"Don't let this get you down," says Alex. "It's just one person, one object; it doesn't mean the museum is a bad idea."

"But you heard what she said," I reply. "Some things are thrown away for a reason. What if all we're doing is storing up other people's pain? Perhaps she's right; perhaps in part, by taking in so many discarded items, Barclay had allowed the museum to become less a celebration of people's ordinary lives and more a repository for their sorrows. And now, here I am, all these years later, trying to encourage visitors to take a tour of what could be, in essence, the physical reminders of some of the darkest points in other people's lives."

23

When my alarm wakes me the following morning, for the first time in a very long while I don't immediately leap out of bed excited at the prospect of a day at the museum. Instead, my first thought, as I lie under the covers next to Guy, is exactly the same as the thought I'd had before drifting off to sleep last night: "Am I wasting my time?" Perhaps I'd be feeling different had yesterday's visitor figures been anything to shout about. But despite spending yet more money on social media advertising and flyers, we still only had a total of six people through the doors, two of whom were friends of mine who had stopped by hoping to say hello.

So right now, I don't feel much like doing anything other than rolling over and going back to sleep, let alone trekking all the way over to Peckham to face yet another day of disappointment. Instead, I could spend my Sunday going out for a lovely brunch with Guy, or while away the afternoon with Luce amongst the flea markets of Brick Lane. I could even just stay here in bed eating chocolate and watching rubbish TV all day on my laptop. But I don't, not because I think today will be any different, but because despite it all I feel like I owe it to Paul, Dec, Angel, and Alex. They've all given up so much of their spare time, so much of their energy, for something that I persuaded them was a good idea.

By nine, I'm at the museum, by ten the doors are open for another day, and by midday, not a single soul has crossed the threshold.

"Are you okay?"

I give my head a shake and look at Alex. I'd been lost in thought about my future. Wondering whether I'd left it too late to retrain to do something useful, like teaching or nursing. Something that might give me the sense of purpose I'm looking for, something that might make me feel like I'm not just here on this planet to take up space or make up the numbers.

"I'm sorry, I was miles away there."

"Not back in Maidstone with that woman, I hope?"

I smile. "Maybe a little bit."

"I told you yesterday, you shouldn't let it get in your head. For every Denise, there's a Stephen, or maybe even multiple Stephens. You can't let one bad experience color—"

Alex stops and we both look up in surprise as a young family of five—mum, dad, two primary-school-aged girls, and a toddler asleep in a stroller—come in through the entrance as if it's the most natural thing in the world.

"Hi there," says the mum. "We are okay to come in, aren't we?"

"Yes, yes, of course," I say brightly. "Please, make yourselves at home. There's an activity sheet if your children would like to do it?"

Two small faces look up at me and nod solemnly and so I grab the sheets, two clipboards, and pencils and hand them over.

"And what do we say to the nice lady?" prompts the dad.

"Thank you," the girls quietly chorus.

"You're welcome," I reply. "Please, take all the time you need to look around, and if you've got any questions, just ask."

I can't quite believe it. An entire family have chosen the Museum of Ordinary People for their Sunday afternoon outing. I want to hug them, genuinely squeeze them, and tell them just how grateful I am they've come. Instead, I just smile and walk back over to Alex, barely able to contain my joy.

"See," says Alex with a grin. "I told you things would start looking up."

"You did, didn't you? You're clearly a lot wiser than I am. I know it's pathetic to get this excited over one family but, Alex, this is exactly what I've been hoping for."

The family, I discover over the course of their visit, are called the Ade-bayos, and the mum and dad are both teachers at a local primary school. They tell me that they decided to come to the museum after having a flyer pushed through their door a couple of weeks ago. "We would've come earlier," the dad says, "because from the look of the flyer it sounded really quirky and interesting, but you know what life's like: with birthday parties and family visiting, it's hard to squeeze in the things you really want to do."

They stay for over an hour, asking all sorts of detailed questions about how the museum came to be and some of the exhibits that had piqued their curiosity. When I go through the girls' activity sheets, their responses to the final question, "What object would you like to see on display at the Museum of Ordinary People?" are so sweet, it takes me back a bit. The older girl, Imani, has chosen her granny's cake tins "because I love her cakes so much," while her sister has chosen a fluffy toy duck that she won at a fair when she was five: "Ducky is my favorite toy and I lost him on the bus last year and it made me sad. But I wouldn't be sad if he was being looked after in a place like this."

Before they leave, the girls hand me pictures of the motorcycle sidecar and the fifties wedding dress, their favorite exhibits from the collection, as a thank you. I proudly Blu Tack them to the wall above the children's activity table where they were created, and as if that isn't enough, the mum asks about the possibility of booking me to go and give a talk about the museum to her school.

"I just think the kids would all get a real kick out of it," she says. "We're always trying to find new ways to get them to really engage with history."

I give her my details and on the way out, not only does the girls' dad hand each of them a ten-pound note to drop into the transparent plastic donation box attached to the wall, but they also take the time to write in the visitor's book, the first time this has ever happened.

The moment I'm sure they've gone, I race across to read what they've written and straightaway there's a lump in my throat: "Such a special and unusual museum! Kids and parents alike loved it. The staff were brilliant, so knowledgeable and friendly too. Will definitely recommend to friends and family. Can't wait to make a return visit!"

While it's only the smallest of victories, to me it feels like winning gold at the Olympics. I'm so happy that even after I've talked Alex's ears off, I'm so full of energy that on my way to the station it's all I can do to stop myself from hugging old ladies, kissing babies, and giving a high five to a group of dodgy-looking teens that I pass on the way. In celebratory mood, on my way home I head to Marks and Spencer Simply Food and splash out on some really nice dinner for Guy and me, and the most expensive bottle of wine I can afford.

Reaching the apartment, I let myself in and immediately call out to Guy, who I find sitting at the dining table with his laptop open. Waltzing over to him, I pop the carrier bag with the wine and food on the table, plant a kiss on his cheek, and throw my arms around his neck, squeezing him tight.

"Someone's in a good mood," he says. "What's happened? Have you discovered a Rembrandt in that museum of yours?"

"Not exactly, but I did have something good happen today."

"Go on then, I'm all ears."

I sit down on his lap, then tell him all about the Adebayos and what a boost their visit had given me.

"You should've seen their faces, Guy. They really got it; they weren't just being polite. It was so good to see, complete strangers connecting with the museum just like I'd always hoped they would."

Guy looks at me confused. "I don't understand, so was the arrival of this family the beginning of a big rush or something?"

I feel myself deflate slightly. "Well, not exactly, but it was just nice to see people getting it, that's all."

"So, how many people did you actually have through the doors today?"

I feel myself deflate even further. "Including the Adebayos?"

Guy nods.

"Six."

Guy's face falls. "And if you exclude the family that came in?"

"One," I admit reluctantly as my last puff of joy leaves me. "And he only came in to use the loo and left straight afterward."

"So, all this," he says, glancing at the carrier bag, which has toppled over slightly, revealing the pack of sirloin steaks and the bottle of white Burgundy, "is to celebrate the fact that one family came to see your museum today?"

Feeling foolish, I get off Guy's lap. "I just wanted a win, that's all. I just needed to feel good about the museum for once. But I suppose you're right; it wasn't anything to shout about."

Grabbing the carrier bag, I walk over to the kitchen and empty the lot into the bin. Guy immediately gets to his feet and comes over to me.

"I'm sorry," he says. "I shouldn't have poured cold water on your good news like that."

"So then why did you?"

He sighs. "I don't know...I know this museum thing means a lot to you but I...just miss you, that's all. I feel like I barely see you these days because you're pouring all of your time and energy into that place and so to hear that it's all been just for five people feels a bit...I don't know...a bit of a waste."

"I know it's been difficult, and I know how patient you're being, I really do, but it's not always going to be just five people, is it? One day all the sacrifices are going to pay off. Word's going to get out about the museum soon, I just know it."

"But when? You've had your big launch and since then you've barely had anyone through the door. All I'm trying to say is that maybe it's a case of right idea, wrong time; all I'm trying to say is that maybe it's time to call it quits so that we can just get on with our lives."

I don't say anything in response; instead, swallowing down my pride, I fish the packets of food and bottle of wine out of the bin, wash them off under the tap and set about making a meal that now feels more like a consolation than a celebration. We eat it sitting at the dining table, and between bites of food and sips of wine we talk about the house move and how different things will be once it's ours.

"Just think how happy we'll be, sitting in our brand-new house in our brand-new neighborhood," says Guy at one point. "It'll be like a new beginning for us both; we'll be Guy and Jess 2.0, new and improved, ready to start the next chapter of our lives together."

At work the following morning all I can think about is Guy's comments about wasting my time on the museum. Is he right? Is it time to call it quits on the museum? After all, we've been open for three weekends now, and by this time I'd hoped things would really be taking off but instead here I am deluding myself that a solitary family of five visiting the museum is something to celebrate. I feel bad, not just for Alex, Paul, Dec, and Angel, but for Guy too. One way or another they've all made sacrifices for the museum but to encourage them to make any more when the project is so clearly doomed to failure just feels selfish. Guy's right, I need to draw a line under this. I need to give people back their lives, and maybe even get on with mine. It was a nice try, and it wasn't as if I hadn't given it my all, but clearly this time round it just isn't enough.

I pick up my phone to call Alex and tell him about my decision, but before I can even look up his number, my phone vibrates.

"Hi, am I speaking to Jess Baxter?"

The voice at the end of the line is female but it's not one I recognize.

"Yes, you are. Who's this?"

"My name's Rachel Cross, and I'm calling from the *Peckham Courier*."

"Oh right. How can I help?"

"Well, if it's okay, we were rather hoping to put together a feature about you and your museum."

24

Hi, Christine, have you got a minute?" I say, poking my head round the office manager's door.

"Not really," she says without looking up from her computer screen. "Is it urgent?"

"Sort of," I say, edging farther into the room. "I know it's short notice but I really need to book the day off on Wednesday."

"Wednesday," she repeats, still not looking at me. "As in the day after tomorrow?"

"Yes. I wouldn't ask but it's a bit of an emergency. I've already spoken to the part-timers and they're both more than happy to cover my shift."

"That's all very well," says Christine icily, "but it's not up to them; it's up to me. And anyway, you know as well as I do that it's company policy for all requests for time off unless for bereavement leave to be submitted in writing no less than a month in advance."

"I know but can't you make an exception just this once? It's really important."

"Important how?"

I hesitate for a moment, unsure whether to confide in her about the museum, but then I look at the sour expression on her face and I just know she wouldn't understand.

"It's a complication to do with the sale of my late mum's house," I say, almost but not quite playing the dead mum card.

"I see," she says. "Well, that's unfortunate but I'm afraid that makes no difference. I cannot in all good conscience authorize a day off against company policy at such short notice. Now, if that's all?"

The real reason I need the day off is because Wednesday afternoon is the only time the journalist from the *Peckham Courier* can do the interview. I had tried asking whether it would be possible to do a weekend or evening instead but had been so frightened of putting her off and losing the opportunity altogether that in the end I'd agreed to the time and date suggested, then crossed my fingers, hoping I could make it work.

If this had been Surita, my old office manager, my request would have been dealt with in a matter of seconds. I would have told her what I needed; then without even checking the roster, Surita would've said, "Yeah, no problem, leave it with me," and we would've spent the next ten minutes catching up with each other over a coffee. But Surita had left London and moved to the North East to be closer to her daughter, who had just had a baby, and now her role is being done by suck-up supreme Christine, who had once been a lowly receptionist like me but had now risen through the ranks.

"Right," I say tersely, "thank you for your time," and then without another word I leave the office having already made up my mind that whether Christine likes it or not I am going to take the day off on Wednesday anyway. I will just have to cross my fingers and hope I'll still have a job at the end of it.

When Wednesday morning comes round, I leave for work with Guy as usual without telling him about my plans for the day. Much like Christine, Guy is a stickler for rules and I know he would never approve of me pulling a sickie, least of all for the benefit of the museum that he thinks is doomed anyway. As it is, these days, with his focus on his job promotion and trying to secure a completion date for the house move, it's all he can do not to roll his eyes whenever I mention anything museum-related. Last week in the middle of a spat about missing paperwork for the house move, he even said, "Honestly, Jess, I know it's ridiculous but I almost feel like there are three of us in this relationship, you, me, and that junkyard of yours."

At the station, Guy kisses me goodbye and as he begins his usual walk to work I look around for somewhere quiet to make my call. Spying a café, I duck into the loos and call work, leaving a message on the office voice mail. "Hi," I say, trying my best to sound weak and feeble, "Jess here. I'm not feeling great I'm afraid. Must have been something I ate. I won't be in today, sorry. Hopefully it's just a twenty-four-hour thing. I'll be in touch if not."

Leaving the café instead of getting on the DLR as I do every day, I join the Jubilee line. Later as I make my way to the overland train, I find myself looking furtively around, just in case I see someone from work or anyone who might know Guy.

"Maybe he's right," I think as I board the train to Peckham. "All this sneaking around behind his back, all the secrets I'm keeping from him, perhaps I am having an affair of sorts after all."

I spend the morning making sure everything at the museum is in place and looking its best for the journalist's arrival. With Alex working, Angel at university, and Paul and Dec out on a house clearance, I have the place to myself. I swap some of the exhibits for ones I think might look better in photographs and, spotting a few typos, I print out a few new information labels and even spend a good half hour cleaning the loos just in case.

The journalist, Rachel Cross, arrives a little after midday. She's small and smartly dressed in a charcoal-gray trouser suit. Taking her through to the office, I make us both a coffee and then give her a tour of the museum. Though I try my best to be witty and informative, pointing out some of the highlights of the collection I thought she might want to feature in the article, she doesn't seem anywhere near as bowled over as I'd hoped. Instead, if anything, she seems quite underwhelmed, and I'm beginning to worry she's simply going to call her editor and tell them that we're not worth the printing ink.

"So," she says, stifling a yawn as she places her phone on the table between us to record the interview, "tell me how this all started."

I clear my throat. "Well, I suppose it all began with—"

A sudden knock at the entrance to the museum cuts me off, and for a moment I wonder whether it's Paul and Dec messing about but then I remember they're out on a job and there's nobody here but me.

"Do you want to get that?" asks Rachel.

"No, it's fine. The museum's closed today and I'm not—"

The knock comes again, louder this time, and not just once but several times in a row. Whoever it is clearly isn't going to give up any time soon.

Apologizing, I hurry over to the entrance and I'm surprised to find a smartly dressed elderly lady on the doorstep brandishing a walking stick in a manner indicating that she'd been using it to bash the door with.

"Excuse me, dear. Do you work here?"

"Yes, are you looking for Paul or Dec?"

The woman frowns. "I don't know a Paul or Dec. No, dear, I'm looking for the museum."

"Oh, you're in the right place but I'm afraid we're not open today." I point to the sign on the door. "It's Saturdays and Sundays only at the moment."

"I can't be coming back then," says the old woman brusquely. "It took me all I had just to get here today and I've enough going on already." Edging herself inside, she says, "You carry on doing what you're doing, love. Don't mind me," and without any further debate she begins looking around the museum.

I'm torn. Though I could do without this right now, the last thing I need is for the journalist to write a story about me turning away a pensioner. Reasoning that she can't get up to much trouble, I close the door and try my best to put a positive spin on things for the benefit of Rachel.

"Sorry about that," I say, "just a member of the public desperate to get a look at the museum. I did try to explain that we're currently only open at the weekends but she simply can't wait. I hope you don't mind."

We continue the interview, with me trying my very best to be effusive and charming, while Rachel remains businesslike and perhaps a little bored. But then just as I'm about to outline the museum's mission statement, the old woman interrupts.

"Sorry to bother you again, love. Are you in charge here?"

"Yes," I say, a little grandly for the benefit of the journalist. "I'm the curator."

"Good," replies the old woman, and then eyes the journalist expectantly as though waiting for her to declare her role in the operation.

"Hi, I'm Rachel," she says. "Are you local?"

"The name's Ivy," declares the old woman. "Ivy Foster and I'm Peckham born and bred as were my mum and dad, their parents, and their parents before them." She turns her attention back to me. "Anyway, now that I've had a look around I was wondering if you might be able to help me."

I'm just working out how to tell Ivy that I'm in the middle of something quite important when she takes out a photograph from her bag and hands it to me. It's a snap of a family: mum, dad, and two young boys, sitting around a table at Christmas all smiling and holding up their drinks to the camera. Judging by the clothes and décor, I guess it must have been taken at some point in the late sixties or early seventies. But lovely as it is, I'm not entirely sure what Ivy wants me to say about it.

"It's wonderful," I say, and show it to Rachel.

"Is that you in the picture with your family?" she asks Ivy.

"Yes, Christmas 1967. I was thirty-one then and the boys were seven and eleven."

"It's such a great photo," says Rachel, handing it back to her. "So authentic."

Ivy pulls a puzzled face and then turns her attention back to me. "So, will you take it then?"

"You want me to take the photograph?" I ask, confused.

Ivy tuts as though I'm being particularly dense.

"What would I want you to take the photograph for?" she snaps, and, thrusting the picture back into my hands, points to the center of it. "Of course I'm not talking about the photograph! I'm talking about the table."

"What about the table?"

"My granddaughter told me that she looked this place up on the Internet and apparently you look after things for people."

The zombie *Time Out* article strikes again, I think. It has to be. None of the flyers we'd distributed mentioned accepting donations. I can only hope the *Peckham Courier* feature will stick around for as long.

"And well, that's what I'd like you to do: look after my Harry's table."

Without further prompting, she waves me out of my chair, sits down, and launches into the story of the table: how it had been made by her late husband a little after they'd moved into their first home together in the fifties.

"He wasn't exactly the best carpenter in the world," she says. "In fact, for as long as I can remember, I've had to wedge a piece of cardboard under one leg just to keep it from wobbling. But we had so many happy times around that table as a family, and mind you, a few sad ones too... that I just can't bear the thought of it being thrown away. My place is too big to manage on my own since my Harry passed away last year so I'm moving into sheltered accommodation next week, and there's no way that dining table is going to fit. I'd ask my boys to take it but one lives in Finland and the other has only got a tiny flat, so if you can't take it, the only place for it is the dump." She pulls a tissue out of her sleeve and briskly dabs at her eyes.

"Of course we'll look after it for you," I say impulsively, even though I have no idea where we are going to put it.

"You will?" exclaims Ivy. "Oh, that's such a weight off my mind. Come here and let me give you a hug." Mid-embrace I hear a click and turn to see Rachel holding her camera and grinning.

"You can't fake photos like that," she says. "Photos like that are what keep local papers alive. I think I've just found my hook for the feature."

The first thing I do once Ivy and Rachel have gone is lock all the doors, quietly count to ten, and then scream, "Yessss!!!" at the top of my voice. And the very next thing I do is call Alex.

"It went better than I could ever have imagined," I say, and I tell him all about Ivy and her table. "Thank goodness for belligerent old ladies!"

"That's fantastic," says Alex. "I couldn't be happier for you. You deserve it." He pauses and then adds, "Actually, you're not the only one who's had some good news."

"Oh? What's happened?"

"I might have had a bit of a breakthrough with my hunt to find out more about Barclay," he says. "I think I've just found the closest thing he had to a friend. I'm going to go and see him. Do you fancy coming?"

"When are you thinking?"

"Well, there's no time like the present. How about right now?"

25

THEN

Since the call from the charity shop manager yesterday, this supposed diary of Mum's had been all I could think about. Mum wasn't at all the sort of person to keep a diary. She was far too practical and pragmatic for that. I'd kept one briefly in my teens after getting one from Luce for Christmas but I'd never stuck with it. After a week or so of documenting every mundane detail of my life, I'd grown bored and instead it had become a repository for doodles and to-do lists. I'd tried again in my mid-twenties, after spotting a particularly alluring day-to-a-page diary in Paperchase. It had a pale green silk cover and marbled end pages, and was so exquisitely beautiful that even though I couldn't strictly afford it, I'd found it impossible to resist. I think I managed to record my daily thoughts in it for all of three days before I gave up and it eventually joined the small but not insignificant pile of beautiful abandoned notebooks that now lived in a carrier bag in the wardrobe.

Getting in the car, I drove over to the charity shop and, as I entered, was grateful to see that the mean manicured volunteer was nowhere to be seen. The personable young man in her stead greeted me with a smile when I asked to speak to the manager, before pointing me in the direction of the back room. The manager, a tall, gray-haired woman who carried herself with the air of a retired teacher, seemed to know who I was straightaway.

"Here you go," she said, handing the diary to me. Holding it in my hands, I stared at it blankly. It was about the size of a paperback, the cover, a navy-blue faux leather, embossed with the words "five-year diary" in gold lettering. It looked worn and well used; the gold edging on the pages had faded in places over time, but it failed to ignite a single spark of recognition until I flicked it open, and felt my heart lurch at the sight of Mum's unmistakable neat boxy handwriting.

"So, it's yours then?" asked the manager.

I nodded mutely.

"Well, that's good news. You wouldn't believe the things we come across in bags of donations: false teeth, money, car keys, the lot. I'm just glad we were able to reunite you with it."

Once outside I sat in the car for a while, turning the diary over in my hands. Part of me was desperate to open it up straightaway and read it, to trace my fingers over the words she'd written, to hear her voice in my head and feel close to her. But another part of me, the part that had felt uncomfortable going through her private correspondence and her underwear drawer, felt like it was wrong, an intrusion somehow. This was the dilemma before me—to read, or not to read?—and I wrestled with the question all the way home, but as I pulled up outside Mum's I saw two burly men knocking on the front door and the question slipped away.

"All right, love," said the bigger of the two. "We're here to pick up some furniture?"

I looked at their T-shirts, emblazoned with the name of a local hospice charity, and though I realized who they were, I was confused.

"I was told you'd be coming tomorrow."

The man looked down at his clipboard. "It's not what's down here. Do you want us to come back another day?"

"How about tomorrow?"

He shook his head woefully as if I'd just asked him to give me a kidney. "We're fully booked up for the rest of the week, could do Monday if you like."

"I'm only here until the weekend."

"Don't know what to tell you then, love."

I thought briefly about the mess in all the rooms and how much I'd have to run around clearing things away, but then it occurred to me that they probably wouldn't care one way or the other. Anyway, I needed this stuff gone; I couldn't come back and do this a second time.

"Fine, come in and I'll show you what's going."

I pointed out Mum's three-piece suite and the coffee table in the living room. Then in the back room I showed them the huge shelving unit that had always been home to my Encyclopedia Britannica, which now sat lined up in piles next to the radiator along with everything else I'd cleared out of it. I was worried they might think it was a bit too dated to be of use (I couldn't even remember where Mum got it) but they agreed to take it along with the dining table.

I was just about to show them what was going from upstairs when my phone rang. It was Luce.

"Don't worry, love," said the smaller of the two men. "You carry on and get that, and we'll make a start."

As they headed back to the living room, I stepped out into the garden to take the call, grateful that I didn't have to watch the furniture Mum worked so hard for being taken away.

"I can only imagine how gutting it must be," said Luce after I told her what was happening. "But I think you should try to remember that it's for a good cause. They do such amazing work at the hospice and I don't doubt for a moment that your mum would've approved. Anyway, aside from that, how are you? Is there much left to do?"

I looked back toward the house and thought about the piles of Mum's things dotted around the place that I'd yet to decide what to do with. "I'm getting there, but I'm glad I gave myself a whole week to do this. Anything less would've been impossible."

"And you're absolutely sure you still don't want any help? I could start laying the groundwork for a sickie as soon as we're done talking and be with you by the end of the day no problem. Just say the word."

I smiled. "Thanks, but I think I'll be fine." I paused as I realized I was still holding on to Mum's diary. "Before you go, there is something you could help me with. It's a bit of a moral dilemma. I didn't know, but it turns out Mum kept a diary."

"Like a full-on 'Dear Diary, here are my innermost thoughts' type of thing?"

"I don't really know," I said. "I flicked it open, saw her handwriting, and then I sort of froze and shut it again."

"Because you feel like it would be an intrusion to read it?"

"Sort of. I mean she didn't write it for me; she wrote it for herself. If the tables were turned, I'm not sure how I'd feel about someone reading my diary."

"Even me? I'm shocked! I thought we told each other everything."

I laughed, grateful for the light relief. "Especially you. Not that I keep a diary anyway, so it's a bit of a moot point."

"If I kept a diary, I'd let you read it," said Luce matter-of-factly. "That said, it would mainly be full of rants about the people I work with, so I'm not sure how edifying it would be. But if your question is should you read your mum's diary, then my answer is yes, absolutely. I mean, maybe not now, not while you're still in the middle of things, but yeah, when you're feeling stronger you should definitely read it. You and your mum were so close I can't think for a minute that she'd mind."

By the time Luce and I were done, the men from the hospice had loaded all of the furniture from the front room into the van and were just getting started on the back room. Flicking on the kettle, I made them a drink and then took them upstairs to show them everything that was going from the bedrooms. The bedframes and wardrobes, the chests of drawers and bedside tables. For a moment, as we stood in my bedroom, I thought about telling them to leave my lovely old art nouveau-style desk. It was the first piece of furniture Mum let me choose for myself from a junk shop on the edge of town when I was fourteen. I'd studied for both my GCSEs and my A-levels at that desk and it meant a lot to me. But then I thought about the logistics of getting it down to London, and then

I thought about the look on Guy's face when it appeared in the living room rubbing shoulders with his designer furniture, and knew it would never work. So, I told them to take the desk and the office chair with it, resigned once again to the fact that I couldn't keep everything.

It took them a full hour to get all the stuff loaded onto the van, and after watching them leave, I walked around the house taking in the impact of their morning's work. With the furniture gone the rooms were strange and echoey, the marks on the walls and indentations on the carpet bearing witness to what used to be there. It almost felt as if the furniture was still there but had somehow been rendered invisible, and later as I wandered around the house, I found myself unable to walk across the spaces where it all used to be.

That night, lying on the mattress on the floor in my room, my attention returned to Mum's diary. Picking it up, my desire to be comforted by her proved so strong that I finally made the decision to read it.

At random I opened it and flicked to a page near the end dated 4th March 1995, which would've been my seventh birthday:

Jess turned seven today. Can't quite believe how quickly the time is flying by. I took her and her friends to McDonald's after school and then everyone came back here for cake. She told me it was the best birthday she'd ever had and that she can't wait to be eight!

I found myself smiling and crying at the same time as I read. I remembered that day like it was yesterday. Waking up the moment it got light, getting out of bed to knock on Mum's door, and then climbing in beside her. I remembered the excitement as she opened up her wardrobe door and brought out a stack of presents from underneath a pile of jumpers where she'd hidden them. I remembered being overwhelmed with excitement as I unwrapped the Beanie Babies I'd been so desperate to have in my possession. I remembered how special I'd felt at school wearing the "I am 7" badge from the card she'd given me. I even remembered how Luce and I had ordered exactly the same Happy Meal and how delighted we'd been when we'd found we had exactly the same Pocahontas toy in our boxes.

It was such a lovely memory, a reminder of how wonderful the past had been. But when I thought about the future, how from now on every birthday, every Christmas, every celebration would be without Mum, I realized that Luce was right. Perhaps I wasn't strong enough right now to be brought so vividly back to the past, no matter how comforting it was there. And so, I closed the book and, clutching it to my chest, I shut my eyes and imagined that I was holding on to Mum.

26

NOW

This is it," says Alex, pointing to a green-and-white sign on the wall next to the entrance to the building, "Hawthorn Court."

We both look down the short driveway to an ugly single-story brick construction with almost no redeeming features other than the well-tended gardens that surround it, which are full of neatly trimmed shrubs, bushes, and the best-stocked bird feeders I have ever seen.

"Are you ready?" I ask, looking at Alex.

"For what?"

"To find out why Barclay left you everything he owned."

On the way over Alex had told me how, while looking through some of Barclay's papers, he'd noticed the same name, Ted Enfield, cropping up on invoices. After a bit of digging he'd discovered that Ted used to run an antique furniture stall at Spitalfields Market and Barclay must have been one of his regular suppliers. "I don't know if I'm right," he'd said, "but I got the feeling they might have been friends, as on all the invoices there's a running joke about whose turn it would be to get the next round in." And now, after a bit of detective work on Alex's part, he had managed to track Ted down to this residential care home in Croydon.

Making our way to the main entrance, Alex presses the buzzer several times to no avail but then a middle-aged couple carrying a large bunch of flowers and several presents arrive.

"Don't bother with the buzzer," says the woman. "They're always too busy to answer at this time of day." She sighs and adds, "Just tap in the code for us: it's 4-3-2-1."

I smile at Alex, enter the code, and as we step inside, the first thing I notice is the heat. Despite the fact that it's a relatively mild day, for some reason all the radiators are on full blast. The second thing I notice is the smell, an unpleasant aroma of cheap pine disinfectant combined with the faint scent of boiled cabbage.

"Can I help you?" asks a healthcare assistant after Alex and I have wandered up and down the corridor several times.

"Yes, please," I say. "We're looking for a Mr. Ted Enfield."

"Are you a relative?" she asks.

"I'm his great-niece," I reply, wishing I too had brought gifts like the couple Alex and I had met at the entrance. It seems almost churlish to arrive at a place like this empty-handed. "I've been away traveling for a couple of years, so I'm desperate to see him."

"Oh, okay," says the care assistant. "Just follow me and I'll take you to him."

We follow the young woman back down the corridor and through a set of double doors that lead to a day room, a large rectangular space dominated by a flat-screen TV with chairs lined up against the wall, all of which are occupied by elderly people in various states of consciousness. We walk through to a quieter seating area where a man in a wheelchair sits looking out of the window watching an empty bird feeder.

"Hiya, Ted," says the care assistant brightly, "look who I've got here for you."

Turning his head, Ted looks from the care assistant to Alex and me, then back again.

"Who did you say it was again?" he asks, maneuvering his wheelchair around to get a better look at us.

"Your great-niece..."

"Jess," I say as the care assistant looks at me expectantly.

"Oh, Jess!" says Ted warmly. "What a lovely surprise! It's wonderful to see you. How long has it been?"

"Too long," I say, thinking quickly. "Far too long."

The moment the care assistant is out of earshot, Ted lets out a laugh so raucous that I worry he might choke.

"That has got to be the best fun I've had in ages," he says once he's recovered himself. "So, come on then, who are you really?"

Ted's mind, despite his physical frailties, is clearly still as sharp as a tack.

"Sorry about the deception," says Alex. "We're here about an old friend of yours. Thomas Barclay? We were hoping you might be able to tell us something about him."

"Old Tommo!" says Ted. "How is the old goat? Is he well?"

Alex and I exchange pointed glances.

"I'm afraid he passed away six months ago," says Alex.

Ted shakes his head mournfully. "Now, that is sad news. He was a good bloke was old Tommo. So, are you related to him or something?"

"Not exactly," says Alex. "The thing is I never actually met Mr. Barclay, but for some reason I'm trying to get to the bottom of, he mentioned me in his will. In fact, he did more than mention me; he left me everything he owned. And well, the thing is, I have no idea why and I was hoping you might be able to shed some light on things for me."

Ted studies Alex's face keenly, taking in his scars but stopping short of commenting on them. "What did you say your name was?"

"Alex, Alex Brody."

Ted shakes his head. "Doesn't ring any bells, I'm afraid. Mind you, my memory isn't what it used to be these days."

Without saying anything more, he begins wheeling his chair in the direction of the exit. "Come on then, you pair," he says when he realizes we aren't following him. "I think I've got a couple of photos of Tommo back in my room somewhere."

We follow him out of the day room, through several sets of fire doors, and down a long corridor to his room, a rectangular box with a single bed, wardrobe, and an armchair facing a chest of drawers with a small TV perched on top.

"Welcome to *mi casa*," he says, winking at me before taking out a small shoebox from his wardrobe. "Here he is," he says after a few minutes rooting through the contents. "That's Tommo there at my eightieth about five years ago. It was a good night that was. We all had such a laugh. My daughter really pulled out all the stops sorting out a cake and making sure all my pals were there."

"It looks like you're having a great time," I say. "So how long had you and Mr. Barclay been friends?"

Ted smiles. "Let me think. Must be a good twenty years or so, I reckon."

"So, I'm guessing you met through your stall in Spitalfields?" asks Alex.

"Funnily enough, no," says Ted.

"Oh right," says Alex. "It's just that when I was going through his stuff, I found duplicates of a number of invoices he'd sent you."

"Oh, we did a lot of business together. He always put aside the best stuff for me, he had a really good eye, and in return I would point people looking for a house clearance in his direction. In fact, he did mine when I moved into this place after my wife passed away. Bless his heart, he even put my wife's granddad's old workbench in that lock-up of his when I couldn't find a home for it. Three kids, twelve grandkids, and three great-grandkids and not one of them would take it. Would've been lost to history if it hadn't been for Tommo."

I smile. "I know the workbench you mean. It's a lovely old thing, full of scrapes, dents, and gouges. It was obviously well used."

"So, it's still in the lock-up, is it?"

"Safe and sound," I say.

"Oh, that's good," says Ted. "I'd have felt awful if it'd just ended up in a dump somewhere."

"So, you were telling us where you knew Tommo from," says Alex, trying to get Ted back on topic.

"Oh yeah, like I said, while we were in the same sort of trade, that's not how I met him."

"So where did you meet?" asks Alex.

Ted gives a sniff. "Alcoholics Anonymous."

Across the space of the next hour, as we sit in Ted's room surrounded by the few objects he's been able to hang on to from his old life, he tells Alex and me about his own battle with drinking. It had started in the eighties when Ted's imported-furniture business had failed and his house was repossessed. But what had begun, in Ted's words, as "a bit of over-indulgence" had quickly spiraled into dependency and before he knew it, he was starting and ending his day with a drink. It wasn't until his wife threatened to leave and take their two young children with her that he finally took stock of just how far he had fallen, and on the advice of his GP he had attended his first AA meeting at a local community center.

"The first time I went," he says, "no word of a lie, I was so terrified my knees were knocking like a bailiff on overtime. But it was the best thing I ever did. It saved my marriage, it saved my relationship with my kids, and I don't doubt for a minute that it saved my life too."

Ted explains that he'd been six years sober and attending meetings in a church hall in Camberwell when the huge frame of Thomas Barclay had first come through the doors. "He was a big chap," says Ted, "like a heavyweight boxer, and tall with it, but I could tell from looking at him that he was just as terrified as the next bloke. To begin with, he'd always leave the meeting the minute it was over, before I could even say hello, but thankfully he kept coming back and as the weeks went by he stayed a little longer each time. It was hard work getting more than two words out of him mind, but eventually we found out we were sort of in the same line of business and we became friends after that. He still wasn't much of a talker. I think Tommo was always more comfortable listening than he was talking. I got the feeling that he was a deeply troubled man but he never went into detail apart from one time when he told me he'd let a lot of people down in his life. I told him that was true for every alcoholic on the planet and he just smiled sort of sadly. I pressed him on it but he clammed straight up and I got the impression there was a lot more to it."

We stay chatting with Ted for a little while longer but then he suddenly looks tired and so we thank him for his time and tell him we need to be going.

"I wasn't expecting that, were you?" I say to Alex as we leave the home and make our way back to the station.

"Took me by surprise too," admits Alex. "I wasn't sure what to say. Even though he's okay now, Ted's story was really sad. He's obviously been through a lot in his life. But I'm not quite sure this visit has brought me any closer to knowing why Barclay put me in his will."

"Not directly, I suppose," I say thoughtfully. "But at the very least we know a bit more about the man…and his demons…That's something."

Alex shrugs. "I suppose."

We walk along, deep in thought, for a few minutes. "What do you think Barclay was hinting at saying he'd 'let people down'?" I ask as we approach the station. "Do you think he had some sort of criminal past? Could he have ripped off somebody in your family somehow or owed them money and that's why he left everything to you? From time to time you read about burglars being remorseful about what they've put people through and wanting to make amends somehow; maybe it was something like that?"

"Maybe," says Alex, sounding unconvinced. "But then again, if that was the case, why not leave me a letter explaining, why be so mysterious? It's almost as if he didn't want me to know."

The following day I head into work, loudly proclaiming, whenever Christine is in earshot, just how awful my food poisoning had been and how I'm never taking a chance on cooking raw prawns again. While I'm not totally convinced that Christine buys my act, neither does she say anything to me about it, and for that I am grateful.

When Saturday comes round, I catch the train to Peckham as usual and spend the journey trying to work out what else I can do to raise the museum's profile. While the *Courier* feature is certainly a good one to have under our belt, as it isn't due to come out until next week, chances are we're looking at yet another quiet weekend. It's just so frustrating, knowing that people would enjoy the museum so much if only they knew it existed and made the effort to come. Short of knocking on front doors and dragging people down to the museum myself, I'm at a loss about what to do next.

After a quick catch-up over coffee with Alex, I check my watch, and seeing that it's already five to ten, we start our usual opening-up routine. I walk down to the museum, switch on the lights, and check over the room to make sure everything is in order while Alex grabs the pavement sign and heads outside to place it near the front entrance. I'm just switching on the projector when Alex returns wearing a huge grin.

"What's up?"

"I think you should come and see for yourself."

He unlocks the museum door and pushes it open.

"What am I looking at exactly?" I ask, staring at the open doorway and the brick wall of the garage opposite.

"Look round the corner," he prompts.

I poke my head out of the door and to my surprise there's a queue of about a dozen people standing at the side of the building, all staring back at me.

"Are you open yet?" asks an elderly man standing at the front of the queue.

"Could you just give me a minute?" I say, holding up a finger, and then I quickly duck back inside, looking at Alex for an explanation. "What's going on?"

"The feature in the paper," he says. "There must have been some sort of mix-up because according to the people I've just spoken to in the queue, it came out yesterday."

Alex shows me a copy of the paper he's just borrowed. While we're not on the front cover as I'd hoped, the huge picture of Ivy and her table on page three along with the headline "Plight of the Round Table!—Quirky Museum Saves Gran's Beloved Furniture" more than makes up for it.

I look at Alex, then cast my gaze back toward the door. "And all these people have come to see the museum?" I ask, barely able to believe what is happening.

"You've done it, Jess," says Alex. "You've absolutely done it. Word about the museum is finally getting out there."

27

For the next seven hours, we're so rushed off our feet that I don't even stop for lunch. Every time I think the queue might be reaching its end, there's a fresh influx of visitors. While most acknowledge that they've heard about the museum through the *Peckham Courier* article, a good number refer to the flyers that had been distributed weeks earlier, indicating that like most things in life, intention only ever turns into action when given a bit of a push. Another unexpected boost has come in the form of the weather. Marketing plans for museums are all well and good but there are few things that draw people out of their homes in search of something to do than a spot of unseasonably warm London weather.

It's a little after five when, exhausted, I finally close the door behind the last of the museum's visitors but instead of collapsing in the first chair I see, I race over to Paul and Dec. In a bid to make sure the museum didn't get overcrowded, I had stationed them by the door on "clicker duty," a task they have bizarrely relished.

"So, come on then," I say excitedly, "how many did we have through?"

I hold my breath as everyone gathers around Paul.

"One hundred and eighty-six!" he announces.

I can't believe what I'm hearing. "Are you joking? Are you sure you haven't made a mistake?"

He leans across and shows me the number on his tally counter so I can see for myself. There's no doubt about it. He's right.

"I can't believe it!" I say, my eyes brimming with tears of joy. "One hundred and eighty-six total strangers came to see our little museum!" I look over at Alex to see him grinning back at me.

"I always knew you'd do it," he says. "Well done, you. Well done, everyone."

Quite whose idea it is to go to the pub is anyone's guess, but half an hour after closing up the museum we are all packed around a table at the Crown, a traditional pub five minutes' walk from Barclay and Sons. Despite the fact that payday is still two long weeks away and I'm already very close to going into the red, I'm so brimming with happiness that I insist on paying not only for the first round, but every subsequent one too.

With each new round of drinks, as the small group becomes louder and more ebullient, trading amusing stories and telling raucous jokes, I feel on top of the world. Guy was wrong; the museum isn't a failure. Finally, after all our hard work, after all the long hours, it's a success.

I stand up and am about to insist on paying for yet more drinks when my phone rings.

"Guy!" I scream a little too loudly.

"Jess?" he says in a bemused tone. "I was just checking you're all right. It's after eight. You're usually back by now."

"I know…and I'm sorry…but, Guy…Guy, the most wonderful thing happened today. We had loads of people in the museum! Loads of them! Over two hundred…okay…not exactly over two hundred…more like a hundred and something, but that's nearly two hundred, isn't it? Anyway, doesn't matter. People came, Guy. People came to the museum and so we're in the pub celebrating."

"I suppose congratulations are in order," he says flatly. "Well done, I'm pleased for you. Your museum is a success."

"And I'd never have been able to do it without you," I say. "You've been so amazingly patient, but it's been worth it. Why don't you grab an Uber and join us?"

"Maybe another time," he says. "I've got some work I need to be getting on with."

"On a Saturday night? Awww, come on, Guy, work can wait. Please come down."

"I'll see you later," he says firmly, putting an end to any further debate. "Just text me when you're on your way home, okay?"

For a moment I think about heading home after all because it's clear that Guy's in a bit of a mood, but then Dec appears and shoves a double gin and tonic into my hand and says, "This round's on us to say well done!" And as he pats me on the back, it dawns on me that I deserve this. I deserve this moment and there's no way I'm going to let Guy spoil it.

One by one over the course of the evening the group starts to disperse. First Angel leaves to meet up with friends in Camberwell, then Dec announces he's due at a friend's birthday bash at an Indian restaurant in Dagenham, and Paul follows not long after when his wife rings to find out where he is.

"Looks like the party's over," I say to Alex sadly after Paul's hasty exit. "Don't feel you have to stick around if you've got somewhere you need to be."

"Not likely," says Alex. "There's nothing waiting for me at home but an empty flat and a ready meal for one."

"Have you always lived alone?" I ask, considering him as he takes a sip from his glass. For someone I've spent so much time with over the past few weeks, frustratingly I still feel like I don't know very much about him at all.

"I lived in a few houses and flat shares when I first moved to London, but ever since I got my own place I've lived alone."

"No girlfriend?"

The question had seemed innocent enough when it had occurred to me, but the moment it leaves my lips I regret asking it.

"Sorry," I splutter, "that's an incredibly nosey question, isn't it? Please, forget I said anything."

Alex falls silent and for a moment I worry I've really offended him, but then as if the words are suddenly escaping from him against his will, he says, "Actually, I've ... well ... I've never had one."

I don't know what to say to this and I don't think he does either, and so there's another long awkward silence.

"I'm so sorry," I say eventually. "It was rude of me. I shouldn't have pried like that."

Alex takes another sip from his glass. "You weren't being rude, Jess; you weren't being anything of the kind. It's a reasonable question. Most men my age would either be in a relationship or have a string of them behind them by now . . . It just so happens that I haven't."

There's another long silence as we both feel the weight of his words.

"It's not for want of trying on my part," he says with a jocularity that sounds hollow. "There was a girl at uni I really liked and a housemate I grew close to when I first moved to London, but it turns out I'm not exactly what most women think of as 'boyfriend material.'"

There's a real sadness in Alex's eyes and he looks so desolate, so lost, that for a moment I want nothing more than to put my arms around him and tell him everything will be all right.

"Well, it's their loss," I say, wanting to bolster his spirits, but somehow it just sounds patronizing and Alex looks unconvinced.

"Yeah, right. You'll never believe this but a while back I got so fed up of being alone I actually set up a profile on Tinder." He pauses and scratches idly at a wet patch on the beer mat next to him. "I don't know why I did it really. I suppose things were going well with my therapy, and I was trying to push myself to do more than ever. I suppose at best I thought I'd be ignored and at worst . . . well . . . you know, the usual sort of thing. But I convinced myself it was worth a shot, you know all that 'it's better to try and fail than never try at all' stuff."

"So, what happened?" I ask gently, tensing as I imagine the million different ways such an endeavor might have gone wrong.

"Well, after a few days of absolutely no interest I got a match. Her name was Becks; she was thirty-seven and lived in north London. At first I wondered if she was just some teenager somewhere trolling me but the longer we talked, the more convinced I became that she was real.

I couldn't believe it; I'd made no attempt to hide my scars on my profile picture and yet here was a real-life woman interested in me."

I sit perfectly still, breath bated, not wanting to interrupt him. This is the most Alex has opened up to me since the night of the launch party and, judging from the fragility of his voice, the most he's opened up to anyone in a long while.

"After a few days of messaging," he continues, "she suggested meeting up and so we arranged to have lunch one Saturday at a pub in Highgate. That day I got ready and trekked all the way over there to meet her. The pub was rammed, and of course, the moment I stepped inside, I could feel people staring. But I told myself that I didn't care. I told myself that it would all be worth it. All I needed to do was just hang on. So, I got a drink, found myself a table, and waited. I didn't worry too much when she was ten minutes late; you know what getting around London can be like. I didn't even worry when she still hadn't arrived after half an hour. But when an hour came and went without her messaging, I knew it was time to call it a day and of course that's exactly when my phone buzzed."

Alex stops and, taking out his phone, scrolls through his messages, then turns the screen to me. I read the message:

Hi Alex, so sorry to mess you around like this but I'm afraid I won't be meeting you today. The truth is I was here when you arrived, sitting at a table near the back, but when I saw you looking for me, I don't know, I suppose I suddenly realized that I'm not quite as brave as I thought. I really have enjoyed messaging you these past few weeks. And I'm sure you're a lovely soul who deserves nothing less than to be with a nice girl who will make you happy. Sadly, however, I'm afraid that girl won't be me. Please, please, don't think too poorly of me. I'm so sorry to have let you down like this, but I'm sure you'll agree that this way will be far better for both of us in the long run. Once again, I can only apologize. Please don't think too badly of me, all best wishes, Becks.

Without saying anything, I place Alex's phone facedown on the table and rest my hand on his.

"Oh, Alex, what a rotten thing to go through. Why have you kept her text all this time? You should delete that thing right now. She doesn't deserve room on your phone, let alone in your head."

"I don't know," he says gloomily. "I suppose I keep it as a reminder."

"A reminder of what?"

He looks at me mournfully.

"Not to want things I can't have."

That night I fall asleep thinking about poor Alex and how lonely he must be, and the following morning before we open I try to talk to him about it but it's as if he's avoiding me. Eventually I come to the conclusion that perhaps he feels like he's said too much; not wanting him to feel bad about opening up to me, I just let things be.

The day's figures end up being better than even yesterday's and we have over two hundred people come through the doors. In addition, social media and website inquiries are through the roof, and I can't wait to see if this success will continue next weekend too. But then at work the following day I'm in the middle of replying to a woman who wants to bring her women's group for a visit on Sunday, when Guy calls.

"Great news," he says. "Annabel's had the baby; it's a boy! They've called him Zachary Henry."

"Wow, you're an uncle," I say. "I'm so pleased for you. Leave it to me, and I'll jump on Etsy and get Annabel and the baby a little gift from us both."

"Great, get it express delivered so that we can take it with us when we go and see them at the weekend."

"At the weekend?"

"That's okay, isn't it? I've told my parents we'll stay with them and then zip over to welcome the new arrival. Besides anything else it would be great to have a weekend together without that museum of yours getting in the way."

I feel a flicker of annoyance over Guy's barbed comment about the museum but the last thing I want right now is a fight. Anyway, he's every right to be excited about meeting his new nephew and as his partner I should be too.

"Of course it's okay. Can't wait to meet the little fella. When would we go exactly?"

"I was thinking we'd probably leave first thing Saturday and come back some time on Sunday afternoon. I've got a couple of early meetings on Monday, so I can't be too late."

"That sounds perfect."

28

It's coming up to midday on Saturday as Guy turns off a quiet country lane and begins heading down his parents' sweeping drive past fields and outbuildings until he pulls up outside their imposing Grade II listed manor house, parking the rental car next to a brand-new shiny black Range Rover.

"It's so good to see you, Jessica," says Guy's mother, Susannah, kissing me on the cheek while the family's overexcited Labradors, Ariel and Thunder, run around us barking good-naturedly.

"Now, now," says Guy's father, Hugh, grabbing one of the dogs by the collar, "I'm sure Jessica will play with you later if you don't get your filthy paws all over her lovely dress."

"It feels like such a long time since we last saw you," says Susannah as Guy and Hugh empty the car trunk of bags and presents. "It's got to be coming up on six months now, hasn't it?"

"Probably," I say apologetically. "Life's just been so hectic."

"I'm sure it has," she replies. "And of course, you've not long had the first anniversary of losing your poor mother. Those sorts of milestones are always tough to get through. How are you, my dear? I do ask Guy every time we speak, of course, but you know how men are with details. All I ever get out of him is a light and breezy, 'She's fine,' and then he moves the conversation along."

"I still have some bad days," I admit. "But generally speaking I'm okay.

And thank you again for the lovely flowers you sent on the anniversary; it was very thoughtful of you."

"It's the least we could do," she says, resting a comforting hand on my shoulder. "After all, we're practically family, aren't we?"

Following Susannah into the house, I remember how nervous I'd been on my first visit here three years ago. Although Guy had warned me beforehand that his parents' house was "quite impressive," that hadn't prepared me for just how grand it was. It has six bedrooms, a boating lake, and its own woodland. It has not just one but two tennis courts and a swimming pool. That first visit, I'd spent most of the weekend getting constantly lost and having to call Guy to ask him to come and rescue me. And even now as Susannah leads me through the vast hallway and up the grand staircase to the bedroom that will be ours for the weekend, I'm still overawed by the scale of everything.

"I'll just give you a moment to unpack," says Susannah, preparing to leave the room, "and if you need anything, we'll be down in the kitchen."

I thank her profusely, and as soon as she's gone I take out my phone, as I'm dying to know how things are going back in Peckham. But the moment I look at the screen I recall my promise of a museum-free weekend to Guy, and throwing it on to the bed, I head back downstairs and join everyone in the kitchen.

For the next hour I catch up on all of Hugh and Susannah's news while Guy and I help them prepare food to take over to Annabel and Theo's house. Then once we're done we load the food, along with presents we've brought with us, into Hugh and Susannah's brand-new Range Rover and make the short journey over to the next village.

With its honey-colored Cotswold stone, wisteria-clad frontage, and thatched roof, Guy's sister's house, though a more modest affair than that of her parents, is still undeniably impressive. As we greet the new parents and unload the car, I take a moment to marvel at just how lovely the place is. It's the sort of house most people imagine whenever they think of escaping the city and moving to the country, the picture-perfect

English idyll. And while I agree it's a lovely place to visit, I know in my heart I could never live in a place like this. I'd miss the hustle and bustle of the city too much and I think the peace and quiet would eventually drive me mad.

"So where is the young chap?" asks Hugh as we all stand in the kitchen. "Don't say he's moved out of home already?"

Annabel laughs and waggles the baby monitor in her hand. "He's just napping in his Moses basket in the drawing room at the moment. I'll run and fetch him the second he wakes so you can see him."

"In the meantime," says Theo, "what would everybody like to drink?"

As Guy and Theo make the drinks and Susannah and Hugh set out the food, I take the opportunity to give Annabel the presents we've bought.

"I wasn't sure what you needed," I say apologetically as Annabel unwraps one of the gifts, "but I saw these on Etsy and they were just so cute I couldn't resist."

"Oh, they're simply gorgeous," says Annabel, holding up the tiny pair of bright red handmade baby shoes. She turns to her husband. "Look, darling, look what Jess and Guy have bought for Zachary. Aren't they adorable?"

"Very cute," says Theo. "And they'll go wonderfully with that red and blue outfit my parents bought for him."

As if on cue, the baby monitor issues a piercing cry. "He's awake," says Annabel, grabbing my hand. "Why don't you come with me and I'll introduce you?"

I follow her into the tastefully decorated room and watch as she scoops the wriggling bundle up into her arms. "Hello, little man," she says softly, "come and say hello to your aunt Jess."

Without warning, she hands the baby to me. I can't remember the last time I held a baby and can't quite believe how small he is, how fragile.

"He's just gorgeous, isn't he?" whispers Annabel.

"He's perfect," I say, gazing down at him.

"Isn't he just? Mum and Dad are completely besotted. Come on, let's take him to meet his uncle."

With the baby still in my arms I follow Annabel carefully back into the kitchen and within seconds I'm surrounded by everyone, all straining to get a closer look.

"He must like you," says Theo. "Any time anyone but his mum picks him up he wriggles like an eel."

"Clearly you're a natural," says Hugh.

I smile uncomfortably. "I'm not so sure about that. I'm completely terrified I'm going to break him. Anyone else like a turn?"

The rest of the afternoon is filled with delicious food, fawning over the baby, and a short walk to the village pub. As much as I try to join in with the conversations going on all around me, I can't help but feel a little stab of sorrow. This is the longest I've spent around a family since losing Mum, and even though Guy's family couldn't have been more different, it made me feel nostalgic all the same. What I wouldn't give to enjoy a lazy afternoon making lunch with Mum in our kitchen followed by a walk in the park down the road, then returning home to slouch on the sofa in front of an old movie on TV. Pure bliss. Instead, here I am with a family the polar opposite, nice people admittedly, but somehow I doubt the day will come when I'll ever truly feel at ease with them, like they're real family.

I wake early the next morning to the sun streaming through a chink in the curtains, and not wanting to disturb Guy, I slip out of bed, dress, and creep quietly downstairs with the aim of enjoying a solitary walk around the enormous garden before breakfast. I remember from previous visits just how beautiful it is and I'm keen to see what, if anything, has changed.

"Morning, early bird," says a voice from behind me. I turn to see Susannah, already dressed and ready for the day, framed by the doorway cradling a mug of coffee.

"Going anywhere special?"

"I hope you don't mind. I was just going to take a little stroll around your lovely garden."

"What a good idea," she says. "It really is quite breathtaking at this time of day. Would you mind if I tag along? I'd love to show you all the work we've done since your last visit."

As we make our way through the grounds followed by the dogs, Susannah chats amiably about the garden, pointing out the newly landscaped area leading down to the tennis courts, and tells me all about the problems they've had with flooding around the boating lake.

"It's all sorted now of course," she says as we come to a halt at the water's edge and look out across the perfectly still surface mirroring the clear blue sky above. "But for a while Hugh and I were tearing our hair out."

"It's beautiful," I say, suddenly aware that after a weekend with Guy's parents I'm running out of adjectives to describe their rarefied existence. Everything, from the home they live in to their brand-new grandson, is beautiful, a fact they simultaneously seem to appreciate and yet somehow take for granted.

"Anyway," says Susannah, "enough about this old place. Tell me about the house you and Guy are buying. It all sounds very exciting."

"It is. I can't wait to get in there."

"Guy sent us the details. It looks very impressive. A perfect family home."

This last bit feels pointed somehow and I'm not sure how to respond, but then one of the dogs jumps into the water, quickly followed by the other, and the moment is lost.

"Guy's told me all about this museum of yours," Susannah continues as we watch the dogs frolicking in the water. "It's been keeping you very busy, I hear."

"Quite busy. But it's effectively a start-up, so there's been a lot of work involved getting it off the ground."

"And am I right in thinking you only have another four months before it's sold?"

"Yes, but it's going so well at the moment that I'm hopeful we can find a way to keep it going somehow."

"Oh, I see, and then what?" I look at her, puzzled by the question, and she adds, "I suppose what I mean to say is, what's your ultimate aim?"

"I don't know really. I suppose I'd like to find a permanent home for the collection."

"With you at the helm?"

"Ideally, I think I'd hate the idea of handing it all over to someone else."

Susannah mulls over my response. "And children?"

"Sorry?"

"Is having children part of your plan?"

I feel myself flush with embarrassment. "Well, yes, I suppose...at some point."

"Guy definitely wants children," says Susannah. "He hasn't said as much but you only had to see how he was with Zachary yesterday to understand how much he wants them."

"Yes...well, we haven't even got the house yet...so all of that is still quite a way off."

Susannah gently places a hand on my arm. "I know you must feel like I'm speaking out of turn here but if you ever do become a mother, you'll learn that your children's happiness will always override any sense of impropriety. I suppose what I'm trying to say, Jess, is that I just don't feel that starting a family is high on your list of priorities at the moment whereas for Guy I think it's right at the top. Obviously, this is between you and my son, but I'm just wondering if you're being totally honest with him. This museum thing, I can see you're really devoted to it—your face lights up whenever you talk about it—but I can't help but feel as if it's taking you in another direction, one that might lead you away from Guy. For you two to have a future together you need to be on the same page, and I think perhaps if you aren't, then, for both your sakes, you should tell him sooner rather than later. Difficult though it will be, it will be kinder in the long run."

29

Making the decision to dismiss Guy's mum's caution as the misguided efforts of a new grandmother with babies on the brain, I don't tell Guy what she said. Instead, going to great lengths to pretend that our conversation had never happened, we all enjoy a leisurely breakfast followed by a huge lunch, before Guy and I head back to London later in the afternoon.

On the way we chat about the new house, how much we are looking forward to moving, and even speculate how long it will take for everything to come together so that we can finally exchange contracts. Being so busy with the museum in recent weeks, I've barely given any thought to the move and what it will mean for us. It's almost as if I've filed it away in a box at the back of my mind marked, "Deal with later." It all still seems so unreal, so theoretical, that even though I field calls from solicitors and fill in paperwork, I can't imagine a time will come when this will all be done and dusted. But here in the car talking about it with Guy it suddenly starts to feel much more concrete, more real. This is not a drill, this is not a daydream, I really am buying an insanely expensive house with my boyfriend and I find myself veering between excitement and terror at the prospect.

The moment we reach home I explain that I need to swing by the museum to catch up with work and although I can see Guy is disappointed, having work to catch up with himself, he doesn't say anything. And so, borrowing the hire car, I make my way over to Peckham to find out how things have gone.

"Here she is," jokes Paul as I come through the doors of the museum just as the last visitors are leaving. "Swanning in like the Queen of Sheba once all the hard work's been done."

"Sorry," I reply. "If I could have been here, I would have, believe me."

"I'm only pulling your leg, sweetheart," he says. "You missed a cracking couple of days though."

"Really?"

"Yeah," says Angel, coming over with the tally sheet. "Eighty-five yesterday and ninety-one today. And interestingly most people haven't mentioned the article as being part of their reason for visiting; it seems to be either they got a flyer or heard about it through word of mouth."

"That's brilliant," I say, scanning the sheet before heading over to the visitor's book that now has several pages covered in glowing comments.

After looking through the feedback forms, I gather everyone around. "You've all done such a brilliant job," I say, barely able to contain my delight. "The responses from visitors have been amazing. People giving us top marks for friendliness and expertise. Results like this are all down to you, and the hard work you've put in."

"And you too," says Alex with a smile. "You've been the one leading us."

I feel myself flushing. "I'm not sure about that," I say. "But I am sure that I couldn't be prouder of you all right now if I tried."

There's a real spring in my step the following morning, which even the prospect of another week at Capital Tower can't remove. Letting myself into the building, I make my way straight to the staff room, but no sooner have I slipped off my coat than the door opens to reveal Christine, the office manager.

"Morning, Christine," I say cheerfully. "Did you have a good weekend?"

"Yes, thank you," she says tersely. "Could I have a word with you in my office, please?"

"I'm not late, am I?" I ask, checking my watch. "It's still only five to eight."

"No, you're not late," she says frostily. "At least not today, but as I said, I'd like to speak to you in my office."

As I follow her, I frantically run through all the things I might have done to have rattled her cage. Looking back over the past few weeks, I'd been guilty of quite a number of infractions. Not only had I been late several times, having overslept after working all weekend at the museum, but I'd also been caught using my private phone on reception making calls about Mum's house sale and the Greenwich house purchase, as well as using the office photocopier to print out museum feedback forms when the one at Barclay and Sons finally gave up the ghost.

"Look," I say as I sit down opposite Christine in her office, "I'm sorry, I haven't exactly been a model employee lately. I've had a lot on and—"

"Let me stop you there," she says brusquely. "The week before last I declined your last-minute request to take the day off, and yet lo and behold you called in sick. Correct?"

"I know how it looks, Christine. But it was just a coincidence. Thankfully it was just a touch of food poisoning and I was back in the next day."

Christine says nothing but instead reaches into her desk drawer and takes out a copy of the *Peckham Courier*. Without a word she flicks the newspaper open and slides it toward me. "I take it you accept that this is you?"

I stare at the picture of myself next to Ivy and the dining table.

"Yes," I say, wondering where she's going with this.

"And can I ask you when this picture was taken? And before you answer, please bear in mind I've already spoken to the journalist in question."

My heart sinks. "Look, I know I was in the wrong doing what I did but come on, be fair. I did ask you for the day off, and I even found people to cover me. You just didn't want to help."

Christine gives a sniff. "Well, even if I were to put that incident to one side, your regular lateness and continual contravention of office policy along with countless other misdemeanors mean you've left me with no choice but to suspend you immediately and escalate the matter to human resources."

I look at her trying to work out what I might say to placate her but then it dawns on me that I don't want to. The only thing I really want to tell her is where she can stuff her job.

"I'll save you the call," I say, calmly standing up. "I quit."

Grabbing my things, I turn and leave and spend the next half an hour walking around central London, propelled purely by the adrenaline from my showdown with Christine. Finally, I crash down in a small café in Covent Garden and there, over a comforting hot chocolate, I call Luce and tell her everything.

"You just walked out?" she says incredulously.

"I know," I say despondently, scooping a mouthful of cream from the top of my drink. "What was I thinking? But I just saw red and thought, screw it, keep your job."

"Do you know how many times I've dreamed of doing that when I'm having a bad day?" says Luce. "And you've actually gone and done it. You're my absolute hero. I should get you a medal or something."

I shovel the spoonful of cream into my mouth, hoping it might make me feel less wretched, but it doesn't. "I don't feel like much of a hero. I feel like an idiot. It was a really stupid thing to do. Guy is going to lose it when I tell him what I've done. We combined my salary, pitiful though it is, with his to get our mortgage offer, so all that will be up in the air now too."

"But still," says Luce mischievously, "didn't a tiny bit of you enjoy it? That woman sounds like a nightmare."

"She is, very much so. But I was in the wrong and I should've just sucked it up instead of making things worse."

"Don't worry, I'm sure it'll all be fine. You know what my mum always says, 'Everything happens for a reason.'"

Luce spends another ten minutes talking me off the ledge but then she has to go into a meeting and so I sit for another hour in the café wondering what on earth I'm going to do. I even half toy with the idea of going into the museum, but in the end decide to go home via the supermarket. I pick up a few things to make Guy's favorite meal, and by the time he walks through the door that evening the apartment is filled with the delicious aroma of lamb shanks gently braising in a red wine sauce.

"That smells amazing," he says, coming to join me in the kitchen. "Is it what I think it is? What are we celebrating? Don't tell me you've finally got a completion date for your mum's place?"

I shake my head and, handing him a glass of wine, decide against waiting until after the meal is over as I'd planned.

"I've got something I need to tell you," I say, feeling sick with nerves. "I...I...I quit my job today."

"You did what?"

"They were going to sack me anyway, so I saved them the trouble and quit."

"Sack you? What for? I know you've been late leaving a few days but they can't sack you for that. I'm going to call Josh. Let's see how quickly they back down once they get a letter from a top-notch law firm." He reaches for his phone but I put my hand out to stop him.

"It's not just about my being late." I sigh heavily. "My head hasn't really been in the game since taking on the museum and dealing with Mum's house sale and the move. There's been so much to do, and I've been so exhausted, and to make matters worse, you know that article about the museum I managed to get into the paper?" Guy nods warily. "Well, the journalist could only do a weekday for the interview and so I asked for the time off work but they said no, so I pulled a sickie and took it off anyway."

Guy looks at me, his eyes full of fury. "So, let me get this straight: you've thrown away your job, thereby putting our house move in jeopardy, all because of that blasted museum?"

"The house won't be in jeopardy," I say quickly. "I'll sign up with an agency first thing in the morning. It won't be a problem. I promise."

"You don't get it, do you?" snaps Guy. "The mortgage company can withdraw their offer at any point, even after we've exchanged contracts, if our financial circumstances change. If you'd been paying attention and not had your head full of that ridiculous junk shop, you'd remember that the mortgage guy explained all that to us."

"Guy," I say quietly, and reach for his hand, but he snatches it away the moment I touch it. "I really am sorry. I'll fix this, I promise."

"You will, will you? What are you going to do? Waltz back into work in the morning and pretend like you didn't just tell your boss what she could do with her job?"

"How about we just don't tell the mortgage company? It's not like anyone else is going to tell them, is it?"

"Aside from the fact that we're contractually obliged to tell them, that's a great idea." Guy sighs and leans against the kitchen counter, arms folded. I stand next to him and put my arms around him but he doesn't respond, and so I step back.

"You know what really hurts?" he says after a while.

I say nothing. Instead I look down at the floor.

"It's how low down our future is on your list of priorities."

"Of course it's not," I say quickly. "It is a priority. I'm putting all of Mum's money into it, aren't I?"

"You say that like you're doing me a favor. Like you're indulging me rather than investing in our life together. Is that what you're doing?"

"Look, I know you're angry, and I know I've probably gone about this all wrong but the museum . . . it just means so much to me. You love your job, it gives you direction, it gives you purpose, and that's great. But, Guy, I've been so lost, so lost for so long, and the museum has really helped. It's given me something to aim for, to hope for."

"And what about our hopes, our future? Mum told me, you know. About the conversation she had with you. Is it true? Is it true that you don't want to start a family?"

"I never said that."

"Then what did you say?"

"I didn't say anything. Because it's none of her business. It's between the two of us."

"Then tell me now," says Guy. "Do you ever want to start a family?"

There's a long silence as I think how best to say what needs to be said. "I love you, Guy, really I do, and maybe I'll want kids one day. But right now, I can't say when, or even if, that will ever happen."

He looks at me stunned, as if I've just slapped him across the face. "I wouldn't have believed it if I hadn't heard it for myself. Well, thank you for your honesty at least, even if it has been a long time coming."

I try to hold him again but he pulls away from me, marches into the bedroom, and starts throwing clothes into an overnight bag.

"Guy, where are you going?"

"I don't know," he says. "I feel like I don't know anything any more. All this time I thought we were on the same page, wanting the same things, but it seems like I was wrong. I think right now we need to give each other some space . . . to work out exactly what it is we both really want."

30

THEN

Setting down my morning mug of coffee on Mum's kitchen counter, I went through my mental tick list. Yesterday had been a really productive day. I'd not only defrosted the freezer and emptied the understairs cupboard, but I'd also made three more charity shop runs, plus two trips to the local dump as the trash was now almost full to overflowing and I still had the mattress I was sleeping on to get rid of before I left.

My phone, which I'd left in the bedroom, rang. I raced up the stairs to answer it. It was Guy calling me on his way to work. We chatted for a while and then he said, "So, any idea what time you'll be home tomorrow? It's just that some of the cycling boys are planning to do the Windsor loop but obviously if you're going to be home early, I'd much rather see you."

While the day ahead was looking quite busy, I couldn't imagine that I wouldn't be in a position to leave first thing in the morning and be back in London before lunch.

"I've no idea," I said, surprising myself, "but chances are it'll be pretty late. You go for your ride and I'll see you when you get back."

"Are you sure?"

"Absolutely. There's no point in you hanging around all day when I'm not sure what time I'll be home. I'd much rather you have a good time and anyway, we'll still have Saturday night to enjoy and a nice relaxing Sunday too."

When the call was over, I leaned against the sink trying to work out why it was I hadn't been honest with Guy. Perhaps I was being selfless and just didn't like the idea of his weekend plans being spoiled because of me. But the longer I thought about it, the more I began to wonder if perhaps my reasoning wasn't entirely altruistic. The fact of the matter was this week had been so insanely intense, so draining, both emotionally and physically, I couldn't help thinking that I'd need time to decompress when I got home, something I wasn't sure I'd be able to do if Guy was around. I felt terrible for thinking like that, for wanting to keep him at arm's length, but I knew we'd both be better for it if I could have just a little time to breathe, to be, before there was any attempt to resume normality.

As I washed out my coffee mug, I stared through the kitchen window out into the garden and thought about how often Mum and Gran had stood there looking at the same view, and how when it sold this would be someone else's kitchen, someone's else's view. I couldn't imagine it, another family inhabiting this house, another set of people living out their lives underneath this roof, people who'd never met Mum or known anything about her. I felt like getting one of those blue plaques made like the ones English Heritage put up on the front of notable buildings: "Maria Anne Baxter, 1961–2018, mother, daughter, shop worker, and friend, lived here."

A knock at the door brought me back to reality and I opened it to find a young woman wearing a black hijab with two small children, a baby girl in a stroller and a boy of about three holding his mum's hand, looking back at me.

"Hello there, sorry to disturb you. I messaged you yesterday on Facebook. I've come about the things you are giving away."

"Of course, come in and I'll get them for you."

The idea to get rid of some of Mum's stuff by using social media had come to me late on Wednesday evening. Over the past few days it had slowly begun to dawn on me that there was a growing pile of things gathering in the back room that I knew charity shops wouldn't take but which I didn't feel right throwing away, given that they were still useful. There was the vacuum cleaner, for example, the iron too, plus the microwave, all a few years old but still in perfect working order. The idea of trying to sell them on eBay made me feel exhausted, which is how I came to put a notice on the local community Facebook page.

The woman followed me inside and although I tried to chat to the little boy, he just stared at me wide-eyed, saying nothing. The woman told me she and her family had recently relocated to Northampton and now lived in a flat on the other side of town. "The flat is nice," she said in heavily accented English, "but the vacuum cleaner that we had was very old and has now stopped working. And a new one is too expensive."

I got out the vacuum cleaner and even gave her a quick demo to show that it worked and how to empty the bag. She was so ridiculously grateful that I also gave her the microwave I was going to take home with me and the kettle and toaster too. She explained that there was no way she'd be able to get all of the stuff home on the bus but I told her it wasn't a problem, then loaded everything into the back of the car, along with two sets of Mum's curtains, and drove the woman and her family home.

By lunchtime, I'd given away the DVD player, clothes rack, and two boxes of unopened sixty-watt bulbs to a couple of dreadlocked students; all the gardening tools to a young woman working for a community regeneration project; the fridge-freezer to a bloke with a van, who I suspected was some sort of dodgy landlord; and the ironing board, a set of heated rollers, and two unopened boxes of bathroom tiles to a middle-aged woman and her twenty-something daughter, who were clearly disappointed to have missed out on what I overheard them refer to as "all the best stuff."

I was just figuring out what to have for lunch now that I was without a kettle, toaster, or microwave when Luce called, and so I told her all about my morning.

"You know you can go over to my mum and dad's any time you like and help yourself to whatever you want, don't you? In fact, why don't you think about staying over there tonight? It can't be any fun with the house stripped bare, and I know my folks would love to have you."

"It's a lovely thought," I said, "but to be honest, tonight's my last night sleeping here and I've got it all planned out: fish and chips and a glass of rosé for tea, any old eighties movie I can get hold of to watch on my laptop, and then an early night."

"Sounds perfect," said Luce. "Are you sure you don't want any company? I know Mum and Dad can be a bit much but I could always blow off my plans with Leon for tonight, jump on a train after work, and come back with you tomorrow."

"It's tempting but I'm sort of thinking of this as my last goodbye. Or at least one of them. Maybe before it sells, me and you could come up to Northampton and camp out here, visit all of our old haunts and make a weekend of it. How does that sound?"

"Like an excellent plan," said Luce. "Count me in."

Despite the plans that I'd shared with Luce, by the time I finished for the day I was so tired that the thought of even the short walk to the local chip shop felt insurmountable. Instead, I ordered a curry and a four-pack of beers to be delivered and ate sitting on the mattress on the floor in my room, half watching some TV show I'd downloaded on to my laptop but mostly thinking about how by this time tomorrow I'd be back home.

Heading downstairs, I disposed of my takeaway containers and then caught sight of the large cardboard box I'd brought down from the loft earlier in the week. Mum had used it to store several summer-weight duvets, but having put them in the trash, I'd set it aside for all the things I was planning to take back to London with me. So far, it was empty, the prospective candidates for inclusion dotted around the back room. I'd thought this would be a task I'd complete in the morning, reasoning that in the cold light of day I might be more discerning, but weirdly reenergized by the two beers I'd drunk, I told myself there was no time like the present and got stuck in.

First in was the pile of Mum's scarves I'd saved after clearing out her wardrobe, followed by a few ornaments that I couldn't bear to part with, including a ceramic duck with a broken beak that had once belonged to my grandparents and a small blue vase that Mum had bought when we went on holiday to Anglesey when I was twelve. I carefully placed in her makeup bag still full of its contents, along with the potato masher and her Mason Cash-style mixing bowl, both of which reminded me of the fun we'd had cooking together.

In went a few of her favorite LPs on vinyl that she'd resisted giving away, even though it was a long time since she'd owned a record player. There was Michael Jackson's greatest hits, Prince's *Purple Rain*, and last but not least, Madonna's *True Blue*. I added a folder crammed full of official documents—everything from her birth certificate through to her most recent wage slips—and a shoebox full of mementos Mum had collected over the years that I'd found at the back of the cupboard in the back room. It was full of homemade birthday cards and my primary-school paintings, ancient Christmas cards from friends and family that must have meant something to her, and even concert ticket stubs of bands I'd never heard of from when she was a teenager. Next into the box went a carrier bag bursting with family photos, snaps of me growing up, pictures of Mum with her various hairstyles over the years, and a handful of my grandparents taken when they first came to England. And then finally, on the top, I placed Mum's diary and then closed the lid.

The only thing not in the box that I wanted to take was the set of encyclopedias piled up on the floor near the door. Purchased second-hand, they hadn't been in all that great condition to begin with, but now all these years later the cover on the spines of some of the volumes was coming away or had long since disappeared altogether. Their pages, once white, had now yellowed with age and smelled heavily of dust and mildew. And while I hadn't looked through any of the books in over a decade, I had a strong feeling that this particular edition, from the early seventies, might not only be woefully out of date in terms of its scientific declarations but also culturally insensitive, if not downright racist, too.

By rights I should have put them straight into the dumpster but every time I thought about it, I just couldn't bring myself to do it. And so, I found some shopping bags, filled them with the books, and then stood back and stared. It was a sobering sight: fifty-six years and an entire home distilled down to a single cardboard box and five tote bags.

The next day, along with everything else, I loaded the encyclopedias into the back of the hire car and brought them back to London, never once imagining that the decision to hold on to them would lead me to the Museum of Ordinary People.

31

NOW

When I open my eyes the next day, the first thing I do is reach out a hand to Guy's side of the bed, but instead of his warm body all I feel is a cold, empty space. In that instant any hope that last night had been just a bad dream evaporates, leaving me no choice but to face up to the stark reality of the situation. Guy is gone.

As he'd packed his bags last night, I'd tried everything I could to get him to stay. I'd begged, pleaded, and cried but he'd carried on throwing things into his overnight bag all the same. Finally, at the front door I'd asked him if we were over, to which he'd replied once again that he needed time and space to think. "Then do it here," I'd pleaded. "Just don't go, don't leave me." But he shook his head and without another word he turned and left.

In the first few moments alone in the apartment, all I did was sob, wondering if this was it, if this was the end. Guy was gone, I was alone, and I had no one to blame but myself. I should've taken the dressing-down from Christine. I should've just told her that I was sorry and that it would never happen again. I should've been honest with Guy about the newspaper interview, and perhaps he could've helped me come up with a solution that wouldn't have ended with me losing my job.

Of course I'd thought about calling Luce and telling her everything that had happened, but the last thing I needed was to listen to her bad-mouthing Guy. What I'd really wanted, what I'd really needed, was to be able to pick up the phone, call my lovely mum, who always knew what to say, and pour my heart out to her. But I couldn't, because she wasn't there any more; she was gone. At that moment I'd never felt more alone, more adrift in the world, so completely and utterly without consolation. Eventually I'd crawled into bed, pulled the covers over my head, and there in the darkness I'd cried myself to sleep. And now here I am awake at the beginning of a brand-new day, without Guy, without a job, and without hope.

Hoping that Guy might have messaged while I was asleep, I check my phone but there's nothing. No message telling me he was wrong and wants to come back. No message telling me he misses me. Not even a message telling me to have a good day. Instead, there's a message from Deliveroo offering twenty percent off my next order and one from the bank telling me I'm about to exceed my overdraft limit.

Tempting as it is to roll over and do nothing more constructive than wallow in self-pity all day, I tell myself I need to make this right. With great effort, I force myself out of bed and into the shower and give myself a stern talking-to. Guy left because I'd lost my job; therefore, it seems obvious that the simplest way to start repairing the damage between us is to get myself another as soon as possible. Maybe then he'll see that I do care about him, that I do care about our future, and he'll come home and we'll be happy again.

Getting out of the shower, I make myself presentable and then as soon as I'm ready and feeling at least half human, I call up my old temp agency, the one I used to use all the time before I got the job at Capital Tower. While it's been years since I'd last contacted them, thankfully Molly, the woman I used to deal with, is still there, and after a bit of a catch-up, she tells me about a temp gig staffing the reception desk at an insurance company over in Hammersmith that sounds right up my street. I ask when it starts and she replies, "Two hours ago," and so grabbing my bag, I slip on my coat and head straight out of the door.

My first day at Monarch Alliance Insurance goes well. The girls who staff the desk along with me are nice, and the office building is so like Capital Tower, everything from the glass atrium to the fake potted palms in the comfortable waiting area, that if I squint I can almost imagine I'm back there and that the past twenty-four hours haven't happened at all. But they have, and when I leave work and return home to an empty apartment, there's no mistaking this fact.

That night I don't feel up to cooking and so the closest I come to meal preparation is pouring milk over a bowl of granola, which I eat with the TV on because even though there's nothing on that I want to watch, the sound of people talking makes me feel just that little bit less lonely.

I've barely had more than a few mouthfuls when my phone vibrates. I leap up so quickly to grab it from the coffee table that I spill milk everywhere, but as I check the screen it's not Guy, as I'd hoped, but Luce asking when I'm free to meet up. I tap out a quick reply telling her that I'm not feeling great at the moment, but knowing Luce, she'll guess something's up, and so I take a deep breath, call her, and tell her about me and Guy.

"I'm so sorry, mate," she says. "Do you want me to come over? I'm supposed to be seeing Leon's brother's band tonight but I'll happily cancel or you could come with us, you know, take your mind off things."

"Thanks, but I think I'm just going to get an early night. Anyway, if Guy comes back, I want to make sure I'm home."

There's a pause and then she asks, "And do you think that's likely?"

"I don't know," I say. "But I've got to hope."

But Guy doesn't come back that night, or the one after, and when I'm not staring at the phone hoping he'll call or message, all I do is get up, go to work, come home, and go to bed. I don't go into the museum after work as I usually do, and when Alex and Angel text me separately, asking if I'm okay, I tap out a quick reply telling them I'm feeling a bit under the weather and that I hope to be back up to strength soon. When Audrey messages me at work on Thursday, asking to meet up with me for a quick drink that evening, I'm about to use the same excuse but as I'm typing out my reply my phone pings again with another message from her. "PS. I've got some good news for you! Really good news!" I look at the message, wondering what this good news might be, and curiosity gets the better of me so I agree to meet her at the Museum Tavern straight after work.

"Here you go," says Audrey, setting down my gin and tonic. "I know you didn't ask for it but I told the barman to make it a double."

"Thanks," I say gratefully, looking around the pub, packed full of after-work drinkers. "It's just what I need right now."

Audrey raises an eyebrow. "Bad day?"

I consider telling her about Guy but then think better of it. "Let's just say it's been more of a bad week."

"Well, I'm sorry to hear that but I think I might have something that will cheer you up, well, two things actually."

"Is it anything to do with the violin?" Since handing it over to Audrey, I'd been itching to know more about it but I hadn't wanted to hassle her when she was doing me such a big favor.

"Well, no, although I have passed it along to a friend of a friend of mine whose specialty is musical instruments, so hopefully she'll be getting back to me soon. No, I had a couple of things I wanted to talk to you about, the main being that I've heard about a job going at the British Museum that would be perfect for you. It's only a junior position and the pay isn't great but what it would be is a foot in the door. And while obviously I couldn't guarantee that you'd get the job, I could definitely put in a good word for you."

I can't believe it, after all this time, after so long dreaming about it, the possibility of a job at the British Museum. I'm lost for words.

"Wow, that's amazing. When's the deadline?"

"The end of the month. So you have a little time to get your ducks in a row."

"And do you think they'd be okay with me..."

Audrey finishes off my sentence. "Carrying on with your museum?" I nod. "Well, while I can't say for sure, I doubt that would be the case. Institutions like the British Museum aren't particularly renowned for letting curators have their own side hustles."

This is typical of my luck right now. My dream job but the only way I can do it is to lose the thing that's brought me the most joy since losing Mum. It's a tough call, but I make it nonetheless.

"In that case, it's probably best if I don't apply for it. Even though there's only four months left before I have to close the Museum of Ordinary People, I've come too far and sacrificed so much not to see it through."

As the words leave my lips, I immediately think about Guy. How would he feel if he heard what I'd just said? Would he think I was choosing the museum over him? Before I even have chance to consider what this might mean, Audrey says, "I had an inkling you might say that, which brings me to my second piece of good news."

Reaching into the tote bag slung over the back of her chair, she takes out a brown A4 envelope and hands it to me with a dramatic flourish.

"I happened to get wind of some funding this morning that's available for new innovative cultural projects," she says as I open the envelope. "In particular those hoping to engage a wider audience, and I thought of you straightaway. There's some information about it here and all the details you need to apply. Completing the application would be a tight turnaround I'm afraid, and the competition will be fierce, but it's definitely worth a try. And perhaps if you were successful, you'd be able to rent some new premises, pay yourself a decent wage, and ensure the survival of your museum for the next couple of years at least."

The thought that my little project might have a life after the sale of Barclay and Sons is a dream I haven't allowed myself to entertain. And as I quickly scan through the paperwork, I feel a little buzz of excitement. It will take a lot of work, and I'll need to prove all sorts of things about the museum's viability and benefit to the wider community but I'm surprised to find that I feel undaunted. I'd learned a lot in the past couple of months and my confidence has grown too and I don't doubt for a moment that I can do this.

But then I remember Guy.

If I did get this money, if the museum got to live a little bit longer, what would that mean for us? Would he be prepared to support me, to accept that this was something I needed to do, or would he take it as a signal that I'm choosing my own happiness over our future?

"Something wrong?"

Taking a sip of my drink, I look at Audrey trying to read my troubled expression, then tell her all about losing my job, Guy leaving, and how he blames all of our troubles on the museum.

"So," I say in conclusion, "it's complicated."

"It certainly sounds like it." She pauses, considering me, and for a moment I feel like an artifact under scrutiny. She leans forward in her chair. "I don't want to speak out of turn but would you mind if I gave you a tiny piece of advice? Don't let fear dictate your decision-making. I did for many years, and I can tell you from experience that it doesn't make for a happy life."

She doesn't elaborate and I don't pry; instead we talk for a little while longer about the politics of academia, her students, and a book proposal she's working on, and then finally we part ways.

"You look after yourself, Jess Baxter, and that's an order," says Audrey, giving me a hug. "And spend some time thinking about what it is that you want to do, before you start taking anybody else into account."

I head home, and spend much of the journey flicking through the funding application and scribbling notes in the margins. My head is buzzing with ideas, and I can't wait to get home and really get stuck into it. Reaching the apartment, I let myself in, already mentally preparing myself for a late night in front of my laptop, but then as I kick off my shoes I look up and to my surprise there on the sofa is Guy.

32

"Guy, I wasn't expecting you. If I'd known you were coming, I'd have—"

"It's my fault," he says, getting to his feet. "I should've called first."

"This is your home. You don't need to book an appointment."

He smiles softly and lifts his gaze so that his eyes meet mine, albeit briefly. He looks so lost, so unsure of himself that I want to hold him, to hug him, to tell him that everything's going to be okay, but I can't. Even though he's standing right in front of me, it's like there's a million miles between us.

"Have you eaten?" I ask after a while.

"I grabbed a quick bite after work. You?"

"To be honest, my appetite hasn't been up to much lately."

There's another long silence, and not for the first time in our relationship I wish I could see inside his head, read his thoughts, know exactly what it is he's thinking instead of having to guess or piece things together like a forensic detective.

"Where have you been staying?"

"At Josh's. I just told him we were having problems. He didn't ask for any details and I didn't elaborate."

"Maybe you should have. Sometimes it's good to talk. It can give you a little bit of perspective."

"Maybe," he says, and then slumps down on the sofa as if even the act of standing is too exhausting.

"I've really missed you, you know," I say, sitting down next to him and taking his hand in mine. "I've lost count of the times I picked up my phone to call you."

He smiles sadly. "I was the same."

"Then why didn't you?"

"I didn't think it would have been helpful."

We sit in silence. He seems determined to remain distant, as though afraid to drop his guard, even for a moment.

"I've got another job," I say, even though he hasn't asked. "Working on reception at an insurance company over in Hammersmith. It's only temporary at the moment but I think there's a good chance something permanent might come up soon."

"Oh, that's good."

"And how's work been for you?"

"Fine."

"Any news on the promotion?"

He shakes his head and I leave it a moment, hoping he'll say more, but he doesn't. How weird it is that just a week ago we'd have been chatting away amiably about anything and everything, and yet now, here we are talking like two strangers in a dentist's waiting room.

"Guy, can you look at me, please?"

Slowly, very slowly, he turns to me.

"I'm sorry, okay? You were right, I have been distracted by the museum, and I have been neglecting you...us...and it's not right. I've just got to get better at managing my time, that's all, and I can, I will."

Turning away, Guy sighs heavily. "But it's not just a matter of time management, is it? It's not just a question of better scheduling either. It's about what we both want, and I just can't help thinking that at this stage in our lives we want different things."

"But I want you. I want our life together."

"Then prove it."

"How?"

He pauses, as if carefully weighing the words he's about to say. "Give up the museum. That's what I want. From the day you got involved with that place you've been like a different person. It's like a switch has been flipped in you somewhere, and it's all you can think about."

I take a deep breath in a bid to remain calm. "But we've been through all this. You know I only have a few months to make a success of it; you know how much work was involved in turning it around. Of course it's absorbed a lot of my time, but that was to be expected. We're open now, people are coming through the doors, and yes, it's still keeping me busy but that doesn't mean I don't love you; it doesn't mean I don't care about us."

"But it's not just the time it's eaten up; it's who you've become in the process. It's a side of you I've never seen before. To be honest, lately every time I've looked at you I've found myself thinking: who is this person and what has she done with my girlfriend?"

"But I'm still the same."

"Are you? Because the person I fell in love with would never have lied to me."

"Are you talking about when I met up with Alex to pitch my idea? I explained all that at the time."

"And what about the newspaper interview and skipping work too? Anyway it goes deeper than that, Jess. Last year, when we were having problems, what do you think that was about?"

His question takes me by surprise. "I don't know, I just thought we were going through a bit of a rough patch like all couples do. We got through it, didn't we? Why are you bringing it up now?"

"Because it wasn't just a rough patch; it was me being sick and tired of the way we were just drifting along. It felt like every weekend that summer we were at some wedding or other watching friends making a commitment to each other, couples that had in some cases been together for less time than we had, and yet there we were, congratulating them for doing the thing we hadn't been able to do ourselves."

"You wanted us to get married?"

Guy shrugs. "I just wanted us not to be treading water."

"So why didn't you say anything?"

"Because up to that point I'd assumed we were on the same page. But the more I thought about us, the more I started to see that though you seemed happy enough, it was almost as if you had no interest at all in moving things forward."

I open my mouth to protest but he cuts me off.

"When things were at their worst last year, I really did think it was over between us but then your mum died, and overnight, all the things I'd been worrying about seemed so trivial. All I wanted was for you to be okay."

"And I wouldn't have been without you," I say, taking his hand. "You were amazing. You are amazing."

He smiles sadly and lets go of my hand. "If I'm so great, then why does it feel like I'm the only one thinking about our future? It was my idea for us to get a place together and my idea to make an offer on the Greenwich house. Was any of it ever what you really wanted? Lately, to be honest, I've been thinking you'd sooner have invested your mum's money into that pile of junk over in Peckham than use it to build a future with me."

My initial instinct is to jump to my own defense but the longer I sit here, the deeper his words sink in, the more I begin to realize that actually he might be right. I don't think I have been as committed to our relationship as I should've been, as much as he deserved me to be. Had I always been this way? I try to think of the last time before the museum came into my life when I'd felt sure of myself, certain about what I wanted. Thinking back, it must have been before Mum told me about her cancer, because after that I don't remember being sure about anything, anything at all.

I look at Guy, suddenly aware of how much I'm to blame for the mess we're in.

"This is all my fault," I tell him. "I'm not trying to make excuses... but listening to you talk makes me wonder if I've been committed to anything since my life got knocked off track when Mum got ill all those years ago. Before then, I'd had everything carefully planned out. I'd known exactly what I wanted and how I was going to get it and then just like that everything changed."

Guy sits up. "Changed, changed how?"

"I don't know... I got lost, I suppose... I lost my focus, my drive, my confidence. Instead I just drifted from one poorly paid job to another, until I finally washed up doing the receptionist thing at Capital Tower."

"And so what, are you saying you just drifted into me?"

"No, of course not. You were the best thing that had happened to me in a long time... I loved you, Guy, and I still do. But thinking about it now, I can see you're right... I was content for us just to stay as we were, not because I didn't love you, but because on some level I think I must have stopped making plans for the future at all."

"But then the museum came along."

I nod and bite my lip. "All this time I'd thought I was done with chasing career dreams but it turns out I was wrong. The museum... it stirred something up in me... something I'd thought long gone."

"And it's more important to you than I am?"

"No, not at all. I love you, Guy, and I want to be with you but I also want to see where the museum will take me. Why does this have to be a case of either or?"

"Because I want to start the next chapter of our lives and I can't see any way the museum isn't going to interfere with that. I mean you've only been involved with it for a few months and look where we are now."

"So you're not prepared to wait?"

"For how long? Until the six months at Barclay and Sons is over? Until you find a permanent home for that collection of rubbish? Would you happily walk away from it then? Or would you always be wanting to build it up, make it bigger, better?"

I don't say anything; I can't. He's right. I can't imagine walking away from the museum. I have to see this through wherever it leads me, and I have no idea how long that will take.

"And there's my answer," he says after a while. He looks at me and I feel compelled to meet his gaze. "I think if things had been different, if we'd met once you'd achieved everything you'd wanted to achieve, we could've been really happy, you and I. But the fact is we didn't, and we have to deal with things the way they are. You shouldn't have to settle for second best, Jess; you deserve your happy ending. But the thing is, so do I."

*   *   *

It's late when I arrive at Luce and Leon's in Brixton. I pay the taxi driver, who watches with an air of detachment as I struggle with the suitcase that half an hour earlier I'd frantically stuffed with a few of my things, all the while wearing a rucksack that is also full to bursting. Eventually, and without his help, I manage to get the case out of the cab, and the moment I slam the door shut he drives off without giving me a backward glance.

Wheeling the case up the path to Luce and Leon's front door, I ring the buzzer for their flat, and in no time at all I hear the sound of footsteps racing down the stairs. Finally, the door flies open, Luce appears, and without saying a word she wraps me in a huge hug that feels like the very definition of safety, and I finally let go of all the tears I've been holding back since I left the apartment.

"I'm so sorry," she says as she sits cradling me on the sofa while I sob ceaselessly. "I'm so sorry this is happening to you." But I'm just so overcome with it all that I can't speak; I can't even begin to form the words. And so, she just carries on holding me, until eventually I fall asleep.

When I wake the following morning, I'm lying on Luce and Leon's sofa covered in not one but two duvets. With the exception of the ticking of the clock above their fireplace, the flat is completely silent. I check my watch and to my horror discover it's after eleven. I pick up my phone to call work but then I spot a handwritten note from Luce on the coffee table in front of me. "Morning, Ace Face," it says, "don't worry about work. I found their number in your phone and called them first thing and told them you've got a stomach bug. And don't worry about anything else because I'm going to be with you every step of the way. I couldn't take the day off work to be with you because I've got a big meeting I can't get out of but I'll try and get away early. Leon's out all day, so you should have the place to yourself. Feel free to raid the fridge. Love you to the moon and back, L xx."

It's just after seven when Luce gets home from work loaded down with carrier bags, one containing some sort of delicious-smelling takeaway and another that makes a distinctive clinking sound that can only be multiple bottles of wine. Under her arm is wedged a huge bunch of flowers, which, after setting the carrier bags down on the coffee table, she presents to me.

"You shouldn't have," I say, gratefully receiving them, and then after making her close her eyes, I go to the kitchen to retrieve the bunch I'd bought for her when I'd gone for a walk earlier this afternoon.

"For you," I say, presenting them to her. "To say thank you, for everything. I honestly don't know what I'd do without you."

At this I start to cry and she puts her arms around me.

"Hey, come on, don't cry. What you need is some good food, some cold wine, and some crap telly. Leon's gone to stay at his brother's tonight so we can slob out on the sofa without him judging us."

And that's exactly what we do; we eat, we drink, we watch back-to-back episodes of *The Real Housewives of Beverly Hills* until finally we fall asleep somewhere around midnight.

I wake up about an hour later needing the loo, Luce snoring softly beside me. I carefully navigate my way to and from the bathroom, picking up the spare duvets along the way, which I drape over the two of us, but no matter how hard I try I simply can't get back to sleep. As I lie wide awake in the darkness I can't help but feel like some sort of cautionary tale, the person your parents warn you'll become if you make the wrong choices. Here I am at the age of thirty-one, with no money, no career, no relationship, and now no home. For a moment I seriously consider calling Guy and telling him that I'll give up the museum. But the longer I lie here composing speeches in my head, the more I realize that I could never give up the museum without resenting him, because to give up on it would be too much like giving up on myself.

When I eventually drop off, I sleep badly, tossing and turning all night, and I awake in the morning to hear the sound of Luce snoring in her own bed. I think about the day ahead, and though I know Luce will want to spoil me I feel like I need a distraction, something to focus on: in short, I need the museum.

I shower and get ready as quietly as I can so as not to wake Luce, then, slipping on my jacket, start writing her a note but then I hear the bedroom door open. I turn to see a bleary-eyed Luce, bare-legged and wearing one of Leon's old band T-shirts, looking at me.

"And where do you think you're going?"

"To the museum. It's my shift today. But even if it wasn't, I think I'd go in anyway. I just need to keep busy."

"I know you do, mate," says Luce. "But at this rate you're going to burn yourself out. Listen, you're not sleeping, you're barely eating, you need to take the weekend off to rest; otherwise, you're going to make yourself ill. I'm sure someone will cover for you and we can have a nice lazy day here."

"I can't say I'm not tempted but I really could do with the distraction. Hope that's okay?"

"Of course," says Luce. "But know this: when you get back, there will be more wine, more food, and more *Housewives* waiting for you."

On the way to Peckham I make a conscious effort to put aside all thoughts of Guy and my uncertain future, and instead think about the museum. Rather optimistically I've brought the funding application with me to work on if I've got a spare minute, but to be honest I'm not sure I have the headspace for it right now. What I need is to absorb myself in something practical, something physical, something that gets me out of my head for a while, and so I make a decision to go ahead with some of the changes I've been planning for the exhibition. Much as it's tempting to keep things as they are, given that people are coming through the museum's doors, my gut instinct isn't to play it safe, but to keep things fresh, keep visitors on their toes, and showcase as much of the rest of the collection as I can before we run out of time.

Reaching Peckham, I get off the bus and I'm so busy typing a to-do list for the day on my phone that I accidentally bump into a couple locked in an embrace near the station.

"Oh, I'm sorry," I say automatically. "My fault, I—" then stop suddenly as it dawns on me that the couple aren't strangers as I'd first thought but in fact two people that I know very well indeed.

33

Jess," says Alex, looking mortified, and then quickly removes his arms from around Angel as if I've just caught him doing something he shouldn't.

"Hi," I reply, not quite sure what else to say. Alex and Angel are a couple? I had no idea. When did this happen? How had this happened? I have so many questions.

"Hi, Jess," says Angel, shooting a puzzled look at Alex as if she can't quite understand why he is acting so strangely. Turning back to me, she asks, "Are you feeling better now? Alex and I didn't think you'd be in today."

"I wasn't going to be," I say. "But when I woke up this morning I felt a bit better, so I thought I'd give it a go."

"Well, it's good to see you," says Alex, and then even though I haven't asked, he adds, "One of Angel's friends was playing a gig last night over in Camden, and she asked me along."

"They weren't that good, to be honest, but I'm glad we went." She gives Alex a shy smile and then goes to take his hand but he quickly shoves both of his into his jacket pockets.

"I think we should get going," he says, avoiding Angel's questioning look, and then without waiting for a reply he starts walking in the direction of the museum.

For a moment, I don't know what to do, and neither, it seems, does Angel. Finally, we exchange an uncertain look, as if we both know that something has happened but aren't entirely sure what, and then word-lessly we both fall in step behind Alex. Feeling awkward, I try my best to make conversation, asking them both more about the band they'd been to see, but Alex barely says a word, and Angel seems distracted. Unable to bear the silence, I start babbling and tell a long and involved story about the time I went to Glastonbury, lost my friends on the Friday night, didn't see them again until Monday morning, and yet somehow still managed to have an absolutely amazing weekend.

As soon as we reach Barclay and Sons, Alex and Angel head off in opposite directions without even looking at one another. Alex disap-pears to the office, closing the door behind him, while Angel makes her way straight down to the museum, leaving me alone by the entrance unsure what has just happened. Suddenly, I feel as if I might cry and so I dash to the loo, and the moment the door closes behind me I burst into tears.

As I wash my face and attempt to regain my composure, I try to get to the bottom of why I feel so upset. Is it because Alex and Angel are together? I can't see why that should be the case. Yes, seeing them together like that had surprised me but Alex is such a lovely, kind, gener-ous, and warm-hearted person that all I want is for him to be happy. It can't be that. The only reason that makes sense, the only one that feels right, is that my tears were all down to Guy, to the fact it's been less than forty-eight hours since we split up, less than two days since my whole world turned upside down. Perhaps I should've followed Luce's advice and stayed home today after all. Perhaps I'm simply not ready to be back in the world quite so soon.

I decide, since I'm here already, to work the morning and see how I feel and so after making myself look presentable, I join Angel down at the museum and start making the changes I've been planning. With the help of Paul and Dec, who had arrived while I'd been in the loo, we swap over the motorcycle sidecar for Ted Enfield's father-in-law's workbench; the elegant forties wedding dress for a hideous, yet somehow still charm-ing, coffee-and-cream-colored meringue affair from the eighties; and exchange some of the suitcases on the display for others that have yet to see the light of day.

By the time we're finished it's nearly ten o'clock, and when Paul opens the doors once again there's a queue of people waiting to come in. First in line is a group of smartly dressed pensioners from a local lunch club who seem utterly entranced by the idea of the museum. Then there's a group of university art students who had been recommended to come by their tutor. Finally, there's a group of Cub Scouts who I'm told are here as part of their bid to earn their local knowledge badge. Everyone, no matter their age or reason, seems to have a good time, and I'm busy all morning answering questions, listening to reminiscences, and fielding queries about volunteer opportunities.

When my stomach starts rumbling at just before one, I suddenly remember that I haven't had any breakfast. Grabbing my bag, I head out to get a sandwich from the café down the road but as I open the door I bump into Alex coming the other way. Things have been so busy I've barely seen him all morning, but now that we're face-to-face I feel our earlier awkwardness return.

"Oh, hi, just popping out to the café to get some lunch."

Alex holds up the paper bag in his hand. "I've just come from there. Sorry, I should've asked if you wanted anything."

"It's fine. I could do with some fresh air."

I move to carry on past him but he says, "Look, Jess, about this morning, me and Angel…"

"Alex," I say, not wanting him to feel like he owes me an explanation. "Honestly, you don't have to say anything to me. I'm really happy for you. Angel is a lovely girl and I think you make a great couple."

He opens his mouth as if to say something but then his expression changes as if he's thought better of it.

"Okay," he says. "Well, I suppose I'll catch you later, then."

A thought crosses my mind. "Actually, before you go, can I ask a quick favor? I don't really want to go into it right now but long story short… Guy and I … we … well … we've split up."

Alex's face fills with concern. "Jess, I'm so sorry. I had no idea. What are you doing here? You should be at home looking after yourself."

"It's okay, I'm better keeping busy. Less time to think about things."

"Well, is there anything I can do to help? What's the favor you mentioned? Whatever it is, it's yours."

I smile; he really is such a lovely person. "Don't be too nice, or you'll set me off. The thing is I need to move my things out of Guy's asap and I was wondering if there's any chance I could borrow the van?"

"I can do better than that," he says. "Let me know when you want to move and me, Paul, and Dec will help you do it."

That night back at Luce and Leon's, I contact Guy and across half a dozen messages we agree for me to go and get my things on Monday evening as he'll be away in Brussels for work. The exchange is purely functional, and though I ask how he is, he doesn't acknowledge the question. I get the feeling that now that the hard part is done all he really wants to do is move on with his life without me; all he really wants to do is draw a line under this whole sorry mess.

On Monday after work I head straight to the apartment to make a start on packing before Alex and the boys arrive with the van. Letting myself in, I turn on the lights and as I look around I'm struck by the fact that nothing much has changed. Guy hasn't suddenly become a slob because he's heartbroken we're over. In fact, the place looks as immaculate as ever, perhaps even more so without me here making it untidy.

In the hallway I open one of the cupboards and start to remove my things. It's sobering, seeing all the boxes of my belongings that I'd moved in with two years ago still packed away in there, as though living here had only ever been a temporary arrangement, a stop on the way to somewhere else. Perhaps the boxes are telling me I'd always known deep down that it wouldn't work out between us. Then again, perhaps they're telling me a plainer truth, that I could never have been truly happy here while so many of the things I loved and that brought me joy were hidden away. Either way, I tell myself that this will never happen again. Wherever I end up, whether it's a tiny bedroom in a shared house or a flat all to myself, I'm going to put my own stamp on the next place I live. I'm going to make it my own and not apologize to anyone for doing so.

Half an hour later as I balance on a dining chair, tugging at a black bin liner stuck fast on something in the cupboard at the top of the wardrobe, the door buzzer sounds. Determined not to be defeated I give one last sharp tug, which only succeeds in ripping it open and showering a bizarre mix of items (clothes, CDs, shoes, books, scented candles) across the bedroom floor.

Leaving the room looking like a bombsite, I go into the hallway and check the intercom video screen to see Alex, Dec, and Paul looking back at me. "Come on up," I say, pressing the button to let them in, and then, leaving the front door ajar, I return to the bedroom and start clearing up.

"You never told us you lived in a palace!" I hear Paul's booming voice comment as he, Alex, and Dec come in. "This place is like a posh hotel! You must be gutted you've got to leave it."

As I emerge from the bedroom, I catch Alex remonstratively shaking his head at Paul and he looks mortified when he sees me.

"It's okay," I say, smiling. "Paul's right, this place is like a hotel and there are some things I'll definitely miss about it, the views for one." I walk over to the kitchen and as I fill the kettle I think about how easy it is to get attached to things even when you don't mean to. Sometimes things and places get under your skin even when you tell yourself they won't.

"Thanks for helping me out today," I say, taking out four mugs from the cupboard. "I really do appreciate it."

"It's no problem," says Alex. "We're just glad we're able to help."

Once they've finished their drinks, Alex, Paul, and Dec make a start on taking the boxes and bags I've assembled in the hallway down to the van, while I carry on clearing up the spill from the bedroom and empty the cupboards of the last of my things. Once I'm done I make one final sweep of the apartment, checking drawers and scanning shelves, which is when I catch sight of the silver-framed photo of Mum on the sideboard.

Sitting down on the sofa, I stare at the picture, wishing she were here to talk to. I know she'd tell me that everything happens for a reason. I know she'd tell me that I'll get through this. I know she'd tell me that every-thing will be okay in the end. But I just wish I could hear her say it herself.

Standing up, I take the photo out to the hallway and scan the remain-ing boxes until I find the one I'm looking for, the one full of Mum's things I'd brought back after clearing her house. I take out a couple of her scarves and carefully wrap them around the photograph for protec-tion before slipping it into the box. As I do so, I suddenly remember the diary and I don't know why; perhaps it's because I so long to hear her voice, or perhaps it's because I realize that I might finally be ready to read it, but I take it out and put it into my bag. As I close the lid of the box, Alex, Paul, and Dec return.

"What next?" asks Dec. "The sofa?"

"That's Guy's," I explain.

"Okay, then," says Paul, "how about the dining table?"

"That's his too."

"So, what else is coming, then?" asks Dec, and so I gesture to the small pile of bags and boxes that remain in the hallway.

Paul raises an eyebrow. "Really? How long did you say you lived here again?"

"You don't have to answer that," says Alex, shooting me an agonized look. "We'll take this stuff down now and we'll meet you in the van when you're ready."

After they've gone I take one last tour around the apartment and I'm shocked by how little difference the removal of my belongings has made. With the wardrobe doors closed and the bathroom cupboard shut, aside from an empty space on a shelf here and there, almost nothing appears to have changed. It's as if I never lived here, it's as if I never made an impact, it's as if this entire apartment is a holiday let, and now the holiday is over there's nothing left for me to do other than return my keys. Laying them down on the kitchen counter, I look around this place that was once my home before opening the front door and pulling it closed behind me for the very last time.

34

Alex very kindly lets me store all my things at Barclay and Sons, and once we're done I thank the boys for their help and prepare to head back to Luce and Leon's but then I sense Alex hanging back wanting to talk to me.

"Are you okay?" he asks once we're alone.

I give him a smile. "I will be. Thanks so much for your help tonight; you've been a real friend."

"Really, it's nothing. I wish I could do more. I can't begin to imagine how difficult this must be for you."

"It is," I admit. "But if I'm honest, it was a long time coming. Guy and I weren't right for each other but we just didn't have the guts to admit it until it was too late." I start to get upset, and Alex moves to comfort me but then my phone vibrates.

"I think that's my Uber. I'd better go."

Alex is silent for a moment, and once again I'm struck by the sense that he wants to tell me something, but in the end all he says is, "If you need anything, anything at all, just ask, okay?"

His expression is so full of concern and his words so heartfelt that I have to blink back my tears. "Thank you, thank you so much, I will," I say, and then turning round, I head for the door and moments later I'm in the back of a car, alone with my thoughts, flashes of late-night Peckham speeding past the window.

*   *   *

No matter how hard I try that night, I can't get to sleep, my head is so full of thoughts about the future, about the question marks hanging over the rest of my life. Where am I going to live? What am I going to do after the museum closes? And self-pityingly, will I be alone forever? Unable to come up with any answers, I get up and, grabbing the museum funding application from my bag, tell myself that now is as good a time as any to get going on this, especially as the deadline is now only a few days away.

In the days that follow, between work and the museum, I spend every spare moment on the funding bid. At first it feels like it's going well but as the deadline for submission draws closer, my confidence begins to fail and I feel like all I'm doing is going round in circles. Finally, the night before it's due in, when by rights all I should've been doing was adding a few finishing touches, I read the whole thing through at Luce and Leon's dining table while they sit on the sofa watching TV. It's awful. Absolute drivel. And I'm so disappointed that I throw my hands up in the air and officially admit defeat.

"What's wrong?" asks Luce as I slam the lid of my laptop shut and lay my head down on the table.

"I can't do this stupid funding bid thing Audrey gave me. I'm not going to bother."

Luce pauses the TV and comes over to me. "Listen, mate, you've been at this since forever. Why don't you nip down to the liquor store, grab us a bottle or two of wine, and me and Leon will take a look at what you've done so far."

Leon smiles. "I bet it's not half as bad as you think it is. I can't begin to tell you how many times I've thought about deleting my thesis, quitting my PhD, and running away to live a simpler life somewhere else. But then Luce tells me I'm being stupid and all I need to do is take a break, and I have to admit more often than not, she's right."

Reluctantly I take their advice, and slipping on my coat I head out into the cool night air, cringing at the thought of someone other than me reading my terrible attempt to persuade experts in their field, people who spend all day every day looking at funding bids, to choose mine.

Reaching the liquor store, I spend an inordinately long time choosing wine and snacks in a bid to avoid any chance of returning to the flat while they're still reading it. In the end I take so long that the shopkeeper starts giving me funny looks and so I quickly grab two bottles of merlot, because it's Luce's favorite, and five random packets of family-sized snacks, pay for them, and then head back to the flat.

"Okay," says Luce once I've poured out three glasses of wine and decanted a large packet of Doritos into a bowl. "I'm not going to lie; it's not great. It's more a three-thousand-word stream of consciousness ramble than a succinct and well-argued funding bid but after everything you've been through that's hardly surprising. But on a positive note, there's enough good stuff in there that with a bit of judicious editing and a couple of lines here and there, I think Leon and I can sort it out for you."

Too tired to protest, I ask them what I can do to help.

"Nothing right now," says Luce. "Just watch some telly and let me and Leon do our thing."

I can't watch TV, and so instead I spend the next couple of hours pacing the flat, simultaneously desperate to help but keen not to get in the way. Then finally, Luce calls me over and asks me to read the rejigged funding bid.

"We haven't really changed the content," explains Leon. "Just given it some structure, that's all. Tell us what you think."

Nervously, I sit down in front of the laptop, aware that if this isn't any good I'll lose my one and only chance to save the museum. But as I begin to read what they've done, I start to feel more hopeful. Somehow, they've managed to get to the heart of what I really wanted to say in a way that I'd been struggling to achieve and there's a clarity and persuasiveness to my arguments that had previously been buried in jargon.

"It's perfect," I say as I reach the last line. "Absolutely perfect." I stand up and give them both the biggest hugs I can manage. "You're both amazing. I don't know how I'll ever be able to repay you."

"You don't have to," says Luce. "It's just what friends do, isn't it? It's what we've always done. We look out for each other."

"Sorry to interrupt this beautiful moment," says Leon, "but if I'm not mistaken, Jess needs to press send pretty soon; otherwise, perfect or not, we'll be too late."

I check my watch. Leon's right; it's five minutes to midnight.

"I feel like I should say something momentous," I say, with my finger hovering over the return key, "but I don't know what?"

"I know," says Luce. "How about dedicating it to Maria Anne Baxter?"

"That's perfect," I say. "This one's for you, Mum." And then, taking a deep breath, I press send.

With the funding bid off my plate, there's a danger that I might allow myself to start thinking about Guy again and so in an effort to keep my mind occupied, in my spare time I take the opportunity to do a bit of conservation work. Ironically, the first thing I start working on is a wedding album from the sixties. It's a beautiful thing that comes with its own presentation box, which sadly is coming apart, the album inside spotted with water stains and patches of mildew.

The photos themselves, however, are in quite good condition and I don't know whether it's because I'm single now or because I just want so badly to believe in love, but I find myself getting drawn into this couple's story. They look so happy, as if they really are each other's best friend, and even though I know the fate of their wedding album, that Barclay found it in a dumpster outside a block of flats in Basingstoke, I like to think that somehow their love survived the test of time.

The following day as I'm waiting in line at the Pret round the corner from work to pay for my lunch, I find myself thinking about the couple from the wedding album again. While I know that with a single swipe on a dating app I could be with someone tomorrow, I wonder whether I'll ever have a connection like they did. The groom clearly adores his bride and she him, and it's not hard to imagine that they would do anything to see the other happy. That's the kind of love I want. That's the kind of love I need. I'd sooner be alone forever than settle for anything less.

Arriving at the front of the queue, I set down my sandwich and drink and reach for my phone to pay, when it rings and I'm forced to do that awkward dance you have to do when you want to answer a call but don't want to be rude to the person at the till. By the time I've finished apologizing, the call has gone through to voice mail, and so as I take my tray and look around for somewhere to sit, I listen to the message and the next thing I do is call Luce.

"You're never going to believe it," I tell her, "but after all this time, all this heartache, the solicitor dealing with Mum's house sale just called. I've finally got a completion date."

"I bet that was a bit of a shock," says Luce that evening when we pick up the conversation in the kitchen while I'm cooking dinner for her and Leon.

"Just a bit. When something takes so long to happen, you start to believe it never will. And I think it's thrown me a little."

She takes a sip of the beer she's been drinking. "It's only natural. It's the end of an era." She gives me a hug. "But don't forget you'll always have a home at Mum and Dad's and they won't be happy unless you come to us for Christmas again this year."

I think about the prospect of Christmas, my first without Guy, but quickly put the brakes on this depressing train of thought. Instead, I think about a conversation Luce and I had a while ago.

"Do you remember, when I first put the house on the market and we talked about going back to say one last goodbye?"

Luce nods. "I like your thinking."

"So you fancy it then?"

"Count me in."

"Great, it'll have to be this weekend though because the sale goes through a week on Friday. Does that work for you?"

Luce groans. "Typical! It's Leon's dad's seventieth birthday thing this weekend. Just me, him, and sixteen members of his crazy extended family stuck in a house on the Pembrokeshire coast. You know if it was up to me, I'd skip it in a heartbeat, but when Leon booked it he threatened to dump me if I tried to wriggle out of it."

"Don't worry, it's not a big deal."

"Maybe we could go another weekend and stay at my mum and dad's instead? I know it wouldn't be the same but it's got to be better than nothing."

"It's fine, really it is. I think I'll go anyway; we can visit your folks and make a weekend of it some other time."

"You've just been through this miserable time with Guy, and now you want to spend the weekend back at your mum's alone? Are you some sort of glutton for punishment? Come on, Jess, even you must see how much of a terrible idea that is!"

I sigh heavily. Maybe she does have a point after all. This will be the first time I've been back to the house since clearing it. It will be completely bare, stripped of all the comforts of what used to be my home. With Luce with me, we could've at least had some fun remembering all the good times we had there, but alone I can't imagine I'll do anything other than spiral into sadness.

"You might be right," I say, giving the pot of veggie chili I'm making a stir. "As much as I wanted to say one last goodbye to the house, I'm not sure doing it alone is the right thing."

"Well," says Luce thoughtfully, "maybe you don't have to do it alone. How about asking Alex? He'd go with you, wouldn't he?"

I consider the question. Luce is right. Hadn't he told me when he'd helped me move out of Guy's that if I needed anything, all I needed to do was ask? But then again, he's with Angel now, and the last thing I want to do is cause any problems between them.

"I think he probably would," I say in answer to Luce's question, "but I'm not sure asking him would be the right thing to do."

"Why, because you fancy him?" says Luce, giving me a cheeky wink. "I remember that glint in your eye when you first talked about him."

I sigh and roll my eyes. "There was no glint, just you and your overactive imagination. No, remember I told you he and Angel are together now."

"But I don't see any reason why that should make a difference. You've just said you don't fancy him, and he's got a girlfriend, and this is the twenty-first century after all. Just because he's a bloke doesn't mean you're trying to seduce him; the bottom line is you're friends, aren't you? And this weekend a friend is what you need."

"I don't know," I say. "I don't want to make things weird between us."

"Why would it? Think about it, if Alex was a woman, you wouldn't even give it a second thought. In fact, if you really think about it, it would be weird if you didn't ask him."

While I'm not entirely convinced by all of Luce's crazy logic, I have to admit that some of it makes sense. Perhaps I'm overthinking it; perhaps I'm making it into a bigger deal than it should be.

"Okay," I say finally, "I'll put it to him and see what he says."

After we've eaten I call Alex and after we've chatted for a while I ask my big question.

"Listen, I don't know how you're fixed, and feel free to say no, but I've just heard that the sale of my mum's house in Northampton is completing next Friday and so I'm planning on taking one last trip there this weekend to sort of say goodbye. Anyway, I was wondering, as my unofficial road buddy, if you'd fancy coming along? Obviously, the house is empty, there won't be anywhere to sit, and you'll probably have to sleep on an air bed, but in exchange I can promise you an all-expenses-paid meal out at the Punjab Palace, if not the best Indian restaurant in town, then at the very least the best within a five-minute walk of my mum's. So, what do you say?"

There's a brief pause, one long enough for me to imagine I've overstepped the mark and that right now Alex is trying to think of a way to turn me down gently, but then to my surprise and without any reference to Angel at all he says, "Yeah, I'd love to; count me in."

35

Here we are," I say, nodding toward Mum's pale green front door. "Number thirty-seven Arnold Street, former home of Jess Baxter, chief curator of the Museum of Ordinary People. Maybe there'll be a blue plaque here one day, but I won't hold my breath."

Alex and I have done a lot of talking in the two hours it's taken us to drive here, mostly about the museum but also subjects as diverse as cooking, architecture, and the bewildering intricacies of Dec's love life (we both agree that he needs to pick one girl and stick with her). The one thing we hadn't talked about was Angel, and even now I can't work out whether that's because he still feels awkward about sharing details of their relationship or whether he's worried I will.

Unloading our bags from the trunk, and then fishing around in my jacket pocket, I locate the keys and open the front door. As we stand in the empty living room, I feel even more unsettled than I had when I'd first arrived here all that time ago to clear the house. Now on top of dealing with the loss of Mum there's also the absence of her familiar furniture and belongings to contend with.

"I'm sorry," I say, turning to Alex, "it's not exactly what you'd call a welcoming sight, is it?"

"It's okay," he says. "You did say it would be like indoor camping."

"I'd offer to give you the guided tour but there's not much to see."

Alex smiles. "Then why don't you tell me how it used to look and I'll use my imagination."

I don't quite know how to respond. It's such a delightful thing to say that I can't help smiling and yet at the same time I'm not sure if he's being serious.

"You don't mean that, do you?"

He sets down his bag on the floor, on the spot where the sofa used to be, and grins. "Do I look like I'm joking? Stop dawdling and get to it, Baxter!"

I begin describing the room as it had been, placing every piece of furniture, picture, and ornament exactly where I remember it in my mind's eye. Each description elicits a flood of memories about Mum, my childhood, and the fun we'd had here, and it really lifts my spirits.

As I take him through the back room to the kitchen, I'm surprised to find a bulging blue IKEA bag on the counter. I peer inside and see teabags, milk, mugs, sugar, biscuits, and even a kettle. I pick up the note beside it and as I read it I can't help but smile:

Hi Love, thought you might need a few things for your weekend. Do you and your friend fancy coming to ours for tea tonight? Say seven-ish? Nothing fancy, just a bit of pasta and salad, but it'll save you the bother and expense of getting a takeaway. You wouldn't have to stay all evening. It would just be nice to catch up. All our love, Maggie and Dougie xxx.

"This is all Luce's parents' doing," I say, taking out the kettle. "Aren't they sweet?"

"Yeah, it's really thoughtful." Alex smiles, unpacking the contents of the bag onto the counter.

"They've also invited us round for dinner too."

"Do you want to go?"

"Only if you'd be okay with it. They've been so good, checking on the house and sorting things out for me. But we don't have to if you don't want to. They're so lovely they won't be offended. What do you think?"

"Sounds good."

"Are you sure?" I say, suddenly remembering the museum launch party and the thoughtless assumptions I'd made. "Like I said, you really don't have to."

Alex smiles and as if reading my mind, he says, "You don't have to worry, Jess, really. I'll be fine. So where are we starting this farewell tour of yours?"

It's a good question. Should we go to the market square so I can buy us a bag of piping-hot fresh doughnuts like Mum used to treat us to after a busy morning's shopping when I was little? Or perhaps we should head straight to the museum and art gallery so I can show Alex where my love affair with the past began? But then it strikes me that today would be a good opportunity to do something I've been meaning to do for months.

"If you don't mind, I think I'd like to visit Mum."

"It's not just Mum who's here," I explain to Alex as I pull off the busy highway and in past the stone pillars guarding the entrance to Kingsthorpe Cemetery, "but my grandparents too. They came over from Trinidad in the fifties, settled in Northampton in the sixties, and didn't budge after that and neither did Mum."

"So you've some deep roots here then?"

"I suppose so, but it's not the same now everyone's gone; the older you get, the more home becomes about people rather than place, I think. The older you get, the more roots are about where you want to be rather than where you come from."

Reaching into the car, I grab the three large bunches of flowers I've brought with me and then Alex and I walk in silence along the tarmac pathway, every now and again passing someone tending a grave or sitting in silent contemplation on a bench. After a five-minute walk we turn off the main path and, after wending our way past various memorials, finally come to a stop in front of a modest white headstone with Mum's name and dates of birth and death inscribed in gold below a simple stylized flower.

"It looks better than I thought it would," I say, gently tracing my fingers along its edges. Although the funeral directors had called to ask if I wanted to be present when the headstone was being laid, I'd declined and so this is the first time I've seen it in place. "I think Mum would've approved. She didn't like anything too fussy or sentimental."

I lay the flowers down at the base and then stare at the headstone trying to work out exactly how I feel about being here.

"Are you okay?" asks Alex gently.

"It's strange. I know she's here physically but I just don't really feel anything."

"There's no reason why you should. Our memories of people tend to be bound up in places we used to go with them or things that belonged to them perhaps, not where they're finally laid to rest."

"I suppose that must be it. She's at home pottering around the kitchen, she's in the garden yanking up the weeds, she's in the volumes of my encyclopedia as I turn their pages. If I'm sure of anything, it's that she's not here."

"For what it's worth," says Alex, "I haven't visited my parents' graves in years for pretty much the same reason. My gran used to take me once a year when I was growing up, the annual pilgrimage to Sutton Coldfield, but I haven't been back since I went to university. I just didn't see the point. I never felt like they were there."

I reach out and take his hand. "You must miss them terribly."

"I was so young when they died and it was so long ago that my memories of them are hazy at best. But yes, I do miss them. I miss them every single day."

We spend what's left of the day visiting old haunts of mine. I treat Alex to hot doughnuts from the same stall run by what bizarrely looks like exactly the same woman from my childhood days. Afterward we go for coffee at Oslo, the café Luce and I hung out at virtually every day after senior year. We attempt to visit the museum and art gallery only to discover that it's closed for refurbishment and so instead finish the day at Abington Park and visit the museum there, another one of my all-time favorite places. Finally, we head back to Mum's, and after a brief pitstop to make ourselves look presentable, we go across to Maggie and Dougie's for dinner.

"Aww, you shouldn't have," exclaims Maggie as Alex hands her the bottle of wine we've brought with us. I watch carefully as Dougie and Maggie turn to Alex and smile politely, but thankfully they show no reaction to his scars. Either they'd seen us through the window earlier in the day or more likely Luce had briefed them in advance; whatever the reason, I'm relieved.

"And it looks like the good stuff too," says Dougie over Maggie's shoulder. "Not that I know much about wine. I just buy whatever's on offer."

Dougie takes our coats and Maggie ushers us into the living room, where I make the introductions.

"Pleased to meet you both," says Alex. "Jess has told me so much about you."

"All good, I hope," says Dougie.

"Absolutely," says Alex. "But I'm hoping she'll tell me the truth now that I've met you."

Dougie and Maggie burst out laughing. "Oh, I do like a good sense of humor," says Maggie. "It's one of the things that first attracted me to Dougie."

"Well, that," says Dougie, "and the fact that I had a Kawasaki Z900." He smiles fondly at the memory. "Now, that was a great machine. Do you like bikes at all, Alex?"

"I've never been on one, but some of those vintage models are real beauties."

"That's what I keep telling Dougie," says Maggie with a wink. "Us vintage models can show the younger ones a thing or two!"

They both start laughing again and I feel a flood of warmth as I remember how much Mum would laugh when she was around them both. Dougie pours us all a glass of wine and then corners Alex with a photo album full of pictures of the various cars and motorbikes he's owned over the years.

"I think that's our cue to leave," whispers Maggie, steering me in the direction of the kitchen. "I need to check on the lasagne; it was almost done last time I looked, just needed a bit of crisping up on top."

As I decant bags of salad into a bowl, Maggie opens the oven. "About another fifteen minutes, I reckon," she declares, turning up the temperature. Grabbing her glass, she takes a sip of her wine. "So have you and your friend had a nice afternoon?"

"Yes, thank you, it was lovely."

"He is just a friend, isn't he? It's so hard to tell what's what with you young people sometimes."

I smile, embarrassed. "Yes, we're just friends. When Luce couldn't make it, Alex very kindly stepped in."

"Aww, that's nice," says Maggie, and then lowering her voice unnecessarily adds, "Luce told me about you and Guy. I am sorry, love. It's such a shame when relationships end. Are you coping okay?"

"The truth is I've been so busy over the past couple of weeks I've barely had time to think about it all. But to be fair that's probably more by design than accident. I like being busy; it keeps me from thinking too much. But I'm okay, thanks. It was just one of those things. It wasn't meant to be."

Maggie goes to the fridge, takes out a packet of garlic bread, opens it, and slips both baguettes into the oven.

"So is your friend Alex single?" she asks, wiping her hands on her apron.

"No, he's recently started seeing someone."

"Oh, that's a surprise."

I look at her, wondering if she's implying no one would want to date Alex because of his scars.

"What do you mean?"

"Nothing really, just that he's clearly taken with you."

"He isn't," I say quickly. "We're just friends."

"Well, that might be what you think but I'd check with him if I were you. I'm not usually far off the mark about these things."

I don't say anything and thankfully Maggie changes the subject and we chat easily until the oven timer goes off.

"Give the boys a shout and let them know dinner's ready, will you?" she says, wrestling the dish out of the oven. "I should think Alex is bored to tears by now anyway."

Maggie has always been a good cook and this meal doesn't disappoint. As we eat, Dougie and Maggie take great delight in regaling Alex with stories from my past, including the time I broke my ankle while climbing a lamppost in a bid to disprove the theory of one of the older boys from the road that girls couldn't climb because their boobs got in the way.

"And I'd do it again," I say defiantly. "No one tells me what I can and can't do."

Dougie tops up our glasses, then sits back down and sighs. "It'll be the end of an era seeing someone else moving into your mum's."

Maggie nudges him with her elbow and frowns. "Don't mind him, he's too morose for his own good. More's to the point, have you any idea what you'll do when the sale goes through? Do you think you'll buy a place in London?"

"I'll probably rent to begin with and then see where I am."

"London's so expensive," says Dougie. "I keep saying to Luce and Leon that they should move over this way. Maybe you could come with them, get a job in town, and then you could all come round to ours every week for Sunday dinner."

"It's tempting," I say, and smile. "And I can't say I'm much looking forward to flat hunting in London after all these years, but I've made a life there and I don't think it would feel right coming back."

"Well, I don't want to sound like a broken record," says Dougie, "but don't forget there'll always be a home for you here."

It's after nine as Alex and I prepare to leave, having stuffed ourselves not only with Maggie's delicious melt-in-the-middle chocolate pudding but also on the cheeseboard she had insisted on wheeling out.

"Thanks so much for having us," I say as the taxi Dougie ordered beeps its horn outside. "Not just for tonight but for everything you've done to help me since Mum died."

"We wanted to help," says Maggie. "We only wish we could do more. And don't worry about bringing the kettle and stuff back; we'll pick them up when we drop off our keys."

Feeling like I'm saying goodbye forever, I hug them both tightly, and as Alex and I climb into the waiting taxi, Dougie and Maggie stand on their doorstep waving enthusiastically as if we're traveling to the other side of the world.

"That was nice," says Alex. "They seem like good people and it's obvious how much they care about you."

"They're the absolute best," I say. "I suppose they're the closest thing to family I've got now."

I fall silent, wondering about the next time I'll see them. They said I had an open invitation to come back, and I'm sure I will at some point in the future, but for now I can't imagine how it will feel to be back in the road and see another family popping in and out of number thirty-seven.

36

Getting out of the taxi, we head straight to the White Horse, which used to be an old haunt of mine and Luce's. It's Saturday-night busy, loud music fills the air, and the place is packed full of young people at the start of their big night out. At the bar I scan the room trying to find something familiar to lock on to but the truth is, everything from the décor to the layout has changed. The seats where we used to sit have been replaced by a dining area, the floorboards that were always sticky underfoot from decades of spilt drinks have been stripped back and lacquered, even the clientele has been transformed from grungy students to a slightly more glamorous set, with girls in vertiginous heels and boys dressed in too-tight jeans.

"It feels so weird being back here," I shout over the music as we wait to be served. "I think the last time must have been with Luce about six years ago. We've always meant to come again but never got around to it."

We're served eventually and, despite the crowds at the bar, manage to find a table to sit at. "I bet this is bringing back memories," says Alex, looking around the room.

"Sure is. I had my first ever underage drink in this place. I've got a horrible feeling it was something disgusting like cider and black currant."

He pulls a face. "That sounds revolting."

"It was pretty sickly but more importantly it was cheap and we weren't fussy. What was your poison growing up?"

"To be honest, I didn't drink much when I was younger."

"Not even when you were a rebellious teenager?"

Alex shakes his head. "I mean, I wasn't a hermit or anything. At least not back then. I had a couple of friends who I used to hang out with at the weekends playing video games. But then they started going out instead and though I tried it a couple of times, it just wasn't for me."

For a moment he looks lost in thought and there's something so sorrowful about his expression that I feel guilty for bringing up the subject. It must have been a really tough time for him. You're self-conscious enough as a teenager as it is, without scars that make you stand out so visibly to contend with.

I am about to apologize when my phone rings. "It's Luce. She's probably checking on how dinner with her parents went. Do you mind if I take it? I'll be quick."

"Be my guest. I'll be right here."

I stand up and go outside where it's quieter.

Luce jumps straight into the conversation. "Were they a nightmare?"

"Anything but, they were lovely."

"And my dad didn't say anything cringeworthy about Alex, did he?"

"Nope, I think he quite liked him actually. He even got out his car and motorbike pics to show him."

Luce groans. "He didn't, did he? He tried that on Leon the first time I brought him home. Leon doesn't know one end of a car from another and yet Dad talked to him about them solidly for a whole afternoon!"

"How's things your end? Is the birthday bash going well?"

"There's only been two fights and one hysterical outburst so far, which for Leon's family is pretty good going. Where are you? I can hear music."

"I'll give you one guess."

"The White Horse!"

"Got it in one."

"Still grim?"

"No, sadly gentrified beyond all recognition. Mind you, I haven't been to the loos yet, so there's an outside chance that your infamous 'Luce and Steve-o, forever' carving will still be underneath the tampon dispenser."

Luce laughs. "Steve-o Walsh! I wonder where he is now? Have you seen anyone you recognize?"

"I thought I saw Julie Packwood working in the back of Boots pharmacy earlier today but I couldn't get close enough to be sure."

"I wouldn't trust Julie Packwood with my drinks order, let alone my prescription. Do you remember when she tried to poison Anna Clarke by pouring ink into her Diet Coke just because she thought Anna was flirting with her boyfriend? That girl was a maniac."

Not wanting to leave Alex stranded alone too long, I wind up the call as quickly as I can, promising to text Luce the moment I see anyone from our school days, before heading back inside.

The pub seems even busier than before and so rather than fight my way back over to Alex I decide to go to the bar to get another round of drinks instead. I've only been waiting a few minutes when I feel a tap on my shoulder and turn to see a face I haven't seen in a very long time.

"Jess?" slurs the man. "Jess Baxter. It is you, isn't it?"

The man in front of me is tall and muscular. His arms and neck are covered in tattoos and his T-shirt and jeans are so unbelievably tight that I wonder how he can even breathe. To top it all, he reeks heavily of beer and expensive aftershave and despite the years, I know instantly who he is. He's my old secondary school's chief Lothario, Jamie Parsons.

"Hi, Jamie," I say, plastering a smile on my face. Of all the people I could have bumped into tonight, why did it have to be him? When I was at school, practically all the girls in my year had been in love with him but he was always a bit too egotistical for my liking. I wonder how drunk he is, and how quickly I might be able to get this whole encounter over and done with.

"How are you?"

"All the better for seeing you, love," he says, making no attempt to disguise his leering looks. "Talk about long time no see. You look good. Really good. When did you get back in town?"

"I'm not back. I'm just here for the weekend. Trying to have a quiet drink. Anyway, it was good to see you." I turn back to the bar, hoping he'll get the message, but then I feel a hand on my shoulder and my heart sinks as I reluctantly turn back to face him.

"So, what are you drinking? Have anything you like. It's on me."

"That's kind of you, but I'm fine really, thanks."

"Oh, come on, Jess. Just have one little drink with me for old time's sake. I haven't seen you in years. I'm sure we've got loads to catch up on."

"Like I said, I'm fine."

"Oh, I see, it's like that, is it?" he says as I attempt to turn back to the bar. "You and that other one...Lucy...what's her face, you pair always thought you were better than the rest of us, didn't you? Far too good for this place."

I fight the urge to defend myself. Ever since I'd left for university I'd heard whispers of people from back home saying similar sorts of things about me and Luce. I wanted to say to him that leaving your hometown didn't mean that you thought you were better than the people you left behind; it just meant you wanted to be part of a bigger world. Still, there's no point in explaining any of this to a drunken Jamie Parsons. Or a sober one, for that matter.

"Look," I say firmly. "Just leave it, okay? It was nice talking to you."

He grabs my arm and tries to pull me toward him. "Well, if it was so nice, why won't you just have a little drink with me? We could have a laugh and talk about old times."

I wrench my arm from his grip. "I've already told you I'm—"

"Everything okay?"

I turn to see Alex standing behind me and straightaway I know that this is going to end badly.

"I'm fine," I say quickly. "I just bumped into an old school mate, that's all. You go back to the table and I'll see you in a second, okay?"

Alex doesn't move; instead he glances at Jamie, who regards him unsteadily.

"What happened to your face, mate? It's a right mess."

I feel sick. Why did I ever think this would be a good idea?

"Come on, Alex, let's go," I say, grabbing him by the arm, but he doesn't move. Instead, he stands staring at Jamie in a manner that makes me feel afraid something awful is about to happen.

"Looks like your crispy-faced friend thinks he's a hard man," says Jamie. "Is that right, mate?"

Alex says nothing but this only seems to spur Jamie on.

"Are you seriously telling me this guy is the best you could do after going off to university and moving to London?" says Jamie. He shakes his head and laughs. "You can definitely do better than this freak. Why don't you stay here with me and let this bloke crawl back under whichever rock you found him?" He makes another grab for my arm but before he can make contact, Alex throws a punch that sends Jamie staggering backward into a group of drinkers near the bar and in an instant the whole place is in uproar.

All around people are screaming, shouting, and pushing, desperately trying to escape the commotion. In the confusion more fights break out as drinks are spilled and girlfriends knocked over. The bar staff, who seem well accustomed to dealing with such occurrences, coolly summon the security over their radios and in no time at all, three burly doormen are wading through the crowds of startled drinkers into the center of the action, which now appears to consist of Jamie and all the people he's crashed into after Alex's blow. I grab Alex's hand and, aware that we need to put as much distance between us and this place as possible, I almost drag him toward the main exit and out onto the street. Once we're outside we break into a run.

Without looking back, I pull Alex along through the back alleys and side streets of town until we're far enough away for me to finally feel like we might be safe. I'm just so angry with myself. What was I thinking taking Alex to the White Horse? If ever there was a place guaranteed to be full of people like Jamie Parsons, the White Horse was it.

I look around to get my bearings and realize we're just across the road from Becket's Park. This was a place I'd picnicked in with Mum as a toddler, smoked illicit cigarettes with Luce as a teenager, and sat reading pretentious novels as an undergraduate home for the summer.

"Let's duck in there," I say, pointing to the park. "We can catch our breath and I'll call us a taxi."

The main road is full of Saturday-night traffic but eventually we get to the other side before hopping over the low fence into the park. There's barely anyone else around, just us and a couple of late-night dog walkers, and we walk deeper into the park until eventually we reach a bench overlooking the river, where we both slump down breathing heavily. I can't remember the last time I've run so hard for so long and my lungs feel like they're on fire.

When I turn to Alex, I see that he is shaking and as I put an arm around him, I wonder if he might be in shock.

"I'm so sorry, Alex. This is all my fault. Are you okay?"

He says nothing, instead sits there shivering, his gaze fixed on the inky-black water before us. Finally, he turns to me, his expression furious.

"I'm so sick of this," he spits. "Why can't people just leave me alone?"

"This is my fault, Alex. I should've known better than to drag you out to a pub in the middle of town on a Saturday night when all the idiots are out. I don't know what I was thinking."

"It wasn't your fault. This sort of thing follows me wherever I go. I had the same thing happen last weekend when I was out with Angel. Some guys started making comments while we were waiting for her mates."

"People are idiots when they're drunk."

"They're only saying what everyone else is thinking. People are repulsed by me, I can see it on their faces, and in their minds it makes me somehow less human. So they think they can say whatever they want and look at me however they like and I've got no choice but to let them. Well, I'm tired of it, Jess. I just can't take it any more."

He leans forward, his head hung low. "I've had this virtually my whole life. At primary school the other kids used to call me names constantly and it only got worse when I went to secondary. I didn't make any friends at all at college; everyone just gave me a wide berth and talked about me behind my back, and it was pretty much the same story at university. People just couldn't seem to get past my scars, as though that was all I was, as though there was nothing more to me than how I looked. In the end I just gave up trying to live a normal life. After all what was the point? Instead, I tried my best to keep people at a distance. I bought my flat, went freelance, and made sure I had as little face-to-face interaction with people as possible. Every now and again, of course, I'd get a little resentful, so I'd put my head above the parapet only to wish I hadn't."

I put my arm through his. "I'm so sorry, Alex. I'm sorry people are so shallow and insensitive. You're an amazing person and you deserve more than that."

"Do I?" Alex sighs heavily. "Sometimes I'm not so sure. Sometimes... sometimes, if I'm honest, I wish I'd died in the fire too."

My breath catches in my throat as he turns to face me. As if reading my thoughts, he says, "It's how I got my scars. I was in a fire when I was little. A fire that killed both my parents and destroyed my home."

37

I listen intently as the story of that terrible night pours out of him.

"It had been just another ordinary day," he begins. "I'd been to school as usual, stayed late for football practice, and then Mum picked me up and took me home. We had sausage and mash for tea when Dad got back from work, and then he played football in the garden with me until Mum called me for a shower and then bed." He pauses and smiles. "I remember I'd just started reading *The Twits* by Roald Dahl and I was loving it so much that I wanted to stay up and carry on but Mum said no because it was a school night. She said good night and even now I can remember the floral smell of her perfume and the sensation of her hair tickling my face as she bent down to kiss me. As she turned out the light, she whispered in my ear that she loved me and then she left the room. That was the last time I ever saw her."

I take Alex's hand in mine and together we stare out across the water in silence. I want nothing more than to put my arms around him and comfort him but he's so lost in thought, in his memories, that I'm afraid the slightest movement will stop him in his tracks. This is clearly something he needs to tell me and so I keep quiet and wait until he's ready to continue.

"When I woke up, it was like I was still dreaming; nothing made sense. There was smoke in the room but I couldn't understand why, and there was shouting outside the house but I couldn't make out what they were saying. I thought I was having a nightmare and I tried to call out to

Mum and Dad but all I could do was cough. Finally, it dawned on me that I really was awake, that this really was happening. I got out of bed, desperate to find my parents so they could hug me and tell me everything would be okay. I opened my bedroom door and that was the last thing I remember."

He pauses again and I squeeze his hand in a vain attempt to comfort him. I want to be strong for him. I want him to know that he can lean on me.

A dog walker passes by followed by a young couple holding hands and Alex waits until they have gone before he continues.

"The next thing I knew I woke up in hospital, covered in dressings. A nurse told me I'd been in a fire but wouldn't say where my mum and dad were. Then my grandmother was standing by the bed holding my hand and crying as she told me that both my parents were gone. I don't really remember much about that time. Everything just seemed so confused and unreal, like the world had been turned upside down. I didn't understand how it was possible for me to go to sleep one night and then wake up the next day without my parents, without my home, and with half my skin burned away."

He tells me he can barely remember his parents' funeral, even less the countless operations that came before and after it. When he was finally released from hospital, a small part of him had still been convinced that there had been some mistake, that he would be going home to his parents. Instead, his grandmother took him to live with her in Hertfordshire, and it was only then he fully realized that his old life had gone for good.

"My gran was a wonderful person but even so, taking me on when she was so much older must have been a real challenge for her but she never once complained. Though she must have been reeling from the loss of my mum and dad, she gave her all to me. She was never anything but kind and loving and did everything in her power to give me the happiest childhood she could manage. Even so, life was never the same. How could it be? I suppose that night, along with my mum and dad, I'd lost that childish belief that everything will always be all right; now I lived in a world where nightmares could come true. For years afterward I used to dream about that night, about the fire. It would always be the same: I'd feel happy and content as Mum put me to bed and then the fire happened and I'd wake up screaming."

I can barely breathe as I listen to Alex. I suppose I'd assumed in that way you do when you're left to fill in the blanks of someone's story that he'd been in some sort of accident, perhaps a car crash when he was a teenager, but nothing like this. I can't believe how someone who has been through such horrors can still be standing, let alone be the kind, generous person I know Alex to be. Without thinking, without weighing up the consequences, I place a hand gently on either side of his face, his scarred skin strange and unfamiliar to my touch; then I gently turn his head toward me and kiss him.

"I'm so sorry," I say, pulling away from him, feeling ashamed and embarrassed, as though I'd taken advantage of his vulnerability. "I shouldn't have done that. I don't know what I was thinking. You and Angel—"

"There is no me and Angel," says Alex, eyes fixed once again on the river. "At least, not any more. She dumped me. But to be fair I totally had it coming."

I'm confused. "You had it coming? Why?"

Alex looks down at the ground. "After that day when Angel and I bumped into you near the station and I was acting so weirdly…she guessed."

"Guessed what?" I say before I can stop myself. On some level I already know the answer, but it's one I haven't wanted to admit to myself. It seems obvious to me now, all the time we'd spent together, how close we'd become, how easy we were in each other's company. How could I have not seen this? Was I really that skilled in self-deception?

I look at Alex, and he meets my gaze briefly, then looks away.

"I think I liked you from the day I met you," he says. "Actually, forget that, I know I did. But you were with Guy and…I don't know…" He doesn't finish his sentence; instead it lingers between us like our breath in the cold night air.

I open my mouth to speak but he cuts me off straightaway.

"Look, there's no need to say anything," he says. "Let's just move on." He gets to his feet. "Come on," he says, holding a hand out for me. "It's freezing; let's get you home."

I want to protest, I want to tell him that we should talk this over, but I feel like I need to respect his wishes. I feel like I need to give him the time to process everything that's happened.

And so I take his hand and we walk home, each of us, I suspect, keen to prolong the intimacy that's grown between us and at the same time grateful for the opportunity to think.

Had I always secretly had feelings for Alex? It's something I haven't allowed myself to consider properly until now. I'd been so moved by his revelation about the fire and his parents that for a single moment I'd acted without thinking. I recall our first meeting at Barclay and Sons, how intrigued I'd been by the mystery of him. I'd simply put it down to the feelings that seeing the Museum of Ordinary People had sparked in me but had it been more than that? Had Guy been right to be jealous? Had he been able to see what I couldn't? Then there was the night of the launch party, the time Alex had first opened up to me. Had I felt something between us then, something that once again I'd written off as being nothing more than compassion? And now here I am, walking hand in hand with him, having discovered that he has feelings for me and had since the day that we met. I feel elated and confused; I feel like I want to kiss him again and yet angry with myself for the one we've already shared.

When we finally reach Mum's, I let us in, wondering where exactly this night will end. The last thing on earth I want to do is ruin the friendship we have by making the kind of mistake that we'll find impossible to come back from.

"I'm really tired," I say quickly before I can change my mind. "I'm going to get off to bed if you don't mind."

Alex nods, and I study his face, desperate to know what he's thinking, but it's impossible to tell.

"I think I'm going to do the same," he says. "It's been a long day and I'm shattered."

We take our bags upstairs and I show Alex to my old room and help him inflate his air bed. The whole situation is horribly awkward and so I try to defuse the tension between us by gabbling incessantly about childhood camping trips, the bronze Duke of Edinburgh expedition when I got lost for three hours, and the time Luce and I almost floated out to sea on an air mattress while on holiday in Marbella. When it comes to inflating my air bed, I politely decline Alex's offer, feeling like I might explode with embarrassment if I had to go through it again in Mum's room. Instead, I tell him he can use the bathroom first and while he's brushing his teeth I go downstairs to lock up. As I head back upstairs, Alex emerges from the bathroom smelling of soap and toothpaste.

"Well, I suppose I'll say good night then," he says, but then neither of us quite knows how to be with each other. Finally, I step toward him and hug him tightly, burying my face into his chest, and then before anything can happen I let go and head straight into the bathroom, closing the door behind me.

Despite being utterly exhausted, sleep eludes me, and I don't think it's just the air bed that's to blame. For a while I imagine how easy it would be to just get up and walk over to Alex's room, to throw caution to the wind, to worry about the details in the morning. But I know I can't do that, for Alex's sake as well as my own. When we get together, if we get together, I don't want it to be something we've rushed into without thinking. I don't want this to turn out to be a mistake, a spur of the moment decision we'll later regret. I'm not sure I could handle that and I'm not sure Alex could either.

Lying in bed, I put in my AirPods and try listening to *In Our Time* but that doesn't help. At a loss, I even try counting sheep but when I reach two hundred I feel like I'm even more awake than ever. I briefly consider going downstairs to make myself a cup of tea but I don't want to wake

Alex. Resigned to the fact that whether I like it or not I'm not going to sleep, I reach for my phone and start scrolling through Instagram, but ten minutes in a message pops up warning me that my battery is running low. In the darkness I search for my bag and start rooting around inside for my charger, but then my hand brushes against something that feels like a book and that's when I remember that I brought Mum's diary with me.

38

With my phone plugged in and the flashlight function switched on, I stare at the diary's navy-blue cover. I think back to the last time I opened its pages when I was clearing Mum's house and recall the profound effect reading her words had on me. Is now the right time to read it? Am I any stronger than I was back then? I'm not sure. Part of me is almost afraid of doing it, afraid that I might set myself back somehow, reopening wounds that are only now very slowly starting to heal. But I long to hear Mum's voice again if only through the pages of her diary. There is no perfect time to do something like this, although I realize I've been waiting for one. The perfect time will never come and so I reason it might as well be now.

I open the diary, and just as before, the sight of Mum's handwriting takes my breath away. These are her words, written in her own hand, and while nowhere near the same as having her here, I find the sight of them soothing.

As I turn the pages, it quickly becomes clear that rather than being a daily diary as I'd first thought, this five-year diary had been repurposed as more of an occasional journal. Its entries are sporadic, covering a period of about ten years from the mid-eighties when Mum would've been in her early twenties through to the mid-nineties when she would've been around my age.

One entry I flick to is about Mum's shock when Luce's next-door neighbors, the Grahams, had their house repossessed. Another is about a day out we took to a local steam railway and another about coming to see me at a Mother's Day assembly at school. So much time, so many memories, some of which I'd lived through myself, others I only knew of through Mum.

For a moment I think I might be in danger of becoming maudlin, so I close the diary and lean over to return it to my bag, but then a thought occurs to me: if the diary covers the period before I was born, then it might include entries about when Mum met my dad. And although I already know the story, the temptation to see their relationship unfolding in Mum's own words proves impossible to resist.

Flicking through the diary from the beginning, I scan the pages until I find the first entry that mentions him. It's dated 11th July 1986:

Went out with Andrea and Cathy from work for a drink, ended up chatting with some Americans based at RAF Croughton. Two of them were very loud and sure of themselves but I got talking to a guy called Joe, who was much quieter but lovely and very funny. I think he quite likes me.

I close my eyes and picture Mum out on the town just like any other young woman, carefree and happy. In the box I took back to London with me, there are so many photos of her from that time looking like a complete eighties fox in her ripped Levis, cropped jacket, and big hair and I completely understand why my dad fell for her.

I open the diary up again and continue reading and within a few entries it's clear that Mum is already falling in love.

Went out with Joe again tonight. He told me all about where he comes from in America and what it's like and even talked about taking me over there to meet his family next summer. I'm really starting to think he feels the same way about me as I do about him. Who knows, maybe this time next year I'll be in another country? Me, Maria Baxter, in the USA!

I can't help but feel sorry for Mum. Her words about Joe are so hopeful that I almost want to jump into the pages and tell her to be careful, to hold back, because I know she's about to have her heart broken. The irony is, of course, that had I been able to issue such a warning, I would never have been born.

But in the entries that follow she seems so happy and every meeting is so lovingly documented that for a split second, even though I know they don't, I convince myself that perhaps things might end well after all. But then I reach the part where Mum and Joe split up:

> I can't believe it. Joe's gone without saying a word. He's been
> redeployed to Germany. I only found out through talking to one of
> his friends from the base. I thought I meant something to him, like
> he does to me. I can't believe I've been such a fool.

Her confusion and pain are so awful to witness that I find myself shedding a little tear. My poor mum, going through this terrible time and not even realizing there's worse to come with the news that she's pregnant. I scan through the next lot of entries looking for the first mention of her pregnancy but there isn't one. Instead, of the sporadic entries dated across the next few months, most are focused on her sadness at the split and the rest record everyday events like birthdays, job changes, and Dougie and Maggie moving in across the road.

In fact, it's not until a year later that I come across an entry I think might be related to Joe again.

> Last night I made a mistake, a terrible mistake. I can't believe I let it
> happen. It's not like I'm a stupid kid. I'm old enough to know better.
> Still, it won't happen again. We're both agreed on that.

The next entry that catches my eye comes a month and a half later and reads:

I can't believe it. I'm pregnant. I was so sure this was all behind me. And now this. I don't know what I'm going to do. I've got no idea at all.

I read the date on this entry again, and do the math in my head. Give or take a few weeks, it's nine months before I was born. I flick through the previous entries again and double-check in case I've missed any mention of Joe getting back in touch but there is none. He's just not there.

Sitting up in bed, I run my fingers through my hair trying to work it all out. Had Joe and Mum reunited briefly in the year after they'd split? It's the only explanation that makes sense. But if that is what happened, why is there no mention of it in the diary? And what's more, why had Mum never told me this part of the story? Granted, she'd only ever given me the briefest of outlines about her relationship with my dad, but even so this seems like a detail she would've mentioned. After all, she had no reason to lie.

When morning comes around, Alex taps on my door to see if I'm awake and the first thing I do is tell him about reading the diary and my confusion over Joe.

"Maybe he came back to visit her," Alex suggests. "Just because it's not in the diary doesn't mean it didn't happen."

"I'm sure you're right, but at the same time I feel like something's off somehow. She wrote about the early days with my dad, she wrote about the breakup too, but when it comes to my conception there's no context at all. It just seems odd, almost as if she was hiding something."

"Maybe she was," says Alex. "Then again maybe she wasn't. It's impossible to know...unless..."

"What?"

"Well, you could try asking Maggie before we leave. After all, with them being such old friends and so close, if anyone knows, surely it'll be her."

"You're right. I suppose it's the next best thing to asking Mum." I check my watch. It's early, but not too early, and anyway Luce is always telling me how her folks aren't ones to lie in, even at the weekend. "How about we pop over now and get Maggie to clear this all up for me, and then I'll take you somewhere nice for breakfast?"

A short while later Alex and I are standing on Maggie and Dougie's doorstep. I ring the doorbell and wait, and then ring it again, but it's only when I'm about to ring for a third time that it dawns on me that their car isn't anywhere to be seen.

"They must be out," I say to Alex, "which is probably a good thing. I'm not quite sure what they would've made of me banging on their door asking mad questions about Mum this early on a Sunday morn—"

I stop short as the door opens and Dougie appears wearing a pair of old jeans and a crumpled T-shirt, a pair of hedge clippers in his hand.

"Oh, hello, love," he says. "I thought I heard someone at the door but I wasn't sure." He looks at Alex and smiles warmly. "Sorry about the state of me. I was in the garden, just doing a bit of tidying up. Come on in, both of you."

"Actually," I say, "it's only a quick thing and I don't want to take up too much of your time. Is Maggie in?"

Dougie shakes his head. "No, love, she's gone power walking or whatever you call it, with one of her friends from work. She's usually home by eleven if you want to come back, unless it's anything I can help with." He exchanges a grin with Alex. "I know I'm no Maggie but I do have my uses."

I hesitate, thinking over his offer. Granted, Mum is unlikely to have confided in Dougie but I can't imagine that Maggie wouldn't have shared this information with him at some point.

"This is going to sound mad," I say, "but I was reading Mum's diary last night."

Dougie raises an eyebrow. "Your mum kept a diary?"

"Sort of, it was more an off-and-on type of thing, from when she was younger. Anyway, last night I decided to read it for the first time and I noticed something odd."

"Odd, how do you mean?"

"It's just that...Mum always told me that she found out she was pregnant with me after she and my dad broke up."

Dougie nods. "That's right, isn't it?"

"That's what I thought," I continue. "But the thing is, according to the diary, Mum and Joe broke up a whole eighteen months before I was born. It makes no sense and I was just wondering if you or Maggie knew anything that could shed any light on it."

Dougie rubs his chin and looks thoughtful. "Sorry, love, nothing springs to mind, I'm afraid. Have you thought that maybe the dates in the diary are wrong?"

"No," I say, "it's definitely not that."

He sighs. "Well, I can't help you then. Sorry to be of no use."

"Don't worry, we're not going straightaway. I'll pop back over when Maggie's back and ask her."

Dougie shakes his head and pulls a face as if this is a bad idea. "To be honest, I think your Mum's house selling has made Mags a bit fragile, you know, brought it all back about your mum again, so I wouldn't mention it if I were you. Tell you what, leave it with me and when things are a bit more settled, I'll bring it up and if she knows anything, I'll get her to give you a ring."

Although he's trying to sound casual, there's something odd about his demeanor, as if he's working really hard to appear calm.

"Are you sure she'll get upset?" I say, watching Dougie's face carefully for his reaction. "I mean, it is only me asking."

"Definitely," says Dougie. "Like I said, it's hit her really hard."

His answer comes a little too quickly and is delivered a touch too firmly for me to believe him. I decide to press him just a little bit more.

"I'll tell you what, how about I give her a call just to say goodbye and then I'll try and drop my dad into the conversation just casually, and see how she reacts."

Before he can reply, I pull my phone out of my pocket, dial Maggie's number, and as it rings all the color drains from Dougie's face. And in that instant something in my head clicks into place. But it can't be. It just can't. It's just too crazy for words.

"Joe's not my dad, is he?" I say, unable to believe what I'm about to say. "You are."

39

Dougie's sense of disbelief is writ large across his features as he looks at Alex. "What's going on here? Is this some sort of wind-up?"

"No, just a statement of fact," I say, sensing Alex's disquiet.

"Facts!" snorts Dougie. "What facts? Are you trying to say your mum wrote down in her diary that I'm your dad?"

The incredulity in his voice suddenly makes me feel a lot less sure of myself.

"You know as well as I do that your dad was a Yank from the airbase."

"I certainly know that's what Mum told me. But like I said, the dates just don't add up and your reaction just now . . . well, I think you're hiding something."

"My reaction?" scoffs Dougie. "Is that what you're basing this whole accusation on?" He shakes his head sadly as if I've let him down in the worst way possible. "What have I done to deserve this? I've never been anything but good to you and your mum."

"I know, and if I'm wrong, then . . . well . . . I'm sorry. But I'm not. I can see it in your eyes, Dougie. You're scared, scared of me calling Maggie and asking her about it."

"I'm not scared of anything," he says dismissively. "By all means, call Maggie and ask her whatever you like. I've got nothing to hide."

I reach for my phone again and Dougie starts to rant. "You're losing the plot, Jess; this must be the grief talking. Can you even hear yourself? You sound like one of those crackpot conspiracy theorists. How can I be your dad? I've known you all your life. Just look at me, you know me, you know this isn't true." He turns to Alex as though appealing to the voice of reason. "Come on, mate, make her see sense. Next she'll be saying lizards from outer space are running the world. Come on, tell her she's talking—"

He stops abruptly and glares at me as the sound of me calling Maggie fills the air.

"Stop," he says abruptly, all his fight and bluster evaporating in an instant. "Just stop and put away your phone and I promise...I promise I'll tell you everything."

Without speaking, he moves back inside the house and we all sit down in the living room, me and Alex on one sofa, and Dougie in the armchair nearest the fire, looking like a man with the weight of the world on his shoulders.

"It was 1987," he begins, "Maggie and I had only been married for a couple of years but things hadn't been great between us. We'd been together since we were sixteen and I think she was wondering if she'd settled down too soon. Anyway, to cut a long story short, we were arguing a lot and she left me and went back to her mum's. I genuinely thought we were finished."

I'm stunned. "You and Maggie split up? I didn't know that."

"Well, it's not something you really like to talk about, is it?" he says. "The only people who knew, apart from your mum, were Maggie's parents and mine. Anyway, I was really down about it and one night I was coming home from work when I bumped into your mum and it all just came out. I told her everything. And it felt so good not to have to keep everything bottled up inside, to have someone to confide in that I kept making excuses to see her so I could talk to her. Your mum was having a difficult time too. It had been a year since she'd split up with Joe, and she was missing him something rotten. To make matters worse, your grand-dad was really poorly at the time, so she had a lot on her plate. Anyway, one night, when we were both at our lowest, I invited her over just for a chat, like. Of course, we had a drink or two to lift our spirits and one thing led to another and the inevitable happened. Afterward we both agreed it had been a mistake and vowed not to let it happen again."

"And did it?" I ask, fervently hoping this isn't a prelude to a confession of a lifelong affair.

Thankfully Dougie shakes his head. "No, it was the strangest thing. The very next day, Maggie called and told me she'd had a change of heart. She wanted to come home and for us to make a go of it, so that's what we did. She moved back in, we tried to put the past behind us, and for a while, things were great. But then out of the blue one day, I'm coming out of work and there's your mum waiting for me at the gates. Straight-away I knew something was up, because since that night we'd made a massive effort to steer clear of each other. The only time I'd see her was when Maggie asked her over or arranged for her to come out with us. I couldn't believe it when she told me she was pregnant, not least because I'd only just found out that Maggie was expecting too."

I sit back and close my eyes. This whole story from beginning to end is a mess.

"At first I didn't know what to think. I didn't know what to say, but by the time I'd gathered my wits about me I knew what I wanted to happen. I'm not proud of it but I told her she should get rid of it."

"Of me, you mean?" I snap.

"I didn't mean . . . Look that's not how I wanted it to come out . . . What I meant to say is that . . . well . . . I was desperate. I'd only just got Maggie back and now here was your mum with a bombshell that was sure to blow everything apart all over again. Anyway, it didn't matter what I thought; your mum was having none of it. I remember by this time we were sitting in a café, just the two of us, and she said to me, 'I'm keeping this baby, and there's nothing you can say to change my mind. It's not what I'd planned, it's not the way I saw things turning out, but there you go, it is what it is and we're just going to have to deal with it.'

"She said she didn't want anything from me; she told me she was only letting me know out of common decency. She told me that the last thing she wanted was to come between Maggie and me and was happy to pretend that nothing had ever happened. Things were still up in the air when we parted but then a few days later Maggie took me aside and told me that Maria was pregnant. Your mum hadn't gone into the details and Maggie didn't push her; all she said was that she'd met someone but it hadn't worked out. Maggie said to me at the time that she thought maybe the American had come back briefly and that your mum didn't want to talk about it."

"But I don't understand, Mum was one of the most honest people I know and she and Maggie were so close. How could she have lied to her for so long?"

"I think it's exactly because they were so close that your mum couldn't bear to tell her. It really messed her up for a while, and there were times when I felt sure she was just going to come out with it. It was horrible, Jess, horrible for the both of us, but what could we do?"

"Not live across the road from one another for starters," I say bitterly.

"You don't know how hard I tried over the years to persuade Maggie to move but she wouldn't hear of it. It wasn't just that she loved the road and all the people in it; the fact was she felt like she wanted to be a support to your mum. Yes, times had changed, it wasn't that unusual to be a single mother, but that didn't mean it wouldn't be hard, and Maggie could see that and she wanted to help her friend."

"So, you just kept on lying to her? Poor Maggie. Poor Luce. What were you both thinking?"

"We were thinking that yes, we'd made a mess of things but that somehow we could make them right. It's not like we'd had an affair—Maggie and I were split up at the time—and it's not like anything ever happened between us again. It was just an impossible situation and we had to make the best of it because the only alternative was breaking the heart of the one person we both cared about."

"But I still don't understand. How could you stand by watching me grow up, knowing all the time I was your daughter, and not say a single word? All those years, all that pretense, how could you live with yourself?"

"It wasn't easy," says Dougie. "In fact, there were times I wanted to give up the whole charade. Seeing you and Luce playing in the garden, knowing you were both mine but that I could only ever claim one of you, it nearly killed me. But there was just too much at stake. Too many lives at risk of being ruined forever and I just couldn't do that."

"But to keep up the pretense for over thirty years, that takes some doing."

"I know this is probably the last thing you want to hear but the strange thing is, the longer it went on, the easier it was to believe the lie. Like I said, your mum and I were never in a relationship; it was just one night, one time, which made it easier to convince myself that it had never really happened, that I wasn't your dad. I was more like . . . I don't know, some sort of uncle, there to help make up for the fact that your real dad wasn't around. To have told Maggie, to have ruined Luce's life just for the relief of getting it all out in the open would've been selfish."

"Would it? Surely selfish was watching your eldest daughter go her whole life thinking she didn't have a dad who cared about her."

"I did everything I could for you," says Dougie. "I got money to your mum whenever I could, I made sure you came on holiday with us even if it wasn't every year, I did everything I could do under the circumstances to take care of you."

"And yet you let Mum struggle all those years, watching her having to scrimp and save to buy me a winter coat and new school shoes or scrabbling around to pay for repairs to the house. For so many years she had to be so careful with her money that whenever she treated me to something nice I would be absolutely racked with guilt."

"I'm sorry, Jess, I really am, but like I said, I did everything I could. When I had extra money, I gave it to your mum. I tried to help her, to help you, whenever I could."

I get to my feet, feeling like my whole body is shaking with rage. "Alex, let's go. I can't do this."

Alex stands up and takes my hand. "Of course."

"Jess, wait, please," says Dougie, getting to his feet too. "I know this has all been a horrible shock, but neither me nor your mother meant to hurt you; you've got to believe that."

"But you have hurt me, haven't you? Okay so I might not be a kid any more, but this still hurts all the same. You and Mum lied to me, Dougie; you lied to me all my life in the worst way possible, and I'm not sure I can ever forgive either of you for what you've done."

I turn and start walking toward the front door but then I feel Dougie's hand on my arm.

"Please, Jess," he says, his eyes full of terror at the thought that his world is about to fall apart. "I'm begging you, promise me you won't breathe a word of this to Luce or Maggie. It will destroy them."

I look at this man I used to trust and look up to, this man who has been the closest thing I've ever had to a dad, and feel nothing but contempt. I'm so confused and have so much I still want to say and as I stand looking at him, something that has been bubbling away at the back of my mind ever since he'd said it suddenly comes to the fore.

"You know how you said you tried to help me, what exactly did you mean?"

Dougie looks confused. "What do you mean, love?"

"You said you helped Mum and that you helped me. How?"

He waves a dismissive hand. "I don't know, like I said, by giving her money when I had it to spare, looking out for you, helping out around the house, giving you things I thought you might need. I just—"

I hold up a hand. "It was you, wasn't it?"

"What?"

"The encyclopedias. It was you who bought them for me all those years ago."

He sighs. "Your mum was always telling me how smart you were, and how much you wanted to go to university so that you could be in charge of a museum, and when I saw them in the junk shop near the racecourse I thought of you straightaway."

I look at Dougie, my heart breaking, and want nothing more than to be as far away from this man as possible. Reading my mind, he darts to the door, barring my exit.

"Jess," he pleads, "Jess, promise me you won't tell Luce and Maggie about this. Promise me, please, I'm begging you. It'll destroy them."

"I'm not going to say a word," I reply, feeling strangely calm. "You are. You and Mum might have been happy to live a lie all these years but I'm not. So, either you come clean and tell them everything, or I will."

40

Dougie is banging on Mum's front door with such fury that the whole house is shaking, and his cries to be let in are so loud that when I look through the upstairs window all I can see is the twitching of net curtains and the shifting of blinds. Mrs. O'Connor doesn't even attempt to conceal her curiosity; instead she stands, front door wide open, gawking for all she's worth.

"Do you think I should go out and try and calm him down?" I ask Alex.

"He's in no state to listen to reason," he replies. "Let's just get our things together and leave."

As I frantically pack, I'm struck by the thought that this is nothing like the goodbye to Mum's house I'd imagined. The one I'd planned had been far more sedate and thoughtful. I'd pictured myself visiting each room in turn, reliving happy memories, and bidding the place a proper farewell. Instead, I feel like a criminal fleeing the scene of a crime, even more so as I planned out an escape route in my head.

"Let's go through the back," I say to Alex as Dougie continues to pound the door, and grabbing our bags, we head downstairs and through the kitchen to the back door. "This way," I say, pointing in the direction of the shared access that runs across all the gardens. "It'll take us farther up the road. We'll still have to make a dash for it but maybe by the time he notices us we'll be in the car with the engine running."

When we emerge onto the street, disconcertingly Dougie is nowhere to be seen. Just as we're about to make a break for the car, he suddenly appears from inside his house. Ignoring the onlookers, he strides across the road to Mum's front door and that's the moment I remember he still has a set of keys.

"Now," I say, grasping Alex's hand as Dougie lets himself into Mum's and we race toward the car. In my hurry I drop the keys and they land underneath a neighbor's van. I snatch them up almost immediately but the delay is enough that Dougie is back on the street before we reach the car.

"Jess! Stop!" he yells, spotting us straightaway. "Jess, please! Wait! Just give me five minutes! That's all. I'm begging you, just five minutes!"

Ignoring him, I try to get the car open but he's next to us before I know where I am and tries to make a grab for the keys.

"You better back off, mate!" says Alex, stepping in between us.

"Jess, please!" yells Dougie, ignoring Alex. "I'm not trying to hurt you. I just want to talk."

"I mean it," says Alex, taking hold of Dougie by his shirt. "You either calm down or I'll knock you down."

Dougie opens his mouth to protest but then he stops and something about his demeanor changes. A look of horror flashes across his face. "It's Maggie!" he hisses urgently, and I look behind me to see Maggie's car making its way toward us. For a split second it's impossible to know what, if anything, she's seen but then slowing down, she pulls up next to us, winds down her window, and switches off her radio.

"What's going on here then?" she asks, nodding toward our bags. "You two aren't going already, are you?"

I look at Dougie, now trying his hardest to appear relaxed, and he shoots me a pleading glance. "Actually, I'm afraid we do have to go," I reply. "I did try calling a couple of times but you didn't pick up. The long and short of it is, Alex has got a bit of a work emergency and we need to get off. I'm so sorry."

"Oh, that is a shame," says Maggie. "I was hoping I could talk you into going for lunch at the Keepers. They do a great buffet on a Sunday.

Maybe next time, eh? Anyway, you hang on there so at least I can have a proper goodbye."

"Please, Jess," implores Dougie, his voice lowered, as Maggie parks the car a few houses down the road. "Please, don't say anything to her."

"Fine, but what I said before stands. You need to tell her, Dougie. You need to tell her or I will."

As Maggie walks toward us, we all try our best to look normal but I'm not sure how good a job we do because her first words are "What's wrong with you lot? You've got faces like wet dogs, the lot of you."

"We're just feeling sad that we've had to cut the visit short," I say quickly.

"I know, love," says Maggie, giving me a hug. "But you'll be back to see us soon, won't you?"

"Of course."

She steps forward and hugs Alex. "So lovely to meet you. Like I say, you and Jess are welcome to come and stay with us any time you like, aren't they, Dougie?"

"Of course," says Dougie, holding out his hand for Alex to shake.

As Alex reluctantly shakes Dougie's hand, Maggie turns and wraps me in another huge embrace. "Now, young lady, I'm not going to say goodbye because I'm going to see you soon, aren't I? And remember, as long as we're here you'll always have a home in Arnold Street."

I bury my face into her hair and whisper, "I'll miss you, Maggie. Thanks for everything."

As Dougie moves in to give me a hug, I drop the car keys and thankfully the distraction of retrieving them from underneath the car means I'm able to avoid his embrace. Getting into the car, I start the engine, and then with one last wave to Maggie, I pull away, leaving behind Mum's house and Arnold Street, all too aware that while it might feel like I've made my escape, the repercussions of the events of the past twenty-four hours will catch up with me one way or another.

"I'm so sorry for dragging you into my drama, Alex," I say as we hit the highway. "And here was me thinking we'd have a nice quiet weekend."

"There's no need to apologize. None of this is your doing. How did you even figure out it was Dougie in the first place?"

"It was his reaction," I say. "I've known the man my entire life, and I'd thought he was about as straightforward as they come. So when he started acting so weirdly when I talked about asking Maggie about my dad, I just knew something was up. I can't believe, I don't want to, I mean...it means Mum kept this huge thing from me my whole life...It means that for all these years, she and Dougie have been lying to all of us, to me, to Maggie, to Luce...It means that Luce and I...well...all this time we've been sisters...It's all so crazy I just don't want to believe it. But what choice do I have now? I can't unknow what I know. No matter how much I want to."

I feel Alex looking at me. "Do you think Dougie will do the right thing and tell them?"

"I have no idea," I reply. "I thought I knew him; I thought I knew my mum. Now I have no idea what to think about anything at all. Maybe he'll tell them, maybe he won't, but I wasn't bluffing—if he doesn't, I will."

For the rest of the journey all I can think about is Luce and how this whole situation is going to devastate her. Part of me wonders if I should've guessed, but it wasn't as if we look alike. I have light brown skin; Luce is pale. I have black hair; Luce is blond. And to be honest, if anyone had asked me, I would've said that Luce looked far more like Maggie than she did her dad, and people had always told me that I looked so much like Mum that I'd never really given much thought to what, if anything, my dad might have contributed to my appearance. What a mess. What an absolute mess.

By the time I pull up in front of Alex's building, I'm exhausted, not just from the drive that was plagued with traffic jams and diversions but by the endless loop of thoughts swirling around my head. In the space of twenty-four hours, my whole world has turned upside down and I no longer feel like I know which way is up.

"Look," says Alex, putting his hand on mine, "I don't know if you've made any decisions…about…well, about anything really, but I'm guessing right now the last thing you want to do is go back to Luce's. It's completely up to you but I just want you to know that you can stay with me until you work it all out. You can have the bed; I'm happy to sleep on the sofa. I just want you to have somewhere safe to sort your head out."

He's right, I can't go back to Luce's until this is all resolved, whatever that entails. I'd made it clear to Dougie that it's up to him to tell Maggie and Luce, but if he doesn't, then I'll have no choice but to do it myself. And in the meantime, I can't even risk messaging Luce, let alone see her in the flesh. She knows me too well for me to keep anything from her, especially something of this magnitude.

"You're right," I say. "I can't go back to Luce's. I'll have to text her with some excuse. But even so, that doesn't mean I can just take over your life."

"You're not taking over anything. I'm inviting you in." He smiles. "You know, like they do with vampires in horror films."

I groan and lean my head on his shoulder. "It's all such a nightmare, a huge knot that feels like it's impossible to untangle."

"So, don't try. At least not yet. It's a lot to process. What you need right now is rest and some space and you can have both of those at mine. And just to be clear, you and me, what happened this weekend, we can put that on hold while you get yourself sorted. That's all I care about, making sure you're okay."

I know there are a hundred reasons why I should turn down Alex's kind offer and sort somewhere else out to stay instead, but I'm just so tired, so drained, so everything that I just say, "Thanks, Alex, you don't know how much this means to me."

Emptying our bags out of the car, we take everything up to Alex's flat and dump it in the hallway. While I slump on the sofa, he disappears to the kitchen and emerges a short while later carrying a tray laden with two mugs of tea and a plate of biscuits.

"I can rustle up some real food later if you're hungry," he says, setting down the tray. "But I thought you might be in need of a quick energy boost."

He flicks on the TV and we sit in companionable silence half watching a nature documentary, but then just as I feel myself starting to relax, my phone rings.

"It's Angel," I say, checking the screen, and in that instant I feel suddenly guilty. After all, I was the reason she had dumped Alex.

"It's fine," says Alex, as if reading my mind. "Angel and I are good; after she dumped me, we had a long talk and sorted everything out. If she's calling, I promise you, it's not because of me. In fact, I'm pretty sure she's seeing the lead singer in that band she took me to watch."

"That's a relief," I say, and so taking a deep breath, I answer the call but before she even says a word, I sense that something's not right.

"Jess," she says breathlessly. "I'm so glad you picked up. It's all kicking off at the museum. Some bloke from the council's here saying he's come to shut us down and now Paul's in a shouting match with him."

I feel sick. I've been dreading something like this happening since the day we opened our doors. But then the more time that elapsed, the more time we were open, the more I just assumed that we were lucky and the council had bigger fish to fry, but now it seems our luck has run out.

"Don't worry," I say, trying my best to sound calm, even though that's the last thing I feel, "and don't let Paul do anything stupid. I'm going to jump in the car right now and I'll be there as soon as I can."

41

As I bring the car to an abrupt halt in front of Barclay and Sons, the first thing I notice is the queue of disgruntled visitors waiting to go inside the museum. Some are clearly debating whether to give up, while others walk past Alex and me having already made up their minds. And the second thing I notice is a panicked Angel standing at the entrance.

"I'm so glad you're here," she says, her voice shaky, her eyes wet with tears. "You'd better come through quickly. I've got a horrible feeling there's going to be a fight."

Running the length of the warehouse, Alex and I burst into the museum to the most bewildering of scenes: Paul is shouting at a thin balding man clutching a clipboard, who in turn is giving as good as he gets. Between them, hands outstretched to keep the warring parties separate, is a desperate-looking Dec. To make matters worse, huddled in groups around the edges of the room, looking equal parts horrified and intrigued, are several dozen visitors. I'm mortified. This is the kind of thing that could permanently ruin our reputation.

"What do you think you're playing at?" I yell breathlessly just as a toddler coloring at the table in the children's activity area starts to cry. "Look at you, two grown men screaming at each other like kids in a playground. Stop it immediately!"

Much to my surprise they both do as I command, each looking sheepishly at their feet. Taking a deep breath, I turn to address the onlookers.

"I'm so sorry about this, ladies and gentlemen, boys and girls. This is all a misunderstanding, I'm sure; please carry on enjoying the museum."

As the man with the clipboard takes a step toward me, I turn to look at him and recognize him vaguely. It's a man Angel had pointed out to me in the museum a couple of weeks ago as she'd thought there was something odd about him.

He fixes me with a stern gaze. "Are you in charge here?"

"Yes," I reply, determined to keep my cool. I hold out my hand. "I'm Jess Baxter, head curator. How can I help?"

"This bloke's beyond help," spits Paul as the man from the council pointedly ignores my outstretched hand. "Throwing his weight around like a jumped-up dictator. You're wasting your breath trying to reason with him, Jess. I've tried, believe me."

"Come on, mate," says Alex, putting a hand on Paul's shoulder and guiding him toward the office. "Best leave Jess to it. She'll get it sorted."

"Right," I say once Alex and Paul have left the room, "if you wouldn't mind just following me into the back, we can find somewhere to discuss this more privately."

"No need," says the man brusquely. "There's nothing to discuss. I'm here to enforce an official order to close you down."

Despite my earlier intention, I feel myself fill with both panic and outrage.

"Are you serious?" I snap. "Have you really got nothing better to do with your time? Shouldn't you be out there chasing down people traffickers or slum landlords instead of harassing a harmless museum?"

The enforcement officer remains expressionless. "Your business has been under investigation for several weeks now and we've found you to be in breach of numerous health and safety regulations, not to mention your total lack of any relevant permits." He removes a thick envelope from his clipboard and hands it to me. "It's all detailed in this document, as is the contact information you'll need if you wish to lodge an appeal. But I must advise you that as of this moment you are required by law to cease

operating and if you ignore this order, you are at risk of not only incur-
ring a fine of up to £50,000 but also prosecution and imprisonment."

"But can't we just talk about this?" I plead. "Isn't there something we
can do?"

"As I've said, Miss…" He looks at me expectantly.

"Baxter."

"Yes…Ms. Baxter, all you need to know is detailed in the document
I've presented you with. I'm going to leave now, and I suggest that you
close the premises immediately, because if I return later this afternoon
and find you still trading, I will have no choice but to put the matter into
the hands of the police."

With that he turns and leaves and I'm so angry at the injustice of it all
that part of me wants to chase after him and square up to him just like
Paul had done. I hate bullies and this guy has all the hallmarks of one.
But as much as yelling at him might make me feel better, the more ratio-
nal part of me knows that it would only make the situation worse. It's
just so unfair. Okay, so we don't have any official paperwork but it isn't
as if we haven't gone to great lengths to make sure everyone who visits is
safe. I've even downloaded and carried out one of the council's own risk
assessments. All the fire exits are clearly marked, we have a fully stocked
first-aid kit, Paul and Dec have installed a ramp for wheelchair access, and
we constantly keep a tab on numbers in and out to prevent overcrowding.
Really, what harm are we doing?

With everyone in the room looking at me, I know I've got to do something and so even though it breaks my heart, I clear my throat and make
an announcement.

"Apologies, everyone, I'm sorry you've had to witness this. Unfortunately, due to circumstances beyond our control, with immediate effect
the Museum of Ordinary People is going to have to close. But I assure
you, we'll be back open in no time at all, so please keep an eye on our
social media channels for further updates. Once again, please accept our
sincerest apologies and we hope to see you all back here very soon."

*   *   *

With the help of Dec and Angel, I usher everyone toward the exit. Then, once the door is locked, I gather the team together in the museum.

"So, what now?" demands Paul, still clearly riled from his encounter with the man from the council. "We're just going to let them win?"

"No," I reply, "of course not, but the last thing we need is a fine or trouble with the police. We're going to fight this; we're going to fight this with everything we've got. The council can't just shut us down like that. Not when we're of such benefit to the community. I don't know what it is yet, but there has to be some way round it, there just has to be."

One by one, Angel, Paul, and Dec go their separate ways, leaving Alex and me alone.

"Are you okay?" he asks, putting an arm around my shoulder. "I can't believe this has happened today of all days."

"I know. I tried to sound positive for the sake of the team, but to be honest, I'm not sure how much more I can take."

"I know it's tough," he says. "And while I don't know what to do about this thing with Dougie, how about first thing in the morning I try and get us in to see the solicitor who dealt with Barclay's estate? I've dealt with him a couple of times and he seems to know his stuff and at least he'll know some of the background."

"Good idea," I say, and for a moment I feel quite calm but then I check my phone to see if, during all this afternoon's chaos, I've missed any calls but there's nothing. This means either Dougie still hasn't confessed or he has and Luce doesn't want anything to do with me. Ordinarily she'd be the first person I'd call in a crisis, but now because of Dougie, because of Mum, I can't. Catching sight of my encyclopedias, I'm suddenly filled with a rage of such intensity that it demands action. Grabbing a chair and a broom from the corner, I reach up and begin knocking them off the shelf one by one.

"Jess, what are you doing?" cries Alex as I take another swipe at the shelf, sending yet more books tumbling to the ground.

"What I should've done a long time ago," I say, and then I get off the chair, scoop as many of the books as I can carry into my arms, and then dump them in the large bin by the entrance. "Denise Gastrell was right. Some things, it turns out, are thrown away with good reason. And if I never see these encyclopedias again, it'll be too soon."

The following morning after a sleepless night I call Molly at the temp agency and tell her I won't be available for the rest of the week. She's understandably furious and tells me not to bother calling her again for work but I've just got too much on my plate to worry about that right now. Later, Alex and I make our way over to Chedworth, French and Field, the solicitors just off Peckham High Street who Alex tells me dealt with Thomas Barclay's will.

"Good to see you again, Mr. Brody," says the plump, bespectacled man in a well-tailored pinstripe suit who greets us. He offers me his hand. "David Moorcroft, pleased to meet you."

"Hi," I say, shaking his hand. "I'm Jess, Jess Baxter."

Indicating for us both to sit down, he resumes his position behind his desk, straightens the yellow notepad before him, picks up his pen, and peers over his glasses.

"I gather from the message relayed to me that there's been some sort of emergency. How exactly may I be of help to you today?"

"It's about this," I say, handing him the twenty-three-page council enforcement order. Taking it from me, he adjusts his glasses and then promptly begins scanning through it. The wait is excruciating but after several minutes, during which he jots down numerous notes, Mr. Moorcroft finally looks up.

"So, according to this document, you've been running a...museum from the premises. Is that correct?" he says with a slight hint of disbelief in his voice.

"The museum was already there," I explain.

"It was Mr. Barclay's pet project," continues Alex. "It's been there for a number of years, although not quite on the same scale as it is now."

"We hold our hands up and admit that we didn't have all of the permissions and paperwork you usually need for this," I explain. "And we're more than willing to get them, but surely there's got to be some way of doing this that doesn't involve the museum closing down. We've all put far too much into this project for things to end this way. Surely there's something we can do, some sort of precedent that can be invoked to get them off our backs?"

Mr. Moorcroft glances down at his notes, flicks through several pages of the enforcement order, underlines a few sections, then sits back in his chair thoughtfully.

"While I freely admit this isn't exactly my field of expertise, I'm afraid to say that in my professional opinion there's nothing that can be done in the immediate other than comply with the order and close your museum. On your own admission you haven't followed any of the planning regulations, so I'm afraid to say that legally speaking you haven't a leg to stand on."

A jolt of anger rises up within me. First Dougie, now this. I'm tired of people telling me what I can and can't do. "And if we don't close?"

A hint of a smile plays on Mr. Moorcroft's lips as he peers over the top of his glasses. "In that case, Ms. Baxter, you would be breaking the law and would as a result face a number of penalties up to and including extensive fines and the possibility of incarceration."

"But isn't there anyone we can appeal to?" asks Alex. "Someone with some weight, some influence, who could help us out? What about the mayor? What if we start a petition and collect signatures?"

"All commendable avenues to explore, I'm sure," says Mr. Moorcroft, "but none of them will actually mean your museum can legally remain open in the interim. I'm afraid you will still have to close and remain so until the issues in the enforcement notice have been addressed."

"But surely this doesn't have to mean the end," says Angel after I finish telling the team about the meeting with the solicitor back at Barclay and Sons. "I mean, think about it, we could mount an appeal to the council.

You know, try and persuade them to let us stay open while we get every-thing sorted."

"We could write letters to the local MP," adds Dec. "My nan and her mates did that when they tried to shut down the pensioners' lunch club at the community center. It didn't work, mind, but it's still worth a try."

"Definitely," says Angel. "And we could back it up with an online petition."

"Whatever happens," says Paul, "we've got to do something, anything at all. I just hate the idea of that jumped-up little jerk thinking he's got the better of us. I think we should open next week as usual and just let them try and close us down! Could you imagine it, a whole bunch of coppers and the council all ganging up against one little museum? We wouldn't just get in the local papers; something like that would make the *Standard*, maybe even the national news."

I hold up my hand. "I get that you're upset, Paul, we all are, but I don't think getting on the wrong side of the police and council is the right way to go about saving the museum. This is by no means over, you've come up with some really great ideas, but don't forget about the funding appli-cation. I've got a good feeling about it, a really good feeling, and I just know we're going to get that money and the museum will be safe. But for now let's just sit tight, and wait for the cavalry to arrive."

I feel like I've said enough to calm everyone's nerves and then one by one they head home, leaving Alex and me alone.

"You sounded really hopeful there," says Alex. "Do you really think we'll get the money or were you bluffing?"

"I wish I could bluff that well; if I could, maybe I'd be more of a gam-bler but I wasn't lying. I really do think we're in with a good chance. I mean, there's not another museum like us in the country; they'd be crazy not to give it to us."

Just then my phone buzzes with a message and Alex and I exchange a wary glance. As I look at the screen, my stomach tightens when I see who the message is from. It's Luce. The last exchange we'd had was last night when I'd messaged her to say Alex and I were extending our trip for a couple of days to follow up a lead we'd had about one of the exhibits. As much as I'd hated lying to her, I'd needed an excuse that wouldn't set alarm bells ringing and it was the best I could come up with at the time.

While I hope beyond hope that her message is just an ordinary every-day one, if Dougie has told her, then I can only hope that she doesn't hate me. Taking a deep breath, I open the text and all it says is "We need to talk." A message devoid of her usual warmth could mean only one thing: Luce knows and one way or another blames me, and everything we are to each other and everything we will be in the future is at stake.

42

Under normal circumstances the prospect of an evening in Luce's company at our favorite bar would be a welcome one. The opportunity to catch up, offload, and sample a decent cocktail menu was a balm for even the worst of days. But as I sit waiting for her, there's a knot in my stomach, a feeling of dread in my every muscle, a physical sign, as if one is needed, of how the events of the past forty-eight hours have changed everything.

When Luce arrives, for the first time in my life I feel awkward with her. I stand up to greet her but she casts a glance in my direction so withering that it's clear there will be no hugging and so I sit back down and try my best not to cry.

"I need a drink," says Luce.

"What would you like?" I say, reaching for my purse.

"Anything, I don't care. Whatever it is, just make it a double."

As I wait to be served at the bar, I look around. Everyone seems to be laughing, joking, and catching up with each other's news, but even from across the room I can see that Luce would rather be anywhere in the world but here.

I order two double gin and tonics and as the barman prepares them I think about how the evening might go. I have to make her see that what happened between our parents doesn't have to ruin our friendship. I have to make her see that we're stronger than that. We've been through too much together to throw it all away over something that happened before either of us were even born. If I don't, if things go badly, I could end up losing her forever.

Determined to save our friendship, I set Luce's drink down in front of her. She doesn't thank me; in fact, she doesn't even look at me. Instead she just stares at the table and I feel like she's signaling that it's my responsibility to get this conversation started.

I pick up my glass, cradling it in my hands. "How are you?"

"You mean since I found out that my dad's a cheating scumbag, your mum's a whore, and we're half sisters?" She laughs bitterly. "I'm doing fine. You?"

"Look, I know this isn't easy—"

Luce snorts. "Easy? Of course it isn't easy! The whole thing is a total disaster. The moment I heard Dad's voice I knew something was wrong. My first thought was that something had happened to Mum, and when he told me she was fine, my second thought was 'He's dying. He's calling to tell me that he's had some horrible diagnosis and he's got six months to live.'" She pauses and looks at her glass but doesn't touch it. "I know it's a horrible thing to say but honestly, right now, I wish that had been the reason he was calling. I can't help feeling that would've been a million times easier to deal with than this."

"I'm so sorry," I say, feeling like this is all my fault, like I'd made the wrong decision forcing Dougie's hand.

"Are you?" she snaps. "You know, when he finally came out with it, when he told me what this was all about, I genuinely thought he was winding me up. I thought to myself, 'Damn, and there was me thinking I'd got a dark sense of humor.' But then he started to cry, and that's when I knew he was serious. That's when I knew what your mum had done."

"My mum?" I say defensively. "My mum didn't *do* anything, at least not on her own."

Luce shakes her head. "Why couldn't she have just left Dad alone? Why couldn't she have found someone else's shoulder to cry on? If she had, none of this mess would have happened."

"And I wouldn't be here," I reply, suddenly aware that I'm the mistake here, not Luce. It's my existence tearing apart her family, not hers. I mean to take just a sip of my drink to calm my nerves but end up knocking back nearly half of it in one go while Luce's remains untouched on the table. "Look," I continue, setting down my glass. "I get that you're upset, and of course you have every right to be. But can't you see I'm upset too? I didn't have a clue about any of this until yesterday. I had no idea at all. But the moment he told me the truth I knew that I couldn't keep it from you. I knew you deserved better than that. I didn't want this coming between us. That's why I told him he had to tell you."

"Well, I wish you hadn't," spits Luce. "At least then I wouldn't feel like I do right now, like my whole world is collapsing around my ears." She shakes her head bitterly, as tears begin rolling down her face and she wipes them away angrily with the back of her hand. "My mum, my poor lovely mum," she continues miserably. "The first thing I did after getting off the phone with Dad was call her. Oh, Jess, you should've heard her, it was horrible, absolutely horrible. She can't make any more sense of it than I can. All she kept saying over and over was 'How could they do this to me?' She's been betrayed by her husband and the woman she'd thought was her best friend. Honestly, Jess, I have no idea how your mum could've lived with herself, especially after all my mum did for her over the years."

"Mum's not here to defend herself," I say, trying my best to remain calm. It's funny but as mixed up as my feelings toward Mum are right now, I feel like I can't just sit here and listen to her being bad-mouthed like this. "She's not here to tell us her side of the story in person but from her diary and what Dougie said it's clear that neither of them ever meant this to happen. It wasn't an affair, it wasn't meant to hurt anyone, it was just one of those things."

"Oh, yeah, we've all been there, haven't we? Accidentally getting knocked up by your best friend's husband and then raising his baby across the road from his actual family like it's the most normal thing in the world!" She shakes her head. "Your mum was nothing but a liar, a liar and a cheat."

I glare at Luce across the table. "Dougie could've told your mum the truth when it happened or at any other time over the past thirty-odd years but he chose not to. So, if we're talking liars, maybe don't make out like my mum's the only one."

The force of my words and their unequivocal delivery are like a knock-out punch just before the bell signaling the end of the round and Luce sits back in her chair, defeated. I take no pleasure in my victory; in this situation there can be no winners, not when our friendship is at stake. Neither of us speaks for several moments and then finally Luce says, "I'm pregnant."

Her words stop me in my tracks. I look at her untouched drink and suddenly it all makes sense.

"I hadn't been feeling right for a couple of days," she says. "Anyway, just to rule it out, yesterday morning I thought I'd go and buy a pregnancy test but of course I was away with Leon and his stupid family, which made it much harder than it should've been. Every time I tried to leave the cottage, either Leon or some relative would get it into their head that I needed company and would come with me. It took me five attempts, but eventually I managed to sneak out to the local village and pick one up. I took it in the loo at the cottage while they were all singing happy birthday to his dad. I couldn't believe it when I saw it was positive."

"And how do you feel now?"

Luce falls silent for a moment and then says, "Terrified obviously but weirdly kind of happy too."

"And Leon?"

"He's over the moon. He's already talking about us moving out of London for the baby. To be honest, I think it's sort of given him a bit of clarity. He's gone from dithering about his future to suddenly being absolutely certain about what he wants. He's only known for twenty-four hours and he's already got half a dozen job applications on the go."

"Oh, Luce, I'm so happy for you," I say, meaning every word. Much as I know that having kids hadn't been part of her immediate life plan, I know she'll make a great mum, and as her best friend all I want to do is support and help her.

I lean forward and take her hand in mine, desperately wishing things could just go back to how they were. "Please tell me that we can work this out, that we can put this behind us. Please say you'll forgive me, Luce; please say you won't let this be the end. I don't think I could bear it."

For a moment as I see her hesitate my heart fills with hope but then slowly, very slowly, she withdraws her hand from mine and shakes her head. "I can't…I can't…promise that, Jess," she says falteringly. "I just can't. There's still so much to process, so much to deal with." She stands up and gathers her things. "The only thing I can promise is that I'll try. That's the best I can do right now. Until then, I just need some time to think. When you want to get your stuff, give Leon a call to arrange it and I'll make sure I'm out when you come."

"How did it go?" asks Alex when I arrive back at his flat.

"Not great," I say, and tell him everything.

"Coming out of the blue like that plus finding out she's pregnant, I think it's probably shock more than anything that's making her act like this. She probably just needs time."

Suddenly my heart feels heavy, like somehow it's been turned into lead. Perhaps this is my punishment for forcing a secret out into the open that had lain buried for the past thirty years. "I don't know what I was expecting, really. I just wanted to get through this somehow. It felt so awful seeing her hurt like that and knowing that in part I'm the cause."

Alex puts his arms around me, holding me tight. "You aren't the cause; none of this is your fault and given time Luce will see that."

"But what if she doesn't? What if she and Maggie blame me for blowing their family apart? What if they never forgive me?"

"Then we'll deal with it as best we can. You're not on your own, Jess, don't forget that. I'm right here with you."

That night I toss and turn in bed, going over and over everything in my head. I can't believe what a mess my life is right now. I can't believe how quickly everything has fallen apart. In the space of just a few days I've had to close the museum, lost my best friend together with Maggie and Dougie, and all the lovely memories I had of Mum, which now seem tainted by the truth, or rather the lack of it.

Why hadn't she felt she could be honest with me? I can understand her wanting to protect me when I was a kid but how many opportunities had passed by since I'd become an adult? She could have told me. It wouldn't have been easy to accept but I'm sure I would have come round eventually. But because she hadn't trusted me, because she'd chosen to keep this secret, now I'll never know her reasoning, and I'll never know how I would've reacted if she'd just given me the chance.

When I awake the following morning, it's as if the thoughts in my head have been churning around all night, even though I haven't been conscious to witness them. Almost straightaway I'm back thinking about Luce, about Dougie and Maggie, about Mum, and I'm so overwhelmed with it all that I can't imagine a day will come when this horrible situation will be behind me.

Throwing on some clothes, I go in search of Alex and find him sitting at his desk in the living room, his eyes fixed to his computer screen.

"Jess, you're up," he says excitedly as he turns toward me. "I wanted to wake you but I knew you needed the rest. I've been going through some more of Barclay's paperwork and look what I found."

He holds up some sort of official-looking document.

"What is it?"

"It's Barclay's decree absolute."

"Wow, we didn't even know he'd been married let alone divorced."

"But that's not the best part. This was in a folder full of paperwork he must have had to submit to his solicitor. And this one right here"— he holds up another piece of paper—"has got his wife's name and date of birth on it: Elizabeth Jane MacDonald born in Lanarkshire on 5th May 1950."

I know my brain's on a go-slow this morning but I can't quite work out why Alex is so excited. "Does her name ring some bells for you, then?"

"None whatsoever, but the thing is now we've got a name and date of birth for someone who really knew Barclay well, and better than that, I've just this minute found out where she lives."

43

Twenty-three Newbury Crescent is an unassuming thirties semi-detatched home in the middle of a quiet tree-lined street in a suburb of Solihull, half-way between Birmingham and Coventry. If we're right, it's the home of Elizabeth MacDonald, ex-wife of Thomas Barclay, the one person who might be able to shed light on why he left everything he owned to Alex.

"We don't have to do this, you know," I say, turning to Alex sitting in the passenger seat. "If I've learned anything over the past few days, it's that not every secret has to be uncovered, not all truths have to be exposed. I mean it, just say the word and I'll happily turn the car around, head back to London, and we'll never mention Mr. Barclay or his will again."

Alex nods thoughtfully. "I won't lie, it's tempting. All night I've been going over everything in my head. I mean, what if I've got it all wrong? What if I find out today that, I don't know, my situation is a bit like yours and Barclay was my real dad or something? What would that mean for me? What would it mean for the way I feel about my parents?" He closes his eyes and draws a deep breath as if he's carrying the weight of the world on his shoulders. "It doesn't really bear thinking about."

"Then don't do it. Take it from me, the truth is highly overrated."

"I don't believe that for a second," says Alex. "And I don't think you do either. Whatever the truth is, whatever I discover, I know my parents loved me, and so I've just got to hang on to that because at the end of the day, it's all I've got."

His words are so honest, so heartfelt, that tears prick at my eyes as I think about Mum. Regardless of what happened between her and Dougie all those years ago, I know she loved and cherished me more than life itself. Shouldn't this be enough for me to overlook this one thing? Shouldn't this be enough for me to forgive her when she's not here to seek my forgiveness for herself?

He pauses and we both look up at the house.

"Are you ready?" Alex nods. "Okay then," I say, and then, hand in hand, we walk up the front path of number twenty-three, past a gleaming silver Skoda parked on the driveway, and after taking a deep breath Alex rings the bell.

After a short wait the door opens to reveal a small, smartly dressed woman with neatly styled silver hair. She's wearing a long cream cardigan over a pale blue shirtdress.

"Hello," she says somewhat guardedly in a light Scottish burr. "Can I help you?"

I wait for Alex to speak but he suddenly freezes up and so I step forward.

"Hi, so sorry to bother you," I say, trying my best to sound affable. "You wouldn't happen to be Elizabeth MacDonald, formerly married to Thomas Anthony Barclay, would you?"

The woman's expression darkens. "I am as it happens. And who might you be?"

"Sorry," I say, "I probably should have led with that. My name's Jess Baxter and this is going to sound strange but your ex-husband, Thomas Barclay, left everything he owned to my friend Alex here and we were just sort of wondering whether you would be able to shed any light on why he might have done such a thing."

"What do you mean 'left'?" asks Elizabeth.

Alex and I exchange a horrified glance as it dawns on us that we hadn't even considered the possibility that the news of Barclay's passing wouldn't have reached her.

"I'm so sorry," says Alex, "we just assumed you knew already. I'm afraid Mr. Barclay passed away a few months ago."

Clearly shocked, Elizabeth simply stares at us for several moments. Finally, she manages to gather herself enough to utter, "Tommy...Tommy's dead?"

Alex nods. "I'm afraid so. From what I gather it was a heart attack."

"Oh, I can't believe it," says Elizabeth, shaking her head sadly. "I mean I haven't seen him in the best part of twenty years but still...you just imagine people carrying on forever, don't you?" She pauses and stares at Alex. "And you say he left you everything he owned?"

Alex nods. "To the best of my knowledge I'd never met him or had any connection to him and quite frankly it's driving me crazy trying to figure out why. So, when I came across some old paperwork with your name and date of birth on it, I used it to track you down through the electoral register and we drove up from London, and well, here we are."

Elizabeth raises an eyebrow. "Well, I'm not sure what I can tell you that will shed any light on anything but you might as well come in and have a cup of tea since you've come all this way."

Following her inside, we're led to a long through-lounge just as neat and well presented as the woman herself. There's a black-and-white photograph of a couple, hanging above the fireplace, who I assume are Elizabeth's parents, a few other framed pictures on the mantelpiece featuring smiling children, and a larger one of a tall white-haired man with his arm around Elizabeth's shoulders.

"Do you take sugar?" asks Elizabeth, returning to the room carrying a tray of tea things. "It's just that I don't and neither does my partner, Hugh. We both cut it out after Hugh was diagnosed with diabetes, so the little I have got is a bit lumpy."

"Don't worry," I say. "Neither of us take sugar."

Elizabeth pours the tea and then sits back in her chair and looks at Alex. "Tommy's gone then, eh? I still can't quite believe it. And you say you'd never met him?"

Alex shakes his head. "I've seen pictures but no, I never met the man."

"And how about your parents, do they not have any ideas?"

"They both died when I was young. I was brought up by my

grandmother, but she passed away five years ago and there's no one else left to ask."

"Oh, I'm so sorry. So much loss in such a young life. I lost my father in a car accident when I was only twenty and I still miss him now, fifty years later." She pauses and takes a sip of her tea. "Well, what would you like to know about Tommy? Like I said, I haven't seen him for a very long time but we were married for fifteen years, most of them good apart from the ones when he was drinking." She eyes us both. "Did you know he was an alcoholic?"

Alex nods. "One of his friends told us."

"It was a real shame," says Elizabeth. "But hardly surprising, given some of the things he had to deal with in his job. The stories he would tell me sometimes..." She shakes her head. "Absolutely awful. Enough to drive anyone to drink."

I look at Alex to find that he's already looking at me.

"What did he do for a living that was so awful?" he asks, just as I'm about to put the same question to Elizabeth.

"Don't you know? It was the job he did all of our married life," she says. "He was a fireman."

I look over at Alex, quite unable to believe what I've heard, and it's clear from his expression that he feels exactly the same.

"He was... he was a fireman?" Alex repeats.

"It was all he'd ever wanted to be," says Elizabeth. "Tommy and I met at school. I was born in Scotland and my family moved down to London when I was twelve for my dad's work. Tommy was one of the first people I met on my first day at school. He was such a joker, a real 'life and soul of the party' type. But he was kind as well. It was no wonder I fell for him. One day we had a careers lesson and the teacher asked Tommy what he wanted to be and he point-blank refused to say. I think he was shy and didn't want all the other boys teasing him. But on the way home that evening he turned to me and said, 'I'm going to be a fireman one day,' and I said, 'Isn't that quite a difficult job to get?' He looked me in the eye and said, 'It doesn't matter how hard it is. I'm going to do it.' And sure enough he did, signed up the day he turned eighteen. When we were together, he always used to joke that it was the second-best day of his life..." She pauses and then adds shyly, "The first being the day he married me."

She stops and looks at Alex. "Have I said something wrong? You look like you've seen a ghost."

"I'm...I'm fine," he says shakily. "It's just...you know when I told you my parents had passed away?" Elizabeth nods. "Well, what I didn't tell you was that they died in a house fire."

"Oh, I'm so sorry to hear that," she says gently. "You must have been devastated. What a horrible thing to have happened." She pauses, then adds, "And were you in that fire too? I noticed your scars straightaway when I answered the door but of course I didn't like to say anything."

"I was," says Alex, breathing deeply. "Though I don't remember much about it. I was just six at the time. And everything I know about what happened I learned from my gran. There was a fire started by a heater accidentally left on downstairs. We were all asleep upstairs at the time. Apparently, it got out of control quite quickly and by the time the fire brigade arrived, things were pretty bad. Somehow they managed to pull me out and take me to safety but it was too late to save my parents."

Ashen-faced, Elizabeth carefully puts down her cup on the coffee table in front of her and stares at Alex intently.

"Sorry to ask, but when exactly did this happen?"

"It was the night of Sunday, April sixteenth, 1989."

"And it happened where? Down in London?"

"No, Lichfield, where I was born."

Elizabeth takes off her glasses, covers her eyes with her hand, and sits in silence for a moment as though she is unearthing some long-buried memory. When she finally opens her eyes again, they're wet with tears.

"Are you okay?" I ask gently.

"No, not really," says Elizabeth. She reaches across to the box of tissues on the side table next to her, pulls out several, dabs her eyes, and then slips her glasses back on.

"This is such a shock," she murmurs. "At my age you wake up and you think you know more or less exactly what each day is going to bring but I never expected this; I never expected this at all."

"What is it?" I prompt. "What's wrong?"

"I think... I think I might know why Tommy left you everything he owned," she says. "It's just too much of a coincidence otherwise," she continues as if talking to herself. "It's the only way this all makes sense." As she pauses again, I silently will her to carry on with the story. "He never forgot you, you know," she says a moment later, addressing Alex directly. "For months afterward he'd dream about that night; sometimes he'd even wake up screaming."

"What is it that you're saying exactly?" asks Alex.

"Tommy was one of the firemen on duty that night, the night of the fire at your parents' house. It was Tommy who rescued you from the blaze."

My mind is reeling. I'd never have guessed the connection between Alex and Barclay in a million years. It's all too fantastic to believe. A fireman so touched by the tragedy of a young boy losing his parents that he leaves him everything in his will. I reach over and rest my hand on Alex's.

"So, Mr. Barclay... Tommy... he was the one who saved me from the fire?"

Elizabeth nods. "It was the last night of a four-day shift when the call came in. The crew went out immediately but by the time they arrived the fire had really taken hold. Worse still, they quickly learned that you and your parents were still inside. Tommy didn't hesitate; once he knew there were lives at risk he went straight in." She pauses and twists the tissue in her hands. "Tommy told me afterward it was one of the worst fires he'd ever dealt with. The smoke was so thick that he couldn't even see his own hands in front of his face and the fire was so fierce he could feel the heat through his protective gear. He found you lying badly burned and unconscious at the top of the stairs, whisked you up into his arms, and took you straight outside. Then without any thought for his own safety he went back inside to try and find your parents, but by that time the roof had started to collapse and he was forced to turn back. They tried everything they could, but it was too late."

I don't need to look at Alex to know that he's deeply affected by Elizabeth's recounting of that night. His hand is shaking in mine as he listens, his foot bouncing up and down nervously.

"I remember when he came home afterward," continues Elizabeth. "He was like a changed man. Haunted he was. He couldn't sleep, he could barely eat, and when the time came for him to go back on duty he point-blank refused. He said he couldn't do it any more, said he wasn't fit to do the job and was going to resign. Sure enough he did and after that it didn't take long for our marriage to fall apart."

I sense there's more to the story than Elizabeth is letting on. "But I don't understand. Why out of all the fires he'd attended over the years did this one affect him so deeply?"

Elizabeth briefly closes her eyes again and draws a deep breath before replying. "Because it was the only one he'd ever attended while drunk."

44

Elizabeth tells us how the stress of the job had taken its toll over the years, leading Barclay to become increasingly dependent on alcohol. "You might think it's strange but though we were married, I had no idea that Tommy had started drinking. Afterward, when he told me everything, I learned that it had all started back in 1987. You're probably too young to remember, but it was in all the papers at the time, the Clapgate Factory fire. A chemical factory on the outskirts of Tamworth caught light and things got so bad that all crews in the surrounding areas were called to respond, including men from Tommy's station. He lost three friends that night, and was never the same again.

"He said that to begin with he was always quite disciplined about his drinking, only ever touching alcohol on his days off, never when he was on duty. But around the time of the fire that killed your parents, he lost his mum to cancer. He took it really hard and that's when things escalated. He started needing a drink before he went to work, and he even drank while on shift too, although nobody had the faintest idea. He said at first it didn't seem to matter so much. You'd be surprised by how few life-threatening fires there actually are. Most of the time when he was on duty, he was either training, maintaining equipment, giving talks, or attending the occasional false alarm, so there was no risk anyone could get hurt. When he'd crossed this line, what he didn't foresee was the fact that one day he might face an actual fire while he'd been drinking, and unfortunately that time came on the night of your parents' fire."

Alex sits forward in his chair. "Are you saying that my mum and dad might still be alive if he hadn't been drunk? That he's responsible for their deaths?"

"Not at all," says Elizabeth emphatically. "The day after the fire, he went into work and told his bosses all about his drinking and was immediately suspended. There was a thorough investigation and after talking to everyone involved and going over reports from the night, the investigators concluded that Tommy's drinking had no bearing on the outcome whatsoever. In fact, they said that if it hadn't been for him, there would have been no survivors at all. Tommy didn't care about some report though; the day he got it he just tore it up and threw it in the bin along with all of his medals and bravery awards. As far as he was concerned, he was guilty, and there was nothing anyone could say or do to convince him otherwise."

She sits back in her chair and rubs a hand over her forehead. "He never went back to the station after that. Instead, he'd just sit at home day after day drinking, and the marriage couldn't really take the strain. When he left, he signed over the house and everything in it to me. Said I'd earned it for putting up with him for so long. Then he kissed me on the cheek, told me he was going back down to London to work with his dad, and that was the last time I ever saw him. We had a little bit of correspondence at the time of the divorce, but it was all very businesslike; he didn't contest anything."

I turn to look at Alex. "Are you okay?"

He nods. "It's just a lot to take in." He stands up and looks at Elizabeth. "Well, thank you for seeing us. I'm really sorry to have taken up so much of your time."

"It's no problem at all," she replies, getting to her feet. "It might have been painful for me to remember but it must have been ten times worse for you."

I stand up too, and together we all make our way to the front door.

"Thanks so much for your time," I say.

"It's no bother; I'm just glad I could help." She turns and looks at Alex. "I'm sure you must be feeling so many different things at the moment about Tommy, and I'm not about to start making excuses for him because it's not my place. But what I will say is this: if Tommy left everything he had to you, it was because he knew how much you'd lost and wanted to try and make up for it somehow. So please, accept his gift in the spirit in which it was given. Enjoy it, make use of it, live a good life and be happy."

I wait until we're in the car and Elizabeth has closed her front door before I speak.

I reach out and rest my hand on Alex's knee. "Are you okay?"

"To be honest, I really don't know. I can't believe it, after all this time, all those theories and none of them anywhere near the truth."

"Do you regret coming?"

He thinks for a moment. "I don't know...I don't think so...Like I said...it's a lot to take in. I mean...I know what Elizabeth said about the investigation and everything, but the fact remains Barclay was drunk that night. If he hadn't been, would my parents still be alive?" He shakes his head sadly. "My life could've been so different, so much fuller, so much richer, so much happier. Was it his fault all that was taken away? Or is he the only reason I'm here at all? I can't figure out if he's a villain or a hero, whether I should hate him or be eternally grateful." He looks at me mournfully, as if his heart is breaking. "Jess, tell me what I should think."

I bite my lip, wishing I had an answer that would comfort him, that would give him peace. "I can't do that. Only you know what you think but for what it's worth, I think hate is far more destructive than gratitude, and you should choose the one that ultimately isn't going to ruin what you've spent so long building."

We make the journey home in thoughtful silence and when we finally reach Walthamstow, I make him dinner and then we sit cuddled up on the sofa in front of the TV. Eventually he falls asleep in my arms, and though I'm wide awake I don't move, content to hold him while he rests, hoping to be as much of a comfort to him as he's been to me.

*   *   *

We spend the following day hanging out together at Alex's flat, and even though it's clear he's still processing everything that we learned from Elizabeth, he doesn't seem ready to talk about it yet and so I don't push him. The following day, however, sensing that he might need some time alone, I head to the museum, more out of habit than necessity. Paul and Dec must be out on a job because when I arrive there's no sign of the van. Making my way down to the museum, I walk around taking in all the objects and come to a stop in front of one of the latest additions to the collection. It's a 1960s Blaupunkt radiogram. I smile as I recall the middle-aged woman who had brought it in just two weeks ago. The radiogram, which no longer works, had belonged to her late parents, who had moved to Peckham from Jamaica in the 1960s. When her dad died, the woman had been unable to part with it when she'd cleared his flat. "I couldn't get rid it of it," she'd told me. "Just seeing it reminded me of when I was young. There was always music, dancing and laughter in our house, it was such a lovely, fun place to be."

The woman had held on to it for the longest time but now that her family had grown up, she was moving to a smaller place and simply didn't have the space to keep it. "Nobody wants old things like this," she'd said, "and certainly not if they're broken. I hated the idea of something that had brought so much joy and happiness to my family being taken to the dump, but what choice did I have? So, when I heard about your museum from a friend, it was like the answer to a prayer, like my parents' memory could live on."

I stroke a hand across its dark mahogany surface replete with all the dents and scratches of something that has been much used and well loved. Without the museum this beautiful object with all of its memories would be lost forever like so many of the things that have come to rest here. What will happen to them all if we can't open again? Who will care for them? Where will all the stories attached to them go?

I look over at the bin near the exit, the one where I'd dumped my encyclopedias, and feel like a hypocrite. In my anger I'd thrown away a link to the past that, whether good or bad, was in the end still mine. Worse still, I'd tried to counsel Alex on the danger of allowing yourself to be consumed by hatred, when the truth was my own anger toward Mum was just as corrosive. Desperate to make amends, I rush over to the bin and take the lid off but it's too late, it's empty, and I can only imagine that by now the encyclopedias are in a dump somewhere buried beneath several tons of rubbish, several tons of stuff that nobody wants any more.

Just then my phone rings, and I'm so lost in thought the sound of it makes me jump. I check the screen, assuming it's Alex, but to my surprise it's Maggie.

My heart starts to race. Part of me wants to let it go to voice mail, unsure whether I can handle whatever it is she has to say. But another part of me feels that after all she's done for me, the least I can do is hear her out.

"Hi, Jess, I hope I'm not disturbing you."

"Of course you're not." I draw a deep breath, determined to face this head-on. "Listen, Maggie, before you say anything I just want to tell you how sorry I am for everything that's happened. I should've kept my mouth shut."

"Oh, Jess," she sighs. "None of this mess is of your making, sweetheart, and I hate the idea you even think it might be. No, if anyone's to blame here, it's me, your mum, and Dougie."

"You? You're not to blame for anything. What have you ever done?"

"It was all so long ago, but since Dougie told me, all I've done is go over and over it in my mind. Back when...you know...it happened, I was going through a bit of a difficult time myself. Dougie and I got together very young, and I suppose I got it into my head that I'd settled down too early or something, that I was missing out on life. Anyway, I was horrible to Dougie, telling him I didn't love him, making him feel like there was no hope we'd ever get back together again, when the truth was, I think I just needed some time to grow up a little bit."

"But that's no excuse for what they did," I say, "and even if it was, how could that justify them keeping such a secret for so long?"

"It doesn't. And if I'm honest, I'm not sure I'll ever forgive Dougie for this. It's a mess, a right mess, and it's broken my heart, it's broken Luce's, and I know it's broken yours too."

"How is Luce doing? I don't know if she told you but we met up the other day. Things were said, and well, she hasn't spoken to me since and I'm not sure she ever will."

"She will, love, she'll come round. With this and the baby and everything, she's got a lot on her plate. It's just hard for her, that's all. Hard for all of us really. It's part of the reason I'm calling, to see how you are. I know I should've done it earlier, and for that I'm sorry."

I'm completely taken aback. "You're worried about me? I thought you'd hate me, and never want to speak to me again."

"Don't be so daft. I could never feel like that about you." There's real warmth in her voice and I almost want to cry. "None of this is your fault. I know you must be just as devastated as we are, but while Luce has got me, who's looking out for you? Of course I'm worried about you; you and your mum, you've always been . . . well, like family to me. I can't just switch that off. I can't stop worrying about you."

"Oh, Maggie, I'm so sorry. I can't stand the thought of losing you and Luce."

"You haven't lost me at all, and as for Luce, she's hurting right now, but she'll come around, I promise. You two have always been so close, and you've gone through too much together to throw it away. Just hang on in there, and I promise things will come right in the end."

I hesitate. "And you and Dougie?"

"I don't know, love, it's too soon to say, but what I do know is that whatever happens, I'm not letting this come between you and me. It's just not going to happen."

On my way back to Walthamstow all I can think about is Maggie and what strength of character she must have. After all she's been through, all she's still going through, the fact that she can find it in her heart to care about me is truly humbling. Her ability to forgive, to look beyond her own pain, is astounding and it's not long before I find myself wondering whether I could show that level of grace toward Mum. After all, I know she never meant any of this to happen, and I can't help but think she would've told me the truth at some point had she not been so cruelly taken away from me. The fact of the matter is Mum's not here to explain the role she played in the things that happened; she's not here to defend herself or indeed beg for anyone's forgiveness. So, I suppose it comes down to a choice: to continue being angry with a dead woman, or make my peace with her and try to hold on to the memory of the wonderful person I know she was. In the end it's really no choice at all. I have to forgive her because if I don't, it will be like losing her all over again and that's something I just can't do.

As I emerge from Walthamstow Central, I decide to pick up something nice for lunch for Alex and me from the bakery just off the High Street, but as I cross the road my phone buzzes to let me know I've got a voice mail. I listen to the message and I'm so shocked I nearly drop my phone. Somehow amidst the commotion of the week I'd completely forgotten what was happening today, but according to the message left by my solicitor, as of half an hour ago my childhood home, thirty-seven Arnold Street, belongs to someone else.

45

"What's wrong?" asks Alex when he comes into the kitchen. "Are you okay? You look like you've had some bad news."

"Mum's house," I tell him. "The sale went through this morning and with everything that's been going on I hadn't even realized."

"It had completely slipped my mind too," he says, putting an arm around me. "Why don't you sit down and I'll make you a tea. You must be in shock."

He's right. I am in shock. In part because of the finality of the house sale going through, but also because of the six-figure sum now sitting in my usually overdrawn bank account. It really is a life-changing amount of money, but even now I'd give the whole lot up in a heartbeat just to be able to talk to Mum again.

"Here you go," says Alex, setting down a mug of tea on the coffee table. "How are you feeling?"

"I'm not sure, to be honest," I say, picking up the mug and holding it to my chest, finding comfort in its warmth. "I can't believe I actually forgot that something so big was happening today."

"It's only to be expected," says Alex. "It's crazy, the amount of things that have gone on over the past few days. You just need to give yourself time, that's all."

I lift the mug to my lips and take a sip. "I just feel like everything's so muddied now. I mean, should I feel happy, should I feel sad? When I first put the house on the market, I thought it would bring me peace, and help me draw a line under my grief so that I could start to move forward. But then Guy wanted us to buy a place together, then of course we split up, then I found out about Mum and Dougie and well... I don't know... it's all so confusing."

"That's completely understandable," says Alex. "You can't know what you feel right now. I mean, it's not like you've won the lottery. The only reason you've got this money is because you've lost your mum and now everything you feel about her is fraught with complication. Maybe don't try and make sense of it right now. Maybe just live with it for a bit."

I set down my tea on the table and reach across to take Alex's hand. He's right. He's absolutely right. This is a complicated situation and there's no point in thinking otherwise, and for a moment I feel quieter, calmer, but it doesn't last very long. Shrugging off my momentary peace of mind like an old coat, I start thinking again about Luce and how hopeless everything feels, and in no time at all I'm in tears, and no matter how hard I try I just can't stop sobbing.

"Just let it all out," he says, holding me tightly. "Don't keep hold of any of it, let it all out."

And that's what I do, I let it all out, and when I'm done, although I feel spent, I'm left with a clarity of mind that I didn't have before.

"Please don't take this the wrong way," I begin. "But I think I'm going to start looking for a place of my own. I think it's what I need right now."

I search Alex's face, worried he's taken this as a sign that this thing between us is over, but thankfully he smiles.

"Is it because I always make your tea too strong?"

I can't help but laugh. "Yes, Alex, it's for exactly that reason."

"I thought so," he replies. "I get it, it's still early days and you've been through so much. You need your own space. But just know there's no mad rush. You can stay as long as you need."

He plants the softest of kisses on my head and holds me tightly. As I close my eyes, I think about how easy it would be to drift into living with Alex, to simply go with the flow. But if I've learned anything at all this past year, it's that even the path of least resistance leads somewhere, and not necessarily to the place you want to end up. I love what's happening between me and Alex, and I really do think it might go the distance, but from now on I'm determined to make my decisions purposefully, mindfully, choosing my life rather than allowing myself to be carried along by its ebb and flow.

The very next day, I begin the search for a new home in Hackney, an area I choose partly because I know people there, but mostly because it was where Luce and I had lived when I'd first moved to London. The idea of being there made me feel close to her in a way, even though in reality we are still very much estranged.

The first flat I see, although perfectly located, is tiny, so much so that there are some rooms the estate agent and I are unable to enter at the same time. The second, a stunning warehouse conversion with lots of wonderful, quirky features, is so far over my ideal budget as to be anything other than a very short-term prospect. And the rest I view are either too small, too run-down, or too expensive to consider.

Then, a few days later, a one-bed Victorian garden flat, just a stone's throw from Hackney Downs Park, comes up for let. As well as being the right price and in the right location, it looks amazing from the photos I view online. Even so, having been through something of a baptism of fire over the last few days, I've learned very quickly how deceptive estate agent photos can be. And so my expectations are low to say the least.

When I arrive, the sharp-suited letting agent is waiting by the entrance and rushes to greet me. As I follow him into the property, he launches into the usual patter telling me how nice the neighborhood is, how sought after properties like this are, and even about a new Peruvian restaurant that's just opened five minutes away. While I'm indifferent to his sales pitch, I can't help but be charmed by the immaculate Minton-tiled floor and original plaster work in spite of my newfound cynicism.

Opening the door to the flat, we head straight to the living room, which, though on the small side, is bright and sunny with a huge bay window adorned with original painted wooden shutters. The honey-colored floorboards have been expertly sanded and varnished, the walls freshly painted white, and the tiled Victorian-style fireplace, though it doesn't look original, has been well chosen and really suits the room.

The bedroom is darker, being at the back of the building, but cozy, with French doors that open out in the garden. The kitchen, though small, has been recently refitted and opposite the built-in cooktop is a window looking out onto a pretty ivy-covered garden wall. Finally, at the end of the kitchen is a compact modern bathroom containing a shower, sink, and loo.

"As you can see," says the letting agent as we return to the kitchen, "it's all been recently refurbished to a high standard by the owners. If you're interested, it's available to move into as soon as we receive your references, deposit, and first month's rent. Feel free to have a wander and I'll meet you back in the hallway when you're ready."

As I take a second walk around all the rooms, I find myself imagining what it might be like to live here. I picture myself waking up on a Saturday morning, perhaps reading the newspaper while enjoying a breakfast of pastries from the café round the corner, or sitting at the little table in the garden with a book on a sunny afternoon. I think I could be happy here. I think this place is exactly what I need.

That weekend, I pick up the keys from the letting agent and then, with the help of Paul, Dec, and Alex, move into my new home.

"That's everything from the van," says Dec, setting down the last of my boxes on the living room floor. He looks around the room. "There's not much here, is there?"

"There's enough to be getting on with," I say. "Once I'm settled I'm going to have you all round for a little housewarming to say thank you for all your help."

"We'll hold you to that," says Paul. "It's been ages since I've had a proper party."

Paul and Dec head back down to the van while Alex and I say goodbye.

"Are you sure you don't want any help unpacking?" he asks.

I shake my head. "That's really sweet of you but I'll be fine. I'll give you a call later, okay?"

We say goodbye with a long, slow kiss, and then Alex leaves. Closing the door behind him, I turn to face all of the boxes, suitcases, and bags of my belongings, and then taking a deep breath, I begin the process of unpacking. I put out my books, arrange my collection of cushions and throws, and put up my framed pictures and posters. I enjoy every moment, every decision about what goes where. It crosses my mind several times that I probably haven't been this happy since we'd finished getting the museum ready for the public, and I wonder if perhaps this room is sort of like the museum of me, telling a little of the story of who I am and the things I treasure.

It's beginning to get dark by the time I've finished unpacking, although there's still one box left untouched, the one filled with everything I brought back from Mum's. I open the lid, peer inside, and can't help but smile as the faint scent of her perfume on her scarves reaches me. Lifting them out, I hold them up to my nose and inhale deeply, the pain of losing her somehow feeling keener than ever. I would've liked her to see this place, I would've liked her to see me happy, but she's gone and all that remains are the things she left behind. So, drying my eyes, I dot these few precious treasures around the room, so that in the only way she can, she'll be here with me.

For a moment after I'm done, I feel a semblance of peace, as if I've given myself permission to love Mum again, as if I no longer have to feel conflicted whenever I think about her. But then I remember Luce, and how this is the longest we've ever gone without speaking, and just like that all the calm I feel disappears. I need to make up with Luce, I need her to forgive me, because without her I don't feel whole, without her I don't feel like me.

Making myself look presentable, I put on a jacket, grab my keys, and head out of the door to the flat, locking it behind me. As I make my way to the front door, my head is full of thoughts about Luce and all the million and one ways I can think of to make things right again. Some are desperate, and involve nothing more complicated than me getting down on my knees and begging her, others are a little more convoluted, more akin to the last five minutes of a cheesy romantic comedy. I don't care what I have to do to make things right with Luce; all I know for sure is that I have to do it.

Reaching out a hand, I open the front door and nearly jump out of my skin when I see Luce standing there, her hand hanging in midair as if she'd been about to ring the doorbell.

"Hello, mate," she says quietly. "Can I come in?"

46

⋙

I like your place," says Luce as we sit in the living room, holding mugs of tea, rather than our usual glasses of wine.

"Thanks, it's getting there, although I do need to get a few more bits of furniture."

Luce smiles. "If only you knew somewhere that had a stack of old furniture that you could buy."

I smile too, relieved to feel a bit of our old easiness return. "I'm hoping to go to Barclay and Sons tomorrow and pick out a few things."

"Funnily enough, I saw a couple of bits I liked there myself when I dropped by yesterday."

"You were at Barclay and Sons?"

"I went looking for you but those two guys, Ant and Dec or whatever, told me you weren't in and that you were moving today."

"They didn't tell me you'd dropped by."

"They wouldn't have done. I made them give me your new address, then swore them to secrecy. Told them I wanted to surprise you."

"Well, you've certainly done that. You won't believe this but I was literally on my way to see you. I hate not seeing you; I hate not being able to talk to you. I need you in my life, Luce. I've always needed you, I always will."

Luce bites her lip and stares at the floor by my feet. "And I need you too...According to Leon, I've been a right nightmare to live with since it all happened...or at least more of a nightmare than usual." She stops and sighs. "I want things to be right between us but I just don't know how to get us there. It's all so complicated; it's all so messy."

Luce looks so pained that I long to reach over and take hold of her hand but I'm not sure how she'll react.

"How's Maggie doing?"

Luce lifts her gaze. "Mum? She says she's fine but I don't see how she can be when Dad's moved out and is living at my uncle's and everything she thought she knew is a lie."

"It must be so hard for her. You know she called me?"

Luce nods. "She said as much. She said she was worried about you."

"I know, I couldn't believe it, she was so lovely to me."

"And I wasn't, was I?" Luce reaches across, takes my hand, and squeezes it. "It was never your fault, Jess, never. I was just angry, that's all. And I didn't know what to do with everything I was feeling."

"And now?"

"And now, I'm pregnant, with no clue what I'm doing, without my best friend by my side, and I'm terrified, Jess, absolutely terrified." A big fat tear forms in the corner of her eye and rolls down her cheek. "I mean, I'm booked in for my first scan in a month and I've got no one to go with apart from the clueless idiot that got me in this state in the first place."

I can't help but laugh. "Oh, Luce, I can't tell you how much I've missed you, how much I've missed us. Please say you'll forgive me; please say we can go back to normal."

Without a word she leans over and wraps me in a huge hug. "Oh, mate," she says, trying and failing to keep any sign of emotion from her voice, "we were a lot of things, but we were never normal."

This moment, thankfully, proves to be the tipping point we've needed and in no time at all she's grilling me about everything she's missed out on over the last two weeks.

"So, all this time," says Luce, "the connection between Alex and this Barclay character was the fact that he was the fireman who rescued him? That's insane. How's Alex doing now he knows?"

"I think he's okay," I say. "It's a lot to take in but he's slowly processing it all. Barclay's ex-wife said something lovely about the fact that he should use what Barclay left him to live a good life and be happy and I think it's excellent advice."

"So does that mean that he's still planning to sell up once the six months is over?"

"We haven't talked about it yet, but I think he should; that money should be Alex's. It's what Barclay wanted and it's what he deserves."

"So, what'll happen to the museum then?"

"Well, right now I'm putting all my hope in that funding you and Leon helped me apply for. If we get it, the Museum of Ordinary People will get to live on somehow, just not at Barclay and Sons."

"You'll get it," says Luce. "I just know you will. And what about you and Alex, do you think you'll make a go of it with him?"

"I'd like to," I say, "but we've both got a lot that we're sorting through."

Luce smiles. "I definitely hear that, but that's life, isn't it? Messy, complicated, and frequently less than ideal. But for what it's worth, even though I haven't met him yet, I have to say, Jess, I like him already. I like the fact that every time you talk about him you smile. I like the fact that he's making it his job to make you happy."

We sit talking until just after midnight and then Luce announces that she ought to be getting home and so she takes out her phone and orders an Uber.

"I'm glad we did this," she says as we wait on the doorstep for her car. "I never feel right when we argue, like I can't rest until we've made peace."

"And we have, haven't we?"

Luce smiles. "Well, I should hope so, because with hapless parents like me and Leon, this baby is going to need its auntie Jess, big-time."

"Just try and keep me away," I say as the driver pulls up across the road, and we embrace one last time. "I'm going to be the best auntie the world has ever seen."

She turns to leave but then stops and looks at me. "I think I get it now."

"Get what?"

"I don't know...about your mum...about why she kept her secret for so long." She puts a hand to her stomach. "You want to do what's best for them...you have to...It's like...I don't know...it's not even a choice; it's something much deeper than that. If she didn't tell you, it wasn't because she was protecting herself; it was because she was trying to protect you."

Before I can find the words to respond she's in the back of the car, and so, even when it begins to rain I remain rooted to the spot until she's disappeared. Finally, I go back inside the flat, feeling physically and emotionally drained. I think about making a mug of tea, or even pouring myself a glass of wine, anything to quiet my racing thoughts. In the end, more out of habit than anything else, I pick up my phone and idly scroll through Instagram, Facebook, and Twitter before finally checking my email. Sandwiched between a discount offer from Superdrug and an invitation to join a new streaming service is the message I've been waiting for, the message I've been hoping for, the message that could guarantee the immediate future of the Museum of Ordinary People. I'm so taken aback by the sight of it that I let out a little scream and then open it:

Dear Ms. Baxter,

Thank you so much for your recent application for funding for the Museum of Ordinary People. As you might expect we were inundated with many outstanding applications from many worthy causes, making the panel's job of creating a shortlist extremely difficult. It is then, with much regret, that we must inform you that although your submission was highly commended, unfortunately on this occasion we have been unable to shortlist the Museum of Ordinary People. We will of course keep you informed of any further funding opportunities and wish you every success for the future.

The following morning, though Alex had offered to do it for me, I gather everyone together in the office at Barclay and Sons and break the bad news. I brace myself for their outrage and upset, but instead there's just a stunned silence, which is somehow much worse.

It's Paul who speaks first. "So, who did get shortlisted then?" he demands. "I bet it was all posh places full of Lord and Lady Whatnot's crown jewels or whatever...places that have already got more money than they know what to do with."

"I'm not really sure," I reply, trying my best to hold it together. "But what I do know is there's no one to blame for this failure except me."

"I'm not having that," says Paul. "No one can say you didn't give it your best shot. You tried, Jess, you really tried, and in my book that counts for something."

"Yeah," chips in Dec, "you did us proud. If anyone's to blame, it's that lot that didn't choose us. You know how things like that work. It's all back-scratching, innit? I bet they all went to the same private school. Makes me sick."

"Don't blame yourself," says Angel. "There's always so much competition for these things, what with all the cuts in arts and culture. But there'll be other chances; there'll be other things to apply for. And in the meantime we'll just get going with the plans we came up with before. You know, writing letters to MPs and setting up petitions and all that? We could even do a fundraiser, you know, raise what we need that way; we'd only need a retweet or two from a celebrity and we could go viral."

I think long and hard about what I'm going to say before speaking. As touching as the boys' outrage and Angel's enthusiasm are, the fact remains that we failed. I'd put forward the best case I could to secure this funding and it hadn't been enough. Maybe the museum isn't as great an idea as I'd always thought; maybe the only thing I've been good at is encouraging people to follow my delusion.

"I hate to say it, guys, but I think it's the end of the road for the Museum of Ordinary People...or at least with me at the helm. Maybe if you get someone else involved...someone who actually knows what they're doing, who knows, you might have some success. But I just don't think I've got it in me. I'm sorry I let you down. I'm sorry that all your hard work was for nothing."

"Now, now, Jess," says Paul, putting an arm around me. "You're just shattered, that's all. Just take a breather and you'll be as right as rain, I promise."

One by one everyone comes and gives me a hug and then finally Alex takes my hand and leads me out of the office.

"Are you okay?"

"I'm sorry, Alex," I say, drying my eyes with a tissue. "I did try to keep it together but I just feel terrible about letting everyone down, especially you. I promised you I'd make a go of things, that I'd make the museum work, but all I've done is waste time and money."

"You've done no such thing," says Alex, putting his arms around me. "You gave it your all; everyone knows that, especially me. But funding or no funding, this doesn't have to mean the end. I'll sell Barclay and Sons as planned, and you can have that money and use it to find a new home for the museum."

"Oh, Alex," I manage to say before my emotions get the better of me. "That's sweet of you, and so typically kind and generous. But I can't ask you to do that. I don't want you to. That money's yours; it's what Barclay wanted, and it's what I want too."

"But what I want is to give it to you. I've been doing a lot of thinking since we found out about my connection to Barclay, and the one thing I'm certain of is that I want the museum to carry on." He stops and smiles. "I admit I didn't get it at first. I admit that to begin with I thought it was the maddest idea I'd ever heard. But then you showed me the good it could do; you showed me that saving people's treasures, no matter how ordinary they might seem, is a kindness that's worth more than any amount of money. We have to carry on, you have to carry on, you can't give up, not now."

Grateful as I am for Alex's faith in me, the truth is I don't share it. But rather than argue the point here and now, I ask Alex if he'll give me a moment and then I head down to the museum for what I know in my heart will be the last time.

Reaching the entrance, I open the door and turn on the lights, to find the museum exactly as I'd left it, almost as if it's been waiting for me to come and say goodbye. I walk slowly along each of the aisles, stopping every now and again to straighten the folds of a wedding dress, turn the page of a photo album, or adjust one of the labels. As I walk, I think about the people this motley collection of objects represent and the lives they've lived and people they've loved.

I hear the sound of a phone ringing and I'm so distracted it takes me a moment to realize that it's my own. While I've never spoken to the person on the other end of the line before, what they have to say to me takes my breath away. The moment I end the call, I rush out of the museum and burst into the office, where thankfully everyone is still gathered.

"I'm so glad you're all still here," I say breathlessly. "I've just had the strangest call and it's a long story, but do you remember the violin... you know the one I gave Audrey to investigate? Well, I've just had some pretty incredible news about it and I...well...I wondered if you'd all be up for taking a trip with me."

"A trip?" says Alex, looking confused. "Where to?"

"Paris," I reply. "I want to take you all to Paris."

Epilogue

The Thomas Barclay Museum of Ordinary People
428–429 High Street, Peckham
(formerly Carphone Warehouse)

47

"Hi, everyone," I say after loudly tapping the microphone to get their attention. "Thanks so much for coming down tonight to help celebrate the official reopening of what we're now calling the Thomas Barclay Museum of Ordinary People."

At this there's a smattering of applause and a few whoops, started off I suspect by Audrey, who winks at me and raises her glass when I look over at her.

"To cut a long story short, last year some friends and I tried to start our own museum, a museum like no other: a museum dedicated to ordinary people and their treasured belongings. Though the project was a success in many ways, in others it was a total failure, and before we'd even been open six months we were forced to close by the council. I won't lie, I took it hard, even more so when we were turned down for some funding we'd applied for, funding that could have enabled us to keep going.

"Anyway, I was ready to throw in the towel when out of the blue I got a phone call from a man I'd never met about a broken and battered violin that Mr. Barclay had saved from a dumpster. This call changed everything and to continue the story I'd like to call to the stage Mr. Szymon Meyer."

I turn to my left and smile as Szymon, dressed smartly in a gray three-piece suit, his white hair neatly trimmed and brushed into place, joins me at the microphone.

"Good evening, everyone," he begins. "As Jess has just said, I called her after my friend Richard, a luthier, sent me some pictures of a violin he'd had passed on to him by a curator at the Horniman Museum. Richard and I have been friends for many years after meeting at one of my exhibitions and so when he saw this violin he knew it would be something I'd be interested in.

"When I got round to looking at the photographs, I observed that the instrument had much in common with the many violins in my own collection. There was water damage indicating it had been played outside in all weathers, it had clearly been made out of the remains of several different instruments, and there was evidence of many rudimentary repairs. To me these were all indicators that this was indeed one of these very special instruments that I collect and I couldn't wait to see the violin for myself. I was thrilled when Jess, Alex, and the rest of the team, who I now consider friends, very kindly agreed to bring it to me in Paris where I live."

Pausing, Szymon nods toward Paul, who presses a button on the laptop, and a photo of the violin appears on the screen behind us.

"As you will see, to the untrained eye this instrument looks fit for nothing but the rubbish dump." He nods again and the picture changes to some grainy video footage. "The images here were taken via an endoscope, which as you will see in a moment was inserted inside the violin."

Right on cue there is a moment of blackness as the camera disappears through one of the f-holes in the violin. At first, it's hard to tell what the images on the screen relate to, but they gradually become clearer and sharper, revealing what looks like the hull of an old-fashioned sailing ship that has been through many storms.

"This hole here," Szymon explains, directing our attention with a laser pointer, "is where the end pin should be." He points to another spot on the screen. "And this area here is where the sound post should stand." As the endoscope is pushed farther into the body of the instrument, a number of dark spots appear on the screen. "Here we see evidence of woodworm, which is no surprise given the violin's age and condition." Finally, the camera moves farther upward and another image appears. At first, it's hard to make out but gradually it becomes apparent that it is in fact a small, but unmistakable, star of David etched into the wood.

There's a collective intake of breath as it slowly dawns on everyone exactly what they're looking at.

"My interest in these violins began back in the late eighties when my uncle Yaakov passed away," continues Szymon, the audience transfixed. "He'd settled in Paris after the war, and worked as an apprentice tailor before eventually going on to have a little shop of his own. I lived with him for a short while when I first moved from Jerusalem to Paris in the sixties, and even worked in his shop for a year or so, but tailoring wasn't really my forte. My uncle never had a family of his own, and so when he died it fell to me to handle his estate and part of this of course involved emptying his tiny apartment in Le Marais. Amongst his things, I came across a violin hidden away in a cupboard. It was a curious thing; though missing its strings and looking very much the worse for wear, it was quite beautiful really, covered in intricate carvings, more elaborate versions of the star of David you've just seen."

"In all the time I'd spent with my uncle, I'd never seen this violin, let alone heard him play. It was only when I asked my father about it that the whole story came tumbling out. How Yaakov had once been a musician regularly playing the violin at weddings and celebrations as part of a sort of folk ensemble, but then came the war, and everything that followed."

As the audience considers the weight of his words, I feel a silence expand and fill the room.

"Of the eighty thousand French Jews sent to Auschwitz, my uncle was one of only two thousand who survived. Though he never spoke to me about it, my father told me that his brother had been forced to join one of a number of orchestras at the prison camp and it was his belief that it was most likely his ability as a musician that had saved him. And while sadly we can only speculate as to why he never played the violin again, I don't think it takes much imagination to understand his reasoning."

Szymon pauses and takes a moment to compose himself. "As it dawned on me how easily this important piece of history could have been lost forever, I began to wonder if there might be more violins like my uncle's out there, violins that had survived that horrific time, beautiful instruments that had borne witness to such terrible atrocities. That's when I began my search, which turned into a hobby, which over the years has, I suppose, become something of an obsession.

"I came across my second violin through a friend I made while trying to discover more about my uncle's instrument. Though I had no direct familial connection to it, I fell in love with that violin too. Over time word spread, and people who knew about my interest began to alert me to the whereabouts of other violins.

"Some were German instruments that their Jewish owners could no longer bear to have in their possession, others had been crafted in the death camps themselves, but all of them, whatever their quality, whatever their origin, had a story to tell about the people who had played them. Today I have eleven violins in my collection, which form the basis of an exhibition that has toured the globe several times over, my modest attempt to ensure the world is never allowed to forget what happened." Szymon looks at me and smiles. "And, thanks to the work of Jess, Alex, the late Mr. Barclay, and the Museum of Ordinary People, I now have one more violin to help me tell this story."

There's a flurry of applause and then the room falls silent as Szymon continues. "When I first met Jess and Alex in Paris, they were on the verge of giving up on their museum. It seemed that at every turn there was some insurmountable obstacle, some thing or other standing in their way. They were closed down by the council. They failed to secure funding. In short, they felt as though they had come to the end of the road. But in discovering the history of this violin, this beautiful instrument that had either been lost or abandoned, they came to see once again the value of their work, of the Museum of Ordinary People."

He goes on to tell the audience a quick history of the past few months, how on returning to the UK Alex had gone ahead with the sale of Barclay and Sons and how with the money raised, together with a sizable donation from me, we'd set up a charitable foundation to fund a new version of the museum. Instead of having a permanent base, embodying the spirit of the Museum of Ordinary People, we'd made the decision to utilize an empty retail space in Peckham to display the collection, thereby bringing it to the people. He continues by telling the audience that this is only stage one of our plan, how in partnership with local councils we're negotiating low-cost short-term leases for premises not just here in London, but across the country. Finally, he explains our vision, how one day we hope there will be a Museum of Ordinary People in every town, on every High Street, dedicated to honoring the memories of the ordinary people who lived there through the objects they loved.

"So many people only see value in the things that will fetch large sums at auction," he says in conclusion, "the objects made or owned by the rich and famous. But Jess, like myself, sees the world somewhat differently. We give value to the overlooked, to the ordinary, to that which the world thinks of as commonplace. And we do this in the hope that the lives and the stories of the people these seemingly unremarkable things once belonged to will be treasured and remembered long after they're gone. So please join me in showing your appreciation to Jess, Alex, and the Thomas Barclay Museum of Ordinary People."

There's a huge round of applause, and as I stand at the side of the stage holding Alex's hand tightly, I can't help but grin as I look out into the appreciative audience. There's so much good will in the room, so many people who want this project to be a success, that it's quite overwhelming. There are old familiar faces, like Audrey, Paul, Dec, and Angel, alongside new friends we've made in the course of getting this version of the museum off the ground. Even Guy has turned up to cheer me on along with his glamorous new girlfriend. But the biggest surprise is the sight of Luce and Leon and their beautiful newborn baby girl, my niece, Florence, making her first public appearance since we'd welcomed her into the world a week ago. And as I walk toward them past all manner of exhibits, both old and new, I cast a glance at the shelf holding my encyclopedias, the ones I'd thrown away, the ones that Alex had secretly rescued and tucked away for safekeeping.

While it might be true that some things are thrown away with good reason, it's equally true that some things are saved for a purpose. Mr.

Barclay saved Alex, and strange as it might sound, the Museum of Ordinary People saved me. And because we were saved, countless treasures—like my encyclopedias once destined for the dumpster, the trash, or the dump—will now get to live on. And although the objects themselves are no replacement for the people we ache for, they are a reminder of the fact that those people were here, and they mattered and will be missed.

Acknowledgments

Firstly, I'd like to thank you, the reader, for picking up this book! In a world where there are so many great books and so little time, it says a lot that you've chosen mine and I hope you've enjoyed spending time with Jess, Alex, and the rest of the gang at the Museum of Ordinary People. In addition, I'd like to say a special thank you to those of you who have been with me since the beginning and the days of *My Legendary Girlfriend*. And in addition to that addition (if I'm allowed to say that!), I'd like to thank all the readers who have joined me along the way. The stories of where, when, and how people have discovered my books over the years never cease to fascinate me, so if we ever do bump into each other IRL, even if I'm running late for a train, feel free to stop me and share!

Another huge debt of thanks is due to Steve and his lovely wife Gratz, of Moseley Vintage Hub, without whom you'd be holding nothing but a book of blank pages! Steve and Gratz are vintage furniture dealers and longtime friends of mine and it was their story, about coming across a dumpster full of items so personal that they felt compelled to at least try to save a few, that was the inspiration for *The Museum of Ordinary People*.

More thanks, as always, are due to Nick and Ariella, my dream team editor and agent. They're always so encouraging when they hear what my next book is about and their feedback and advice are utterly invaluable. Thanks too to everyone at Hodder (special mentions to Alice, Jenny, and Priyal), United Agents (special mentions to Molly and Jenny), and Grand

Central Publishing (special mentions to Beth and Kirsiah) for all their amazing work, so much of which often goes unseen and unacknowledged but for which I'm incredibly grateful.

Finally, thanks as always to my wife, for absolutely everything. I could list all that she does but, to be honest, it would be so long it would practically be a book in itself.

And finally, finally, thanks to Lucy Malone and Jolie Booth, whose existence I was completely unaware of until I'd finished this book because, in a twist fit for a thriller, it turned out there already is a real-life Museum of Ordinary People. Sadly, it's not housed in the back of a dilapidated warehouse in Peckham but you can find out more about the Museum of Ordinary People and the amazing work they're up to at www.museumofordinarypeople.com.

Reading Group Guide

Discussion Questions

1. Jess decides to put her encyclopedias on display in the Museum of Ordinary People because they symbolize her mother's love and encouragement. Discuss the significance of the other objects that get brought into the museum and which had the most emotional impact.

2. The museum was a breaking point in Jess's relationship with Guy, leading them to go their separate ways. Do you think their breakup was inevitable? Or was the museum the root cause of their separation?

3. What lessons can be taken away from Jess's relationship with Guy? Why is their incompatibility important in the story?

4. What social commentary might the author be trying to make about Jess's race and class, and the trials and tribulations that she had to face as compared to Guy?

5. Before she has a chance to curate the Museum of Ordinary People, Jess often acknowledges that she's not able to follow her dreams. What was holding her back? What finally spurred her to take risks, from quitting her stable job to trying to build the museum from the ground up?

6. Alex and Luce's unrelenting support gives Jess some of the strength and reassurance she needs in curating the museum. Who is your biggest supporter in your life? What would you say to them if they were here?

7. The Museum of Ordinary People is deeply concerned with the preservation of memory. In what ways has the museum acted as a safe haven for its operators and patrons?

8. Paul and Dec act as a comedic and compassionate duo. How have they been a positive influence in the story?

9. Discuss the ways in which grief and hope manifest throughout the narrative. How have each of the characters healed and changed?

10. Luce's parents, Dougie and Maggie, are important parental figures in the story. In what ways is their presence important and impactful?

11. Throughout the course of the novel, there are plenty of friendships that flourish. Which platonic relationships felt the most impactful to the story?

12. Family, both chosen and found, is a recurring theme. In what moment in the novel did you find this to be the most effective or moving?

13. Why does Alex need someone like Jess to help overcome his fears about his scars? Why does Jess need someone like Alex to help curate the museum?

Author Q&A

1. What inspired you to write *The Museum of Ordinary People*?

A good friend told me a story about how he was walking past a dumpster outside a house that was being cleared. Curious, he stopped and looked at what was being thrown out and found a bag full of personal items like letters and postcards. He told me it felt wrong that these things, which had clearly been cherished, should end up in a landfill and so he took them home even though he had no connection to the owner. This story stuck with me and I started to think about how sad it was that personal possessions people had once really treasured should become so disposable once their owners passed away. This got me to wondering what would happen if a place existed to look after these forgotten things, something like a museum dedicated to preserving the treasures of the lives of ordinary people.

2. Throughout the course of the book, Jess creates a community around herself that supports her goals and helps her flourish in life. Who in your life makes up your chosen community for mutual support?

Not long after I became an author, I was asked to contribute to a short story collection for the charity WarChild, and a number of us who wrote pieces for this became firm friends. We had our own secret message board in the days before social media and we even had an annual office Christmas party (which is still going to this day) because, of course, as full-time writers working from home we didn't have any other option! What I particularly love about this group is the support it offers. We've been there for each other through good times and bad and it absolutely means the world to me.

3. *The Museum of Ordinary People* celebrates the ordinariness of everyday people and everyday life. Why was that message so important to you to write about?

From monarchs to presidents, and actors to authors, there is no dearth of institutions willing to look after your belongings after your death if you're rich, famous, or influential. There's an immediate sense that everything these illustrious people owned has some sort of intrinsic value because of who they were and what they did in life. But when it comes to ordinary people, there's no such assumption. Their things, unless kept and treasured by family members, are thrown away, almost as if their lives didn't matter, almost as if to say that they didn't count for anything. To me this just feels wrong, and while I appreciate that not everything can be kept, I find the idea of a place that might value such things comforting in the extreme.

4. Jess shows that sometimes people lose their way in life. Did you ever have a moment where you felt you lost your way in life?

I think we can all feel a bit lost in life sometimes, especially when it comes to our careers. It's such a big question: What do I want to do with the rest of my life? I mean, how are you supposed to answer that? I started out as a journalist, and there were lots of reasons to love what I did, but as my career advanced I found myself editing other people's work instead of doing the thing I loved, which of course was writing. It wasn't until I left my full-time job and picked up the half-written novel I'd begun in my early twenties that it dawned on me that journalism wasn't the answer; writing books was. So getting lost isn't always a bad thing if eventually it helps you find your way.

5. Do you have a favorite museum that you like to go to? What about it do you love?

The thing I love about museums is the way they can transport you out of the world you live in. It's as if one moment you're inhabiting the real world, with all its trials and tribulations, and then you step through the doors of a museum and you're somewhere else entirely. A place where you're asked to do nothing more than to look at and enjoy a celebration of things from the past. My favorite has to be Birmingham Museum and Art Gallery in my hometown because it was the very first museum I ever went to and I have a lot of fond memories of going there across the years. They used to have a forty-foot-tall papier-mâché T. Rex in their collection, and the first time I saw it I was five and was terrified as I thought it was real! The first time I took my own kids there I tried to find it, only to be told that decades of wear and tear had taken their toll and it had begun to fall apart and so had been thrown away! Such a waste! Even in pieces I think it definitely would have found a home in the Museum of Ordinary People.